SPIDER STAR

SPIDER
STAR

MIKE
BROTHERTON

A TOM DOHERTY
ASSOCIATES BOOK
NEW YORK

TOR®

This is a work of fiction. All of the characters, organizations, and events portrayed in this novel are either products of the author's imagination or are used fictitiously.

SPIDER STAR

Copyright © 2008 by Michael S. Brotherton

All rights reserved, including the right to reproduce this book, or portions thereof, in any form.

Edited by Beth Meacham

A Tor Book
Published by Tom Doherty Associates, LLC
175 Fifth Avenue
New York, NY 10010

Tor® is a registered trademark of Tom Doherty Associates, LLC.

ISBN-13: 978-0-7653-1125-2

Printed in the United States of America

ACKNOWLEDGMENTS

I would like to thank Ski Antonucci for sparking the core idea of this book, once upon a time; Neil Cornish for keeping me from straying in an unproductive direction; open-minded astrophysicists David Eichler and Robert Foot for their speculative papers; and Eric Nylund, Jeremy Tolbert, Leah Cutter, Bob Berrington, Öjvind Bernander, and Scott Humphries for their helpful feedback on early drafts.

SPIDER STAR

PROLOGUE:
PANDORA'S BOX

ARGO, POLLUX SYSTEM, 2433 AD
BARREN BUTTES ARCHEOLOGICAL STATION,
PROCESSING LAB

Two of the most important things ever to happen to Virginia Denton occurred on the same day, almost at the same moment. At the time she was unaware of the importance of either event.

Every day seemed important to Virginia then—and there was certainly a case that her work could never be as important again. They had found a virtual treasure trove, artifacts from Dynasty 2c, immediately before the third and final fall of the Argonaut civilization of Argo. Artifacts close to two million years old shouldn't even be recognizable, but Dynasty 2c had reached a level of technology beyond that of Earth in most ways. That was not daunting to Virginia—it was thrilling. Any item potentially provided the opportunity to uncover new science or engineering, beyond even the immense archeological value that was her primary interest.

Today she got to open what she had dubbed "the box," what appeared to be a chest, a meter long and half a meter high and deep. Dull matte gray, unassuming, it awaited her under the hood. She wished she had one of the X-bots to help, but they were all on-site steadily and meticulously uncovering other artifacts, work for which they were immeasurably better suited than humans, and she wasn't going to wait—she'd been promising herself this treat. She only had the hood's robotic manipulators for reliable assistance, as Virginia didn't count on her summer student. Anatole was still new enough that she didn't yet trust him with anything too critical. Besides, his boundless enthusiasm, barely an exaggeration in truth, was not limited to archeology; that quality had seemed a plus when she'd selected him for the position—broad interests often seemed advantageous to her—but she was seeing the downside today. The kid could be scatterbrained.

Anatole, at the moment, was across the lab watching the New Colchis satellite feed. There was some sort of event—Virginia hadn't followed it closely—involving the unexpected arrival of a ship from Earth. Although the event was already a continent and a small ocean away, it seemed even more distant with the unopened box before her.

A Pandora's box, she thought, chewing on her hair, then dismissing the notion. Greek mythology had seeped into the naming of everything in the Pollux system, from its planets to its inhabitants, and sometimes into more than just the naming. Pollux was one of the two stars that, from Earth, made up the core of the constellation of Gemini, the twins. Castor was the other star. In the myths, Pollux and Castor had been twin sailors on Jason's famous ship *Argo* who quested, ill-fatedly, for the Golden Fleece. As occurred all too often with naming things, or renaming things as was the case here, everything was wrong or backward. Now the name of the ship that bore Pollux was the name of a planet in orbit around Pollux, which had never made sense to Virginia. But never mind the ancient history.

She smiled in anticipation as she pulled on the remote gloves. In response, the robot arms under the clean hood twitched, and sprang, hovering, to electric life.

The box had no lid, or opening mechanism, but that was not atypical for artifacts of this material from the site. You just reached out to open such a box and it would open. Random jostling, other contact without intent to open, didn't normally do the job. Nothing magical about it, just differences in the impact and forces, something she could probably program herself with enough time and a smart material like the one before her.

Virginia moved her arms, splitting her attention between a direct visual of the box, and watching the monitor fed by a camera on the robotic hand. She reached for the box, felt the feedback pressure when she touched it, and grabbed and lifted the top.

She grinned, immediate understanding filling her as the lid opened. It wasn't a Pandora's box, full of all evils. Far from it. The box was full of *toys*. There were bright, multicolored round objects, furry eight-armed dolls, plastic disks, and more. Despite the odd assortment, she was sure it was a toy box—alien toys, to be sure, for alien juveniles, but certainly toys. This was fantastic! In those first moments of delight, she couldn't think of anything more important than finding children's toys because, after all, this would be something that would get her into the psyche of the ancient Argonauts at a fundamental level that nothing more adult could do. After all, wouldn't dolls and toy guns be quite revealing about humans?

"Anatole!" she called. "This is wonderful. Come see!"

She panned the camera over the contents, recording three-dimensional information to better than a micron with the laser scanner.

Virginia took a moment to control her overpowering smile. She wondered if any Argonaut child had ever felt such excitement as she did in opening the toy box. The Argonauts had to be more than the ruthless monsters that their extinction indicated.

Where was Anatole? He should be here. Sure he was more distractible than she'd banked on, but this was a golden moment. Virginia was from Earth, second mission, and had signed up to come to Argo. Anatole, on the other hand, had been born locally and like many of his generation seemed to resent it. She supposed she could understand how Earth would sound—high-tech, glamorous, and infinitely enticing to someone who viewed their home world as a backwater. But Earth didn't have ten-million-year-old artifacts. To an archeologist, Earth was the backwater.

She couldn't wait for him. She began lifting artifacts—toys!—into individual containers. They'd be cradlefoamed into place for transport back to the more sophisticated labs of New Colchis arcology.

Giddiness flashed up her spine and lifted her cheeks into a painful smile. She should be going slower, going more carefully, but the Argonaut boxes preserved their contents so well she knew the toys were likely in fine shape. Fine enough for a quick, careful lift anyway.

Hell, they were probably ready to be played with, as fresh as the day alien hands had put them away for the last time.

Breathe. Go slow. As slow as possible, anyway.

Where *was* that kid? "I've got something great!"

A moment later she heard him push open the door and felt the wave of warm, moist air that flowed in with him. She didn't bother looking up, and proceeded to lift out a reflective hexagonal box with no apparent purpose, not one so obvious compared to the figures and spiky balls anyway. What was it? The best stuff was never obvious at first glance. Perhaps this was something exceptional.

"This guy on the feed," Anatole said, "Klingston's his name, he didn't come from Earth. Not directly. He's a Scout, and he met aliens, real live aliens. Living extraterrestrial intelligences!"

Okay, that was intriguing, Virginia admitted. She had become interested in archeology initially as a window into alien cultures, human or otherwise, separated from humanity by time. She was surely as interested in alien intelligences separated by space. An abyss opened before her as large as the universe, a place full of interacting aliens rather than just ancient ruins of lost civilizations. She'd gone into archeology because that was the big show, the only place you could touch those other cultures, but perhaps that wasn't true anymore.

Still, she couldn't think about that now. She could hear about it later, and find out all about this enigmatic and fascinating Klingston, maybe even meet him and pick his brain. But now, now, she had to focus on the toy cradled in the slaved robot's hands.

What she was doing here was still exciting, but her smile had vanished in mixed emotions. Wasn't the world full of wonder?

"Okay," she said, "tell me about it in a minute. Let me get this baby put to bed."

She continued to move the hexagonal box, slowly, steadily, to the scan pad a meter away.

Suddenly, something pricked her arm and she jerked involuntarily. Her smile twisted into a snarl and she exclaimed, "Oh!"

A tenth-of-a-second glance revealed the culprit: a blue stabber had flown in with Anatole, careless Anatole. The stabber inhabited an ecological niche very close to that of the mosquito, and like the mosquito, its bites were masked by a local anesthetic—except that it didn't work on aliens from Earth, like humans. It didn't matter that she didn't dare slap at the Argotian bug because the medical nano in her blood would kill it almost as fast as she turned to look at it. She had jerked, and that was enough.

The box bounced out of the mechanical hands.

"Hey," said Anatole.

The box skittered to an abrupt stop on the scan table.

Virginia's pulse accelerated with a surge of adrenaline.

The box lit up.

Lit up wasn't the right phrase, Virginia realized, given that what appeared was more of a dark cloud above the box, making the box itself appear lighter in contrast. Something floating above the box, and the way it appeared, had triggered the thought as it had reminded her of a holographic monitor powering up. An image materialized.

What materialized looked to be a star field, with something wispy at the center. The field rotated as the wispy thing sharpened and came into focus. As this happened, sound began to emanate from the box. Tones, in a minor key, ominous and deep, passed effortlessly through the whispering pressure hood and resonated in Virginia's chest.

"Cool," said Anatole.

Virginia ignored him, and leaned closer to peer at this alien image. She'd read of two artifacts that had done something like this before, although she hadn't seen one actually activated herself.

On top of the low tones, a sibilant hissing emerged. An Argonaut voice—perhaps more than one. It was a narration, she surmised, explaining the picture crystallizing before her.

The wispy thing was a structure floating in the night, an eight-armed space station of some sort, she thought. The absolute size of the thing was impossible to determine, but the way the image grew so slowly, with so much detail and relief, it seemed like it must be immense.

The hissing, alien voices continued for several minutes, and she noticed a tiny glittering light at the focus of the perspective, approaching the station. A ship? The point of view enlarged, and the narration quickened. The light sharpened into something resembling an attacking silver octopus, but it did seem to be a starship of some kind.

This was a storytelling device, and the story made her feel uncertain, and deeply disturbed. The Argonauts of all eras had only rarely used fiction. Not for education anyway.

The toy before her was interesting, in the most profound way.

"I think this is important," she whispered to Anatole. "Alien-encountering Scouts or not, we're going to make the feed today, too. We're going to have a real story worth telling."

The tiny ship docked with the station, and the toy emitted such a sour, disquieting note that Virginia had an involuntary reaction to try to shut it down. She ignored the feeling, and watched the strange story unfold as best she could follow.

Anatole said, "I wonder if it has a happy ending."

She hoped it did, but wasn't getting that vibe from it. "I doubt it," she whispered. "But neither do most fairy tales. Let's keep watching."

PART ONE

POLLUX SYSTEM, 2453 AD

KNOCKING ON HEAVEN'S DOOR

CHARYBDIS, INNER MOON OF ARGO

Without an atmosphere to create distortion, the stark crags of the Pindus range cast exceptionally sharp shadows across the plains of Charybdis.

Commander Manuel Rusk took a deep breath, admiring the view, even though he breathed only his suit's slightly stinky recycled air. The view was still grand.

"Drop position confirmed, all relays good," Sloan Griffin, his second, said over the public channel from orbit.

He almost felt like it was real, that they were in the Castor 6 system, instead of a training mission on Argo's larger moon. Fine, he'd go with the feeling, treat it as real as he could, since that was the best way to be successful. Here he was, leading an investigation into a five-sigma gravitational anomaly on a planetary moon. Not so exciting, he supposed, although the anomaly was real and worth exploring. Probably just a mineral excess of some sort, a random fluctuation . . .

But maybe not. This was how a buried Argonaut power plant had once been discovered, after all. Definitely worth a look.

"Fan out," Rusk ordered. "Let's proceed through the foothills, systematically, heading north, with Selene and Melinda on the perimeters, at two kilometers, with X-bots trailing in the gaps."

He hopped forward in the light gravity, deliberately moving slowly as he scanned every direction. Compared to the humans, the bots were more likely to find something given their extended spectral capabilities, but they were not foolproof. Humans had millennia of natural selection going for them when it came to hunting the unknown. Rusk was a modern hunter, and had skills that the cyberneticists could not quite duplicate. Yet.

So he hopped, and looked.

With no atmosphere or significant erosion processes, tracks in the dirt would last for millions of years. It might not be so hard to locate something of interest, if it were present. Charybdis had not yet been mapped at the sub-meter resolutions necessary to spot fine details from orbit.

Sixteen individual Argonaut landing sites, plus two long-term bases with associated activity, had been located on Charybdis from satellites. The nearest base was over one hundred kilometers away, not all that far. But anything military, the most interesting sites, might well be designed to avoid detection from orbit, high-resolution imaging or not.

"Rusk," Walter Stubbs's voice floated over the public channel. "I've got something. A hole."

A hole? Okay, worth a look, but it didn't sound so promising for everyone to quit what they were doing. "Walter, I'm on my way. Everyone else keep on. Come, Magellan."

His X-bot, fifty meters to his left and a little behind, closed the distance between them. The bot didn't bounce in the lower gravity like he did, but moved in a sinuous, snakelike manner with its multiple legs undulating beneath as one. Apparently that was more efficient than the more spiderlike way it moved under heavier gravity. The X-bots had a built-in library of movement patterns for a wide range of environments spanning more properties than just surface gravity.

Rusk's head's-up painted a green label STUBBS over the silver-suited figure a short distance away. Stubbs's X-bot, Phyllis, squatted beside him, leaning its sensor-adorned head downward and to the right of the pair.

"What do you have, Walter?" Rusk asked over the short-range channel.

"Phyllis picked up an aberration in the dust at a radius of thirty-four meters. I mean, a nonaberration aberration. I'll let her explain."

Over his HUD, a ghost of a face appeared, one of Phyllis's expert patterns: an older, blond woman with long, straight hair. Rusk couldn't recall the pattern's human name. She said, "There's a circular region of enhanced randomness. That is, it exhibits perfect Gaussian statistical randomness, which happens all the time with large enough samples, but I guess you'd call this anally random."

Walter said, "Especially when there's a big rock at the center, with a hole under it."

Too random? There had to be a chance of getting perfect randomness that wasn't too small. But it did seem to be of interest, potentially. And any protected nook here was worth at least a quick look. "Tell me about the hole."

"It's a hole. It's a meter across, at least ten meters deep, then it slants off. You can't see it from orbit at all."

Rusk considered the situation, the chance that this was something artificial. It seemed like it might be. Under normal circumstances, he would drop everything and allow an archeological team to proceed. But these weren't normal circumstances—he was on a training mission, and directed to play it as honest as if this were a real find, so he should proceed as he would if this were a moon orbiting a planet in the Castor 6 system.

So . . . onward. And downward.

"Magellan," he said, "give me a line."

Rusk turned toward his X-bot and extended a hand. The X-bot responded by taking two of its legs and grabbing a nub in its thorax. The bot pulled out the nub and handed it to Rusk. A filament of high-tension nanocarbon ribbon connected the nub to the X-bot's carriage.

Rusk locked the nub into his belt and stepped to the edge of the hole. "Give me a solid belay," he said.

Wrapping the line around his back, Rusk stepped to the hole, and jumped in.

Jagged rock walls flashed slowly by in the low gravity. His helmet lights followed his head, providing a strange perspective as he looked about during the rappel. When his feet touched the wall, he kicked off, slightly, and continued to drop.

Rusk fell into the hole, trusting his equipment and training. Training was for real, something one could rely upon in the face of any challenge. For one properly prepared, fear was unnecessary. He wouldn't get caught on a sharp outcropping, and he wouldn't twist an ankle with an awkward landing.

He landed, softly, on a flat surface covered in a few millimeters of dust. Flat seemed interesting. He shone his light down, panning around his landing area.

Tracks in the dust. Hundreds of them. Not human prints, either, but the smaller oval prints of suited Argonauts. *Jackpot.* He radioed up calmly, "This is the real deal. Get everyone over here, and get Timothy down here, and an X-bot with Argonaut military expertise."

Timothy knew Argonaut history, such as it was presently understood, and could provide an informed opinion about anything they might find. He'd be a useful human counter to any X-bot perspective. Despite being based on human personalities and expertise, X-bots often lacked the big picture view.

He wished he had an omni-bot, or O-bot, his dream assistant, that could synthesize disparate information more effectively. People had been daydreaming about decent help for the entire history of civilization, and you worked with what you had. X-bots were useful, but their narrow-mindedness sometimes let people down when relied on too much. Still, Earth-based researchers were always improving the things and broadcasting the results to Argo.

Rusk didn't pay much attention to the discussion topside, the logistics of moving down people and bots. His team was competent. Rusk focused on the tracks in the dust. These were at least many hundreds of thousands of years old. Part of him realized that he didn't dare move, but another part of him didn't care. These were mere footprints. His suit was recording them, not only with video but—he picked out a menu on his HUD and eyed the appropriate activation—with scanning lidar. If he were in the Castor 6 system, he'd make high-quality recordings, and proceed despite the destruction his own movements would cause. So he would here, too.

He hadn't come for footprints.

Onward then.

"I'm moving ahead," he said, detaching himself from the drop cable, and oriented himself toward the downward sloping tunnel filled with prints. "Full archival recording engaged."

Rusk shuffled along, slowly, looking at his surroundings. The tunnel itself wasn't natural, he decided. The walls were smooth and round, but not perfectly so, slightly elongated in the horizontal to maybe three meters wide. The ceiling was two and a half meters high at least, and he didn't have to stoop.

It wasn't spooky, exactly, as he didn't think anything had been here in untold millennia, but there were ghosts nonetheless. He was the first here in eons, and he couldn't help but imagine what things might have been like when the Argonauts had abandoned this place. Which era had built the base, and what had ended things here? Had it been war? Economic depression? Or perhaps just a bureaucratic decision?

He didn't know, but speculation made him feel closer to the long-lost beings of Argo, exploring and establishing their presence on their largest moon the way men had done on theirs.

About fifty meters down the tunnel, the passage opened up into what seemed an antechamber, close to ten meters in diameter. While much of the floor was covered with more oval footprints, there were also several flattened areas that looked as if something large and flat, like crates or machines, had once rested there.

Rusk scanned it all.

Opposite the tunnel was something that was clearly a door of some type: a flat indentation in the wall, wide at the bottom, tapering to a rounded top, similar to other Argonaut doors he'd seen in ruins and in videos. "I've got something. Get that X-bot down here, and another to relay."

"Acknowledged," said Timothy.

When Rusk was sure that he'd recorded every detail, he stepped toward the door. He didn't see any obvious way of opening it. It had no handle, or knob. There was no keypad. He supposed it might open with a radio frequency combination, or have a light sensitive lock. Maybe even something much more exotic. In the worst case, they could always force it open one way or another. The team had enough explosives to make an academy of archeologists cringe, but it probably wouldn't come to that.

One thing different about it, though, was a mark. Close to what he perceived as the middle of the door, was a dark indentation. The shape was familiar: like a four-leaf clover from Earth, with the top two leaves larger than the bottom two leaves. It was the Argonaut symbol for *heart,* equivalent to the human symbol with two bulges on top, narrowing to a vee at the bottom. This symbol, he thought he recalled, was associated with one of the primary nation-states during one of the high-tech civilizations. He should know it, and was irritated with himself for not being able to place it exactly. He'd studied this topic extensively for an exam, and he didn't usually forget.

Rusk let it go for the moment.

The question was, for him as training mission commander, should he continue as if he and his team were really in the Castor 6 system, alone and isolated, or recognize that this was an opportunity for some crack archeology team from Argo to take over?

Inside this lunar cavern, inside his helmet, where no one could see, Rusk frowned.

The chance of this sort of discovery was remote enough that it hadn't come up explicitly, and from experience he knew the real answer to the unknown range in possibilities had always been "use your best judgment."

And then he'd be judged in turn, later, with perfect and unforgiving hindsight.

He could argue either position, and he could see those with control over him and his future arguing the opposite positions. He imagined the back-and-forth conversation. He took a deep breath. People in charge always condoned success, when it could be visibly measured, but blasted failure. At this point, he and his team would get credit for the discovery, and credit for the methodology that produced it. Anatole's new algorithm had selected this site as more unnatural, as he defined it, than others. Any additional level of discovery would be a bonus, but only that, on top of the basic find.

He should stop now, he realized, from a political perspective. They'd score points for no additional risk.

As fascinating as Argonaut discoveries were, he'd grown up with them, and nothing here could match the importance of the initial exploration the previous generation had performed. Only something like opening a new solar system, or a multiple system like Castor 6, could compare to that.

Training his team should take precedence over a marginal increase in the archeological understanding of the ancient Argonauts, but it wasn't the safe move. Leading an unsupported team in an alien star system would require safety. He grunted to himself, "Too much second-guessing already." Safe or reckless?

Rusk made his decision. He stepped forward through the

ancient dust, stopping before the doorway and its dark symbol. He raised his hand and, with only a little hesitation, briskly knocked on the surface before him. The surface felt firm, and resonant. A satisfying sensation, even though he couldn't hear any sound. He spoke, but did not broadcast, "Is anyone home? We've arrived. Now I turn you over to the experts to follow with their slow, careful brushes."

Rusk stepped back, satisfied with the state of the universe.

"Rusk?" It was Griffin's voice, relayed to him from orbit. "About six seconds ago we picked up a neutrino pulse."

A *neutrino* pulse? That was far from the easiest thing to detect. And when he knocked? Exactly when he knocked? That seemed unlikely.

"From here you think?" he asked. "And real?"

"Yes," she replied. "Several dozen detections. Really strange, isn't it?"

Neutrinos barely interacted with anything. Gazillions spewed out of Pollux all the time, essentially all of them passing through everything peacefully, including a star and the entire planet of Argo. Spacecraft Cerenkov detectors were small and only picked up neutrinos as a by-product of monitoring dark drives, and without the drives they wouldn't even have known about the burst. Furthermore, Griffin had to have had a good position to intersect with the neutrinos.

A cold sweat trickled down Rusk's forehead, and he couldn't wipe it away because of the helmet. Was it possible that he'd triggered the neutrino pulse, with his simple knocking?

No . . . couldn't be.

"Yes," said Griffin, "I've backtracked the trails, and the ninety-five percent confidence interval is centered within a kilometer of your location. Did anything happen down there in the last few minutes?"

A knock. That's all, but there it was. A giant black spot on his career, for a little knock? Oh . . . how? Ludicrous! And he had decided to play it responsible, to play it safe.

Safe!

He took a few deep breaths. He was probably okay here. What could a neutrino signal do from a lunar base millions of years old, after all?

But a neutrino generator as an alarm system was a very, very strange thing indeed.

A WALK IN THE PARK

HESPERIDES PARK, ARGO

Frank Klingston landed his car in the deserted parking area of Hesperides Park. It seemed they had it all to themselves today. He looked to his wife, Virginia, and caught her smiling back. She was beautiful in the sunlight, with her tanned face, dark hair, and golden hoop earrings, complemented by her gleaming smile. She winked at him. Life was good.

"Dad!" Kenny said, poking his head up from the backseat. "Let's *goooo* already!"

Kenny was his youngest, and at six, much more vocal than his moody older brother Allyn.

"Okay, sport," he said, letting out his grin.

His family poured out of the car and onto the white perma-crete. Virginia rescued the picnic basket from the trunk as he was shutting down the engine. His sons were already patrolling the forest perimeter.

"Hey!" he called. "Don't go too far! Allyn, watch your brother!"

Allyn turned to give him a dirty look. Watching Kenny was far from his favorite job. Kenny was running and jumping about and didn't give him a look at all.

Virginia leaned into him. "It's okay. Nothing's going to hurt them."

He wrapped her in one arm and took the picnic basket in the other as they marched to follow their children. "I suppose not."

Hesperides was a secure park, with ultrasonic barriers tuned to deter the larger predators, and most Argotian life had already learned to give humans a wide berth. Especially young humans, who seemed to enjoy the way even their spit would kill bugs.

A dirt trail wound into the shallow hills above the parking lot. Frank and Virginia followed the path at a stroll, letting the kids pull ahead out of sight, but not quite out of earshot.

This was a special place to them. This had been where they'd met. Frank had been touring Argo, and Virginia had been the archeologist assigned to show him the ruins of Hesperides. "You weren't so happy the first time I came here with you."

Virginia laughed, bright in her yellow sundress. "No, I sure wasn't. I really wanted to meet you, but the request to play docent still stung a bit. Claude Martin was as big an ass then as he is now."

"That's government for you, even here. I'm glad you didn't hold it against me."

"You're lucky I still hold it at all, old man."

He grinned—he *was* lucky she still held it—and cherished what they had.

The trail continued up, and slightly to the right. Spotty light leaked through the canopy, highlighting their way and illuminating the occasional flutterwing. It was also the season for flowerflies, with their overly sweet-and-sour odors coming and going along the trail as they passed mating balls.

Another five minutes of walking brought them to the crest of the hill where it was possible to get a view of the valley. They paused. Everyone did, every time.

Great spikes of dull metal, hundreds of meters tall, sometimes singly and sometimes in sets, thrust upward from the jungle foliage. Some of the sets betrayed patterns that made Frank think of dinosaur skeletons, the colossal remnants of antiquity lost for millions of years. It was as if some vast metallic beast had crawled into this valley and died long ago, its life and flesh leaving it, only the hardest and most stubborn parts persisting. And in some sense, that's what had happened.

"Come on, Frank. The kids are almost down already."

He saw them, two blobs of white t-shirt bouncing along way down the trail.

"Okay," he said, feeling a small ache in his lower back and sweat moistening his hairline. "Let's go."

Downhills were easier on his wind than the uphills, but his back and knees complained more. He was a little too fat and happy, he supposed. So be it. There were things worse in life than being fat and happy.

They descended down the trail and back into jungle, which soon blocked most of the giant metal spikes. Far ahead he heard the mournful wail of an Argotian spider monkey troop. On Earth, spider monkeys had a high-pitched screech that they emitted with no particular organization. On Argo, the alien creatures physically resembled their Earthly namesake, plus a few limbs, but differed significantly by joining their voices together. Together their voices built, harmonized, and, reaching a crescendo, all dropped the call—stone-dead silence within the span of a single human heartbeat. It was usually unnerving to listen to.

"When I first came here with my adviser," Virginia said, "he told me that the monkeys were the ghosts of the Argonauts."

Frank agreed it was a spooky sound, amplified by the presence of the ruins. "Kenny better not have nightmares after begging to come here."

"How could he not beg to come here, after the way you built up how fantastic your first visit was?"

"I was referring more to the company."

"Flatterer," she said, smiling.

The trail led into a small clearing. In the center of the clearing rested a thick, metallic gray slab, half-consumed by some pink pastel rust. On top of the slab stood Allyn, hands on hips, imperiously gazing down at Kenny.

Kenny, at the base of the slab, was jumping up and down. "Let me up! Let me up!"

His hands, at the zenith of his jumps, still missed the slab top by ten centimeters.

Frank thought it was kind of funny, and couldn't keep from smiling.

Virginia elbowed him in the ribs and stepped forward to lift Kenny up.

Kenny squirmed and crawled with every muscle, grunting as he ascended to the top of the slab. When he got there, he carefully rose up, starting from his hands and feet. Then he yowled and began stomping around, raising his small fists in the air. "I'm the king of the ruins!"

Allyn pointedly ignored him.

Virginia caught Frank's smile, and he felt warmed by his family. "Come on, boys. There's more to see before lunch."

"I am the king of the ruins!" Kenny shouted.

Virginia lowered her head and looked at him through her dark bangs. "I think this will do, if *His Majesty* will let us feed him."

"Okay," said Frank. He set the picnic basket onto the slab. Then he made a hitch with his hands and gave his wife a boost, wishing at the last second that he'd pushed her bottom up rather than her boot. Oh well, a lost opportunity that could provide inspiration for helping her down later.

Frank joined them as Virginia was already pulling out the blanket from the basket. He stood on the high slab and looked around. Blue sky, a few puffy clouds floating by, perfect. Some trees cast a shadow onto one end of the slab, so they'd have some shade if it got too hot. Above the trees loomed several nearby spikes, the last remnants of some great structure. Quiet, idyllic, and ancient.

"Pretty cool," said Allyn.

"Isn't it," said Frank.

A spider monkey troop started to howl very close by. Kenny must have jumped a meter—he'd have surely made it onto the slab on his own with that inspiration!

Frank started to laugh, but then stopped himself. There was something odd about the call. An uncharacteristic lack of harmony, perhaps. Odd sounding, at a minimum. Then he caught a glimpse of another oddity. The shadows from the irregular-shaped leaves were not sharp, rather they were asymmetrically blurry, holding shadows within shadows in an unusual pattern of light and dark.

"Da, what's that?" asked Allyn. The boy pointed toward the sun, Pollux. Not quite at Pollux, Frank realized, but a bit off in the direction of the greater of the two moons, Charybdis, its crescent visible just above the trees in the eastern sky.

Pollux, as seen from Argo, was a tinge more yellow than Earth's sun, and appeared half again as large. That bothered Frank sometimes—not because it appeared larger, but because it didn't appear more than slightly larger. Pollux, an evolved giant star, burned helium in its degenerate core, and was an order of magnitude physically larger across than old Sol.

The contacts protecting Frank's eyes automatically polarized and darkened as he turned his attention to Pollux, permitting him to stare almost directly at the star without too much discomfort. A bright, thin line stuck out from the star's disk, like the handle of a lollipop. It was a very strange thing to see and didn't make sense. "I don't know. I've never seen anything like that."

Kenny quietly slipped his hand into Frank's and squeezed.

Frank squeezed back.

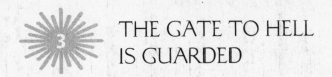

THE GATE TO HELL IS GUARDED

Over the last several hours, Rusk had nearly put the neutrino incident out of his mind.

They were in the midst of hauling up the final X-bot, Theodore, from the hole. The X-bots had thoroughly documented the tunnel with seventeen different scanning technologies, and their Specialist bosses were poring through the data despite rationed oxygen. Rusk himself felt sweaty and grimy, and kept checking his internal suit temperature, although it was always exactly where it belonged. They'd discovered something, and it had been a good day, if a long one.

It's time to leave it for the scientists with the brushes, he thought again, when Griffin called.

"Commander?" Griffin's tinny voice echoed in his stuffy helmet. "I've got something coming in for your ears only."

"Okay." What was this, now? Was he getting reprimanded, or rewarded perhaps, for how he'd handled things before he even returned to Argo? "Patch it through."

"Commander Rusk, acknowledge."

He didn't recognize the voice. That meant it wasn't someone from normal Corps operations. Who else could it be? "Rusk here. Talk to me."

A pause to let the signal travel the light second to Argo and back, maybe even to run through voiceprint verification. The gas mix and pressure were not those of the Argotian atmosphere, and he wondered how easy it would be to account for that in any verification routine.

A click, then, followed by a new voice at a higher volume level. "We have a situation you should be aware of, Manuel." Rusk recognized the deep timber immediately. Claude Martin, Commander-in-Chief of Argo, their branch of the Specialist Corps, and all space operations in the Pollux system. "They woke me up for this, so it must be important, and as I'm rubbing the sleep out of my eyes, I'm starting to agree."

"Sir?" Just like Martin. It was hurry up and wait, even when trying to have a simple conversation with the man. Well, curmudgeonly bureaucrats like him were important to have around, Rusk supposed. He kept thinking he'd figure out why when he got older, and had had that thought for some years now.

His current theory was that it was a combination of slowing mental faculties requiring more start-up time, a minor reminder of power, and being lonely.

Rusk waited with a small sense of relief, knowing that no one would awaken Martin just to chew him out. Still, something that required waking up Martin and contacting him in the middle of an exercise was something both serious and mysterious. Something important was happening somewhere that mattered to him.

"So there's this thing," Martin said. "We don't know what it is, so I'm calling it a thing. That's as good a name as any. It's a thing flying out of the sun at a good fraction of light speed."

Rusk didn't know how to respond to that, so he waited again. He had questions, but imagined he would be supplied with the necessary information.

"Well, here's the crux of the matter. They tell me you sent a neutrino signal a little while ago that went off in the direction of Pollux."

Ah! He was tired, or he'd have made the connection more rapidly. Neutrinos traveled at essentially light speed and could penetrate normal baryonic matter, even the core of a star, with only a small chance of interception. There had been enough time for the neutrinos from this base to have traveled to Pollux.

As soon as Martin stopped speaking, Rusk jumped in. "No sir, we didn't send a signal. Not exactly. We found a hidden Argonaut base on Charybdis, and shortly thereafter a neutrino signal was sent from that base."

A long pause. Then: "You think they're in there, still?"

That was not a thought that had occurred to Rusk, and he should have thought of it hours ago. A secret military base, self-sufficient, shielded, with a handful of long-lived hibernating Argonauts, or their descendants, holding down the fort, so to speak. Interesting. "That seems exceedingly unlikely, but honestly, I don't know, sir. We could find out."

"Well, you'd better I think. That thing, heading out of Pollux, it's heading your way."

"Sir?"

No hesitation now. "This thing. They're telling me it's a great, grand fireball flying out of the sun on a trajectory that's going to smack into your newly found base in a few hours. If there's anything there, I want it. Get in, get everything you can out, now, and get out of there as fast as you can."

It seemed this was not the time for brushes, after all.

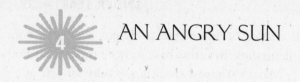

4   AN ANGRY SUN

HESPERIDES PARK, ARGO

Frank resisted the urge to look up, and instead looked at his lovely wife.

Virginia gazed into the azure sky with curiosity playing on her face. "What do you think it is?"

"I don't know," Frank said. This was family time, and he'd left his link in the car to keep the kids from spending all their time on it. He could hike back and get it, he supposed. Frank considered this. He had been waiting for three weeks to get everyone's schedules synchronized for a quality outing, and it certainly was not clear at the moment what was going on. It was likely something innocuous, some comet rounding the star, or a new *Dark Heart* test he hadn't remembered. If it weren't something easily explained like that, they could spend all day hearing wild speculation to no good end.

"Frank," Virginia whispered, arching one eyebrow in that cute way of hers.

He looked over at her.

She held the picnic basket open and leaned it toward him. He made out her link inside.

Of course Virginia had her link with her. With their car several kilometers away, at a semi-remote location, what mother would leave her link behind?

He felt suddenly inadequate as a parent. Why couldn't he always manage to be as thoughtful and protective as his wife? He didn't dwell on the thought. The thing in the sky was likely something innocuous. They could check later if it seemed warranted.

"Come on, boys," he said, shaking his head slightly and looking away from the basket. "Let's have lunch!"

Allyn and Kenny went along with the proposal.

As they dug out sandwiches, cheese, star fruits, and soy sticks,
Frank watched his boys steal glances into the sky every few
minutes. He resisted the urge. It might well be nothing, and
even if it weren't, he no longer played in such big stake games.
Such matters were the province of young men looking for
names for themselves, and sitting around speculating wouldn't
do anyone any good. His big stakes games were behind him, and
his stakes now were here having a picnic with his family, and
that's what he would focus upon.

So he tried to focus on them, the way he imagined Virginia
did every minute without effort. Kenny's pants were too short,
he noticed. Time to get him a new set, or invest in a smart set of
clothes, or two. It wouldn't be a big portion of their quota on
the local nanoforge. And Allyn, why hadn't he started to get interested in girls yet? Or boys? Or *something*? He didn't seem to
be shy, or hiding things, the way some kids did. He looked fine,
a good-looking kid. They didn't have to live up to his fame.
They were fine boys. Of course they were.

His family was *fine*. No reasons to worry.

They ate their food, a little more quietly than usual. Frank's
peanut butter and quixoberry jelly sandwich was on the dry
side, crumbling on his pants. Virginia asked a few leading questions, but his kids had both mastered the monosyllabic reply
and they used it to cover their distraction. It started to get to
him, too.

Above him a fiery line was emerging from the sun.

He finally decided there wasn't much use resisting. How
could the thing going on in the sky not be of interest to them on
Argo? How could it not be important to him personally, and his
family? Maybe being a good parent could also mean focusing on

the world around you, watching for danger. This was unlikely to be dangerous, but perhaps that should always be his first reaction.

He looked to Pollux again.

There was no doubt about it. The line of fire was visibly longer. How much longer? It was probably foreshortened, wasn't it? He knew to think three dimensionally about astronomical objects. Whether foreshortened or not, it had to be growing fast. Argo was nearly six astronomical units away from Pollux and at that distance light took about fifty minutes to reach them. Any visible change in less than an hour meant enormous velocity if in fact the thing was close to the sun.

This thing really could be dangerous.

"Boys," Frank said. "What do you think is going on in the sky?"

"Dunno," said Allyn.

"Space ray gun!" offered Kenny, excitedly.

"That's dumb," said Allyn, lightly punching his brother on the shoulder.

"Allyn!" Virginia warned.

"Sorry, Mom. What do you think it is, Da?"

Frank gestured toward Pollux, and shrugged. "It's nothing, probably, except distracting. But let's find out for sure."

Frank gave Virginia a meaningful look, and after a moment's hesitation and a look back, she dug the link out of the basket.

A few seconds later they were all clustered atop the ancient ruin, under the weird sun, watching the tiny display. There were reports, with lots of graphs and animations—many more than Frank had ever seen growing up on Earth, but the population of Argo was better educated and his kids soaked it all in. The reporter was saying, "The origin of the phenomenon is unclear, but something is emerging from the sun at nearly thirty thousand kilometers per second. Spectral analyses indicates a temperature of . . ."

Frank did the math to make sense of the velocity—that was

10 percent light speed! Incredible. It couldn't be headed for Argo, he realized. If it were headed directly toward Argo it wouldn't extend out so far, and be growing longer. He pondered a little more and thought it could appear to curve away from them and still hit them since the planet was moving in its orbit . . . but the effect wouldn't produce a very large curvature, would it? He wasn't sure.

He used to do calculations like that in his head all the time, and felt old now.

"It's not going to hit us, is it?" Virginia asked.

"I've been thinking about that, and I don't see that it could. It's headed somewhere in our general vicinity, but not at us."

Virginia bit her lip. "Well then," she finally said. "It's not a danger. Let's enjoy the rare spectacle, whatever it is. It's a special event to mark our special picnic day."

Frank looked at his wife, her dark tousled hair and bright eyes, alert yet uncertain. Was this one of those times he was supposed to ignore what she said or to overrule her and suggest they fly home immediately? Being married was good, but not always danger-free. He knew she had to be as desperately curious as he was, but since their first child had been born she had prioritized family in an instinctual manner he wished he could match. His own family background and the years alone in space had blunted whatever instincts he should have had, and he had to constantly work at it, thinking about things she immediately knew. "Okay, we'll make a holiday of it."

"I love you," she whispered quickly.

"Love you, too," he replied, quietly.

"Yuck!" said Kenny. "Mushy!"

Virginia straightened up and said, "Like oatmeal!", which always made Kenny laugh, and this was no exception.

So they finished eating, and watched the sky.

The bright line had grown a little more. The day remained

relatively cloudless and the view became clearer as the line extended farther away from Pollux. It reminded Frank of watching bamboo grow—he'd done that a few times when he'd been on the *Scout 7* in the deep space between the stars and had nothing better to do. Okay, it had been more than a few times.

"What's the line in the sky?" Kenny asked.

"I don't know," Frank said.

"Why not?"

"Not enough data," Frank said.

"Why not?"

"Not enough time to collect it," Frank said. Kenny liked the question game, but thankfully less now that he was older. Frank was happy that Kenny let it drop at that and that Allyn didn't hit his brother.

They continued to watch and Frank worried that, despite the time he was spending with his family, he'd simply become more anxious about what might be happening, hanging out like this. He tried to ignore the feeling. Worrying about worry wasn't productive.

It was a pleasant afternoon, all in all, he decided at one point.

The spider monkey troop had settled down and no longer seemed bothered by the strange lighting. The dark-bristled creatures crawled out into the clearing on their four legs, and, with their four arms, began picking through the soil for bugs and other edibles. Frank still found them interesting to watch although he'd seen similar troops regularly for the nearly twenty years he'd lived on Argo. The spider monkeys moved with a jerky motion that was more reminiscent of birds, or insects, than of Earth mammals. Their movements were arresting to watch. One of the monkeys found a sant nest and yowled. A ripple propagated outward as others moved in to fight for their share of the fat, apparently tasty bugs.

Kenny, giggling, threw a piece of cheese into the troop.

"Kenneth!" Virginia shouted. "Don't do that."

The troop scattered, the rippling circles in reverse. They made a brief unified call of outrage, and then the inner circle dove in for the cheese. They would eat most human food, fight over it even—they were an aggressive species. The colonists, their pets, and livestock had undergone gene therapy to be able to extract nutrition and live off the different combination of amino acids in the Argotian ecology. The life forms of Argo, however, could not as readily digest most Earth food. Especially dairy. Why had he thrown the *cheese* of all his choices? Soon the area would be covered in tiny puddles of pungent monkey crap. Even with their alien biochemistry, the waste from most Argotian animals exuded a foul stench to the human nose.

"Sorry," Kenny said, and continued to giggle, albeit more quietly.

Frank, embarrassed, glanced at Virginia. She didn't say anything, but her stern look revealed a hint of dimple.

"Hey, it's really starting to move," said Allyn.

It was the thing in the sky, of course, not needing explanation. And so it was. The luminous trace etching along was growing faster than bamboo now, clearly moving as he watched it. Also apparent now was that the part of the line extending back to Pollux no longer seemed quite connected. The line had become a pulse.

They watched.

A glowing line drew slowly across the sky, as if God himself had reached down to tear open reality. The finger of God trailing through the heavens. It was awesome to watch, and all the more scary for not knowing its origin. Ancient peoples must have felt similarly watching an eclipse.

"Da," Allyn said. "It's aimed at Charybdis."

And surely enough, it was. The crescent moon was now high overhead. It was smaller than Earth's moon, but closer, and came in at about a third larger, just less than a degree across. At a glance,

Charybdis didn't look all that different from Luna, but the pattern of craters was far from the same, and there were linear patterns, darker latitudinal lines, across the surface, that had no equal on Luna or other moons in Earth's solar system. The origins of the much-studied dark marks were not known.

Away from Pollux, the color of the light of the pulse clarified to a light, bright violet that stood out even in the cerulean blue of the early-afternoon sky.

Frank felt a warm pressure on his knuckles. Kenny's tiny hand wormed its way into his.

Virginia asked, "Did you ever see such a thing?"

"Uh-uh." No, indeed, he had not. He'd traveled longer and farther than any other man alive that he knew of, but this was new. He felt as if he should have something more profound to say, but he didn't. He wasn't often struck wordless.

"I live on another planet from where I was born," she continued, "and I've seen some amazing sights, but this silent, steady scrawl across the sky . . . I'm thunderstruck."

He, too, was awed. He didn't say anything more. The kids started to look spooked though.

The pulse crawled inexorably toward its goal. They watched, minutes passing. The pace accelerated. What had been a barely perceptible motion now seemed fast. Even though it was moving several kilometers per second, fat, round Charybdis appeared to sit still in the sky like the easiest target in the history of target shooting.

"What's going to happen?" asked Kenny.

"I don't know," said Frank. He had always prided himself on the honesty with which he raised his children—no made-up stories, no nonsense answers, no appeals to mythology or mindless tradition, no resorts to tickling to get out of answering a question. Now, however, he desperately wished to reassure his son, reassure himself, but his own sense of integrity wouldn't permit him to do it. He wasn't truly sure if the events warranted being scared, but he was afraid they did. He resisted thinking about that contradiction. Worrying about being worried, afraid he should be scared. He shook his head at himself.

Thankfully, Kenny refrained from pestering him with another question loop.

"Would you look at that," Virginia said.

The pulse quickened, and suddenly its trek across the sky zipped along faster and faster and, proceeding relentlessly, it splashed into the edge of the moon. Splashed, with an intense flash brighter than the sun, making his corneas instantly darken. Disturbing, for more than the obvious reasons, a burst lasting many long seconds, with no sound, no smell, nothing an explosion of this magnitude would generate in an atmosphere. For a few minutes there were two suns in the sky.

Kenny buried his face in Frank's side, holding him tightly.

"Wicked," whispered Allyn.

Frank didn't know what to think as he watched the impact's glow on the edge of Charybdis facing Pollux. The glow was bright, searing. Plumes of molten material blew off the moon's surface and slowly fell back, as if they were watching a distant volcano of fire and black lava.

Without warning, on the opposite side another plume erupted on a beeline through the body. The pulse continued on its fiery way into interplanetary space.

From their feeding spot in the field, the spider monkey troop looked up into the sky and called out in an uncoordinated and mournful cacophony of distress.

Frank said, "Try the link."

"I'm just getting static," Virginia answered.

Frank hoped no one was up there. Still watching the spectacle in the sky, and feeling very concerned, he said "Let's get home."

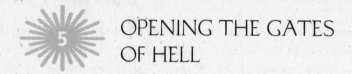

OPENING THE GATES OF HELL

CHARYBDIS, INNER MOON OF ARGO

Rusk looked up at Pollux in the dark sky of Charybdis. Despite the knock-down filters and contrast-enhancers, he couldn't make out this flare, or whatever it was, headed toward them. He supposed that was because it was headed directly at them and was as hot as a sun.

Rusk radioed up to Griffin in orbit. "What's our problem's ETA?"

"One hundred eleven minutes. No accelerations, smooth and steady."

"Keep me informed of any changes."

"Of course," she quipped. "Any progress?"

"I'll let you know. We're about to blow some charges."

"Anything I can do up here?"

Did she really have to be chatty just now? "No."

"Okay. Griffin out."

The disconnect message hit before he could acknowledge. He'd been curt with her, he knew, but he didn't care. She was his junior officer, but also his oldest friend in the Corps. She should be more understanding given the circumstances. It didn't matter at the moment. She was professional, and they had a job to accomplish. Friendships and niceties weren't top priority just now.

She would understand. She'd always be there for him, he knew, no matter how much he might screw anything up. He knew her that well.

A minute later, the trembling of the ground signaled that the explosion had gone off. No sound, no light, just some quivering under his boots. "Report!"

Two X-bots, arms swinging crazily, swarmed down the hole and within a minute relayed video filled Rusk's heads-up display. The Argonaut door stood still, gouged around the sides, but solid.

Well, they had one option left now that the electronics and explosives had failed. "Walter, Anatole. Get your X-bots down there and disassemble that door."

They acknowledged and he summoned Magellan and followed his Specialists down the hole.

Rusk worried a little about the disassembling. He didn't think it was much more dangerous than explosives—less so in many ways—but your average person reacted like twentieth-century people had responded to nukes. Nukes were just bigger bombs with some radioactivity, and could be employed in controlled ways when necessary; tools, like everything else, used or misused by choice. Still, protocol made disassemblers plan C or plan D, never a first or even second option.

The X-bots were already spraying the damned door when Rusk arrived. He and Magellan moved to the opposite side of the room with Walter and Anatole. Walter Stubbs was his nanoexpert, while Anatole Hamilton was his instant expert on everything, a man who probably could make greater contributions to humankind than the Specialist Corps, but had his heart set on the stars.

Magellan stood with the humans and broadcast a very short-range destruct code to protect them from any wayward nano with power reserves beyond spec. Standard procedure.

Rusk gave the go-ahead and the X-bots illuminated the door with microwaves to power the disassemblers. Within moments, the surface began to blacken and sink inward. The trillions of tiny robots were grabbing individual surface atoms and tearing them off, one by one. One centimeter grew to two. Dusty grime piled up at the door's bottom the way termites left sawdust behind their own work. Two centimeters doubled to four.

Rusk watched quietly with the other two men.

After ten minutes, the door had sunk into the wall nearly a meter with no end in sight. Rusk began to doubt, remembering the doomsday clock in the sky above. Should they stop, destruct the nano, and inspect the situation? Perhaps now that they were into the innards of the door they could find a simpler and safer way of opening the thing.

He decided patience was warranted at the moment and that there was no reason to stop yet. Argonauts were not known to use such thick doors, even for the few military bases they'd found, but who knew for sure? This place could be something monumental, like a weapons cache or a genetic ark. Or something greater. He had to have patience and do this job.

The disassemblers now had bored over a meter and a half into the door, making it resemble the start of a tunnel, when Griffin rang him.

He wanted to ignore her, annoyed that she might be communicating something frivolous, just to make up, but he was concerned that the situation had changed up above.

"I've got it," she said.

"Got what?" He wondered about stopping the disassemblers again to inspect the situation.

"The answer to what to do about an obstinate door."

He knew she liked to play games when she knew something he didn't, but this was not the time. "Sloan, what is it?"

"I've got time to look at things you don't up here. Not much for me to do but anticipate emergency flight plans, you know? Well, I was thinking about how Todd is always carrying on about how aggressively sneaky the Argonauts were, so I've been questioning every assumption you've made. I was amplifying the track patterns in the dust, and while there are plenty of tracks that appear to emanate from the door, there are a few that seem to enter from the wall opposite the door."

Rusk checked the countdown, and the numbers weren't getting larger. "And?"

She said nothing, giving him a pause to figure it out for himself. She used to do this while they had studied for exams, and it had annoyed him then, too.

As usual in these cases, she made him stop to think, which was an important thing to do from time to time. So there were tracks coming from another location, which implied another door. A hidden door. They were trying to open a decoy, using their most powerful technology, and wasting their time.

Rusk turned away from their tunneling project to the opposite wall. To his eye, it looked identical to every other wall: smooth, gray, blank. Pointing, he said, "Magellan, destroy this wall."

The X-bot extended two arms to the ceiling to brace itself against two legs on the floor, then with its other four middle arms it began to pummel the wall like a jackhammer. Plan A for *Destroy*.

"What's up?" Anatole asked.

Rusk informed him and Walter while Magellan silently struck the wall, kicking up powdered rock.

Magellan stopped. "I have struck metal," the robot announced.

"Clear the rock away."

A few minutes later a new door became visible, identical to the first, down to the Argonaut heart symbol.

Rusk took a moment to inform Griffin. "You're terrific," he said.

"I know," she replied. "You owe me a drink."

They sent the destruct signal to the deployed disassemblers, rotated 180 degrees, and repeated the procedure on the newly revealed door.

Rusk started counting the minutes, stopped himself, and resumed almost immediately. It wasn't like they'd had a safety margin in the first place.

The newly deployed nano began eating into the real door, centimeter by centimeter, the material sinking into a hazy falling dust.

Suddenly a plume of spraying gas erupted from the center of the door.

Disassemblers blew back into the chamber, hitting the X-bots first, and everywhere else, including the Specialists' thin suits. While the nano required active microwaves to operate, they could still be dangerous for a short time.

Before Rusk could act, Stubbs had shouted "Destruct nano!"

Everyone was quiet for a long moment, breathing heavily.

There were no X-bot malfunctions or suit breaches on first look, and they didn't have time for a complete inspection. Onward. His adrenaline waned, and Rusk felt some elation that they'd finally made some real progress. He promised himself that he'd thank Griffin properly when there was a chance.

The outgassing subsided, revealing a jagged hole in cracked alien metal about three centimeters across. Under their direction, the X-bots inserted their claws and, bracing themselves, pried open the door like he would a can with a busted tab.

There was no illumination inside. Helmet lights showed a small, empty room with another door on the other side. He hoped it to be a real door and not another decoy.

"An airlock, perhaps?" Anatole suggested.

"Could be," Rusk said. "Let's move in and assume that compartments will be pressurized, and avoid using the disassemblers if we can help it. I don't need one blown up my nose."

If each compartment was pressurized, that could slow them down. Doors that might open automatically under normal conditions would sense the pressure difference and refuse to open.

Despite the fact this base had to be at least a million years old, the neutrino pulse indicated operational equipment. Scary technology there, that could last so long. But there was no time to worry about things like booby traps. No time at all. While no one had explicitly said so, he assumed that whatever was coming out of the sun wasn't going to be good news when it arrived.

"I think I can speed this up," Walter said. He was standing by the remains of the door the X-bots had torn apart. "There's a locking mechanism to the lower right of center. The material might be thin enough for brute force, if the systems are still powered."

"Let's give it a try."

At Rusk's order, Magellan extruded a spike from the apex of one claw and thrust it into the indicated spot on the new door. The X-bot popped the arm back, and everyone waited.

Almost immediately, the door unsteadily opened, sliding to the right, in fits and starts. Rusk leaned toward the door to balance himself against the wind coming out. The lock trick seemed to bypass any pressure security. Something breaking their way, finally.

"Good job, Walter."

Walter started to say something, but Griffin overrode the channel. "Safety margin exceeded. You're to drop everything and make for the secondary pickup point."

That was the one closest to this base, so she'd already let the primary pickup deadline pass to give them extra time. He'd trusted her to do this, and hadn't questioned her timetable. But now he had to consider the situation. He was the man on the spot.

Rusk stepped to the threshold of the newly opened door and didn't require his headlamp to scope out the interior. Banks of lighted displays were stacked one over another before the wide, low chairs favored by the extinct Argonauts. The base computers

were definitely active and presumably filled with every secret—
at the least the military sort—known to one of the major fac-
tions of the last civilized era. This could be the key to the demise
of the Argonaut species, and provide countless unknown technologies.

This was extremely important, perhaps as important as any
Castor 6 mission.

"Damn," said Anatole, bumping against Rusk and looking at
the room before them.

"Acknowledge orders," Griffin said.

X-bots could move faster than humans across Charybdis,
even loaded down, so they could stay and work for at least a
few more minutes. There was a problem, however. The X-bots
could never do the excavation correctly on their own. They'd
make the wrong choices about how to rip things apart and how
to prioritize artifacts. And the patterns for the X-bots' experts
on Argonauts tended to be conventional archeologists—which
would have been fine if they were looking for mere artifacts and
had time to be selective, but they had to be looking for military
computers now. A human needed to stay to oversee this. Rusk
held no illusions that it would be safe, or that the base would
even exist after this thing from the sun hit.

"Acknowledged, but I'm exercising my on-the-spot prerogative."

He'd already second-guessed himself once this day, choosing
the politically safe move, and had still blown it. No way he was
going to play it safe now when something this potentially critical was at stake. This military base contained technology that
could control a star.

Inanely, he thought of the phrase, *flare gun,* and forced himself
back to a proper focus. "Walter, Anatole, make for the secondary
pickup site. Leave the exit lines and relays. I'm staying here with
the X-bots to finish this off right."

Anatole started to say something and Walter reached out to flick his helmet sharply.

"Right," said Walter to Rusk, and he turned away.

Walter was always quick to figure things out, especially in times of trouble. Not perfect solutions, but effective ones. Rusk never reliably beat him at speed chess even though he was otherwise the stronger player.

The men moved off, and Rusk queued up some low-volume electronica music that sounded tinny inside his helmet. It wasn't loud enough to drown out Griffin or anyone else, although she was the one talking incessantly at the moment, but enough to help him focus. More important, it was fast paced.

Onward.

He stepped inside and was startled at the motion of his own reflection in a faded display screen. He swallowed dryly. He recalled Martin's unexpected question about whether or not there might be living Argonauts somehow hanging on in here. Maybe the government knew something he didn't?

No, push it away. If there were aliens sequestered here, they were welcome to crawl out of their hidey-holes and pounce on him. He had a job to do, and he got to it.

This room sported a number of blank display screens and electronic boxes. Rusk started pointing at alien equipment and barking orders at the X-bots. The X-bots in turn jumped at his commands and began slicing things apart. He had them cut open several covers to let him peer inside and see the contents. Power supplies or display technology had to be second priority compared to data storage. He'd studied Argonaut tech enough to make those distinctions, but there was a room full of items, and perhaps a base full of rooms, to select from. When he had to make choices among similar components to salvage, he got input from the X-bot patterns or his team over the communications channel despite the extra delay.

He thought of Walter, his ruthless efficiency under time pressure, and thought about what was good enough.

Another thread of uncertainty dangled in the recesses of his mind. What if the thing headed toward them was nothing? Rarefied plasma, too thin to damage this buried base? What if he were simply tearing up priceless artifacts out of misguided pressure? *Enough doubts,* he thought, recalling Walter's practicality. He'd been authorized to treat the threat seriously.

He was acting like a commander now, and it felt better than the second-guessing that had resulted in the neutrino pulse and this entire fiasco, if that signal had indeed brought the wrath of Apollo down upon them.

The X-bots sprouted nets from their interior arms and piled what they could into improvised carriers. Rusk considered grabbing an armful himself, but realized that the burden would slow him down. If he were already too late to get clear safely, his booty would be doomed, as well. How many minutes had passed now? Too many . . .

"Let's clear out," he ordered.

The X-bots had to go first, he decided. He was the slowest in the chain here, and less valuable in some sense than what the bots carried. Rusk slowed down finally, and realized how deeply he was breathing and how sour the air in his suit had become. He gave himself a stimulant boost, which he thought the situation warranted, and felt invincible a few seconds later.

As he watched the X-bots scramble up the jury-rigged lines, he canceled the music and permitted himself to fully reengage with Griffin.

She was talking. "Castor Lander Gamma, making final burn, landing coordinates site contingency option beta."

She sounded steady, cool, and beautiful. There had been a multi-person discussion about rendezvous options that he hadn't fully listened to and he hadn't sorted out the details. He trusted

Griffin and his team to manage that. They were the ones with the time and information to make those calls.

Rusk looked up the shaft of the hole as he began his ascent, and hoped the contingency site was close, because all he could see of the sky was fire.

It was spooky, but spectacular.

He kept climbing, allowing himself the wonder of watching fire burning in the vacuum of outer space. It wasn't really burning, of course. No more than the surface of a star burned. It was merely blackbody radiation from hot, dense gas. But what was channeling it?

No time to wonder. He decided to climb like a frightened monkey, forcing himself to move into apparent danger. Every instinct made him want to drop back down into the hole and find the deepest cranny in the Argonaut base, but the thing above him would get him for sure if he did that. It exuded an unstoppable quality he couldn't understand on an intellectual level.

Coming out of the hole, Rusk staggered a step or two in an undirected way, scanning around. He finally spotted the X-bots, snaking along with their loads, and he bounced after them.

It was several moments of strange light and shadow before he saw the lander settling into a cloud of moon dust kicked up by its retrorockets.

"Griffin!" he said. He now possessed the quiet insight of a frightened monkey, too.

The lander had barely touched down before the bay doors raised and the X-bots lifted themselves inside.

"Get in, asshole," Griffin ordered.

No arguments on that point given the bolt of fire above. Rusk hopped up quickly in the low surface gravity, falling on his butt in the airlock. The doors fell abruptly behind him and the airlock cycled. Immediately he felt the engines throttle up to launch. No time to strap in, they were taking off.

Rusk staggered up and moved beside Griffin, who was staring out a viewport, goggle-eyed and flushed, her face lit up through her helmet as if she were looking into an open kiln.

He saw the surface of Charybdis rolling underneath the orbiting mother ship. A black and white cratered landscape gave way to lava fields. *Lava fields.* Molten, bubbling rock, glowing hot red, and brighter. Streaming. Popping. Rivers of molten rock slowly snaked away from ground zero, hardening like scabs some distance away from the open wound. Unbelievable.

Charybdis had literally transformed into some junior version of hell.

It wasn't just red, but so many hues of red, orange, and yellow flashing up at him and off the remaining mountains on this small world. It was a boiling soup of a world.

The moon had become soup, for heaven's sake!

This had been a training exercise, and death had come calling.

And Griffin had been there to save him, like an angel swooping from the sky, just like she'd promised.

He put his arm around her, thankful, and wished his performance had earned such loyalty.

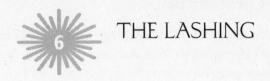

THE LASHING

KLINGSTON HOMESTEAD, ARGO

Frank's house, a low ranch made of rough-hewn wood, nestled below in its lighted yard as they approached, like something out of medieval Earth, nineteenth century, maybe earlier. The arcology of New Colchis two thousand kilometers away at least looked modern, a sturdy composite pyramid reflecting the sky and sea, more like the places he'd lived on Earth before leaving for interstellar space. Looking down on his own house, which in the stark floodlights resembled a giant pile of artfully arranged logs, he felt like he couldn't provide properly for his family. It didn't matter that the disparity between city and country was exaggerated on colony worlds, and it didn't matter that New Colchis wouldn't stand up to what happened on Charybdis any better than his house of sticks.

He landed the car quietly, as smoothly as he could. His boys were asleep in the backseat.

Frank and Virginia carried them inside and put them to bed. They couldn't get Allyn awake enough to get his clothes all the way off, and Kenny had a few tricky moments in the bathroom aiming, but they managed.

Without speaking, he and Virginia made their way to the living room and turned on the feed with the volume on low.

The news was already calling the event "the Lashing," and Frank immediately hated the term. It was a handy, convenient label masking something unknown, powerful, and dangerous. Having labels let people think they understood something, let them throw around terms that were more like iceberg tips and could be infinitely more dangerous. At least it wasn't an acronym. His time as a Scout had led him to really hate acronyms more than most things in the known universe.

Reporter sim Ace, the perfectly coifed androgynous news-caster, broke into one of the expert interviews with an update. Pollux had launched another plasma stream, another Lashing. The sim shrank to a small corner as an obviously magnified im-age of the sun's surface burst into view. While most of the pic-ture shimmered in that big, distant way things appeared when viewed through an atmosphere in real time without corrections, a region near the center churned. Bubbled. Rose. He thought of water spilling from the back of some great reptilian beast emerging from beneath an ancient ocean.

No, a single beast was not the right thing at all as he contin-ued to stare. It was more like a swirling fireworks fountain, spouting up, with streamers of fire flowing away from the dis-turbance. Some kind of school of starfish, or a swarm of some-thing unnatural. It struck him as a group activity, dragging out a plume almost like a geyser, except it kept getting longer.

"Another one?" Virginia whispered into his armpit.

Frank couldn't keep from smiling at his sleepy wife's under-statement, although he felt no mirth. It was his habit to be charmed with her and to show it easily. "Guess so," he said, some sleep in his voice, too.

Assuming this wasn't a planet killer to doom them all (and he didn't have the energy to deal with that), he dimly realized this was one of those defining moments in history that everyone would remember. For the rest of everyone's lives, of those living on Argo anyway, you could ask them exactly where they were and what they were doing the day of the first and second Lashings.

He was happy that he would remember the first being with his family at a picnic.

And now, curled up on the couch with Virginia, in his own

house, with his kids sleeping in their beds, he'd remember the second. If nothing threatened that, he could live with this memory forever. Events were still distant, although this second Lashing was disturbing . . . media speculations about its target . . . time estimates . . .

Frank awoke abruptly from a doze. He was staring straight at a stream of fire and couldn't understand for a moment what he was seeing. He made out the voice of some so-called expert talking about the Lashing (how could you have an expert on something unprecedented?) and it all rushed back again.

But it was still dark outside, Virginia slept quietly on his numb arm, and his boys were safe in their beds. He could almost believe that the previous day's events were unreal.

Frank had to pee. That was a problem he thought he could solve. He shifted to extricate his sleeping arm from under his wife's back.

As usual, she woke up. Easy to sleep, and easy to wake. "What?"

She always said that when awoken. "Going to the bathroom."

"Okay," she said, sitting up.

When he got back, she was more fully awake and leaning in toward the display, her face focused and intent on the dim light and whispering voices.

He was going to suggest they go to bed, but even though they had both fallen asleep earlier, something remarkable and dangerous was transpiring and it would be difficult now. Sometimes the mind forces an escape against the terrible, he knew from experience, but you had to face everything sooner or later. Stroking his beard, he sat down next to Virginia and she leaned back into his shoulder like she had a thousand times before.

"They say this new one is heading toward Charybdis again."

He thought about that for a few seconds. "Good."

"Good?"

"It's not headed for Argo."

She was quiet for a long moment. "Yes. Good."

She settled into him more deeply, and by habit he himself settled in, too. Virginia was smart—smarter than he was, he thought—but he suspected that she was too sleepy to ferret out all the possibilities for destruction offered up by the phenomenon. He'd been enumerating them the night before, and like sheep, they'd driven him unconscious.

She hugged him and said, seemingly absentmindedly, "I feel safer with you here."

That was ridiculous. There was nothing he could do about this weird, destructive force that had simply appeared in the sky. Instead of stating the obvious, he recalled half of a lesson from a counseling session he and Virginia had had several years earlier.

"I appreciate that. I wish I could really do something more," he said.

She squeezed his arm. "You *are*. You're making me feel safer. The kids, too."

He just grunted a half-assed agreement. He didn't try to argue with emotional responses, especially when they were wrong. A hollow sensation crept inside him, between his bowels and his gorge, and dug in.

There was something wrong in the world.

She nestled into his body and her breathing soon told him that she was asleep. Again.

Information trickled in through the feed, slowly, and without many tangible details. What else could he do but sit, wait, and watch?

And sit there he did, becoming a news zombie as the night progressed. Sometimes he'd switch from the main feed to one of the discussion forums, until he tired of that and returned to the news. The display colorlessly illuminated the room with a harsh static that only eventually became softer with twilight. Frank thought he might have dozed a couple of times without fully realizing it.

Virginia abruptly arose without a word and he heard her quiet steps as she padded away barefoot, the water running in the bathroom, and then a quick call—"Come to bed"—and then he only heard the voices on the news again.

He didn't feel the need to move, and decided not to go to bed. The day was already shot, and the prospect of a couple of hours of sleep followed by a half-hearted attempt at work didn't make much sense to him at this point. The news was already saying that country schools were to be canceled anyway, which would likely mean a lot of people wouldn't work, either. He'd figure out with Virginia how to handle it later. Allyn wouldn't want to babysit Kenny—he never did.

He did get up for a minute to go to the bathroom, and stopped by the fridge to grab a beer, one of his darker brews.

Frank paused in the lighted door, a cold bottle labeled KLINGSTON'S KRUD in hand featuring an ugly scribble Kenny had drawn for him, and decided he would try to put in some work today and start a couple of new batches. People might make a run on beer in the next few days, depending on what happened. His experience maintaining a rickety spacecraft with a serviceable microbrewery held together with duct tape and epoxy had given him valuable skills on a colony world like Argo. In the scattered communities outside the New Colchis arcology, someone who could make decent beer was worth every bit as much as a farmer or carpenter. Sometimes more, as he had pleasantly discovered. It was low stress work he could do mostly alone, and he liked it.

The news suddenly changed color and tone and they cut away from an interview with some solar astronomer Frank didn't know. He didn't mind. The man had been worthless for real information like every other expert he'd seen.

Ace, as perfect and chipper as ever, announced, "We now cut to coverage of the impending impact of the second Lashing."

Had that many hours passed already?

He decided to let Virginia sleep. At least one of them could be fully functional. The thought reminded him of when the kids had been young and they'd made those sorts of trade-offs.

A distant part of Frank stepped outside the moment to be critical that Ace hadn't been given a better emergency demeanor, and then to tell himself he shouldn't be drinking beer so early in the morning when such things were happening. So why should he be so critical of some poor anonymous simulation doing their job well enough?

The sim shrank to the corner and was replaced by a luminous lunar view.

The beer, momentarily forgotten in his hand, was getting sweaty. He took a swig and looked again.

The Lashing came quietly into view as it burned its way through the darkness of space.

Ace started speaking lowly and quickly, filling in some numbers they had on what was happening, with a running ticker echoing his words below. The temperature was—

Slap! Ouch! Giggles . . .

"Boo!" Kenny shouted, his little hands splayed on Frank's thigh where they had smacked him. "Got you!"

Frank grimaced and tensed his muscles, heat coming to his face. His stupid kid had to choose *this* moment to interrupt?

But before he let himself say anything, he looked at Kenny's smiling face and his apple cheeks under his thin blond hair, and Frank melted. This here, this little boy, his sweet face with eyes big and unconcerned, this was ultimately why he had remained awake all night, wasn't it?

Before Kenny could sense anything amiss, Frank set down his

beer and scooped his boy into his arms and lifted him above his head.

Kenny giggled uncontrollably.

Frank swept him in, settled him into his lap, and said, "What's the magic word?"

"Abracadabra!" Kenny shouted, as always, correctly. Frank's own parents, likely dead now back on Earth, had always said that *please* was the magic word. Nothing magic about being polite, he'd always thought rebelliously, and Frank preferred teaching magic for magic and polite for polite.

"Right!" Frank pulled Kenny in close, and smelled the clean smell of his morning hair, which puberty wouldn't mar for several years. "Hey boy, I'll tell you something good if you tell me what Mom's up to."

"She's sleeping. I surprise you! Now tell me!"

Fair enough. Frank leaned close and whispered, "There's no school today."

The shriek about shattered his eardrum, and Kenny kicked his little legs against his and the sofa. "Yes!"

If Mom had been sleeping before, he trusted she could get back to sleep easily enough after this interruption. Frank hugged him until he settled down a little and whispered again, "We have to be quiet and let everyone else sleep, okay?"

Kenny nodded his head vigorously and said just a bit loudly, "Okay!"

So what was going on? Frank held his son and peered over Kenny's infinity of cowlicks at the display. Splashing molten rock, lakes of fire, complete devastation of a lunar landscape, as before. Voice-overs were beginning to provide specific details about the impact site and speculation as to why it had been targeted, or if it had been randomly chosen. More break-ins by other cranky voices—likely sleepless as well if they weren't from X-bot patterns, since only one hemisphere of Argo was inhabited—to counter uncertain assumptions underlying earlier statements. A rambling, panicky narration that bit like uncertain piranhas.

And images of utter destruction.

Frank felt a pang of exhaustion and hopelessness, and knew he had to fight it immediately. Just because the narration for hell sucked at his soul didn't mean his soul needed to be full of despair. Let them suck that out, rather than the hope.

With the kids getting up and Virginia sleeping (he hoped), it was time to stop being morosely indulgent. Here he was drinking beer and watching images of distant destruction he could do nothing about. Time to stop watching and worrying, and start living.

Kenny was sitting on the edge of the sofa between his legs, singing a little song to himself and not really watching the news. Better to keep it that way.

"Hey, kiddo, how about some pancakes for breakfast?"

"With booberries?"

Frank loved how he still called them that. "Yes," he said, and did the ghost voice Kenny liked so much, "*with booberries. Boohooberries.*"

Kenny grinned, getting the punch line he so loved. "Don't cry, Daddy. It's okay."

Frank said, "I'm sure it will be, kiddo."

There were three more Lashings that fretful, strange week.

One of the new Lashings hit Charybdis again. Another hit Scylla. The final one passed close to Argo, but safely missed the planet or anything else by thousands of kilometers.

And the sims, patterns, and experts of all stripes kept talking. No one knew why this was happening, how it was happening, or what would come next.

Virginia delayed a trip to visit a dig site, the kids had to resume school but by remote, which kept them busy enough, and Frank more or less managed to stick to his brewing schedule although pickups became erratic. The eggs got collected from the chicken coop, the goats got by, and nothing from the sun got them.

And life went on.

Then a week went by with no Lashings, and things grew stranger.

He imagined it was similar to the way people had once lived under threat of biological attack or nuclear war. Something unusual could happen in the sky and everyone would suddenly die. But mostly it didn't happen, and few worried about it on a daily basis.

Frank kept watching too much news, and started posting anonymously his own thoughts on a couple of the more reasonable link forums. He worried that people might expect him to know more than they did given his relative fame and background, and he'd be a distraction. He also thought he thought too much of himself.

"Why don't you stop obsessing over this for a few minutes and spend some time with your family?" Virginia asked on the way to the kitchen to start dinner.

"Because I'm an old idiot," he said, suspecting it was probably his turn to cook, and trying to remember who had cooked last. If he couldn't remember, it was always him.

"Yeah," she said, smiling. Letting the smile fade, she said, "Come back soon from wherever you are, okay? We need you here."

"Have I been that bad?"

She nodded slowly and deliberately. "Kenny wanted you to read a story for him last night, and you said you would, and he fell asleep waiting. Allyn's cute friend Ashlyn—you met her the other day, remember—and you didn't even embarrass him once. And I was also waiting in bed for you to embarrass me, and had to settle for some old dig reports instead."

"Damn, I'm sorry." He started to get up.

"No, you stay put. You're not ready yet."

Virginia walked over to the sofa, stood behind him, slipped her arms around his neck and whispered in his ear. "I know you had a hard time before, and that you're used to being responsible about taking care of things, responsible to everyone. So I'm giving you some time. But you're not responsible for everything here. Just us, your family, and maybe for getting some beer brewed once in a while."

He took a deep breath, enjoying the warmth of her body against his, the moment of forgetting the crisis. "We could have Lois and Don over for cards."

"No, we can't. You'd be good for an hour, maybe, but then you'd get distracted, or get Don worked up and the two of you would get drunk. Besides I already told them no when Lois called."

"You're right," he said. Then, "You're good to me."

"Yes, I am. Don't forget it."

And off she went to the kitchen, and he heard the pots rattling and the fridge opening. And sooner than he would have guessed, he let the sounds fade to the ongoing Lashing news. At moments during dinner, and later that evening, he felt some guilt, and decided that was a good sign.

Frank went to bed early and while he'd thought he and Virginia might make love, they just cuddled. After she fell asleep, he found himself restless and, after seeking sleep for over an hour, he rose. He hadn't been keeping his family's schedule, and he felt guilty about that.

He checked on the kids. They were fine, asleep. He checked

the security system. No problems there, just three young skitterin bucks bedded down near the perimeter.

Frank strode through the dark house, too tension-filled to be still for long. Easy enough to know you're overdoing it, but another thing to fix the problem.

The ceiling fan spun slowly, the only noise other than his own sounds. He decided not to turn on the news—they'd prattled on with no new information for hours on his last stint, and he didn't want to be caught up in useless details anymore. He was coming out of it enough to know that.

While he admired Virginia for not getting lost in it like him, he could never be like her. She was too focused on the minutiae of immediate tasks. Like a lot of scientists he'd met and worked with, they were often too busy to take new action. She was too much a scientist, always wondering about things and giving them more study without action, and ignoring things that she didn't like, leaving them to be considered in some nebulous "later" that never fully seemed to come. But you couldn't leave things like that. You couldn't just sit back and expect things to work out.

Frank had met aliens. He knew better.

In the voids between stars, the universe was timeless. Nothing seemed to move, and nothing seemed to matter even though it did. Stars, planets, now these were places where things moved fast and you always had to keep an eye open for predators, both day and night. You had to take action sometimes, or you and your family could die in an instant. You couldn't trust yourself to the mercy of others, especially others that were alien. Who could truly know the intent of the other, and trust it?

To the sliding glass doors, back across the living room, even in full darkness, he navigated a well-known path he could see in his mind. Only starlight through the skylights and windows aided him, making him a primitive sailor in his own home. Kind of like the empty years.

A bright blue light blinded him, and made him blink.

Not so bright, but blinding to his dark-adapted eyes. The house computer parsing an incoming message at some urgency level, choosing to alert him and him alone as he was up and walking the premises, letting others sleep.

Frank hadn't maintained his high-up contacts very well, but he'd been important. Maybe someone had thought to call him and tell him something, anything. That would be okay.

He crossed the room to a display to where the camera would only see him from the neck up. He whispered, "I'm here."

The display brightened, casting sharp shadows before it. A tired, gray face with white, bushy eyebrows stared back at him, unblinking. With the sound volume set at a level similar to Frank's whisper, the man on the screen spoke. "Frank, it's Claude."

Claude Martin was not someone he considered a contact. Frank had burned some boosters with Claude, or at least thought he had. "I can see who it is," he said, finally.

"Can you catch the midday shuttle to Colchis the day after tomorrow? I'd like your input on this."

Good, a request this time. Frank relaxed a little, realizing he'd tensed up. Sure, things were chaotic down here, and he hadn't slacked off too much this crazy week; he could afford the time to go if the babysitting situation was solved. But he thought he'd better make Claude work a little. The man wasn't his favorite person.

"You going to tell me anything about what's really going on? Or am I just for show again?"

"Frank, you were never just for show."

Frank waited. Silence was a tool.

The moment dragged.

"In person," Claude said, tersely.

Frank waited again, as if to look like he were considering.

Frank said, "No escort, and nothing on the news. I won't be a PR tool for you."

"Of course not. It's nothing like that at all, Frank."

"I'll see you day after tomorrow."

Claude nodded and turned away, onto the next task, before his image even faded.

Frank felt just a little bad for his token resistance, but that emotion warmed with a quiet satisfaction. There was an action he could take. Maybe it would help quell the cold, hollow feeling settling deep in his heart.

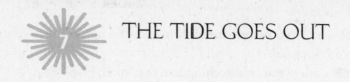

THE TIDE GOES OUT

NEW COLCHIS ARCOLOGY, ARGO

Of the thirty-three bars in New Colchis, Tidepool was not Sloan Griffin's favorite. It was on a lower level, along the outside wall. Half the time the place was underwater, and then it wasn't so bad, with a quiet filtered light in the daytime and a cozy darkness at night. The rest of the time the waves came unevenly, crashing against the sloping wall, an effect she found disquieting and not at all relaxing, especially when drinking.

She thought a good bar should be relaxing all the time, or at least welcoming. But just because she didn't like it didn't mean that others didn't.

The place was Manuel's favorite, for instance. He liked an active, challenging environment, even while she supposed he thought he was relaxing. And, unfortunately, she was sure that this was the sort of place he would pick to deliver bad news given the circumstances.

So she rode the escalators down and across from her New Colchis apartment into the lower zone, and then it was just one slidewalk over. She passed three bars she liked better on the way, and two brew pubs.

She hadn't seen Manuel since the group debriefing several days earlier, and he hadn't replied to her messages. He should have, but he had a decent excuse. They'd been sent on indefinite shore leave with instructions not to speak of their recent exercise. Griffin didn't like the ban, but had to admit that talking would spread rumors and rumors were rarely healthy. Unsupported speculation was already bad enough.

Still, she had her own speculations about Manuel and his mood. In the past, she would have expected him to spend time with her after such a difficult experience, but maybe they weren't as close as she thought they were. Or times were worse than they'd ever been since. He'd been steadily building distance, albeit not a tremendous amount, since he'd been named head of the Castor 6 mission.

As she strolled along the slidewalk, still tired and achy under the full Argotian gravity, she watched the people on the slide and the ones along the mall, in front of the shops and seated at the restaurants. Everyone on the planet had to be under stress. Were they acting normally? Could she just look at them and tell that things were different?

Griffin considered a couple leaning toward each other at a table in front of a pizza parlor. Young, maybe still teenagers, a blond-headed boy and a dark girl. Their hands lingered together on the table, but they weren't holding hands despite the conspiratorial closeness of their heads. Maybe they weren't lovers, and she was seeing sexual tension? Or maybe they were siblings? Then they were gone, carried away by the never-pausing slidewalk. Another couple, middle-aged, stood staring at a window display showcasing holographic clothes flashing over two mannequins. Was it desperate shopping? Or was it normal?

What could be normal now?

She'd seen the surface of a moon explode. Didn't they understand it could happen here? Right here? With only hours' warning?

Maybe they did. Maybe they didn't. Maybe they were in denial, willfully or not. Or maybe it could be characterized in a more positive light. Maybe it was defiance.

But what else could they do? Hide in their apartments? Shriek in terror and run about pulling at their hair?

And it was a very nice day, heading into evening. Sunlight

spilled through the walls and through the light pipes, flashing and sparkling over the diamond beams and fountains, filtered through the sweet-smelling flowering vines, making for a warm and safe feeling. Those raised in the arcology knew nothing but perfect weather, with cleverly crafted artificial lighting helping out the sun on the dark days. Inside was always perfect illumination.

"Hey!" said a woman Griffin was staring past as the slidewalk moved forward.

Griffin smiled and nodded automatically, used to seeing people she knew when out. Argo was not a heavily populated world.

Then she did a mental double take, realizing it wasn't just a casual acquaintance. It really could be strange to see coworkers out of context. She also realized that it was time to leave the slide, and did so immediately, stepping across the slowdown strip. "Selene?"

Selene Madison smiled brightly back at her, nodding a little too much like a mad doll as she twisted her head to one side, then the other. "Like it?"

Specialists had never adopted much of the military formalism that the organization superficially resembled, although she and Manuel had once had an argument about that—their core arose from the original NASA designation of Mission Specialist from their strange mix of military and civilian traditions. Seeing Selene not only in a cute denim miniskirt and red halter top, but sporting a chic asymmetric bob in place of her simple ponytail . . . well, it had thrown her.

Griffin was wearing jeans and an old blouse and felt underdressed. Uniforms for everyone made it easier all around. Especially when you were the one who tended to be in bad clothes when given the choice to select them yourself.

"Yeah, it's great," Griffin said honestly. Even as she said it and meant it, however, she wondered if this was denial again in front of her, or defiance? Selene was competent, but not always tough. It could be either. "You just get here?"

"Uh-huh. Haven't been in yet."

"Well, let's go."

The entrance to Tidepool was sunken in a corner, molded into a rocky grotto, with a stairwell leading down. Griffin took a deep breath and paused at the top of the stairs, then plunged into the soft jazz wafting up to her. The space opened up, broad and low, with the slanting window wall to the left, the long bar on the opposite side, and seating between. It wasn't very crowded but it took a moment before she spotted Manuel and the team at a large table under the water with fish flashing by. There was Manuel and the entire lot of them, out of uniform, inside, dry, and totally out of place.

"Want a drink?" she asked Selene.

"A beer, thanks," Selene answered.

Griffin patted her shoulder, nudging her toward the group, and headed to the bar, delaying things. She tried to tell herself that she just wanted to see the bartender show off, but she knew she was nervous about this meeting. It was all so strange.

Strange was bad. You studied things, figured them out, and then trained until you knew how to respond in any situation. That was her approach and it served her well. But not now.

The bar before her, she considered what to order. While Griffin understood that beer could be a subtle and interesting drink, she never ordered beer at the Tidepool. That wouldn't be any fun, and she needed a taste of fun. She made her choice and labeled it defiance.

The X-bot swung along the overhead monkey bars and gracefully plonked down before her. A dimpled male face winked at her from the pattern display, a name tag beneath saying KEVIN. "What'll it be?"

Griffin said, forcing a smirk, "A beer, whatever you recommend that's on draft, and an Orion Rainbow."

The face on the pattern grinned. "Ah, lass, I think I just fell in love with you!"

She smiled back, more genuinely. Even though the response was all programming, and a bit over the top, it was derived from a real man who was a real expert at what he did, and she responded—at least a little—as if it were the real thing, as she knew she would. It didn't matter that it was an effort to give herself a boost before what might be difficult, or at least depressing.

The X-bot reached over with one tentacle, grabbed a glass with a geckopad, and set it under a tap, flipping the spigot for a slow fill as it withdrew. Now, the race was on.

One tentacle shot straight up, wrapping around a bar and suspending the bot so that all its other appendages were free at the same time. Almost as quickly, six other tentacles reached for six different colored liquor bottles, flipping two in the process, which provided the illusion of juggling. But the Rainbow wasn't about juggling. It was about speed and colors. The colors rained in: red, green, crystal blue, amber, gold, and a dark indigo shot, swirling together, each one containing tasty chemicals to prevent mixing.

The X-bot lowered itself when several tentacles finished their simultaneous pour, allowing it to settle down again. Kevin said, "Here you go, my bonny lass," handing her the beer and the Rainbow.

The drink, still swirling hypnotically, was a bit of a cheat for a pattern to pull off, as it was something no human could make and serve properly. Rusk had told her a few years ago, after first ordering the drink for her, that the Kevin pattern was from a part-time bartender hobbyist, who was also a bot engineer, and had come in from the Earth feed as part of a highly rated cultural enrichment package. All but one of the seven bars in the arcology that had X-bots for bartending used Kevin almost exclusively.

"Make sure these get billed to Manuel Rusk," she said. "He owes me."

"Right-o!" Keven answered.

Griffin let her smile go a little as she took a breath and turned with the drinks to join her team. They huddled around a long table with Rusk at one end. She counted eleven, and she made twelve, so they were all there. At the far end sat Selene, the only open seat next to her. She joined her.

Griffin felt miffed that she wasn't going to sit next to Rusk like she usually did, and that she was waiting for him to shed some light on things as much as anyone. She could tell him he'd gotten charged for the drinks later, she supposed. Or she'd just make him buy her another when they got the chance to talk. He was treating her kind of crappy, and that would be proper.

She took a better look at Rusk. Slightly built and darkly handsome, almost pretty, he was always immaculately groomed and animated in a way that made him seem larger. This day, however, his dark complexion could not hide the circles under his eyes or the stubble on his cheek, and his white dress shirt was rumpled in a way that suggested it had been pulled out of an overnight bag rather than a closet. He slumped at the end of the table, compact, not moving, with an untouched glass of red wine before him.

"Everyone is here," he said softly enough so Griffin had to lean in. Rusk picked up his glass, and sat up straighter. He made slow and deliberate eye contact with each of them, ending with Griffin. He held up his glass and waited for everyone else to do the same. "To the Castor 6 Mission Specialists!"

Then he drank. Everyone followed, with some hesitation, Griffin noticed. Her drink didn't taste quite as good as it looked.

"You were an excellent team," he said. "We would have made spectacular discoveries."

That did it. Half a dozen people started to hurl questions at Rusk. Griffin herself said nothing, but held eye contact with him as he glanced her way, willing for spontaneous telepathy. What *exactly* did he mean?

Rusk broke eye contact. He took another sip of his wine and set it down, slowly, ignoring the questions. He spoke again, quietly, forcing everyone to shut up in order to hear him. "The Castor 6 mission is indeed canceled. I expect to be asked to leave the Corps. I doubt the *Dark Heart* will be going anywhere while Pollux lashes out at us, and I cannot doubt the decision is the correct one."

"Do they blame us?" Walter asked. "Is this punishment? We didn't do anything!"

"We sure did," Anatole said. "We extracted more from that base in less time than any archeologists could have. Those guys would have been killed. They should be thanking us."

Selene asked, "Did the techies get anything useful from the gear we hauled out?"

"I don't know much more than what I've told you," said Rusk. "Claude Martin just informed me this afternoon about the mission. He didn't want me to tell you, not yet, but I convinced him you deserved to know."

"What did he say," Griffin asked, "that led you to believe you'd be asked to leave? And is it just you, or all of us?"

Rusk set down his wine. "Martin said I should prepare for some personnel changes, starting at the top. I'm preparing for that, indeed. But I'm sure we'll still need Specialists."

Lord, that could mean anything. *Martin* could be resigning based on that cryptic statement. But she knew how Manuel took things, and while she didn't know exactly what had happened on Charybdis, she knew he would assume total responsibility for unleashing whatever it was that had been unleashed. Fair or not.

Donovan, her copilot, stood up and pushed back his chair in one fluid motion. Glowering he said, "Why the hell did you have to ask us out here, a public bar, to tell us this?"

"Easy, Mitch," Gina Dorissey, their primary doctor, said, touching his arm.

He shrugged away and leaned closer to Manuel. "Why?"

Manuel, his eyebrows knitting together, peered up at Donovan. "Because I wanted us all together one last time and I didn't think it appropriate for us to be in uniform."

Donovan's body relaxed, a little, as he leaned back, although he continued to frown. "Well, you got your wish. Sorry I don't feel like partying."

"I'm sorry, too," said Manuel.

Through the window behind Donovan, an unusually large sea spider flashed forward to bite a smaller white fish almost completely in half. Its blood was dark in the dark water.

Suddenly everyone was silent, lost in their own thoughts as reality settled in. Castor 6 might as well have been a million light-years away. The mission they'd been preparing for, for years already, would not happen. They might soon be reassigned to other duties, and remain under just as much threat from Pollux as anyone on Argo. Everything was the same as it had been before, and everything was different.

Even though the first sip hadn't been wonderful, Griffin decided there were worse things she could be doing at that moment than drinking a Rainbow, and lifted her glass to her lips. She tried to make eye contact with Manuel again, wanting to tell him that life would go on and they'd all do their best and things would work out, but he only had eyes for his wineglass just then.

Maybe he would want to hear it later, if he hadn't actually given up as completely as it seemed.

And if he didn't, she'd slap the asshole when she got the chance, best friend or not.

ANCIENT HISTORY

"Well, here we go," Frank whispered to his wife as they were ushered into Claude Martin's office. "Remember, you could have stayed home."

"And miss this happy reunion?" she whispered back. "Not a chance. And besides, I figure you owe me at least one decent meal out after all the cooking I've done recently."

"Absolutely," he promised, and then shifted to square his shoulders for the meeting ahead.

Frank had never really liked Claude, and it was things like having to fly partway around the world to New Colchis to see him face-to-face that contributed to that attitude. He resisted the notion that it was because of the man's appearance, and was sure it wasn't entirely that, but Frank always had to steel his face against an involuntary grimace when he saw him.

It wasn't his fault he was old-fashioned. Frank was old, and an artifact of another era.

Claude . . . well, Claude was only part artifact.

Claude crawled across the floor, lifting himself up at the last moment to shake with Frank. Not hands. He used a facsimile of a hand attached to one of his four appendages, which were closer to X-bot tentacles than arms or legs. The hand facsimile was rounded, with a dual ring of extendable nubs, covered in a dark rubbery material that didn't yield as much as flesh but yielded enough to feel fleshy.

The thing about Claude and his modifications that always crept to the front of his mind was that the man had chosen to make them. He hadn't lost his limbs from birth defects or a stupid accident or even extensive frostbite. The way he usually explained it, as often as he could force the opportunity into conversation, was that it was crazy not to trade up when you had the chance. Then he'd make a comparison to poker and laugh in his predictable way. A robot in body and action it seemed to Frank, and not human enough to be in charge of so much.

The Specialist Corps was the power above Argo, and for a colony world that was everything. The man's rank might as well have been emperor or king.

"Good to see you, Frank," he said, with a familiarity that he'd always assumed with Frank, and that Frank had never given him.

"Claude," Frank said.

Claude's smile didn't waver when he turned to greet Virginia, but the way it froze told Frank all he needed to know. He supposed that was another reason he didn't like Claude. Frank had never been particularly good at reading people—the years alone in space certainly hadn't helped—but he'd always felt he knew exactly what Claude was thinking and it was rarely as warm as his outward demeanor. Claude was a robot after all, at least in part, and Frank felt that part extended to his face.

Now his robot-telepathy suggested what was cycling through Claude's mind: *Why dear God did he bring her? I didn't mention her when we spoke and she doesn't need to know anything I'm here to say, at least not on my time. Why is Klingston always so much trouble? I wouldn't even be here if I didn't need something from him, so why can't he just help me already?*

A look and a moment's hesitation from Claude suggested he was thinking about asking Virginia to leave, but instead he bade them both to sit.

"Well, it's no secret we have a problem, is it?" Claude began, with his "we" sounding forced. It seemed ludicrous, but he apparently viewed the threat of cosmic destruction as his own personal problem and was embarrassed to be soliciting input.

"No, it isn't," said Frank.

"What do you know?" asked Virginia.

"I've brought a bot down with me from the *Visionary*." Claude glanced up at the open girders in the ceiling of the Specialists' conference room. "Gerald, give them the briefing."

An X-bot lurking above uncoiled and extended its anterior tentacles pushing it away from the ceiling and toward Frank and Virginia. Gerald reached for the floor with its opposite tentacles, latched on with geckopads, then released its other end. Collapsing and rotating its body, the X-bot faced them like a person, and unfortunately Frank made the connection to Claude himself.

Above the X-bot's composite cylindrical body, in its projection dome, a holographic head manifested. A freckled, redheaded male face of indeterminate age glanced back and forth between Rusk and Griffin and, as the face's lips began to move, a deep resonant voice projected forth from the dome speakers. "Nothing, no matter how well built, stays in one piece for two million years. The greatest mystery of all regarding the technological civilization of the Pollux system is how the Argonauts sailed their planet, if you will, to its present orbit when their sun exhausted its core of hydrogen fuel and began expanding into a red giant."

Personally Frank felt that the greatest mystery was what had happened to the Argonauts themselves, given that they had a civilization capable of taking steps to survive the evolution of their star. He had never quite believed the popular theory that they had annihilated themselves. What kind of intelligent race, when facing extinction, would actually do something like that? What kind of being could press the final button?

They could have just as easily screwed up the planetary migration and set themselves up for long-term failure, Frank figured.

He avoided such discussions with Virginia as she had a vested professional opinion and wasn't very open-minded about it. One part of Frank's formula for a happy marriage was avoiding argument repetition. The one time they'd talked seriously about the fate of the Argonauts, they'd gotten into a fight. He still refused to believe they'd been so nihilistic, those ancient aliens, and thought their demise had to be the result of technological screw-up rather than direct conflict.

The X-bot continued, "This pattern, Thom Kelly, published a paper a few years ago." Finely detailed actuators unfolded out of the X-bot's collar to gesticulate, much as the pattern originator would have waved his hands, as it spoke. "In that paper, I worked from two directions. From the scant data available, mostly hard-to-interpret popular accounts from recovered Argonaut records, and also with physical models. Then I used evolutionary models of Pollux to determine timescales and how Argo's orbital radius needed to change." The X-bot tapped its own transparent projection dome and on cue the face of Gerald faded, to be replaced with a solar system schematic with a bright star in the middle. Moving in coplanar elliptical orbits around the star were six planets, each with its own trace color. The color sequence, Frank realized, was in ROYGBIV spectral order, with warmest colors for the interior terrestrial planets—violet and blue—and the coolest for the exterior giant planets—green, yellow, orange, and red.

"That's this system from the Argonaut era?" Virginia asked.

"Yes," said the X-bot. "Nearly eleven million years ago, just after Pollux exhausted its core of hydrogen fuel, at an age of three gigayears."

Frank had thoroughly investigated the Pollux system before he had decided to abort his scouting mission here. Pollux was younger than Sol, but twice as massive. The old saying that "a candle that burns twice as bright burns half as long" didn't apply to stars—it was more like 38 percent as long. The amount of hydrogen fuel a star had available to burn into helium was indeed proportional to its mass, but more massive stars burned their fuel much faster and varied nonlinearly with the mass. It irritated him that when Earth was three billion years old only the simplest life had arisen, whereas on Argo there had existed not only advanced multicellular life forms, but a civilization that had achieved spaceflight.

His ancestors had been interstellar underachievers.

"I'm speeding up the simulation. Watch for the pink bullets," said the X-bot, pointing. A machine-gun series of pink tracers appeared, streaming in a complex series of orbits that moved primarily past the blue, second innermost planet, Argo, and the fourth planet, the massive yellow gas giant that was Talos. In the time-lapse simulation, the pink bullets traced figure eights, elliptical wheels, and more complex paths. Slowly, as Pollux visibly expanded and cooled into a red giant, the planetary orbits shifted. Talos drifted slowly inward, Argo more rapidly outward.

"What's happening?" Frank asked.

"Forget your celestial mechanics, Klingston?" Martin chided.

The X-bot promptly answered: "The pink bullets are artificial planetoids. Each trip out near Talos they pick up a gravitational assist, coming in behind the giant planet and using its gravity for additional acceleration. This gravity-assist maneuver steals some of the energy from Talos's orbit. When they come back by Argo, they perform the reverse of a gravitational assist leading the planet, and deposit some energy into Argo's orbit, increasing it in a steady, controlled fashion. With this kind of orbital machine you can shift energies quite fast enough to keep a planet occupying its star's habitable zone."

"I follow," said Frank, and he did, as far as this point went. He wasn't stupid, but he was missing the punch line. "But I don't understand how this concerns the Lashing."

The Pollux system faded and Thom Kelly's holographic face

returned, smiling. "It has *everything* to do with the Lashing. In the paper I just described, the planetoids had been assumed to be natural asteroids deflected and maintained in the proper orbits by means of attached propulsion systems. Iron-nickel asteroids with rail drives and moderate nanotech would be capable of doing the job, for instance, or even low-thrust ion drives. We've never found such an object in the Pollux system, but we haven't looked very hard either, and they wouldn't necessarily be easy to locate. This whole scenario would be a dangerous one for the Argonauts to undertake."

"All those close passes of Argo," said Frank, "with dinosaur killer–size rocks. And having the passes orchestrated perfectly over millions of years. It's intimidating."

Virginia added, "And there were several dynasties over those years, we know, a number of powers that rose and fell. Argonaut civilization was not stable over megayears."

Gerald's display shimmered, then morphed from the red-headed Kelly into that of a younger woman with platinum blond hair and a lopsided grin, another pattern. "*Way* not stable! We know the Argonauts fought. A *lot*. We have hard evidence of *at least* fourteen world wars, six of them nuclear. Why, probably the only reason that we're here colonizing Argo instead of the Argonauts colonizing Earth is that they kept blasting themselves back to the Stone Age. *Vicious* little bastards, those Argonauts, make the Mongols look like saints!" Her eyes flashed, a little too much, with glee.

Frank had a moment of sympathy for the woman's husband, assuming the human original had had one.

"Maybe," said Virginia, tightly. Frank knew that she had her own ideas, but wouldn't deign to argue with a simulation that couldn't change its mind on such basic premises.

"One of those planetoids would make an excellent weapon," Frank suggested, trying to get things back to the point.

The X-bot's face morphed back to that of Kelly. "Exactly. And do you think the twentieth-century Americans would have trusted the Soviet Union with exclusive control of such a weapon? Or the twenty-third-century Chinese the Indians? And wouldn't the Israelis of any modern century be concerned if the Arabs could deflect, or threaten to deflect, one of the planetoids?"

Frank began to catch on to the punch line of the dark joke. "But we're not talking about planetoids, are we?"

The face in the dome smiled sadly, and simulated or not, the emotion came across powerfully. "No, we're not. After the Lashing, we reconfigured the Kishimoto Gravitational Array satellites and combined their observations with all other available data, primarily helioseismology, sunspot patterns, that sort of thing. The Lashing task force intuits this."

Gerald's projection dome darkened and in the resulting gloom a new simulation ignited. The first thing that Frank thought of looking at the new display was a swarm of bees. He'd not seen such creatures for decades—Argo had no bees or near equivalent—but he had once trained in Arizona, and had run into so-called killer bees on a hike. They had annoyed him, but not killed him, as he had modern biodefenses and had run away—a caution they had drilled into Scouts in those days that he had since lost.

He had looked up killer bees after his encounter. The introduction of African bees into the hives of European bees in the Americas had once been considered a good idea, as African bees produced more honey (a tasty food he hadn't had in decades), but they were also much more aggressive. The insects often swarmed chaotically and produced an angry, discordant noise. Before human modifications became common, such swarms really had killed people.

The current image was not of bees, he was sure, but a static-filled, red-hued image of swarming . . . somethings. Frank shifted his head to change perspective. He asked the X-bot, "What am I looking at?"

"A three-dimensional map of the interior of Pollux. And before you ask, no one knows what those are except that they are mass concentrations. Somehow they move without significant viscosity in the very dense, very hot plasma at the core. Clearly, though, they are neither rocky nor metallic planetoids surviving as they do within the center of a star, and apparently surviving there for a very, very long time."

"The Lashing," Frank said.

"Yes," said Claude Martin.

"Now." The swarm shrank suddenly, and all the particles were simultaneously near their minimum radial position in their orbits. All but two, that is, and those two were locked in a tight orbit with each other and shot out at high velocity. The field of view expanded to follow them as they barreled toward the star's surface and beyond. "A gravitationally bound binary was ejected carrying an electrically charged field, pulling super-heated plasma with it from the stellar core. That's what hit Charybdis, and what has apparently hit both moons before. We're also fairly certain that six anomalous zones on Argo represent artifacts of past planetary impact, and we're suspicious of ten other regions."

"Will it keep happening?" Virginia asked.

"It seems so," Claude answered. "But we don't know when or in what direction. Right now the theorists are discouraged about the prospects for exact prediction, but it is early in this deadly game. We have some information we recovered, I won't say from where just yet, that explains what's going on and why."

He continued, cutting off the X-bot as it tried to jump in. "The technology that once served to move Argo away from Pollux during its expansion was converted into a weapon. It's a doomsday weapon that has been triggered, and is now a sword of Damocles hanging over our heads, with no one to turn it off but ourselves. Furthermore, this weapon is apparently not an Argonaut technology."

That was worth the trip.

Claude held up an appendage to stall Virginia's protest. "The details jibe with information we've recently acquired dealing with the so-called *Saga of the Spider Star,* with which I believe you're quite familiar, at least the children's version."

Frank thought Virginia's eyes were going to bug out of her head. It wasn't a good look for her. "What other versions are there? Dump it!"

Frank had never liked that expression, and had been unhappy to discover it had made its way from Earth to Argo.

Claude seemed ready to dump it. The man's head bobbed as he rocked slightly forward on his artificial limbs, and he seemed to need only the slightest push to fall on his face.

Frank decided to push, both because he wanted to know, and because he felt sorry for Claude, which bothered him. The man had secrets, colossal secrets, that would break Frank if he had to keep them. Men like Claude normally held them effortlessly, but not this one at this time. This secret was fresh and huge and wanted to burst forward, the way everything packed down on Argo inflated in the low pressure of the space station.

"Dump it," ordered Frank.

Claude glanced quickly at the both of them, a slight smile turning his face crooked. "It's all true. The Spider Star is no star, and the Spider Star is no planet, but it is a real place, and its golden heart is the source of all good and evil. And we know where its golden heart beats."

The man's slight smile grew more lopsided, almost into a leer.

Frank looked at Virginia, and, wide-eyed, she looked back, wonder and confusion sliding across her face.

"Really? That's . . . fantastic," she said, turning back to Claude.

Frank was less impressed. "The weapon is from the Spider Star?"

"Tool, weapon, technology beyond our imagination. Call it what you will. This discovery is worth the Lashings, which, after all, haven't actually hurt us." The man's smile eased off, and he said, more quietly, "At least not yet."

"Not yet?" Frank asked.

"The Lashings represent a weapon all right, an ancient device the Argonauts once obtained from other aliens to save themselves, but in the end used to destroy. We've been lucky it has been dormant so long."

"Shit," whispered Frank. Wave after wave of realization washed over him, recalling parts of the story. The implications were enormous.

"Well, tell us everything!" Virginia demanded.

"I'll tell Frank," Claude said, turning to look at him and losing the smile. And now Frank could read nothing in the face. It held a sternness, an intent of purpose, and he felt as if he had a laser sight resting unmoving on his forehead. "I'll tell you everything and you can decide whether or not to share with your wife."

"Why tell me and not her? She's the expert on Argonauts and the fairy tale you're saying is central to Pollux going crazy. Why me?"

"Because you're the one I want to lead the mission to the Spider Star, Frank. We have to go there, like they did, to fix this. It's the only way to be sure that Argo can be safe to live on for the duration. You're the one who must do it."

What was he talking about? He had to snip this early. "Me? I have a family, a farm, and my current expertise is in brewing beer, of all things. You've got a whole cadre of kids already trained for something like this."

"Yes, I do, and they're going, too. But none of them has encountered aliens before and negotiated anything out of them, let alone a dark drive. Shopping at the Spider Star supermarket for control of the magic bullets isn't something we train Specialists to do."

Frank remembered some of the Spider Star story from the last time reading it to Kenny, and tore himself away from Claude's stare to look at his wife.

Shock appeared to fill her body like a storm.

Experiencing a bit of the storm in himself, he said to Claude, "There's no way I can do that, Claude. You'll have to send X-bots."

Feeling a little out of control, Frank abruptly stood and held his hand out to his wife. "We're going to have a nice lunch now. I promised my wife we could have sushi."

Claude was yelling "Frank!" over and over again as Frank walked out without looking back. He was glad he didn't have to drag Virginia, because he would have.

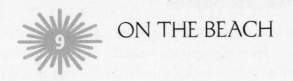

ON THE BEACH

Even though he'd walked for an hour along the coast, the arcology still loomed above Manuel Rusk like a sparkling pyramid, or a man-made mountain. On a world like Argo, it wasn't that hard to get away from it all, to get away from other humans and their devices although they always loomed nearby, but he supposed that getting away from people wasn't his true goal. He really wanted to get away from the known world, not his fellow man. He wanted to visit the alien, and bring it back. He really wanted to explore.

And striding along the rocky beach, poking into its tide pools and its scuttling life, was all he could manage at the moment since the Castor 6 mission had been canceled.

His phone rang with fanfare, and he knew it was Sloan.

He knew he should have turned it off. Against his better judgment, he picked up. "I'm *fine,* all right," he answered.

"Yeah, fuck you, too," she replied sweetly to his snarky response. He loved her for it, but not really that much at this particular moment. "I'm not talking on the phone. I'm coming to see you."

"If you wish."

"Fine, then." Uncaring, he hung up in the middle of her reply, and continued to saunter along the rocky beach. She had his locator code.

A breeze came up and mussed his hair.

Usually he poked at the scrabs and the bellies, experimenting with their reactions, fascinated, but today he just watched them, detached. He was denied interacting with the alien now. He was a rogue planet, flying through free space, ejected from his sun.

He stopped to sit on a rock and consider the steel-gray ocean rolling in under the blue sky. He was a creature out of its element, left in an intermediate world, like that unhealthy-looking scrab in the smelly little tide pool there.

This was reality? This was life? This gray beach under a quasi-alien city? Where did you go when you found yourself in a tide pool?

You could sink back into the ocean, or climb onto the land. He wanted to climb onto the land.

He looked up, searching for a moment, and found Charybdis faint overhead. Was this what people had felt like on Earth when they had seen the moon and couldn't fly there? Just like he felt, now?

He'd had it all, everything he'd worked for and ever wanted. And somehow it had slid through his fingers like beach sand. How? He was a one-in-a-thousand man in most ways, intellectually, physically. He'd been bred and raised for greatness, trained religiously, and damn it all, he knew he was good. No, great. He *was* great.

There was nothing wrong with knowing that and acknowledging it. But it seemed that being great wasn't enough sometimes.

The wind picked up a little more, and he detected a faint brackish odor. He walked on.

He heard the whine of the car fans approaching and knew it was Sloan. He said she could come if she wanted. He wasn't avoiding her, or anyone else. He was simply considering his lot. Sloan knew what was up, his mood, and had come anyway. That was her choice. Anything that happened wasn't entirely his fault.

She at least had the good sense to park away from him and walk up. The wind was bad enough already.

He waited for her, considering, as she approached. He didn't care for the fact that she wore her Specialist uniform and had taken a fleet car. Why would she have done that? She wasn't the type to rub it in.

"Manuel," she said. The breeze shook her short dark hair, but didn't muss it much, and her pretty face undermined her concern and made it seem secondary to him. "We should talk."

There was an understatement, he supposed. He decided to play his expected role. "About what? It's over. No mission. Everything we've worked for, gone. Want some more sad nuggets?"

"Manuel," she chided. She reached out and touched his upper arm. "You know it's bigger than us. The sun is unstable. The entire colony is threatened."

"*Unstable?* Unstable my ass! The sun is outright *attacking* us. Speak the truth. This circumspect coddling is unbecoming for you."

She let go of his arm and took a step back.

Unable to get his face back to a neutral expression, he turned away. He had suspected an outburst was in there, waiting, but he hadn't expected it to pop out so quickly. It had felt good, and he was a little bit ashamed with himself.

He turned away from the ocean to face her fully. "It's our fault. My fault, anyway. I set it off. *Me.* Get it? It doesn't matter that it was a trap, that anyone could have done it. I did it. And now I'm being punished by the gods like some Greek hero."

Her hurt expression changed, and her eyebrows came together. As her eyes flashed she gave him a little shove. "You? A Greek hero? Ha. It's all about you, as usual. This isn't about you now, if it ever was. You, me, New Colchis, we're fighting the ghosts of a civilization more technologically advanced than ours. We need everyone."

He held his face tight, but couldn't keep from glaring at her. What was he supposed to do? Deny it? There was truth in what she said. "You're right, Sloan. Totally right. But I can't do anything more about it. I've tendered my resignation to Martin, as I had to do."

She just stared at him for a moment, like it was a surprise.

"Manuel, you're a fool! You couldn't have done anything worth resigning for. I know you."

"He said to expect changes. That was a clear suggestion. And after Donovan and the others walked out, I knew what I had to do. I explained it all in the resignation letter. You see, I knocked on the trapped door, which set off the neutrino signal."

"You *knocked* on it?" she asked.

"Yes, I did."

She looked deep into his eyes, then smirked. "Well, gee, that was a huge mistake. I'm totally shocked you didn't commit seppuku. What were you thinking?"

"I know!" he exclaimed before realizing she was patronizing him. Maybe he was taking this too seriously, but he had been in charge, and he was responsible. Knocking on an alien door was not something to treat casually. It had been a mistake. Still, it was wrong of her to taunt him now.

They stood there, on the beach, with the source of their eventual doom shining down on their heads, looking at each other from a distance slightly too close to be socially comfortable. Despite the fact that they had been occasional lovers, it was too close for him now. Sloan's eyes weren't soft, not one bit, and belied her soft, pretty face.

Rusk was about to step back when his phone chimed again. He leaned in to take the well-timed call and she moved back as he did so, which was what he wanted.

"What's this nonsense from you?" Claude Martin said, with no preamble.

"I feel resigning is the most appropriate course of action. The Lashings are my fault."

"Bullshit," he said. "We've got a long-term course of action, and you're the only one to lead it."

"Sir?"

"Going to Castor 6 is not an option for us, not now, as I made clear, but we've got somewhere else we need to go."

"Sir?"

"Do you know the Spider Star? It's an Argonaut kid's story."

"A little."

"It's more than a kid's story. You, your crew, you're going there. It'll take as long as the Castor mission, but the payoff should be huge. Rusk, I've got to ask you something."

"Yes, sir?"

"Are you ready not only to meet aliens, but if they won't give us what we need, to take it from them?"

Typical Claude Martin melodrama designed to engage and commit an unsure audience. "I'm not sure I'm the right person. I resigned."

"Bullshit. I'm not accepting your resignation, and you can't afford to give it to me and stay on Argo. Look, I know you take things personally, and take too much to heart sometimes, but you're right for this job. You're the best man for it, a really great leader. It's the same deal as before, but with higher stakes. I need you now. We all need you. So get back in here so we can get working on this, yes?"

Rusk was quiet for a long moment, refusing to answer immediately. Martin let him ride the silence.

Having intellectual integrity, making the right decisions, and living with the consequences . . . those were things that defined him, who he was. His identity. To just come back immediately, without his resignation treated seriously . . . he made a small grunt without thinking.

"Close enough to a yes for me. See you within the hour, okay?"

And Martin ended the call, dumbfounding Rusk.

"I could tell who that was," Sloan said. "What's the new position?"

"Mission commander, same as before," Rusk replied, staring off into the roiling sea. A storm was on the horizon, a front approaching.

"Really? But I thought the mission was off."

"Castor 6 is off. Something else is on, and Martin won't take my resignation."

"Good," she said, moving closer and placing a hand familiarly on his shoulder and leaning into him. Side by side, they looked to the ocean, the wind blowing in their faces.

"I don't know." He let her hand rest there, her body close, and refusing to be rushed, he thought. Had that really been a threat from Claude, buried in there? The man was fond of using both carrot and stick, and he usually got what he wanted. Was there a point to resisting?

If he refused to go back, accepted his lot, who would replace him? If they stayed within the Specialist Corp, it would have to be Griffin. Perhaps Donovan, but more likely Griffin. Did she understand what was going on? She probably didn't overhear the threat, but she knew enough otherwise.

What did her hand on his shoulder and her "good" actually mean? Was she being authentic? Or was she trying to handle him like Martin?

He hated this. Second-guessing himself and others . . . it smacked of insecurity. You picked the best course and stuck to it. His best course was obvious, integrity or not. He'd made the offer. He didn't have to stick to it like a space-quality weld. He and Griffin were close. There was no reason not to take her at face value.

He forged the path, and when necessary she came to rescue him. That was the nature of their relationship.

He took a deep breath, and accepted things.

He reached up, gave her hand a squeeze. "Okay. Let's go back and see what this new mission is all about."

He tried not to let it bother him that she didn't squeeze his hand back. No more second-guessing. It was time to commit. Again. He would lead the Specialists to the Spider Star and whatever awaited them.

What else was he going to do? He really was overqualified to be a beach bum. Everyone on Argo was. He might as well fulfill his ambitions, which were cracked, but not apparently shattered. A man trying to save a doomed land from his own folly was a good basis for a Greek tragedy—he'd be a real hero yet, even if it was the tragic sort.

SAGA OF THE SPIDER STAR

KLINGSTON HOMESTEAD, ARGO

A couple of weeks after the meeting with Claude Martin, Kenny asked for a bedtime story, and he asked for the one that Frank was now obsessing over, the *Saga of the Spider Star.* Why not *Winnie-the-Pooh* or *Little Bunny*? He'd survive those another few dozen times.

Even though the version of the Spider Star story they had was a bit too sophisticated for Kenny, he had heard it at least a dozen times, and it wasn't a reason not to ask for it.

Frank worried Kenny'd heard him and Virginia talking about it, and hoped he hadn't understood too much.

Kenny's Bookie Bear pajamas were so cute, the feet pads gray and dirty as he slipped under the covers, Frank actually almost forgot about the Lashing and how it plagued him with regard to this particular story. He'd do anything for Kenny.

He had made the correct decision, he had no doubt. He was a family man now, and he didn't really know anything, not anything like he was supposed to know. He didn't know anything about the new technologies or protocols the Specialists used these days, and he didn't know much about being part of a team let alone a leader of a team. Yes, he admitted to himself that he'd done something remarkable at one point in his life, but that didn't mean he himself was remarkable, or still remarkable even if he had been in the past. Sometimes the stories he heard about himself got to him, made him feel funny and act worse.

That's the guy who met aliens. Saw them, touched them, smelled them.

He supposed it was one reason he was here, in a remote settlement on a sparsely populated colony world. People acted like his past gave him magic powers, which was light years from the truth. He was still trying to live a life beyond his reputation. Argo had seemed infinitely superior to Earth, and he'd been able to justify the logic of his choice to come here, because he had to. He couldn't share the truth of it, not the real truth, no matter how he tried. The truth itself about anything unusual was hard enough to live up to, but the worse problem, he'd discovered, was that no one could live down a myth. On Earth he wouldn't have stood a chance.

He had a good life here. His kids knew him as Da years before they'd had the smallest inkling of what the whispers and glances had meant, and he loved them for it.

So the Bookie Bear's request was immediately approved and placed in the fast-action basket of Frank's mind, right after bath time.

Frank sat down on the edge of Kenny's bed—bed bubbles were a luxury that you only got for sleeping in the sanitary cage of the arcology—and picked up Kenny's book. He keyed up the saga of the Spider Star.

"Read it with the voices!" Kenny begged, desperate even over the matter of a story.

"I say yes to your request," Frank answered, using one of his regular voices and rhymes, what he imagined a proper librarian ought to sound like.

Kenny giggled.

He took a deep breath, and committed. The Argonauts wrote their stories in eight parts, following a pattern of meaning followed by fact, often leaving out key elements that frustrated human listeners who desired closure. The stories were not always complete, at least compared to a human story. It was like they wrote only what they thought important, not always bothering to connect everything. Perhaps the Argonaut minds knew how to fill in the other parts in a way humans needed to be told.

But also, it seemed, that Argonauts had needed certain things spelled out that Earth children did not.

Was one therefore superior to the other? Or were they simply different? Or was it just more complicated than could be managed on a single axis with superior at one end, and inferior at the other?

Still, it comforted him that the Argonauts, too, told their children stories once upon a time.

Frank shifted fully into storyteller mode, willing his voice to be deep and resonant. He read aloud the title, which humans had placed on the tale, *The Saga of the Spider Star.*

So it began, the same every time.

The first part of an Argonaut story was the preamble, rather similar to the moral that you might find at the end of a fable. It was never anything as pithy as one sentence, but rarely longer than a long paragraph.

" 'The Spider Star is no star, and the Spider Star is no planet, but it is a place anyway, and its golden heart is the source of all good and evil. But mostly evil. For that which comes last, colors all that has come before.' "

"Why?" asked Kenny.

Time to cut that one off immediately. "Because you're going to sleep now without a story if you ask that question again, got it, kiddo?"

Kenny nodded and didn't say anything, but couldn't quite hide a little giggle.

The second part of an Argonaut story gave an overview of the historical and social context of the tale, and varied greatly in length. You would never find a flashback in an Argonaut story. It would be placed in the second part, the backstory, always, if it were required. Generally for children's stories this part was shorter rather than longer.

Frank cleared his throat and continued, slipping into his narrator voice. He'd long ago stopped caring that he put on a faux-British accent for this part.

" 'This story is about the modern voyage, the evil voyage, which came long after the original, ancient voyage that is universally regarded as good. We still enjoy the fruits of that primary effort.

" 'The ancient ones, brave they were. Their names lost to unbeatable time, many dynasties past, yet their deeds immortal. They had troubled times, they did, and worse than ours. The evil was that the life-giving sun, that orb of fire, grew larger. Too much of a good thing is a bad thing. What to do? Burrow beneath the earth? Live under sea? Shrivel and die before that flame like a confused slug-bug? They argued, and fought, and thought, and searched, desperate for the struggle for life that is the purpose of each of us even today.' "

Frank sometimes ad-libbed, making up voices for Argonauts and pretending to argue about what to do, sometimes even asking Kenny for suggestions. He wasn't in the mood to ad-lib tonight. He would read the story straight, at least as straight as the translators had provided it, even if that meant fewer voices. Sometimes the translations seemed overly clunky, or overly poetic, by equal turns, and he wasn't certain he was getting the exact story. How could he tell? Dead human languages were hard enough to translate, never mind the alien ones, despite the recordings they'd found. And he wasn't sure they'd translated for children, and he himself had doubts about the relative intelligence of humans compared to Argonauts. But these were thoughts he always had reading this story, and was sure he'd have again without resolution the next time, too.

Frank proceeded. " 'And then, when the crisis had the most distress, they heard it. A voice in the dark, offering the knowledge to save their world, their home, and their clans. This was the inviting call of the Spider Star, the siren song, speaking for who knows what incomprehensible reasons. The voice whispered from a web in the sky, with the voice of a spider, coming from a star that was not a star. Why the star of a spider? And why a star, not a planet? No one knows, and that is the way of some things. Today we know for certain only that they went, returning many years later with the way to shrink the fattening sun.'"

The story's third part was meaning again, but transitory between the old and the new. It was meaning for vital aspects of the backstory and how they set up the new events.

"'The evil voyage, however, was not born out of the necessity of survival. We Argonauts, fat and bickering, grew again into machine power, and again heard the Spider Star's seductive whisper. Without need for survival, there was desire for strength.

"'It is the way of satisfaction to birth desire, for strength, for dominance, and this is not evil. But to satisfy the new desires utterly, and wholly, and completely, can be, if your rivals are the ones to achieve satisfaction.'"

The fourth part, finally, was what most humans would regard as the start of the real story, and was, in fact, more detailed and meatier than what had come before.

"'Heroes, or antiheroes, depending on your clan, were assembled for the purpose of gaining new power from the Spider Star. The Akkai, their leader, set forth with troops prepared to endure great suffering in return for great reward.

"'The distance vast, their bodies were old when they approached the Spider Star, with children raised to assist them, trained with purpose to be as great as the ones chosen themselves. This place was a spider in space, with a golden heart, in truth, waiting for others to arrive. Was it predatory? Not apparently, not immediately, but wait and see.

"'There was not a place to land, but a place to attach. A

strange place. Attach they did. They were greeted by all manner of beings. Some were as large as kavats, and others merely the size of flutters. Some especially strange ones only had four limbs, but could interact with their surroundings successfully anyway. Together these creatures presented a rainbow of colors, with, however, few immediate indications of hierarchy.' "

"Hierarchy?" Kenny asked. The boy was good. He asked questions every time Frank read the story, and would openly repeat questions about words he'd forgotten. Frank would oblige as long as it wasn't the dreaded *why*.

"Pecking order," Frank said. But that saying wasn't used on Argo, as the birds—or their equivalents here—didn't operate that way. He tried again. "It means who's in charge, then who's second, third, and so on."

"Like Mom, then you, then Allyn, and then me."

Frank couldn't help but smirk, and let it go. There was some truth in that, and it worked fine usually, even though he preferred to think of himself and Virginia as equals in the family pecking order. He continued:

" 'Feasting began, with sharing food animals and the strange creatures of this strange place offering their own strange foods. The Argonauts bided their time, watching and learning of this place, learning unknown details of their ancient predecessors. As nightless days passed, without clear leadership visible among the peoples of the Spider Star, the Argonauts began to plot.' "

Frank tried to remember the types of voices he used for the Argonauts. He always remembered that of their leader, but the other ones he sometimes screwed up. Oh well, Kenny would complain more with delays than with mistakes.

Frank assumed the deep, booming voice of the leader, Akkai. " ' "They are all different, but all equal. They live an easy life, making them weak, and with no sign of mastery of the technology to control a sun. But someone knows. Someone has it." ' "

Slight, whiny voice: " ' "You're right, great one, but what to do? How do we get the power?"

" ' "We ask them," ' " in a third voice, an even tone.

" 'Humor bubbled forth from the group, and Akkai grasped it with four arms. "We did not travel this far to ask. Not from such weak things as we see before us. Taking is the way of all things, and it is our way. He who can take has the right to take, and our enemies earned their own treasure in their day."

" 'Akkai made demands, to either achieve the treasure for the asking, or for an excuse for a fight.' " Frank went ahead and ad-libbed. " ' "Give us your power weak ones!"

" 'The creatures denied such knowledge, although some discussed side deals." Frank couldn't resist a few ad-libs with his sneaky voice. " 'One whispered to them, "I have what you need, Argonauts, but you must do something for me."

" 'Such secret dealings rarely went far. The Argonauts were suspicious and distrustful of aliens. Moreover, they saw little evidence of weaponry. Was it possible this place, large and strange as it was, could be dealt with through force?

" 'Their mission, not for survival but for glory and power, was one with—' " Frank paused to think of a synonym for *latitude,* " 'few rules. They could feel free to fail, which was a small price when weighed against fame forever.

" 'Akkai arranged a series of misunderstandings involving different groups of aliens, letting each grow to anger. A simple matter for an Argonaut leader when dealing with those who do not wage war.

" 'One misunderstanding led to the making of both friends and enemies. Another doubled the numbers in each camp. A third brought around physical conflict, blood, and death.' "

This was one of the especially disturbing parts in the original toy box story that Virginia had discovered, and one of the reasons that the translation for human children contained no pictures.

Most of the story at this point was contained in images, bloody images, that were utterly incompatible with how humans raised children, despite traditional childhood games of army men, cowboys and Indians, and terrorist hunt.

Frank continued, " 'And then understanding shone upon the Argonauts. The place held police, of a mechanical sort, who appeared. Ah, then, police meant more masters, somewhere. But where?

" 'As you must well know, fighting once started does not easily end. Wrong begets wrong, which begets wrong.' " Frank was happy he'd explained begets so many times before, and unhappy with the archaic word used in translation. But, used to pausing here, he slipped in an editorial comment to Kenny. "That's what the Argonauts thought. And that's what your mother and I think, too. So it's better to avoid fighting in the first place."

Still awake somehow, Kenny nodded sagely.

While Frank was happy to see the nod, part of him knew not to trust it. Boys fought, and didn't usually understand this lesson until later in life. *Don't be an alien,* he thought. *Be my son! Be as confused and wrong as I was as a dumb kid! And maybe just a tad more respectful of your parents.*

Frank went on. " 'The police were not weak like the zoo that had greeted them. The police were strong and efficient, and not all the battles went well, despite the expertise of the Argonauts at war, which even today we pride ourselves upon.

" 'Akkai fell. Leaders are of vital importance. While one's heart may pulse with pain for a fellow Argonaut, remember who this is and who this leader acted for. Would that this have been the finale of this tale of woe we now endure!' "

The fourth part often ended on a cliffhanger, or turning point like this one. The fifth part was a pause in the action, to take stock of the events that had unfolded, to point out special meanings, and to foreshadow events to come. Frank took the opportunity to give his son the quick once-over, to make sure he was still being attentive, especially when he'd been so good and quiet aside from the single "why?" earlier. It wasn't the easiest story even for adults to follow.

" 'Sometimes failure may lead to triumph, and ultimate failure to ultimate triumph. The universe is a confusing and complicated arena of conflict.

" 'However, young one, this does not mean that you should not worry about winning! To strive for success is always the goal of an aspiring Argonaut, and to succeed by accident is not a worthy goal.

" 'There is no luck in this world. There is no fate, either. Reality is ever a conflict between the two, the same way it is ever a conflict between good and evil. Dualities simultaneously exist and fail to exist, for it is their nature.

" 'But ever a price for everything, whether good or bad, for life itself is a price to pay.' "

Frank had always thought that part cryptic, even for Argonauts, and meaningless in the way it failed to reach any definite conclusions about anything at all. On Earth he would have referred to it as political speech, or even bullshit. A lot of words, with individual meaning, but ultimately signifying nothing.

The sixth part was better, as it was a continuation of the action.

" 'But their leader falling was not a loss. How it should have been, for our sakes today!

" 'Like a prayer, the battle drew the attention of the godly golden ones, finally, the masters of this place. They were normally on a different level from the mundane affairs of this motley zoo of alien creatures the Argonauts had encountered. But not after this turn of events.

" 'Now, it was finally possible to gain power.

" 'But fighting for power was impossible. For the golden ones were truly great powers, not only for their immense size—' "

Frank read, recalling the image of a giant golden glow looming over a tiny Argonaut in silhouette against a vague glowing foot, " 'but also for their immense knowledge. These beings were beyond us the way we are beyond spider monkeys.

" 'A deal was struck. The Argonauts received their hearts' desire, fame for delivering the power we now suffer beneath, the control over light and dark, life and death, freedom and slavery.

" 'And they lost something. Although we do not know everything, this we know. They lost their home. For despite communicating this power to their power-hungry leaders, they never returned. For there may also be failure in success.' "

Cryptic, cryptic, cryptic, Frank thought. The images and sounds accompanying this last part didn't shed much light on things, but it did help convey a hopeless sense of loss tinged with satisfaction. But Kenny, who had heard the story at least a dozen times, just sat there entranced, accepting the alien non-logic even without the multimedia aids. He worried, a little, that somehow his impressionable son was soaking up alien attitudes the way young children could soak up languages and religious beliefs, fully accepting things that were contradictory and nonsensical and would last them their entire lives. In this case, for a boy growing up on Argo in the shadow of its violent past, was it necessarily a bad thing to develop an intuitive understanding of those who had gone before, and perished?

After all, it wasn't like he was an alien himself. Anything entering his head would be tempered by his humanity, and his upbringing. By him, Frank, and his wife, Virginia. By human parents. He'd be fine in the long run, Frank assured himself.

Kenny's eyes were big and unblinking, and it worried Frank in ways it had never worried him before to watch him sitting quietly, unquestioning.

But still, to an Argonaut, the story was not yet complete. The seventh part outlined the meaning of the closing events.

" 'Nothing is owed to anything, anyone, or even any ideal. There is no justice, or fairness. There is the best you can do for yourself and your clan, and there can be no more. The ideal is to close a deal you can live with, the best you can do. Then even death is not a tragedy, and heroism is abundant. For even heroes may be evil, and the good much less than heroes. Respect the hero, and wish for that in yourself, young one, for the power to act for your clan. You can do no better, for good or evil. And someday, we may be blessed with the power to do evil to enemies of our clan, even though today is their day, and it will be good.' "

Frank didn't necessarily agree with the alien message. He equated *clan* more with *nation state* than with *family*, and nationalism on Earth had caused much strife without any greater good coming of it. Still, it could be nothing but instructive for his kids to try to understand those who had lived on this world before. He also held in reserve the possibility that the translators had blown it, reading the alien words with human biases impossible to ignore.

Were alien concepts of good and evil really the same as the human concepts?

Frank paused, shifting the timbre of his voice to something more somber, and he read the final, eighth part, a brief repetitive section, " 'The Spider Star is no star, and the Spider Star is no planet, but it is a place anyway, and its golden heart is the source of all good and evil. But mostly evil. For that which comes last, colors all that has come before.' "

Silence blossomed.

Kenny was closing his eyes, nearly asleep.

"Good night, kiddo."

The eighth and final part of an Argonaut story, especially in a simpler children's tale, was a restatement of the preamble, often word for word. This part of the structure felt comfortable, echoing as it did the way many Earth stories were told. Allyn had commented on it directly after Frank had spent a few weeks reading *The Hobbit* to him when he'd been younger. Tolkien's story had the alternate title, *There and Back Again,* which signified that the story was about traveling to faraway places and taking those experiences home. There was another old Earth saying, too, that Frank always thought about when dwelling on this topic: *You can never go home again.* He supposed that it was meant metaphorically, since taking it literally didn't make sense.

Frank could have gone home, and returned to Earth following his alien encounter. He'd had the resources and he could have made it, although it would have taken longer. He had no doubt they would have preferred him to have done so, instead of settling out here. If he had done that, tried to go home, he would have never escaped with the amount of peace he had here. He complained about mean old Claude Martin, but the truth was the man didn't have that much power and wasn't that mean. This place was too small to cover up things. Frank could blow him off, and get away with it, especially with the dark drive to hand over, a fait accompli.

He wondered if it had been something like that with the Argonauts. They'd sent back their prize, their Golden Fleece that was the power to rule, but they themselves had not returned home. Was it a transformative experience so powerful they'd been willing to disconnect entirely from their previous lives? Or was it more literal, as it was in the story, and simply the price they had to pay? In essence, giving up their lives for the betterment of their families back home?

He didn't know. How could anyone know?

Frank wandered off to bed himself, having difficulty shaking those last thoughts from his mind. Sleep was slow to come.

A NEW DIRECTIVE

Griffin managed to hide her smile as Rusk began the briefing. He looked sharp and confident again in his uniform, floating tethered before the sixty-two assembled Specialists, all from the senior mission-approved pool. He was alive with purpose as she hadn't seen him since Charybdis.

It was in his eyes. She'd always liked his eyes when they flashed power.

It had taken it long enough to come back, but now that Rusk's confidence had returned, she wouldn't complain.

The conference room possessed an overwhelming view, looking down upon the equator of Argo over the primary settlement of New Colchis, the arcology of eighty thousand plus that shone visibly at night. The space elevator connecting the *Visionary* and Colchis would have been essentially invisible, as thin as it was, but a steady two-way stream of lights on its various elevators traced its location all the way down to an irregular, equatorial island in the Omnigean Sea. The three other continents surrounded the island, and it was still quite a sight that Rusk thought worthy of their colonization.

A semicircular table of polished Earth-mahogany sat "below" the viewport. In some sense having a table in microgravity was ludicrous, but the *Visionary* had been the original colony ship sent to Argo from Earth over a hundred years ago, and while underway on the thirty-four light-year voyage this section had been under rotation. Even in the freefall of orbit, a directional reference was psychologically useful.

So everyone sat, belted to their chairs attached to the faux floor, listening to Mission Director Rusk.

He'd already outlined the basics. The Spider Star, as it turned out, was slightly closer than Castor 6, but at seventeen light-years the mission details weren't all that different. It was still going to be fourteen Specialists and seven X-bots.

He was saying, "But with the changed mission, it can't be the same team as originally chosen for Castor 6. We've been forced to make some changes."

Specialists trained in multiple areas, and were complemented by X-bots and shipboard expert systems, in order to bring to bear as much of the knowledge of modern civilization when they were light-years from it. It was impossible to cover everything, so every mission was a compromise, trying to guess what sort of knowledge would be the most important to have available.

Rusk and Griffin had been intentionally clever and opportunistic in their studies. Both held master-level qualifications in twice as many areas as the average Specialist. He had pioneered new approaches to science in general, seeking patterns to things rather than the details of the things. For instance, biological and social sciences, and some limited aspects of the physical sciences, were really just applications of self-selecting organization and could be categorized as evolutionary studies or, as he preferred to speak of them, antientropic systems. On the other hand, many other areas fell under the laws of conservation of energy, conservation of momentum—where win-lose scenarios were the rule, and conservation principles provided the keys to understanding. He lumped them together under the title of "conservative systems." It was a huge advantage to be able to know which was which, to know when one could be converted to the other, and to operate accordingly. Rusk had parlayed that into a new expertise: entropic synthesis, which also required a certain set of social specialties to effectively interact with other experts.

He could quickly assimilate data and figure out what was going on faster than others, at least in the broadest terms.

Griffin had studied with him in many areas, but had her own strengths that complemented his. Again this was intentional, as they had realized that the better they interlocked the better their chances at a choice mission. She didn't synthesize well, the way he did, but tore things apart, ruthlessly, seizing on discrepant details like a shark smelling blood. He'd made that joke to her once, and she'd adopted it. She was a dissector. She had once explained this to him over a game of pool, something they were both well matched at.

"Imagine a three-dimensional spreadsheet, a data cube basically," she'd said. "You might want to start thinking about two dimensions first, move to three, and then keep going. I just think in however many dimensions are required for the problem. Everything potentially relates to everything else with equal probability, but usually there are more fundamental relationships. I systematically fill in the matrix, make comparisons, and find the sense of things. Trends emerge, but so do the outliers. I guess you focus on the trends. I focus on the outliers and figure out how and why they don't fit, or what extreme trend is manifesting. I like every threat identified, understood—the general trends are predictable, while the individual problems can be unique. That's why I like you so much."

He'd smiled at her, with real warmth then. "You like me?"

"Of course. You're an outlier."

"I'm a threat?" he'd asked.

She'd just smiled, and proceeded to cleverly sink the eight ball early to win the game. "Not at the moment." They'd had sex that night for the first time. They'd continued to have sex over the years, forcibly keeping it sporadic, casual, and nonexclusive. Neither wanted Klingston's sort of problem—family ties—to jeopardize their careers. The Corps frowned on exclusive relationships.

Still, she liked to think of her and Rusk together as a Specialist power couple. She'd helped him revise the crew roster, and was pleased to be in her position now. A few people here would not be pleased with their positions in a few minutes.

"The original mission was optimized for general exploration, with an emphasis on planetary physics and geology. The new mission requires an emphasis on astrobiology, engineering, Argonaut history and culture, as well as some more exotic areas of expertise," said Rusk.

They'd been sure to include several Specialists with combat training, for instance, like Jack Robb, given the Spider Star story.

"Everyone hears it all, right here and now, so there shouldn't be any excuse for continuing rumors. The best one I heard was that I was being replaced by a horse. Well, no. I've tried to keep as many of the Castor 6 personnel as possible. I know everyone here wants to go. Please rest assured the decisions have been made in the best interests of a successful mission in order to make the Argo colony safe once again. In addition to myself, Sloan Griffin remains my second."

She felt a few eyes turn toward her, but kept her own gaze fixed on Rusk. She'd chosen her seat to be able to easily watch who she wanted.

"The others are, in no particular order," Rusk announced, and then rattled off, "Anatole Hamilton, Walter Stubbs, Selene Madison, Jack Robb, Kat Coyner, Mistelle Soon, Timothy Salerno, Gina Dorissey, Gabriella Powers, Melinda Sergevich, Towson Field, and Adrian Slyde."

There was a particular order actually. Adrian Slyde was one of the additions, more of a replacement, for Mitch Donovan. Their backgrounds were similar, specifically both had strong piloting

skills for a variety of craft, but Adrian had studied Argonaut history. Donovan had not.

She watched Donovan start at the completion of the list,
about the way she had expected.

Griffin glanced toward Rusk.

He looked right at Donovan as he spoke. "I know this selection will disappoint some of you, but no one should consider
this a personal slight. You're all talented individuals. We have to
construct the strongest team to travel to the Spider Star, and this
is how it shakes out."

And Donovan sat there, stymied. They expected to hear some
grumblings in private after the briefing, but there was no way
out. The decisions were final, public, and well reasoned. Donovan was good, but he might not be the best colleague when it
would be necessary to trust Rusk. That was just how it was.

Their system was flexible, informal, and merit-based, but hierarchy still ruled the day.

Rusk went on. "The Spider Star team will start meeting tomorrow morning, oh-nine-hundred sharp. I suggest all team
members begin to set their affairs in order. There's less than six
months—"

Rusk's phone rang.

That was odd. Rusk was excellent about his phone manners,
and would have set the device to allow only the highest priority
calls to come through. He looked at the phone for an extended
moment, and answered. What could merit interrupting this
meeting?

"Wait," Rusk said, his face hardening briefly as he listened.
"There's another Lashing detected."

Griffin, and everyone else, waited for it.

"The projection is that this one is headed for Argo."

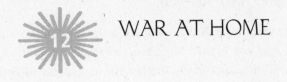

WAR AT HOME

KLINGSTON HOMESTEAD

The experts had predicted it was likely to happen sooner or later, and two months seemed all too soon to Frank.

Pollux was lashing out at Argo itself.

Frank was not a religious man, but he thanked God the Lashing was not going to hit anywhere inhabited, although a couple of digs did require evacuation. It was going to hit some 4,500 kilometers west, well away from their home. But that was a small consolation in the grand scheme of things. There was no evidence that this was going to be the last one.

Orbital cameras, robotic aircraft, and X-bots running mobile ground observatories all prepared to record the event. Military-level shielded equipment and communications lasers promised to stay live even through the interference the Lashing would cause. Despite the fact that they'd been carefully positioned outside the collision vector, all the visual feeds provided the same, ominous perspective: the setting sun was growing to touch them.

And here he was again, watching another event of ultimate destruction from the safety and comfort of his living room, a cold beer in his hand. Virginia was with him tonight—he held her close. The kids had been in bed for an hour.

The images switched from Pollux to overhead shots of the impact region, and all the feeds were focused on one place: Batter's Falls, named one of Argo's nine natural wonders by the original survey team, and within 40 kilometers of ground zero. Batter's Falls was two Niagras in volume with four times the drop. The falls, spewing out of a picturesque gorge, were featured in the immigration literature used to attract colonists from Earth. There was one colony ship, ten thousand hopeful souls, en route to Argo now, and likely the last for some time to come, perhaps forever. The ones en route, they'd never have the chance to see Batter's Falls in person. It was about to be wiped out.

Frank wouldn't see it, either. He hadn't seen it twenty years ago on what he still thought of as his world tour, the trip he'd taken as VIP upon first coming to Argo. For a few months there, he'd had a free ticket to go anywhere and do anything, until the powers that be—Claude Martin—realized that they'd wrung everything out of him they were going to get and his PR value had hit the point of diminishing returns. He'd meant to visit there sometime with Virginia, but they hadn't gone before the kids, and after the kids, well, day trips were hard enough it seemed.

"It's a shame," Virginia whispered from her snuggle spot deep in his armpit.

What an understatement. It was a preview to the future of their home world. He was glad that the lights were down and they weren't looking at each other. While he thought his body hadn't tensed too much, he knew he'd failed to control a sneer and had thought about expanding on what she'd said, to no good end. But maybe anything a person could say was an understatement under the circumstances. And it was possible she wasn't referring to this particular Lashing in general, but the general state of affairs and the chance the human species would have to abandon the colonization efforts on Argo, at least for the foreseeable future.

"Yeah," he said, watching the images of the falls at sunset, lights reflective off the water and pitch shadows behind the rocky outcroppings.

Even though there was no immediate evacuation, they'd have to, in advance of some other Lashing, wouldn't they? Eventually? Somehow? At least start planning it?

How long could it take? And where could they go?

The answers were not obvious.

They had the volume down low, and watched the moving panorama between views of the falls and the growing fire low in the sky that was the sun made too bright and too big. Finally, a spectacular shot from an X-bot moving along the gorge walls, surely a sacrifice ultimately for just this shot: sparkling, spraying water casting a hundred red-hued rainbows between golden cliffs, shadows, and an angry, looming sun.

Pollux blossomed then, scintillating sparks from the water igniting into fireworks, and the snow of static broke the image into indecipherable pieces.

Initially, all in silence.

The feed switched to satellite and high-altitude views, shielded from the electromagnetic interference, and as they did so, revealed roiling clouds of the darkest soot amid the steam and glow of molten rock. After a moment, muted commentary bubbled up, seemingly out of the impact.

Virginia had gestured involuntarily with her free hand, and sat up a little.

After a minute, Frank said, "I'm going to the bathroom." He rose abruptly, and walked away from the carnage of his adopted planet.

Closing the door behind him and sitting down, he was sort of surprised by his action. He just couldn't talk about this with Virginia. He wished he had someone else to talk with. Really talk, without worrying about his relationship or conflicts of interest that could be obstacles to honesty. An old and dear best friend, or maybe a group of guys to hang with at a bar that could actually, occasionally, speak of meaningful things. When he'd married and decided to homestead, he'd elected to forgo such things and invest his time and heart in his family. Virginia was his best friend now, with their shared treasure and obligation of their children. How could he talk to her about what he was really feeling? Speaking about it with her, the conversation would really be about the kids, and he shied away from that thought himself right now.

What, indeed, was he feeling?

He let fevered, nightmarish introspection steal his upper and lower brains, the way he had done, often, when he had been a Scout without impetus to do much of anything right away.

Nothing was certain in this universe, and physical reality could become as much adrift as a relaxed mind. Anything could push it in any direction, from sublime heights of flawless logical design to raw, violent pain every bit as meaningful.

His scout ship, where everything had been the same every day, moment to moment, unless he did something, was not like the universe he lived in now. It had been a lie attacking his mind, constantly, that he had to fight against in anticipation of the time when something very key would change, and he would have to take quick action.

Like now, perhaps.

Argo was under attack, and perhaps it was a faceless, abstract danger that moved slowly and deliberately rather than with intentional swiftness, but it was real danger, and the most powerful destructive force he'd ever witnessed.

Argo, a target of attack.

His home and family, a target of ancient machinations as far beyond in time as a basketball rim remained beyond his ability to dunk no matter how he tried. Or was it?

Frank sat some more, idly thinking. His mind drifted.

What would life be like here? In the future? What future could there be? Would there be daily sun alerts and escape craft available if needed? There couldn't be enough, and the elevator in New Colchis was too slow.

Argo was a target.

A hit this soon after the start of the Lashings, well, there were sure to be more, weren't there? A whole hail of bullets . . . Frank had read that, in the early days of guns, the weapons had been used to execute criminals. What struck him was that some members of the so-called firing squads had been given blanks, and each one could tell themselves that they weren't responsible for the killing shot. But one of them was, every time. One of them always hit with deadly force.

They could move to the arcology and prepare for evacuation if it came to that, he supposed, and move . . . somewhere. It wouldn't be easy. Colonies went one way, and grew, and then became too populous to evacuate completely, at least with any speed. What was going on was unprecedented. They'd have to start planning an exodus, perhaps back to Earth, and that would take time. The incoming colony ships had been disassembled for materials, and would have to be rebuilt—more, given the population growth. Such efforts wouldn't happen overnight. How long would it take? How long could they wait?

Frank didn't want to go back to Earth. He liked it fine on Argo with his family and the life he had built. Farming was satisfying, and brewing consistently interesting. Sure, he didn't have that best friend or circle of drinking buddies, but he had a connection. His children had been born here. It was his home.

That new exploration ship up in orbit, however, the *Dark Heart* . . . that ship with its dark drive that he'd brought with him to Argo, its Bully, wasn't going to go to Earth, or to Castor 6. It was going someplace that might make a difference, if the people riding in it didn't screw it up.

"Frank, are you all right?" Virginia's voice came through the bathroom door.

He wasn't. "I'll be out in a minute," he said, still thinking.

Two days later, ash began to fall like snow. The day after that, Frank suggested to Virginia that they do a flyover, see how bad they were getting hit. School had been canceled, but Allyn could watch Kenny, so Virginia agreed. She'd been saying things about her own upcoming consulting trips that indicated she wasn't happy being very far from the kids at all. Frank understood.

Upon first glance, it looked like winter had struck, blanketing everything under a foot of fine white ash, and it still fell occasionally when the wind blew the right way. The car was rated to fly in sandstorms worse than this, when the wind speeds were as low as they were today, so a short flight wasn't a problem. The garage roof slid away without letting in much ash, and the takeoff was flawless.

They flew north over their pastures.

"Look," she said, leaning out and pointing over the side of the car. "Tracks."

He used the underside cameras and made out animal trails in the ash-covered fields below. He'd expected most of the animals to hunker down and keep out of sight, but they'd have to be foraging for food much harder given the circumstances. "Yeah," he said. "It's going to be challenging to survive, let alone thrive, and we've been lucky here."

"Lucky? To get attacked by the sun? Someone or something set it off. Stars don't do what Pollux did!" said Virginia, in a surprising outburst.

"You're right. They don't. Our bad luck to set up in a system with a bloodthirsty past. For all we know, the Lashings did in the Argonauts."

"I still favor the biological warfare hypothesis."

He couldn't resist this time. "Maybe bio warfare was payback for the Lashings. I mean, how many super-volcano attacks can you really stand before you take desperate measures?"

"One?" she said, quieter than before. "Maybe it'll just stop now."

"Because the ancient Argonauts were known for their restraint?"

Virginia didn't say anything.

Frank flew on, intentionally silent, following a trail of tracks. "We know a few things."

"We do." She changed her tone from accusatory to business. "Are you going to finish that new batch today?"

He didn't want more avoidance. He wanted to have it out, one way or another. Direct, or circumspect. But he wasn't going to talk about his beer, make small talk, that was for sure. They could talk around a subject, but he wasn't going to permit her to change subjects. "It's going to happen again. Maybe soon."

She sighed. "It's a big planet. It isn't likely to hit anywhere important."

He waved his hand at the ash-covered landscape. "Anywhere it hits is a disaster that could make life unsustainable. We're going to see lowered temperatures this year that will affect outdoor crops. Like ours." They had two cornfields to the south. "How many years can we go without summers?"

She was quiet again, and he let her be.

"Look there," he said after a moment. The trail had skirted the edge of the treeline, but he'd been able to follow it. Up ahead he made out a mass of dark bodies in turmoil. As they drew near he could make out what was happening. "Spider monkey troop, attacking one of our goats."

"But why would they do that? They can't eat it. It'll kill them."

"Don't underestimate the desperate. This Lashing has upset everything. I'm landing." He was sorry he sounded as mean as he did, but it bothered him.

Frank set down the car in a billowing poof of ash. He hopped out before it had settled despite Virginia's protests. His goat was being attacked. *His* goat.

"Hey!" he yelled at the swarming beasts. "Hey!"

They ignored him, continuing to pounce on the bleating goat, which tried to turn and buck and fight them off as best it could.

The poor thing was bleeding from a dozen places, but only one of the spider monkeys seemed to have died. Frank surmised that one had been foolish enough to take a bite out of the animal.

He counted eight attackers. They weren't much bigger than medium-size dogs, and Frank was a big man. He didn't worry about himself, and just waded in, grabbing the critters and tossing them as far as he could. He was aware that the ash would cushion their falls, and wished it wasn't there. These things were nasty, snarling creatures right now, and he had a vision of them after Kenny rather than a goat.

He preferred that they get hurt, he realized. Was that wrong?

"Get away!" he yelled, grabbing another one and throwing it high into the air.

The remainder started to scream at him, a more urgent version of their coordinated call. It was scary to be close to it, and to be the target of it. Big men, he knew, could get scared, too. But fear was not an option and it didn't deter his actions.

He chased, grabbed, kicked, whatever he could do to keep them off him and the goat and end their damn infernal call. It was fast, loud, and a good stress reliever given what was going on. He wouldn't have even minded killing a few if it came to that. They'd attacked a creature under his protection.

But they moved away, called at him again, and then moved away some more.

He realized he was warm and breathing heavily, coming down off adrenaline. When he turned around, Virginia was already tending to the bleating goat with a first-aid kit from the trunk.

"You should have stayed in the car," he said.

"You chased them off, and I'm better with the animals than you are. You're bleeding, too."

He looked down at his hands, and sure enough, he had a gash across the back of his hand. Drops of blood had stained the ash on the ground below his hand. He held up his arm and regarded the cut. "I need a bandage."

"I'm almost finished here," she said. "You'll keep for a minute?"

He watched the blood seeping from his hand. "Yeah," he said. It would clot and close soon enough on its own, but he wanted to prevent scarring. Nasty little bastards. He hoped one of them was licking its claws clean right now.

"I'm coming with you," Virginia said abruptly. "You understand?"

It took Frank a moment to realize what she meant. Yeah, he'd been leaning that way since the last Lashing, but he'd wanted to discuss it with her. He'd been half-thinking about the consequences already, enough to know she was being ridiculous.

"Absolutely not. My sons aren't going to grow up with foster parents."

She stared at him, her mouth and eyes wide.

"This isn't fair!" she shrieked to the sky, throwing her hands up in supplication to the universe. "It's supposed to be okay for me to live the rest of my life without you?"

The goat bleated, and stepped back from her. Frank saw tears streaming down his wife's face.

"It's not forever," he said. "Five decades, tops. I can do it in my sleep."

He regretted the comment immediately. She hated it when he made jokes in serious situations, even though he wasn't usually very funny. He thought it relieved tension and sometimes helped put things in perspective. She didn't.

"I'm going to make a sacrifice, too," she said. "I'm an expert on Dynasty 2c, history, culture, language, and the Spider Star story in particular. I found it, after all. I'll go as a pattern. You'll have part of me with you."

That was a nontrivial commitment. Patterning was an involved process, and he would have preferred that she not endure it. But he wasn't about to tell her she couldn't, either. She might start arguing about how he shouldn't defend his family and home.

"Okay," he said. "I'll call Claude tonight and work out the details. I'm going to spend as much time with you and the kids as I can until we go."

"You'd better," she said, choking on her tears, trying to smile, and not entirely succeeding.

Was that it? Was that the whole discussion?

Frank felt another letdown, like there'd been a base of adrenaline he'd been riding for days without being aware of it.

Yes, he was going to go.

Frank looked up at the sun, feeling a little sick.

How does a man challenge the sun and hope to win?

And then he looked back at Virginia, who stared into his eyes, and he knew how.

Kenny had been quiet through dinner, and had run off as soon as dismissed. Frank worried that he'd heard something he shouldn't have when he and Virginia had returned.

He shambled into the tunnel of the hallway, ignoring the pictures of his smiling family adorning the walls, until he came to Kenny's room. A sliver of light peeked out from under the doorway. Frank knocked, hesitatingly, and turned the knob. "Kenny?"

The boy sat with his back to the door, at the worktable in the center of his room, messing around with a three-dimensional wooden puzzle. The sight forced a smile from Frank. With all the video games, robots, and high-tech diversions, his son was playing with the classic toy that Frank loved and Virginia had insisted he'd hate.

Kenny ignored his entry though, and Frank quietly walked across the room and around the table to the other side. He carefully sat on the small chair situated there.

Kenny picked up the pieces, trying to fit them together into a cube. The wood clinked as he pushed in various ways, revealing that he was obviously frustrated. "They won't go, Da," he said.

"I'll help," Frank offered.

"No," Kenny said. "I can do it."

"Okay. I wanted to talk to you about something."

Kenny didn't say anything, just kept fumbling with the pieces: *clink, slide, clink.*

"It looks like I'll have to be going away, not because I want to, but because I have to."

"Why?"

So he was going to be that way tonight. Fair enough. Frank could deal with it. "You remember what we saw happen to the moon? I'm going to go stop that from happening again."

"Why?"

"Because it's dangerous to people. I want people to be safe."

"Why?"

"Because everyone should be safe where they live. Because it's the right thing to do. I'm going to be gone for a long time."

"Why?"

"Because the place we need to go for help is a long, long way away, and we can only go so fast. I'll be a little older when I get back, but you'll be all grown up, an adult, like me and your mom."

Kenny didn't say anything right away, but soon enough came back with, "Why?"

"Because you have to keep on living your life here, learning things, being a good brother, and helping your mom while I'm gone."

Kenny nearly had the puzzle done. It wasn't an easy one, but he had done it many times before. He kept his focus on the puzzle and off Frank, his lower lip sticking out petulantly. After he settled the last piece into place, he twitched, and his hand came smashing down.

The pieces exploded across the table.

As Frank watched with growing horror, Kenny patiently moved to gather the pieces together and started to reassemble the cube, all without saying a word. His anger quivered before Frank with equal amounts of purity and maturity, as well as depths of darkness he didn't know his child harbored.

If he left, would his absence destroy the lives of those he loved as surely as a well-directed Lashing?

It couldn't, it wouldn't. Virginia was a good mother, and together they'd raised their kids reasonably well so far—he knew that even though he worried about the details.

"Kenny," Frank said.

"Why?" said Kenny at once.

There aren't words, Frank thought. *There aren't words for this.*

He nearly got up and left then, swallowed by despair at wanting and needing what was lost to him. Normally he would have just made a ruling, given a punishment, made Kenny behave. But this was a father-son relationship and you couldn't make someone love you unconditionally. He resolved himself to say something, let it out even if he himself didn't know it yet, even if Kenny wouldn't understand it, let it out in a why-proof rush. He opened his mouth. The truth—it was all he had, even if his son was too young to understand it yet. "I'm your father, Kenny. I'm part of you, and you're part of me. We're family, of the same kind. I don't know if this makes sense to you yet, or if it ever will, but I'm doing this because of how much I love you and your brother and how much you mean to me. When I leave, six months from now, you'll—"

"Six months?" Kenny's head swiveled toward him. "Oh, I thought you were leaving tomorrow." Kenny smiled, promptly finished his puzzle, and put it to one side. He put his arms out for Frank.

Frank swept him into his arms into a big bear hug.

"Yoosmoffume," Kenny said.

Frank eased back.

"You're smothering me," Kenny said.

"I love you," said Frank, hugging his son again, almost as tightly.

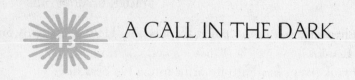

A CALL IN THE DARK

ONBOARD THE *VISIONARY*, ARGO ORBIT

The phone rang, waking Rusk. His eyes flashed open and he unzipped his free-fall bag. His phone would only let emergency calls through when he was asleep, so it had to be something important.

Rusk snaked out an arm and snagged the phone floating on its secure line. "Yes," he answered.

"Manuel." It was Claude Martin. "You sound alert. I was afraid I'd wake you."

Rusk knew that was unlikely. Martin didn't usually care about such niceties, especially when tagging a call as emergency—although maybe he did that for every call? No, Martin was a bit abusive of his power, but not that abusive. Something was up, and the man had intentionally called when he was sleeping. That meant it was going to be something he didn't like.

But he decided to play along with the script. "What is it? A new Lashing?"

"No, thank heavens, no."

They hadn't had a Lashing since the one that hit Argo three days earlier, and there was no way they'd be able to take another aimed at Argo for at least three months. Better yet, three million years.

"Good," Rusk said, letting a little false relief into his voice. *Get on with it, boss.*

"It's just that there's been a development in the mission parameters I thought you should know about immediately. Trust me, you'd be mad if I delayed informing you about this even one single minute."

Rusk waited, looking at nothing in particular in his darkened bunk room onboard the *Visionary,* and said nothing.

"Well, it's a crew change."

A crew change? With only months before departure? No. No. Martin wasn't doing this to him. Again, he gave himself away by his choice of words, and just the fact that he was calling, and calling now. It could have been an injury, or a resignation, something like that requiring a replacement. But no . . . for Martin to pitch it this way meant it was something political.

Something he wouldn't like and something political. And he woke up for this?

"What is it?"

"An opportunity has arisen we can't pass up." Suddenly it was "we," but Rusk said nothing and waited for Martin to continue. "Frank Klingston himself has volunteered to go to the Spider Star with you."

Rusk's hand twitched and sent the phone spinning away from his head. It was a moment before he could haul it back in.

"It's impossible," Rusk answered when he could. "Everything's set, everything's planned. Thank him for his offer, but I'm sure he'll understand why we can't take him."

"Oh no," said Martin. "We can take him. I'm told there's enough of a safety margin with the supplies and weights that it isn't really a big issue."

That wasn't the issue at all, and they both knew it. Sometimes Rusk just wanted to let go and tell Martin that he knew the score, that he'd always known it, and why couldn't they just drop the bullshit and speak frankly. But he never did it. That wasn't how Claude Martin liked things.

Suddenly another thought sparked in Rusk's sleepy head. A space hero like Klingston couldn't be a regular rank-and-file Specialist. "What's Klingston's position supposed to be?"

"Don't worry. You're still mission director."

"What's Klingston?"

"I'm calling him 'executive director.' It's sort of an honorary thing. He'll be a consultant, albeit with some form of veto power. We're still negotiating that part."

Rusk rubbed at his eyes. "Are *we* negotiating?"

"Manuel! I thought you would jump at the chance to have someone like Klingston along. He's field proven!"

And I'm not, Rusk thought, the thing Martin was really implying. But he forced himself away from that unhealthy thought. He knew Martin trusted him and his abilities, and he'd already figured there was a political angle. Sure. Obvious. The mission was announced, but there was little solace in a plan that would take many decades to bear fruit, if at all.

There were plans to build mobile shields to block the Lashings, but no one thought they had a chance of success, or any of the other crazy ideas that had been tossed out. No one wanted to talk of abandoning Argo. Not yet. The Spider Star mission did have a chance in the long run, he believed, but coming immediately after a hit on Argo, the announcement of Klingston tagging along—or perhaps leading, given the title of "executive director"—well, that would help keep public opinion for Martin favorable.

He suspected that his own devastating knock would be announced at some point, after he was on his way, if there was a political angle for Martin to exploit. Sometimes it seemed he intended to remain in charge of Argo forever.

"Look, you don't have to worry about Klingston interfering much," Martin said. "You're still in charge of the ship, the team, and their training. He's not even going to show up until launch."

"What? Why is he even coming then?"

"First you don't want him, and now you're complaining he's not doing enough?"

Martin could be infuriating. Rusk waited on him.

"Klingston's going to be spending as much time with his family as possible. That's nonnegotiable."

Rusk had studiously avoided family connections for years. His parents were workaholics, like many on Argo, so it hadn't been too hard on that end. And keeping his sexual liaisons confined to other Specialists who also wanted to go off-world balanced the other side of the equation.

"Fine," he said, finally. Fighting with Claude Martin on an issue like this had no upside. Not now, anyway, but perhaps later, when he'd have a chance to think. "But I want to sort through the details of Klingston's addition with you later. Get everything spelled out clearly. Okay?"

They'd do that face to face. None of this middle-of-the-night bullshit.

"Okay. Sorry to bother you. You should get back to sleep, Manuel."

Right. That seemed unlikely. He'd have plenty of time to sleep in a few months. "Good night."

"Good night."

Rusk considered calling Sloan or Selene, see if they were up and wanted to come over. That seemed selfish, however, so he resigned himself to working through this new wrinkle. He'd sleep eventually.

He pulled his arms back into the cocoon of his bag, closed his eyes, and thought of Frank Klingston, family man.

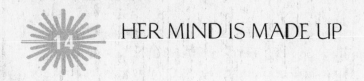

NEW COLCHIS ARCOLOGY, ARGO

Frank held on to Virginia's hand as they walked into the office of the pattern weaver, Dr. Orbos, despite the fact that it was sweaty. Her hands usually got sweaty when she was nervous and once upon a time he had found that charming. It made her transparent in a way he, as a man, appreciated, and was one of his little ways of reading her mind.

The weaver was going to go infinitely beyond his twenty years of little ways in only twenty days.

The waiting room itself was deceptively unassuming: two firm couches, two hanging plants with unkempt tendrils, Monet water lilies in the frame hanging on one wall, and an unmarked door. The color scheme was yellow and lime-green, nothing great or awful, and nothing to startle.

"You don't have to do this," he whispered to her, not sure why he was whispering.

"Bullshit," she said. "This is nothing."

Her sweaty hand told another story.

Getting patterned had been compared to a hundred different things, and none of them good. One infamous quote Frank remembered, although he didn't recall who had said it, suggested that the process was slightly better than driving a steel spike into your own head with a tiny hammer while debating Aristotle on Aristotle. It was the sort of ridiculous thing he would think of at a time like this, and he was happy he suppressed the irrational urge to repeat it to his wife.

Before they could even sit, a calm female voice said, "Please proceed through the door."

No waiting today. They were VIPs. He wished they could wait.

Virginia pulled him to the door that popped open at their approach.

There would be no more waiting.

Today significant and terrible things began to happen, and Frank had no idea when they might end. Not for years to come, unfortunately.

He lived in interesting times. Again.

This is the beginning of the end of my first real life, Frank thought, as he followed Virginia inside.

An hour later Virginia was reclining, her head resting just inside a padded, oval pit at the back of her chair. Her hands rested, clasped, on her chest, moving slowly up and down with her breathing. Her hands clenched for a moment, then relaxed.

Immediately surrounding Virginia on her brightly lit dais were Dr. Orbos, his assistant Dr. Wolfson, and two X-bots. The X-bots both hunkered down by her head, one on each side, tentacles running into the oval pit.

Frank sat on a high stool in the corner and leaned in, listening and worrying. He noticed that the room smelled faintly of ozone, and carried a quiet hum of energy just on the edge of audible.

Over the past hour Virginia had been injected with nanodiagnosticians of three sorts, one for her circulatory system, one for the lymph system, and the last for her nervous system. Chemical and radioactive dyes had also been introduced to heighten the monitoring, along with drugs to help her focus.

As he watched, buds sprouted from the pit like fast-growing

beanstalks and slid into her ears. Just headphones, he remembered, from the demonstration video he'd watched a dozen
times. Hypnotic assistance, which would also filter the noise
from the spinning magnets in the chair when they powered up.

Orbos whispered with Wolfson as Frank glanced at them.
Two middle-aged men, both slightly overweight and graying,
whispering as they stood in their white jackets. Comfortingly
traditional. Frank watched their lips move, but he couldn't make
sense of what they were saying. Too many technical words said
too calmly.

Why was he letting this get to him so? Thousands had been
patterned, and while it wasn't the most pleasant procedure, no
one had ever been hurt by it.

Why couldn't he let go, at least a little? Things would be irre-
versibly bad enough, soon enough, so why make it worse now?

As the X-bots snaked out tiny tentacles to hold open and
moisturize Virginia's eyes, he thought he knew. And when the
lasers splashed rainbows across her face, and she gasped, he was
sure he knew.

Their family, their entire world, was threatened, and they
were both willing to make any sacrifices they could for it. Virginia's sacrifice was symbolic of his own, and he felt it as if it
were his own. His own was going to be much worse, and he was
feeling its pain now, prematurely. But not yet, no need yet, and
he pushed away those thoughts. There was enough now to oc-
cupy his worries.

"You may watch, if you wish," Dr. Orbos said after a moment. "It has begun."

Frank registered the doctor's words and shook his gaze free
of Virginia's transfixed stare. He saw that her lips were moving
although she didn't seem to be speaking.

"Okay," he said.

He fumbled for the visor they'd given him, and set it across his face. The device snuggled to him, and after a brief moment of disorientation, a new world materialized.

He was outside, someplace. He recognized some maroon bushes as Argotian, and the light felt right for Argos as well. A dig stretched before him, delineated by a laser grid and worked by specialized dig bots. That was about all it meant to him, like something he'd seen on a documentary or that Virginia may have showed him shortly after they'd first met.

He heard her then, her voice a distant tide welling up into his awareness. "This is the location of the second significant Dynasty D find, which I visited as an intern for four months. At the time I didn't fully appreciate the difference between C and D, but to be fair to myself, neither did anyone else. The styles were quite similar, and the subtleties would not have kept us from lumping them together when it came to Earth civilizations. I mean, who would separate twenty-first century North America and Europe as separate dynasties, if their governments would have even lent themselves to that designation. That should have been a monumental clue . . ."

She continued on, cataloging the scene with part objective scrutiny and part subjective editorial. Frank had heard her speaking with colleagues on many occasions, and her demeanor was much the same: a seasoned mix of methodical observation and intuitive connections.

Orbos was attempting to learn exactly what Virginia knew and how she thought about her expertise. He tracked her eye movements, her brain activity, her blood, and every chemical and electrical reaction they could measure. Most would map into states that could be interpreted as thoughts, or attitudes, that coupled with Virginia's knowledge base. Eventually there would be a critical point at which a computer model would approach issues the same way as she would and reach very similar conclusions a high fraction of the time.

There would be plenty of trial and error before that point.

This technology had not existed when Frank left Earth for the stars, but he still clearly recalled how Claude Martin had first explained it to him. He flashed to the cyborg leader before him, in his mind's eye, over a glass of red wine and the chess game Frank had won. He had told him that expert knowledge was a combination of pattern recognition and testing procedure, and the first true artificial intelligence had come through chess. Not Deep Blue, which had first defeated a world chess champion (one of the ones named Kar-something), but Mellonhead, which they'd refused to call a program and had installed inside a crash test dummy. Typically silly scientists.

Chess masters almost always immediately knew the right move to make. They had played the game so many times, had seen so many games played, they automatically knew what move was likely the right one. You could either study all the hundreds of thousands of games that chess masters studied, and their outcomes, or study the chess masters, drawing out the patterns. There were fewer patterns.

This was the starting point.

After a few hours, Frank got bored. Virginia didn't. Presumably she found digs and Argonaut dialects fascinating, and she likely did, but she also had the drugs and hypnosis to help. Frank just had love and desperation, and they weren't quite as strong. That was a sobering realization in weeks of sobering realizations.

Slow and methodical, the simulations continued, changing in sophistication, calling for more input and decisions from Virginia.

During a break, Frank asked Orbos, "Claude Martin tells me this is like figuring out how someone plays chess. You can just sit back, figure out their patterns, and duplicate their skills. So why do you need all the brain imaging and drugs? Why not just watch them play chess?"

"Mr. Klingston, have you ever heard of the Chinese room argument?"

"No."

"It's an old argument about artificial intelligence. Basically, was a computer intelligent if it could do something only a human could do, like translate Chinese and carry on a conversation with a native Chinese speaker and have that person not know it was a computer?"

"Okay."

"But what if the computer doing the translation was some guy in a room with a rule book, methodically following the book, and taking an input and producing an output? And the guy never understands a single bit of the conversation—it's all just symbol manipulation. Would that really be intelligent behavior?"

"Who wrote the rule book?"

Orbos tilted his head and gave him a little look. "Sure, the person who wrote the rule book is intelligent, but how about a machine following the rule book?"

"I guess not."

"We could put a bunch of rules into an expert pattern, and duplicate someone's expertise in much the same way as the Chinese room, but when faced with realistic input, rule books often fall short. There isn't a rule for every possible scenario for anything complicated, and who wants a rule book that falls short? So we try to duplicate both the knowledge base and a simple rule book, but also the process by which an expert develops their responses."

"And that requires the brain scans?"

"Oh yes," Orbos said. "You don't get intuitive leaps from rule books, but you do from real experts. And that's the part we're really looking to duplicate. The part that *thinks,* if you will. It's proven difficult. Expert patterns displaying intuitive leaps beyond the range of the input rules is about the best we've done, and it requires some idea of the structure of thought, if you will, that real experts display. Now if you'll excuse me, it's time to start again with your wife."

In the late afternoon, at the end of the last session that involved Virginia trying to translate a new story cube she'd never seen before, using clues from the imagery, Frank was ashamed to find himself exhausted.

He walked over to where she still lay in her examination chair, sans 90 percent of the monitoring devices. He decided he wouldn't even ask her if she wanted to quit.

"What?" she asked, suddenly noticing him.

"Let me take you to dinner," he suggested. "Then you can have a long bath and get to bed."

"What time is it?" she asked.

"A bit after four," he said. "Dinner can be early."

"No, Frank. You need to leave now, or you'll miss the shuttle back south."

"The kids are fine. Elektra and Ionnis said they'd watch them tonight if I didn't get back."

"I don't want our bridge partners watching our kids. Besides, their daughter has a thing for Allyn."

"Really?" Frank smiled.

"He's got that whole distracted, artistic thing going. He thinks he's hopeless, but he'll be a lady-killer. You'd know that if you paid more attention to him."

Frank's smile died.

"I didn't mean that," she said quickly. "But go spend more time with your sons, okay? Let's just keep to the schedule we set. I go back once a week, you come up twice."

"Okay," he agreed. Allyn, a target for girls? Already? Maybe there was a future for his family after all, *if* Argo wasn't destroyed. "We'll stick to the schedule. And hey, one more thing."

"What's that?"

"I appreciate you wanting to do this, and your expertise will likely prove invaluable, but . . ."

"But what?"

Frank wasn't sure how to say this. He was afraid it was going to come out wrong. He forged ahead. "Patterns are often emotionally detached. They're part of a person, but not a person, even though we address them by name and they appear to convey emotions through facial expressions. I don't want to confuse your pattern with you. You know I have a tendency to get short with patterns."

"Don't we all?"

"Okay. But I don't want your pattern called 'Virginia.' Can we call it 'Ginnie' instead?"

He waited, hoping he hadn't stepped on an emotional landmine. Virginia's mother had called her Ginnie well into her teen years, primarily when she thought her daughter was acting childish.

Virginia seemed to consider it, then nodded. "We can do that."

"Thanks." He bent over to kiss her, and she kissed him back more passionately than he expected.

"What was that for?" he asked.

"For considering me." She smiled up at him. "And for love, for the future, and a thousand other things. For the hope of miracles."

"Miracles?"

"Well, the opposite of random bad things like the Lashings, anyway. Random, great, good things. You're my miracle, and I think there are a few more left in my life."

"Mine, too, I hope," Frank said, agreeing.

ASCENSION

Over the next five months, Pollux lashed out eleven more times, without concrete damage to human affairs on Argo.

But even as the fiery attacks spiraled off into space, each one felt like a direct hit on Frank's heart.

As he rode the lift to the orbital station, Frank wished his emotions would go numb, shrivel, and die. He had committed to a path, and they were now a liability. He knew that in the history of humankind there had been many periods when it wasn't uncommon for people to leave their families, often with very uncertain chances of returning. There was exploration. There was work. There was war.

Frank counted his current circumstances as falling under the heading of "war." He knew what he would be fighting for, but when he could focus his thoughts, he realized he didn't fully comprehend what he was fighting against.

The time had passed so quickly! Try as he might to enjoy the days, to memorize every moment, they passed through his hands as easily and quickly as water. Even Allyn had tried to smile more, making an effort, but Frank could barely visualize it now.

The elevator ride took most of a day, and seemed like a year. He'd been given a private car, scooting up at several hundred kilometers per hour. He was glad he'd accepted the offer. He had access to millions of music files, hundreds of thousands of books, tens of thousands of movies, and thousands of games. Jason, his personal X-bot the Specialists had assigned him, squatted nearby, ready to offer conversation with any of the expert patterns it hosted—including Virginia's. He didn't dare start that yet. He also had terabytes of information about the mission, ranging from ship specs, to crew profiles, to decoded and translated Argonaut military files. He should have started studying those materials, but he didn't.

He spent most of the ride quietly crying.

He spent some time considering the golden wedding tattoo around his ring finger.

He drank eight beers.

He didn't think he would do this. He'd had months to prepare himself.

His thoughts circled over the painful loss, moving between Virginia and his sons. He tried to remember the good moments in those days, and tried to ignore the teary, confusing last good-byes. But he couldn't yet, and he let himself wallow in it. After all, chances were good that they'd be dead to him. Virginia might not be alive when he returns, and while his sons would be if the Lashings didn't get them, they'd be strangers, their young memories of him altering into surreality or vanishing altogether with the years.

And to think how this had been for him once, long ago.

Frank had been young, cocky, and more desirous of immortality than living a long, mundane life, and he'd made the same decision that Achilles had made. His parents had actually helped make the decision easy. He had tested them when the manned scouting missions had been announced, and found them wanting:

"I'm thinking about applying for one of the Scout positions," he had said to them at dinner one night while back home in Alaska on holiday from school.

"That's quite bold," his mom had said.

His dad had agreed. "Sure is! Go for it, and tell all the girls."

These responses had struck him as shallow, thoughtless, and without regard for deep feelings for him. After a bite of salmon, he pressed on, suspicious, "I think I've got a chance. I've got the engineering primaries, science secondaries. Psych is good. Top one or two percentile across the board."

"We know," his dad had said. "And we're very proud of you. You get that from your aunt Louise. But don't get your hopes up. They're looking for special people."

"You're special, of course, but don't worry about it," his mom had continued. "You know I tracked down that directory problem. Can you imagine two people named Belinda Sparrowhawk Roche?"

"No, do tell!" his dad had responded, Frank's issue forgotten as if it had meant nothing.

He remembered nearly every detail of that dinner, he'd replayed it in his memory so many times. It still shocked him how much it remained with him, and how it had driven him at that age. His parents were normal people. His mother investigated database anomalies, his father supervised nanoforge feedlines, and they spent their spare time watching TV. Like normal people of the time, they hadn't done much or aspired to much, settling for what they were given by virtue of their place and time of birth.

At least that was the way he had seen it. Frank had always been among the best at everything he'd cared enough to attempt, intellectual or physical, even the artistic. He'd also possessed the curiosity to accompany his talents. And still his normal parents patronized him.

Their attitude had made him quietly furious, and he'd worked his ass off with only one goal in mind: making Scout. He avoided letting any girl get too close, or specializing too much, or doing anything at all that might make him a less-than-optimal choice.

Tens of thousands of applications had been considered with the minimum requirements that Frank had barely managed. He worried his parents were right.

He hadn't been chosen in the first round, but he'd made the supplemental selection.

He slept with scores of women, tossing each aside in rapid succession, and had ignored his parents. He was a minor celebrity and there had been no other future in his mind. Space was his destiny, and he could only depend on himself.

He had not fully appreciated the cost. Years of loneliness, despair, boredom, worry, uncertainty, anxiety, fear, anguish, anger, confusion, isolation, and more, little of it good . . . never again. He thought he'd go mad, and half-believed that he had, several times. Certainly he had to have been mad to do what he'd done when he'd detected the alien ship. That's what he'd heard in debriefings anyway. But he'd done it. Did that really make him special? Did that really mean he should be the one to lead this strange mission?

And while in successive years he had wished many times he had more fully understood what his youthful choices would bring him, his current existence was a consequence of what had come before. Without becoming a Scout, he would never have met Virginia. Without her, Kenny and Allyn would not even exist. He could not regret the past, and could not fully accept the tragedy of the quiet years and his alien encounter, as much as he sometimes, late at night, let himself accept the horror of it all.

Those times had taught him to long for something, and here on Argo he had found it. An acceptance and appreciation for normalcy, and of belonging.

Now it was to be lost to him, and so he grieved.

The elevator climbed into the sky, and his heart sank in response.

Frank had the chance to sleep immediately upon arrival, and being spent, he welcomed the escape. He didn't think he would get to sleep quickly, but he did. One thing about being in space he had always missed was freefall sleep, especially as he'd gotten older. Gravity didn't squeeze his shoulders or press on his back, and there were never morning aches. Although free of aches, he dreamed, unfortunately, of Virginia being a seductive masked alien and awoke unsettled and crying again.

Two hours later, Frank had managed to get up, have a bowel movement, wash up and shave, get dressed, and eat. He was proud of himself in a small way. He hadn't been on the station in years and it took time to remember how to do things in freefall. Moreover, he was now living in his post-family era. He was a single spacer and he had to remember how to be that again, too. The first part was keeping a routine and doing the necessary things that had to be done. Perfect hygiene wasn't essential, but keeping everything else shipboard was.

Well, this trip he wouldn't be alone, so perhaps hygiene was essential.

A woman found her way into his cabin while he was brushing his teeth. "Pleased to meet you, Klingston. I'm Sloan Griffin. Ready to head over to the *Dark Heart* and meet everyone else?"

"Yeah," he said around his toothbrush. He found the vacusink and spit. "Ready as I'll ever be."

"Then let's go," she said, turning and kicking away.

Frank stowed his toothbrush in the medicine cabinet and considered his reflection in the mirror after he closed its door. He looked old and tired, with his face even ruddier than usual and the skin under his eyes noticeably puffy. No trace of young and cocky. He wondered how much his parents had missed him when he'd left Earth, and felt more for them than he had in decades. Then he turned to follow Sloan Griffin into his dark future.

Smile, old man, he thought. *Meet your new life with a smile on your face. It's the least you can do, to make the most of things.*

He would meet the darkness with a smile. If it wasn't a smile, it would be a scream of loss, and that he would not permit himself.

Abracadabra.

MEETINGS AND LEAVINGS

ARGO ORBIT, *DARK HEART*

"We've never met face to face before, Executive Director," Griffin said over her shoulder. "I saw you a few times, at a distance. A sushi place one time, and a play another. I didn't want to bother you."

"Call me Frank, or Klingston," he said. "It would have been fine just to come up. People did it all the time."

"I figured it would be, but I'm polite. Just because you recognize someone doesn't mean you have to rush over and talk to them."

"That's true. I'm sure you recognize people all the time in the arcology."

"Sure, and you nod at them, smile." She was happy that Klingston seemed pleasant so far. From what Claude Martin had said he could be a real bastard to deal with. Rusk had been Klingston's primary contact over the phone, and while he hadn't said anything bad about Klingston, he hadn't said anything to disabuse her of his bastard nature, either. "We're pretty informal in the Corps, Klingston. Everyone's professional and does their job without a lot of the formal signs of hierarchy."

They punted their way down the tube toward the *Visionary*'s space dock. It was a long way out, and she started feeling a bit more microgravity pulling her ahead and a little to the left. "Rusk tells me you met once before."

"Did we?"

She paused at an airlock and started it cycling. "He said it was here, on the *Visionary*, ten or twelve years ago."

"It would have been twelve," he said.

She was in close proximity to Frank and she appreciated for the first time how much space he took up. He wasn't fat, just big, a presence. He smelled good from a recent shower—she realized that this would likely change soon. Everyone would reek of the dens. "Rusk was top graduate and got invited to a lot of the private events that year. You were at one of the receptions."

"That must have been when Claude Martin invited me to head up his latest showpiece, the Bureau of Alien Affairs. I suppose it seems like less of a bullshit deal now than it did to me then."

"Hmmm," she said. "I guess that explains why he didn't speak very well of you when he told me about it. Said you were standoffish and drank a lot."

Klingston laughed, a deep easy chuckle. "I'm sure that was exactly how I was. I'll have to make a better first impression this time around."

The main staging area of the *Dark Heart* hosted a feast. The entire crew was there, eating mutton, soy dogs, pecan pies, pumpkin pudding, six types of fresh fruit, ham, green bean casserole, trout—and that was just what she could make out on the first table. It was a bit of a cheat, since everything was clearly labeled in freefall dispensers and mostly came out in tubes. Everyone's favorites.

"We're bulking up for hibernation already, huh?" Klingston asked.

"Yes," said Griffin, slowly, peering through the floating bodies. "And starting the shots. Be sure to check in with Melinda on the far side of the room. Medical nano for the hibernation. It will activate a number of enzymes, primarily pancreatic triglyceride lipase and pyruvate dehydrogenase kinase isozyme four."

"Just roll off the tongue, don't they?"

"Yeah," she said, blushing. He'd called her on it. She had prepped just in case she got a chance to show off for Klingston. The enzymes governed how stored fatty acids and glucose were conserved, or not, especially in muscles like the heart, which was slowed to just over a beat per minute during hibernation. Hibernation helped preserve muscle tone, but there were mechanical and electrical aids that helped with that part, too.

She recovered quickly, and added, "You'll need to get an implant, as well."

"The tracer?" he asked.

"Yes, so we can locate you and monitor your vitals. We all have them."

"Fine. Let's do it."

"Wait!" she called, grabbing his arm. Rusk was floating their way.

Rusk hit the pair of them, and they ended up in an awkward three-way tumble, none of them having a handhold. She felt like an amateur, and didn't have to imagine what the men felt like—she was touching them. She smiled at the thought.

Rusk was larger than her, and she suspected Klingston weighed pretty close to what she and Rusk weighed together. For a moment the three of them spun together, their own closed system, Klingston their primary.

Rusk laughed, a small forced laugh that didn't contain much mirth to Griffin's familiar ear. Klingston just smiled a fixed smile, and stared at them.

"It's good to have you here," Rusk said.

"Well, I'm here," Klingston replied. "I'm glad you could take care of setting this all up. I respect what you've done."

"Thank you."

Griffin waited for the rest. There was a thing to resolve, and best here and now, in her opinion. "We've got a great, well-trained team."

"I appreciate that. I really do. I just want to help."

"We can't say no to help," Rusk said.

"I—I don't want to interfere. I know this is awkward."

Rusk said nothing, and Griffin decided to let the silence work as well.

Klingston went on. "I'm here to make Argo safe for my family. I'll do what's necessary in my view to do that. I'll leave you alone as much as possible, but I will exercise my best judgment. If I can't do that, I should just stay home."

Griffin felt the man's hand digging into her shoulder. He was going through something. She glanced at Manuel. He was staring back, solemnly, at the bigger man's face.

"I'm going to exercise my best judgment, too. Let's work together for our common goals."

"I couldn't agree more."

It all seemed a little forced to Griffin. They'd both said the right things, but it was strange, and awkward as hell. She supposed it was to be expected. A few days together and hibernation would ease the tension, bring them together. She did believe that both had only the best interests of the mission at heart.

Rusk smiled then, and pushed off the two to take a handhold by the door. "Well then, we can't fail. Let's talk again later and I'll provide a more detailed briefing."

"Yes, let's do that," Frank said. Turning to her he said, "Let's go eat. You have a lot more people to introduce me to."

"Yes I do," she said.

Klingston seemed to be back to being a warm, open person, seemingly genuinely interested in everyone. That was good. He needed to be. These were the people that were going to do the job he wanted done. She only caught a hint of that strange, wide-eyed look one more time in the evening: when he was by himself for a moment, eating blueberries.

Why would blueberries have such a strong impact on a man?

The final days passed quickly, and soon enough came the hour of departure. Griffin, sitting in the command center, running down her checklist, actually thought they were ready—as ready for the unknown as anyone could hope to be.

The years and months of preparation were complete. They were going to do it: leave Argo for an alien world.

She thought Klingston as executive director should say something, anything, to mark the moment, but he remained silent, not preempting the normal launch chatter. She also thought, then, that Rusk might do the same in the absence of any words from Klingston, but Rusk didn't say anything, either. Only Slyde, the lead pilot, the copilots, and herself, in her capacity of second seat, backup systems, spoke, and it was in the timeless, measured cadence of safety that space travel favored.

Fine then, the launch would be an anticlimax, safe and assured. She could appreciate that.

Launching from space dock, however, was the antithesis of traditional, surface-based launches. Planetside, ships sat in deep gravity wells, requiring ass-busting accelerations to reach escape velocity and climb to freedom. Launch was all about fire, thunder, and crushing weight.

There was a better way. At the end of a tether, which was really just an extension of the elevator, a de facto umbilical cord reaching down to Argo and waiting to be severed, a ship was already liberated from the energy-sapping gravity well. The tether swung around with the planet's rotation, swinging the dock around as if it were at the edge of a gargantuan merry-go-round.

Finally, on cue, the docking clamps released the *Dark Heart,* and with a slight rocket-assisted push it slowly slid down the tether away from Argo.

Griffin's stomach fluttered. Einstein's principle of equivalence was that acceleration and gravity were indistinguishable, which was the reason why moving "up" the elevator away from the geosynchronous point felt like "down." As they moved farther down, they felt heavier, being accelerated faster to maintain their circular motion. When the ship was finally released, Newton's first law took over: An object at rest tends to stay at rest and an object in motion tends to stay in motion with the same speed and in the same direction unless acted on by an outside force.

They were in free fall, an easy and cheap launch. It felt like being in orbit.

The clamps had been released when the *Dark Heart*'s release pointed toward a rendezvous with Talos, and there would be additional thrust. Lots of it.

Sometimes, usually in fact, that was it, since most trips were in-system. The gentle release, followed by inertia's relentless progress, and a few weeks, or months, later you blew some rockets to kill your velocity and achieve your destination. Most trips shipped cargo, and advanced planning made super-speed unnecessary.

But this was an interstellar voyage. Interplanetary velocities were insufficient. Fire, thunder, and crushing weight were inevitable at some stage, or else they'd all die en route of old age, if boredom didn't get them first.

Slyde came across the communications channel. "We're going to start pushing in ten seconds."

Griffin swallowed. She didn't feel fear—not exactly. She'd worked through her issues long ago, and merely felt the sort of trepidation she associated with the loss of control. She'd based her life on controlling her environment and making it safe. She sometimes joked with Rusk that it was ironic a security freak such as herself would make a career of exploring the unknown, choosing danger. Wasn't that schizophrenic?

But she was exactly one of the most desirable sorts of people to have along, personally ironic or not, and her success had led her here.

To this moment—when she would be within close range of not just one nuclear explosion, but hundreds.

"Mark," said copilot Slyde. "Dropping eggs."

Eggs. What a misnomer. Eggs were the oldest symbol of creation. They were dropping destruction, and they were going to ride it.

Outside, about now she guessed, came the fire, a flash she didn't see. They didn't have a system that could safely watch in any form of visible light. She was glad that she wasn't in the hibernation dens, in the dimness with eyes wide and staring, waiting for the push that would shore you into the cushions. She had intentionally studied ship systems in order to place herself in a position with some control, or at least the illusion thereof.

Wham! The gentle smack, the first, arrived.

The pusher plate absorbed the blast. The *Dark Heart* lurched forward.

Wham!

Griffin realized that she was squeezing her armrests and clenching her teeth. She forced herself to relax, a task that seemed rather difficult under the circumstances.

Wham!

She breathed deeply, waiting for it to be over, as each explosion pushed her crash chair and accelerated the *Dark Heart* toward their destination.

Wham!

And then a return to zero gravity and a brief moment of silence . . .

Griffin let her breath out as the X-bots made their system checks.

"All systems nominal," Slyde announced.

Griffin grinned, and heard distant cheering.

Good, she thought, *we're really on our way.*

They approached Talos a few days, and a few more "egg rides," later. Griffin was one of the crew with an extensive list of shakedown activities and was not scheduled for immediate hibernation. Even though most were so scheduled, everyone waited until they'd made the big turn at Talos.

Close passage of a super-Jovian gas giant was not to be missed. The *Dark Heart* sported a number of direct observation bays, three observatories featuring an array of telescopes equipped with imagers and spectrographs spanning a large part of the electromagnetic spectrum, and a network that tied all the lounge entertainment displays to the observatories.

Most of the Specialists vied for positions at the windows, passing false rumors about which ones would be oriented which way during passage. The computer jock, Mistelle, had rigged the system to generate random answers in response to queries.

Griffin knew that Rusk would not normally have tolerated such nonsense, but what was normal now? He did nothing, and neither did Klingston. Klingston just sat back (well, metaphorically—he actually spent a lot of time wandering the halls and chatting, being overly social) and let that sort of thing happen.

Even though she knew it must have been driving him crazy, Rusk let it happen, too, deferring to Klingston. She'd always thought he followed the rules a bit too closely, even when following the rules meant allowing others to break the rules.

To Mistelle's chagrin, Slyde announced all the encounter

details, the correct ones, over the PA system as Talos loomed, so several people beat her to the best observing port.

At the appointed time Griffin made her way to one of the secondary portholes. Her duties prevented her from staking out an early spot at one of the primaries with an unobstructed view, so she didn't even try. Specialists wanted to see things for themselves, with their own eyes, or they wouldn't be Specialists. She was going to see it herself, even if it was partially obstructed.

The secondary window was crowded with three people already. The lack of gravity made it relatively easy for all of them to look out, although the ones in the center had to hold on to their fellows for stability. Griffin was thinking about squeezing in when Selene beat her to it.

Fine. She supposed she could move to a tertiary window. There were a few such windows where Talos's second-largest moon, Vulcan, would be worth looking at, even though Talos itself would not be apparent.

As she deliberated, someone drifted up to her and whispered in her ear. "I knew you were working, so I saved you a spot. Come on."

Klingston.

She smiled that he'd thought of her under these circumstances. There were a million other, more important things to do. She supposed he was returning the favor she'd shown him for taking him around his first day. He'd saved her a spot.

Rusk would have never done such a thing. In fact, he'd gone out of his way on a number of occasions to prove he didn't give her any special treatment.

Griffin shook her head and kicked off to follow Klingston to the primary window.

It was packed but, as promised, there was space for two in the center.

"I was going to make sure Manuel had a spot, too, but he told me not to bother," Klingston said. "He's watching the observatory screens. I guess he'd like a more complete look than a live one."

Well, that was like Rusk for sure, to want a more complete look. And he never took handouts of any sort, even when he'd earned them and it was fair.

But it still seemed strange. She knew that on a voyage like this, she would get to know everyone very well and already felt that way about most of the crew, but did Klingston really consider her and Rusk his closest friends onboard? Lord, what had he given up for this?

"Come on, now," Klingston said loudly to everyone as he and Griffin wiggled into place. "Let the spectacle begin!"

As she breathed lightly amid the warm bodies snuggled against the thick diamond window, Griffin reevaluated Klingston again. He had something here, an appreciation of people that showed. He didn't play it hard with lots of rules, the way she or Rusk would, but his approach had its merits.

The encounter *was* spectacular. They wanted to get as close to Talos as they could, without encountering atmospheric drag, in order to use the planet's gravity to adjust their course out of the plane of the ecliptic and on a rendezvous with the Spider Star.

Talos, being more massive and younger than Jupiter, was a warmer planet. Gas giants, at least the super-Jovian planets, were really just failed stars. They weren't really quite in the mass range—Jupiter, for instance, would need to be eighty times more massive before fusion would ignite within its core. But they were in the size range, and took billions of years to fully contract, releasing heat the whole time. Not starlike heat, but enough heat to keep cloud structures especially interesting.

Like Jupiter, Talos displayed one large, prominent storm that had persisted since humans had first imaged the planet. While Jupiter's storm was red, the chronic storm on Talos had more of an orange-gold cast. The cloud colors had to do with trace chemicals, kind of like pigments in the skin, and the chemistry was complex. Colors ran across the planet: bands of deep red, nearly maroon, in regions without high cloud cover; the streaming bands with high clouds featured light yellows. From a distance, the planet did have something of an orange-bronze color, so the name of the bronze giant from the Greek myth of the Argonauts had been a natural.

The encounter was too short. There was something about looking at big things live, big things with infinite, chaotic detail, that cast a hypnotic spell on Griffin. A planet like Talos was beyond her control, but so *far* beyond her control that it didn't bother her and she could enjoy it. She supposed that less controlling people might feel similar about exceptional people or alien animals, but those were not outside her dominion, at least in her opinion.

"That was great," she whispered.

"Yeah," said Klingston.

His diction didn't slip often. Usually he said "yes" rather than "yeah." It could be that he was also moved by the vista of Talos, but she wondered if he was perhaps thinking of the more personal aspects of leaving Argo.

Yeah, catching a glimpse of his somber reflection in the diamond, she thought that likely.

The *Dark Heart* was a Gemini-class starship. The term *Gemini* was inspired by the ancient Greek twins Castor and Pollux, after whom the two primary stars in the Earth constellation were named, and also by the somewhat less ancient two-man space missions of the Americans. The term applied not to the crew, but primarily to the dual star drives.

Earth-based technology had spawned the first: the CNO ramjet. A forward-facing ramscoop collected plasma, fully ionized by laser cannons, from the interstellar medium. This set up old, well understood physics. The scoop's electromagnetic field collected the ions, channeled them toward the heart of the *Dark Heart*, toward the ship's fusion reactor. Concentrated there, confined, the reaction proceeded to explode, providing energy, and, moreover, excessive thrust.

The nuclear reactions that powered the sun were slow, inefficient, following a sequence long ago dubbed the "proton-proton chain." In this sequence, four protons were painstakingly assembled into a single helium atom, releasing energy. It was a brute force approach that relied upon the weak nuclear force to convert a proton into a neutron at precisely the right time—during a high-energy collision, creating stable deuterium as a step in the sequence.

Stars slightly more massive than Earth's sun, like Pollux when it had been on the main sequence burning hydrogen, didn't waste time with the proton-proton chain. The proton-proton chain was a poor person's fusion, slow, relying on that hard step that kept the burn rate to a low four billion kilograms per second. Low efficiency . . . which helped give Earth's sun its long lifetime of ten billion years.

The CNO cycle, now that was a something else. It gave you what you wanted, with only a minimum amount of messing around. Pollux, at nearly twice the mass of the sun and higher core temperatures, burned through its hydrogen fuel in less than a third of the time. The CNO cycle featured a catalyzed reaction in which four hydrogen atoms combined to become helium, with the release of energy, but instead of combining directly, the carbon became nitrogen, which in turn became oxygen. In the end, the catalysts were recovered. The CNO cycle could fuse hydrogen into helium without the slow step, making it much more efficient—10^{18} times more efficient. Other factors complicated the issue and kept stars more massive than the sun from burning through their fuel 10^{18} times faster, but it was still nonlinear.

In any event, 10^{18} was the kind of number that impressed both Griffin and starship engineers. Still, that reaction rate was a million times less efficient than deuterium-to-deuterium reactions. The big bang simply hadn't made enough deuterium to pick up such fuel on the fly.

A fusion reactor sat at the core of the *Dark Heart*. The ramscoop funneled in hydrogen fuel, temperatures in the reactor were the same as at the center of a massive star like Pollux— almost a billion degrees Kelvin—and the heated exhaust was expelled for thrust. In principle the CNO ramjet could accelerate at a small fraction of Earth gravity nearly indefinitely. In practice, there were engineering problems. At around 30 percent lightspeed problems began to appear, particularly with the fuel intake that limited continued acceleration.

That's where the alien technology entered.

The dark drive exerted a force on aetherons, one of several known forms of dark matter. The aetherons were a type of WIMP—weakly interacting massive particle—that invisibly filled the universe. Under normal circumstances, they only interacted with baryonic matter—protons, neutrons, and the like— gravitationally. The alien device somehow managed to push the WIMPs around, violently, to create thrust. It was labeled "the Bully" pretty quickly by nerdy engineers working on understanding the process. Squirting aetherons out the backside allowed the *Dark Heart*'s top speed to push 90 percent light speed. Interestingly, the effect was directionally dependent—the aetherons had a circulation pattern similar to the Milky Way rotation that still had to be mapped at interstellar distances.

Argo, the colony world first getting access to the Bully, would

be a major player in the burgeoning human interstellar civilization. If Argo weren't destroyed . . .

Shortly after Talos, and a few minor course corrections, they'd
reached a high enough velocity that they engaged the first of
two ramscoops. At first the acceleration from the CNO ramscoop was minimal, but it quickly built to several tenths of an
Earth gravity and everyone weighed something again.

Most of the crew began to go to sleep.

Griffin, because of the extra systems checks that were her responsibility, went to bed relatively late. It was the same sort of
problem she'd had with the Talos encounter, but one that she
didn't expect Klingston or Rusk to solve for her.

Hibernation was a stupor. You didn't care when or where
you slept. You found a place, and slept. You woke up at some
point, got up, did some things, and went back to sleep.

Anywhere in the dens would work. The dens had the right
temperature, air circulation, body support, muscle exercise, and
monitoring, to make sure that the hibernation state was effective
in providing optimal metabolic reduction and maintenance.

There were other issues to consider, of course, although they
were not often talked of planetside. Hibernating people snuggled with each other, and often had sexual relations during periods when they were slightly more awake. Everyone was free
of STDs, infertile from their Specialist nanomeds, and expected
to handle it casually if it came up, so to speak. Sometimes, in intermediate metabolic states, erotic dreams could make even the
mildest, repressed personality a sexual aggressor. Wetwalking, it
was called, and those under its spell didn't much care about who
they were with. Again, it was more than tolerated as a side effect
of a physical state that would save years of life, and it was far
from the worst thing in the world.

While she could always move after waking up the first time

six or eight months down the line, it made her selective about where she lay down.

The dens were quite cool, and dark, and smelled more than a little funky. She knew that her sensitivity to the smell of human BO would not persist, but it struck her now. She stripped down, stowed her uniform in her closet, and moved into the den.

The soft floor squished between her toes as she moved forward, hands out, moving slowing as her eyes adjusted to the darkness. She'd prefer to find Rusk, if possible, and if not him, she supposed it didn't matter. Klingston, and a few others, were old enough they might not be so . . . active.

She spotted Rusk and Klingston sleeping nearby each other. She'd been worried they'd conflict with each other, but small and darkly handsome Manuel complemented the big blond Klingston.

Griffin wiped away a tear. Sentimentalism was another side effect of the adaptation. The awful thing about it was that it didn't matter if you knew it was a side effect, you still felt it.

She crawled in between the two men, sinking into the warm, yielding surface, hoping for the best for their mission. They would do great things, she was sure, and save the world. She nearly started to cry, the feeling was so powerful.

Just as she was drifting off, one of the electrostim units crawled across her body and began to work Klingston's muscles. He, and all of them, would be in great shape when they arrived. Griffin then started to wonder about . . . and fell asleep.

PART TWO

THE SPIDER STAR, 2476 AD

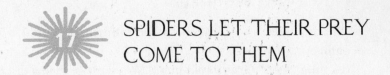

17 · SPIDERS LET THEIR PREY COME TO THEM

ONBOARD THE *DARK HEART*

"Frank," a woman's voice whispered.

A warm hand rubbed his bare shoulder. Irritating. He wished she would stop.

"Frank."

He was in a deep, dark, sleepy place of comfort without worry, without pain, without awareness. Dreams lurked nearby, nonsensical, but comfortable as an old broken-in boot. He liked it.

"Ouch!" he shouted. What had happened? Oh . . . Someone had jabbed a needle in his shoulder! Damn it all.

"Wakey wakey, Frank."

"No." He kept his eyes squeezed shut. Nevertheless, the quiet, safe place receded from him at light speed. Thoughts rushed toward him nearly as fast—thoughts about who he was, what he was doing, and, most important, where he was. He winced.

Black became gray, and the gray became shades of faint color. He willed it away, but reality persisted, calling him from Morpheus to his own now fiendishly strange life.

As executive director, Frank had to wake up earlier than the others, which would make approaching the Spider Star a slow process. They were probably weeks away from the place, at least. If he were so important to the great bloody mission, why couldn't he sleep through the boring parts?

He didn't appreciate it.

But his memories crystallized and he recalled his family, his children, and he realized again why he should care. There were no boring parts. Everything was potentially of great importance.

"We're there?" he croaked to the woman he could now recognize.

"Getting close," Griffin told him. "We've established a distant orbit of the pulsar."

She helped him remove his electrostim bots that had been periodically exercising his muscles while he slept, fending off atrophy, keeping him physically viable. Rising from the soft den floor was difficult, at least psychologically. Climbing the ladder was even harder, despite the lessening gravity as he rose—they were obviously under spin gravity now. He imagined he could hear his joints squeaking.

He felt older. When he reached the restroom and looked in the mirror, he looked older: the orange of his hair was nearly gone, and his wrinkles had perceptively deepened into canyons. The drugs and the hibernation had retarded his metabolism and retarded the aging process, but they had not stopped it completely and they had side effects of their own. He'd been old to start with and he was older now. How old was difficult to say. He had an absolute chronological age that he could in theory calculate, but in practice it would have been best had he had a clock imbedded under his skin at birth. More complex was the issue of his subjective age.

When he'd left Earth, people commonly lived to 130, sometimes 150, with good health and solid activity well into their 120s. Medicine and the supercomputers had been promising indefinite life spans for centuries (although reconciling even Earth time and Argo time was complicated without being aboard an interstellar ship), but that hadn't quite materialized yet. The initial serious efforts had produced an explosion of cancers that had slowed advances to a crawl.

He figured he was probably the equivalent to a well-preserved but natural fifty. Perhaps a few years older than that, he forced himself to admit. Not decrepit, but by no means a young man.

Showering, shaving the hair off his face, off his ears (he hated that!) . . . eventually, he started to feel more like himself again and less like he'd come off a three-day drinking binge—not that he'd done that since the kids had been born. The scent of the soap and the shaving cream was so sharp, so alien, he closed his eyes and wondered where he was for a moment, losing himself for a brief reality vacation. He cleared his bowels, blew his nose, brushed his teeth, and, as he was dressing, began once again to feel that he might indeed have a grasp on the situation and be capable of commanding others.

He wondered how old his sons were now, how old they might look. He shook his head, trying to expel the thought—it was so difficult to determine when *now* was in different places, at different speeds. They would have a measure of success, he promised himself, and when he returned to Argo to reunite with his sons the time lines would by force reconcile. He need not worry about it.

Not now, with the Spider Star looming.

But truly, did it loom? Dressed now in a Specialist uniform that still felt alien, he got himself something to eat and a cup of coffee and walked to the command center of the *Dark Heart*. Griffin and several others were already there, watching him expectantly.

He sat down in his chair, bouncing in the light gravity, feeling tired from the effort. His mind sharpening, he realized that they'd have a substantial backlog of broadcasts from Argo. Relativistic time compression slowed them, but quite a few years of reports should exist. He'd avoided paying attention to them during his brief periods of wakefulness. That dream state was not the time to absorb and process significant news. "Tell me about Argo and the Lashings," he said to Griffin.

"Argo colony is still persistent."

Ah!

"There have been eighty-one new events, according to the

latest report. One passed through the atmosphere of Argo, although Charybdis suffered several hits. The best theories seem to indicate that the moon was a special target, either because of strategic value, or because of its value as an example. Another theory posits that the initial signal from Charybdis gave the Lashing better positional accuracy for the moon."

Frank wondered if this was all a lark, if the Lashings were no threat at all to Argo and the colony. Maybe the bee machine in the heart of Pollux had been meant as a threat, and programmed to hit the moon as a demonstration. But that sort of speculation was pointless—worse than pointless. It held the potential to undermine his entire being, his entire sacrifice, and could not be verified. He forced himself to veer away from the notion.

"Good," he said. And it was good. His mission here was not wasted, at least not yet. He could turn the spotlight of his attention on the matter at hand. "So what's going on here?"

"Nothing, and everything," Griffin answered.

He hated those kind of answers. "When's Rusk waking up?"

"He's been awake for a week," she said. "He insisted. He'll be along soon."

"Undoubtedly," he said, feeling unsure of himself. He knew he was nominally in charge, executive director, but Rusk was mission director; the one training for this for years, the one who had assembled the crew, and the one who best knew their capabilities. Frank still felt himself a pretender to this ambitious, talented young man who lurked in his sudden shadow. All Frank had was the desire to do the right thing and some prior success—to the extent he dared to call it that—dealing with aliens. He supposed that would have to do for now, and forged ahead. "Fill me in on the latest. Start with the nothing and give me a chance to wake up for the something."

She called in an X-bot named Bela to run three floor-to-ceiling displays and began. "The system isn't posing too many surprises from an astrophysical perspective. The primary star is almost nothing, a faded pulsar, about eight kilometers across, cool and long dark."

Griffin pointed at the leftmost screen, which now showed a magnified star field. At first Frank didn't see anything, but then he noticed a distortion. Near the center of the view there was a blank spot, like many other blank spots in the field, but the star pattern seemed to avoid this area a little more systematically as it slowly drifted by. As he watched there was a slight motion and slight brightening of one of the stars on the edge of the blank spot, as it elongated into a tiny arc.

She grinned. "That was a microlensing event we caught last week. The gravitational field of the neutron star is intense enough to warp space. It isn't quite up to black hole standards, but it's close. Now, switching from the optical to the far infrared, the little bugger will pop right out. . . ."

The X-bot anticipated her request and the picture was already changing. The blank spot in the distortion, or rather a very tiny spot in the center of the blank spot, brightened to a dull red pinprick.

"What are those things?" Frank asked, pointing to a handful of faint specks around the neutron star.

"Good eyes," Griffin said. "Bela, stretch the contrast and bring in the supplemental bands."

Faint red lines emerged from the specks, all converging toward a point off the screen to the right. Griffin explained, "They beam microwaves, quite efficiently. It was hard to see anything from them at all. They drag cables as they orbit, at a different rate than the pulsar spin, and the star's magnetic fields induce a massive electrical current. The terawatts of electricity they produce is converted to microwaves and beamed away."

"To where?"

Frank's question cued the next screen. The faint red beams

continued on their path from the first screen onto the second, forming a weblike pattern with its origin at a fuzzy but brightly glowing globe of gold.

"The Spider Star," said Griffin.

So there it was before him, finally, practically in real time. *Its golden heart is the source of all good and evil. But mostly evil.* The heart of so much of his personal pain, the heart of the threat to his adopted home world, to his family. A live glowing heart, beating in its web, nestled in those strings of power, orbiting a dark star, illuminating the gloom of this corner of infinite space. A construct of an alien intelligence vastly older than humankind, similarly approached by another star-spanning race millions of years ago. Had hope kindled brightly in their hearts at its sight? Or had they felt the darkest desperation?

Frank felt both, and shivered.

A box exploded from the Spider Star and filled the third screen, and the alien thing now loomed large—larger—before them. A central sphere, the core of the thing, throbbed slowly, pulsing with its golden energy. A towering shaft speared the core lengthwise, a dark shaft several *thousand* kilometers long along the spin axis, metallic, seamlessly welded into the glow, glinting darkly, connecting to the surrounding arch of permanent night. Six thin spikes thrust from the golden core into the equatorial plane in hexagonal pattern, each spike longer than the dark shaft, each thin and gleaming gold themselves, thickening to a knot at a thousand kilometers, then tapering to invisibility many more thousands of kilometers out. Upon closer inspection he realized that one of the six arms was not lit as brightly as the others, but there didn't appear to be any obvious reason that should be so. A power failure? Fainter, somewhat diffuse lines traced complex patterns between these spikes and the shaft, most concentrated at the knots, a gossamer network invisible to the telescopes orbiting Argo. A fuzzy diffuse halo, wispy golds and darker clouds of gray, inhabited the voids among the gossamer, out to the knots in the spikes, twinkling to nonexistence beyond that limit. Individual lights sparkled, some moving and some not, along the structure's features, an overtone to the golden pulse of the heart of the Spider Star.

"It does indeed have an atmosphere," Bela offered to the overwhelming image. "Many of the astrophysicists spent a lot of time fighting over that point. They all agreed that the spectrum could not arise from any natural mix of gases under any simple set of physical conditions, but the exact nature was less clear. We still don't know how the Spider Star can maintain such an atmosphere—there simply doesn't appear to be enough mass even for something this large."

"It doesn't matter," Rusk said as he strode into the dimmed chamber. "So the alien station has an atmosphere. Perhaps there's a terrestrial core in the center outgassing this strange elemental mix of helium, oxygen, nitrogen, neon, and hydrogen. Perhaps something else. I'm sure this place has lots of puzzling features that we may or may not come to understand. If it does matter, we'll figure it out. We'll achieve our goals in one way or another."

Frank merely grunted at Rusk. The man could have acknowledged him directly instead of coming in with an air of knowing, confident command. That attitude irritated him, as he himself, older and just awake from his long slumber, felt akin to a blind man stumbling through a wet, slick cave. Getting up a week earlier than him . . .

Were things going to be different now that they were away from Argo and on their own?

His irritation seeped away, vulnerable to the power of the image of the living Spider Star. Irritation turned back to uncertainty, laced with awe and fear. This thing projected before him, now so sharp and clear, itself a planet, an artificial planet that dwarfed all the achievements of humankind combined, loomed ominously and churned up childish emotions. What were they, men and women, daring the galaxy? What was humanity, what could they be, compared to civilizations millions of years old? The Argonauts had been one thing. Humans had commandeered their abandoned world and could take comfort in the superiority nature implicitly granted a species that survives compared to a species that extinguishes its own light forever.

Frank realized his mouth was hanging open and decided he ought to do something with it. "What's the plan?" he muttered. "I mean, I know there isn't official protocol for this situation, but remind me what we'd planned."

Fogginess filled his head, made his words awkward. Maybe the aftereffects of hibernation also twisted his emotions toward the maudlin, aiding the alien construct in devastating his self-esteem, his very humanity. Humanity meant nothing next to this.

Griffin answered, "We've been monitoring various chatter across the spectrum. Some of it appears to be automated responses, but others are erratic, less regular, suggesting intelligent communication. Nothing has been directed toward us, so far as we can tell. We will broadcast greetings, with language primers, on detectable bands and await a response. If there's no response, we'll launch spy satellites to study the Spider Star, probe its defenses, if any, and from those reports, construct an approach."

Rusk said, "They dealt with the Argonauts, they'll deal with us."

How could he be so confident? That was millions of years ago, *millions,* before Homo sapiens even existed. Entire species could evolve over that time span. And moreover, they'd dealt with the Argonauts already but their gift had been as deadly as the Trojan Horse. Deadlier; it was still alive and held the potential to drive two civilizations extinct on Argo.

Frank, stupefied, finally said simply, "Okay."

What a meaningless word! An acquiescence to passivity, an acknowledgment of ignorance, a great big nothing. He let it stand. What else could he do now, here? He'd set out with great determination to do the right thing, to protect his loved ones, to protect his own kind on its perilous perch over thirty light-years from Earth. Nothing could protect him now, the entire *Dark Heart,* if they made a misstep. They were ants coming to an elephant.

"Okay," he repeated to this impossible alien monstrosity that confronted them. "Okay."

18 ORBITING THE UNKNOWN

ONBOARD THE *DARK HEART*

Rusk paced. Rusk exercised. Rusk supervised the end of crew hibernation. Rusk made lists of all sorts. Rusk reported to Klingston. Rusk rubbed his chin between thumb and forefinger. And after their messages went out, Rusk waited, but the Spider Star remained silent.

The *Dark Heart* woke up. The Specialists regained their physical form and mental acuity. The ship was checked and rechecked, adjusted, and checked again, until all was exactly as it should be.

Still, the Spider Star remained silent. At least to them.

Sitting with Griffin in one of the lounges, the entertainment system off, he fretted. "We're approaching, closer every second. It does nothing, says nothing. We'll fly by it. If nothing, then we have to take action."

She answered, "We can swing around the pulsar—not too close mind you—and approach a second time."

"And if it remains silent?"

"We'll have to attack, of course," she said, flashing a rare smile.

Her joke irritated him. It wasn't a practical course of action, and the situation did not call for levity. "Ha-ha."

"Come on. You do it to me all the time."

"That was before this. It taunts me and tasks me. The spysats must be sent, and soon."

She frowned a little. "I suppose. If they haven't responded to our broadcasts, they're not likely to be concerned about some smaller craft flybys. Still, I worry about it."

"You worry about everything."

"Want me to stop?"

"Of course not. That would worry *me*." He didn't even smile at his small joke, although it made him feel a little better, and going silent, he pondered for a moment. "Perhaps not knowing what to do now is acceptable. We may soon learn things that suggest our next step."

"We may."

He pondered some more. He had resources to call upon. "Perhaps Klingston has a notion."

"That was the official reason to bring him along. He's had this sort of problem before. Dealing with uncommunicative aliens. He's got to have an idea."

That wasn't quite true, but she didn't know the whole story, the details underlying the fiction the government had spun to make Klingston a hero. Okay, he didn't, either, but he knew enough. The man had simply been bold and lucky—he accepted Klingston at face value there. Who, after all, would downplay such an achievement? He would be happy to know the truth. It would make it easier to run this mission as he saw fit. It wasn't like Klingston was fighting their suggestions much. Still, if an opportunity presented itself, he would divorce Klingston from as much power as he could.

Rusk said, "Well, we have a ship full of brilliant, well-trained people. Someone will have an idea. We'll collect the data, analyze it, and perhaps that will lead to some ideas about how to proceed. We will simply choose from among the best ideas. It's an elementary plan."

Rusk met with the primary probe technician, a woman named Mistelle Soon, one of the additions after the Castor 6 team was broken up; Rusk's X-bot Marlo helped him connect the name and somewhat older face, a little more difficult following a decade of hibernation than he cared to admit. Such things would come back, but slowly. At least he hadn't slept with her and forgotten . . . he thought. He remembered her best as the impressive line on his spreadsheet that had plusses or checks under column headings for reconnaissance probes, software engineering, feedback control systems, celestial mechanics, global positioning, and remote sensing. They conferred about the details of the probe flights and contingency plans in the event of alien activity.

He did not permit himself to dwell long on the concept of "alien activity." One thing at a time.

The plan was to send one probe as a flyby to reconnoiter the far side of the Spider Star. This probe would approach first and most quickly, laser back data from its telescopes, magnetometers, spectrographs, accelerometers, and other instruments. It would fire a small rocket with enough impulse for it to coast to a position on the far side and monitor. They would then launch eight slow probes toward the eight extremities of the station. These probes would creep in simultaneously on cautious trajectories, ease in, and, using one of several technologies, attach. From these locations the probes could sample and test the station material, provide close monitoring, and serve as global positioning relays.

Mistelle seemed giddy with delight at her task, joking incessantly, but Rusk managed to resist the urge to reprimand her. He smiled instead, thinking how Griffin would be pleased with him. He could advise Klingston to formally reprimand her or any other Specialists behaving unprofessionally if there was the slightest problem, and let the old man bring any alienation on himself.

But more likely they were all just suffering from various forms of hibernation hangover.

At the appointed time, everyone met in the assembly hall. The flyby would take many hours, but Rusk knew that it would be good for the group dynamics for everyone to be on hand and discuss their options. Research had shown that after long periods of hibernation, crew members became lonely and disconnected, missing the closeness of the den. Standard policy urged large social events with lots of food: a party.

Things were quiet enough. A party it would be.

The crew members and the X-bots mingled in the same staging area where they had feasted before leaving Argo. The humans snacked on freshly harvested fruit and soy sticks—quite a bit less lavish than the earlier meals. The X-bots congregated among themselves, connecting together with broadband cables and flashing through their legion of personalities as they caught up on the scientific discoveries they had picked up from the Argo feed.

It was indeed becoming a real party, he realized: an arrival party to celebrate the end of the long winter of their voyage through space and time without major incident, an excuse to get everyone together and motivated before events would force them into their separate roles.

With this good-looking, multitalented crew before him, Rusk resisted feeling pride. He knew it was there, but it would serve no purpose at the moment. In fact, he himself had warned everyone in several speeches before launch that humility would likely serve them better. They would do the best they could, and they would succeed as the Argonauts had before, but alien civilizations spanning megayears would certainly dwarf their knowledge and capabilities. He knew that, intellectually.

Rusk found Klingston, clapped him on the back, and hovered nearby to monitor him and his conversation. Rusk smiled as much as he could stand. The young, Argo-born Specialists had never been far from home, let alone close to twenty light-years, and there was a novelty of accomplishment of their travel alone. Rusk himself didn't think much of it—he'd expected to engage in a deep space mission for his whole life. Why should someone feel accomplishment in what one expects?

He was disappointed in most of the conversation. Brilliant people were prone to idle, useless speculation in amazing quantities. Questions ranged from the thoughtful sort, "Do you think this system's unusual galactic orbit indicates the Spider Star is isolated from its parent civilization?" to the foolish, "Over millions of years these aliens must evolve, right?" Rusk smiled, and remained silent. Why would any evolution necessarily occur in a controlled environment? He wouldn't speculate. They didn't know enough yet.

Klingston did though. He'd get these faraway looks and ramble on about so many things, using language that Rusk categorized as "poetic." Did he honestly think that was leadership? This wasn't a job for poets. This was a job for pragmatists who were prepared to do what was necessary. Rusk would make sure that happened, one way or another.

The ship computer announced, "Anomalous data received."

The X-bots disengaged and scuttled to the Specialist most appropriate to help interpret the unusual data: Mistelle.

Rusk jostled across the room to stand at her elbow while Gerald talked to her. Annoyingly, they whispered to each other. What was going on?

Mistelle giggled. "I so knew it!"

"What?" Rusk asked.

"The Spider Star *is* big."

Of course it was. It occupied a volume similar to that of Earth's moon. What was she trying to tell him?

"The flyby probe is deviating from its course. A *lot*. The deviation is consistent with the Spider Star being massive, about half an Earth mass."

Half an Earth mass? That couldn't be right. This was a huge artifact, but there sure wasn't much mass to be seen in the images. Not enough to measure in planetary masses, anyway. How could this be?

She went on, glancing at the updated information feeding into her tablet. "More accurately, the Spider Star masses just under sixty percent an Earth mass."

Sure, the thing was huge, but it was a network of material, a flimsy web of stuff. The filling factor couldn't be more than a fraction of a percent, and the density had to be in the neighborhood of metallic densities, something like ten grams per cubic centimeter. There just *wasn't* enough stuff there to mass so much.

Mistelle continued, thinking aloud, "We didn't know the precise orbital angle of the system, or the mass of the neutron star well enough, to figure out the mass of the Spider Star itself from Doppler shift curves. But we'll be able to confirm using that method soon."

Indeed, that was how the mass of most extrasolar planets had first been determined. Getting the inclination was the hardest part usually, unless the system was edge on and seen to eclipse. When you measured the Doppler shift of an orbiting body, you never knew for sure if you were seeing the result of a nearly maximal Doppler shift in an edge-on orbit, or a minimal projected velocity resulting from a nearly face-on orbit. Face-on orbits had to be watched for long time periods with the highest precision astrometry to find solutions.

There wasn't enough data to figure the thing out, not just yet. Rusk decided not to worry about impossibilities now. He would deal with facts. Fine then, the alien station was massive. He could therefore think of it as a planet, even if it was not a proper planet, at least for the purposes of orbital dynamics—they could orbit the Spider Star. Some smart person here would figure out what was going on soon enough. He asked Mistelle, "Can we convert the flyby to an orbital insertion?"

She whispered to Marlo. While she was doing so, Klingston sidled up to their group, followed by his personal X-bot, Jason. "What's happening?" he asked.

Rusk said nothing. Let Klingston weigh in and demand information be repeated, thus annoying Mistelle. He was executive director, after all.

She piped up happily, "The Spider Star masses half as much as Earth."

"Hmm," said Klingston. "We didn't expect that, did we?"

"No, we didn't! Isn't it exciting?"

"Hmm," said Klingston. "Marlo, go fetch Timothy, Anatole, and Selene over here, will you? Oh, and Einstein, too."

Rusk thought hard. He tended not to think of the crew in terms of their first names, but he gave Klingston points for doing so. He dredged up their expertise through sheer force of will. Timothy Salerno was an expert on Argonaut history and in interpreting their recordings, Anatole Hamilton was a polyglot who had made astounding intuitive leaps in several fields of science, and Selene . . . Selene he knew very well. She didn't have unique expertise like Timothy, or wide-ranging interests like Anatole. Selene had earned her berth through a persistent pattern of dogged logic. During one of her interviews she had confessed that her hero had been Sherlock Holmes, a mythical scientist who ruthlessly applied logic in search of the truth, no matter how outlandish that truth might be. In the unorthodox exams the Corps applied, she had found solutions no one else could, including Anatole and his type, even though she failed many other tests. She was along because she provided the perfect complement to almost everyone else on board.

Einstein was the X-bot loaded with the patterns of Earth's greatest dozen physical scientists of the half century prior to their most recent dump to Argo. Not Albert Einstein himself of course, who had died almost a century before patterning of substantial sort, but his name continued to hold iconic status that no scientist since had achieved. Einstein would be able to quantitatively test and confirm any ideas the Specialists proposed.

While Rusk prided himself on never underestimating anyone, or anything, he admired Klingston's personal approach under these circumstances.

Rusk thought to go check in with Griffin, but when he turned away from the group Klingston put a hand on his shoulder. "Stick around," the older man said. "We might need you."

The gesture and the words filled Rusk with mixed emotions. It felt surprisingly *good* for this old man to reach out to him like that, to make an effort to make him feel important in a way Rusk's own father had never done. Rusk's father had counted himself lucky to have made the Argo expedition and had never had higher aspirations, and could never fathom them in his son. As a result, Rusk had never respected him much, and had often ignored him when he'd grown old enough.

Klingston was a rival and Rusk made sure to keep that fact in mind, always. He hoped that it wouldn't come to direct conflict, and that he'd go along with his plans as they developed.

Klingston's handpicked group assembled, and began to talk. Mistelle filled them in on the probe's flight path—she was obtaining more digits on her mass estimate as the trajectory continued to be consistent with an inverse square law and a large gravitational mass.

Rusk watched and listened as each contributed to the course of discussion, each displaying great listening abilities and managing to contribute where they were able.

Rusk even found himself interjecting points to further the conversation. His particular niche was instigator. When conversation stalled, or started up what appeared to be blind alleys, he couldn't resist nudging them back on course. He normally preferred to think of his primary attribute as leadership, but instigation was closer to the truth in this circumstance.

Was he also a tool in Klingston's hands? Was Klingston everything Claude Martin had promised?

He ignored the dark thoughts and elected to focus on the group effort, to solve the mystery presented to them.

"Einstein, the real Einstein not this X-bot," Anatole was saying, "proposed that the effects of gravity were indistinguishable from the effects of acceleration in his elevator thought experiment. Given his argument, still recognized as valid in the macroscopic limit, even light became subject to gravity."

Rusk himself was talented, very talented. The Anatoles of the Corps were useful as tools, means to an end, but not as leaders. Rusk sensed that this was a dead end. Timothy had been pretty quiet throughout the discussion, but Rusk seconded Klingston's intuition to include him here. The man likely didn't know much about gravity or acceleration, but he knew several versions of the Argonaut accounts of their experience with the Spider Star. "What was it the Argonauts said about the 'placeness' of the Spider Star again? Not from the children's tale, but that other thing from the military records?"

Timothy cleared his throat and said, "The translation isn't all that accurate. There's a technical term that doesn't appear often in other parts of the archival record."

"So tell us what you can," Anatole urged.

Timothy closed his eyes, briefly, wrinkled his blond eyebrows, and recited: " 'The eight-legged place is of course a place, but it is a place having weight not of this world, a weighty place, that encompasses more than one world. The placeness of the eight-legged place is more than unity.' "

"That sounds like a crappy, high-school level translation," Selene said, snorting.

Einstein said, "The translation is consistent with our best understanding."

Timothy smiled. "We know the Argonaut language, major parts of a couple of the major ones anyway. There's no one alive who is fluent, however." He neatly avoided coming across as defensive, which Rusk admired.

Klingston had grown quiet and seemed thoughtful, but showed little inclination to jump in at the moment.

"Does that mean anything to you, Mistelle?" Rusk asked. He hoped they could connect the historical documents with some semblance of physical reality, otherwise it was useless.

"No," she said. "But I suppose it requires a contemporary definition of *placeness*. I imagine it's possible that there are no direct translations for some terms from one alien language to another."

There was a moment of silence, a fleeting sense of doom engendered by the notion of an impossible obstacle in such a simple thing as language. Maybe it was not so simple.

Anatole said, "What if they've built around a condensed object? We can't see to the center of this atmosphere. We can't see past this golden glow in the center of the Spider Star. What if there's another neutron star hidden at the center, or even a black hole. They could dump their garbage on it for fuel."

"But then why would they need the power satellites?" Selene said. "And besides, half an Earth mass would make for a pretty unlikely white dwarf, neutron star, or black hole, wouldn't it?"

That was all true, and the group settled back to silence, thinking. During this pause, Marlo hopped up to whisper in Mistelle's ear. "What?" she squawked.

Everyone waited for more information.

Mistelle stared off, intently, as she processed the information she was receiving. "Apparently the probe orbit is off. The gravitational mass is not concentrated at the center of the Spider Star. Kepler's third law isn't holding."

"Well then," Selene said. "There it is."

Everyone stared at her, until Anatole said, "Right!"

Klingston said, "Mind filling us slower types in on the obvious?"

Selene turned to Klingston and touched his shoulder. "The probe trajectory confirms a large gravitational mass, consistent with the retention of an atmosphere, even though the space station we see isn't massive enough to account for it. The mass can't be some sort of condensed object inside the core of the Spider Star, the close orbit says, since the mass is distributed. Ergo, we have an extended mass we can't see. It must be a form of dark matter."

Rusk never liked people using terms like *ergo* in normal conversation. He supposed it was better than *elementary,* but why not just say *therefore*? Still, he liked the irony here. "You of all people should have thought of it."

"Yes," said Anatole. "It all makes sense. This system is a good match for an evolved black widow pulsar. In some rare binary systems, the more massive stars evolve faster, finally going supernova. The supernova doesn't destroy the secondary star, but its remnant, a young, very hot neutron star emitting a ferocious wind, if close enough, can, over time, blow away its companion— literally. It only takes about a billion years."

"So how does that give us a dark matter planet?" Klingston asked.

Selene spoke, looking at Klingston. "We know that at least eleven types of dark matter exist, mostly WIMPs—weakly interacting massive particles. Some, like neutrinos, aren't very massive, and we've known about them a long time. Others, like the aetherons we collect in the dark drive, no one knew much about before you showed up with the alien device. Three of the types we know of can clump and self-interact. One of those types condensed at the core of the secondary star, and when the pulsar ablated it away to nothingness, the dark matter remained."

"So the aliens built their colossal station in the middle of a gravity sink, just floating around this pulsar, millions of years ago?" Rusk asked.

"Apparently," said Anatole.

"A dark matter planet!" Selene squeezed Klingston's arm. "Isn't it *amazing*?"

Klingston stepped back from her grasp, but not too abruptly, to ask Mistelle something. Rusk thought that was interesting.

Mistelle said loudly, "From the preliminary orbital elements the extent of the dark matter is about five thousand kilometers, something like five times farther out than the normal matter atmosphere. I can't tell yet if the density profile is constant with a sharp edge, like a solid planet, or drops off continuously, like a gaseous sphere. That would help us understand what the stuff is."

"So," said Rusk. He noticed that their group had drawn the attention of much of the crew who hovered about listening for news. "We come looking for an alien space station, and find a dark planet with a golden glow as well. I'll take that as a bonus. We've already had some remarkable discoveries."

"Indeed, it is remarkable," said Klingston. "But we must always keep uppermost in our mind why we are here."

True. But they were also on the singular expedition of their time and Rusk couldn't imagine being anywhere else.

Timothy said, "Say, I know we're broadcasting primes and all the other first-contact protocol and such, but are we sending anything in any of the Argonaut dialects?"

"No," said Klingston. "But that's a good idea. Jason, take care of it."

His X-bot bobbed away to consult with the linguists and communications experts.

The party rolled on, an inefficient but powerful information processing network, a web of deduction. Rusk made the rounds to touch base with everyone—until they knew what they would encounter everyone here was potentially very important and needed to be monitored and stroked. News of the dark matter planet diffused throughout the room and others contributed to fleshing out the details. The secondary probes attached to the Spider arms, as planned, and even more data flowed in. Rusk occasionally saw connections among different groups and brought them together to facilitate synergies among ideas. He fancied himself a webmaster of sorts.

Their information about the Spider Star and its environment doubled every hour, and at some stage Griffin broke up the gaggle of X-bots and had them coordinate the incoming discoveries on a central schematic overlaying the live camera feed. Size scales went up first, then luminosities and energy fluxes in a number of wavebands. Masses, velocities, temperatures, composition, and more sprouted from the diagram like a living, growing tree, with new branches reaching for illumination. It became apparent, for instance, that one of the arms didn't have the same activity and power output as others did. People had fun arguing whether that was intentional or due to breakdowns.

The probes started beaming back high-resolution images, scanning the fields of view of their telescopes down into the Spider Star. Hundred-kilometer-high cloudscapes scattered light burrowing out from the core in some regions, while in others thunderheads flashed lightning at irregular intervals. They glimpsed platforms covered by mirrors shining light onto textured fields of green and maroon—vegetation, or even crops, some argued. Straight, transparent tubes came into focus, connecting some of the platforms at the same level on different arms, filled with lights that moved back and forth, with the highest velocities in between the platforms. Voices bubbled in excitement when some dark specks flashed by; conversations buzzed about whether or not it had been a flock of alien birds. Every moment brought a new discovery and a new mystery.

Standing before his command chair on the central dais, Klingston clapped his hands and shouted for attention. "Heads up, everyone! We're receiving a frequency-modulated radio broadcast. It's in an Argonaut dialect."

Cheers spontaneously erupted from several quarters, although there was not general cheering. Rusk himself felt pensive, cautious. Elation was unwarranted without further information. What did this alien message say?

Klingston bent forward to listen to an X-bot, then rose up to his full height, grinning, and held up a hand to quiet the hum of nervous conversations. "Apparently we have been invited to dock."

About time my career got underway, Rusk thought. *This is definitely the place to be.*

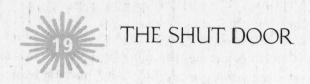

THE SHUT DOOR

"I still say we shouldn't just blindly do everything we're told," Griffin persisted. Why was it always so hard to make the type-A personalities of Specialists listen to caution? They were as eager as newborn puppies that didn't know that pumas or granduluks existed.

Klingston and Rusk exchanged a quick glance, an annoying degree of understanding visibly passing between them.

"Noted," Klingston said. "This is at least a ten-million-year-old artifact displaying technology light-years beyond ours. We're docking *exactly* as instructed."

Annoyingly, Rusk kept his arms crossed and appeared quite determined not to make any objections.

Griffin decided to make one final effort. "How can we dock 'exactly' as requested? Our understanding of ancient Argonaut languages is far from perfect. How many untranslated words did we have in the transmission?"

Klingston looked to Timothy.

Timothy shrugged. "I don't know how we're going to get a better translation whether we wait five minutes, five hours, or five days."

"Let's do it then."

Griffin glowered at Klingston.

He actually noticed. Rusk would have likely ignored her once the decision had been made. Klingston asked, "Would it make you feel better if we had an armed force held in reserve?"

Yes, she admitted to herself, even if that might seem foolish in face of the Spider Star. But should she press Klingston for it? Would he think less of her and her insecurity? No, she decided, she had earned her berth on the *Dark Heart,* and if she didn't express her ideas, she might as well not be there. "Yes, it would."

Klingston nodded. "I want all the Argonaut experts, linguists, philosophers, and negotiators with me. Anyone that doesn't fit those categories with skills you deem useful are yours to prep. Okay?"

"Okay," she said, not feeling as foolish as she feared.

Klingston had Rusk assemble a group to manage the docking itself, including Slyde, the pilot, assorted engineers, and most of the X-bots.

Between Rusk, Klingston, and Griffin, they divided up everyone and every bot. Griffin ended up with Jack Robb, Walter Stubbs, and the X-bot called Drone.

She singled them out and hauled them down to the armory. The *Dark Heart* sported a fully military-quality armory, circa at least the twenty-fourth century, including a wide variety of smart armors and projectile weapons. She had everyone check out their preferred set of defensive and offensive armaments. They didn't question her as much as she feared they might.

In the briefing she said, "We have no idea what we're going to face, and in all likelihood this preparation step is unnecessary. God, I hope so. But we'll be ready to handle something on the scale we can deal with. If something goes wrong at a level larger than that, well, we were screwed before we started."

"Amen," said Robb.

Stubbs muttered agreement. What else could they do?

Using chemical rockets, the *Dark Heart* approached the designated spoke of the Spider Star.

Their docking point was at a corotating point at an altitude of some three thousand kilometers, what would have been a geosynchronous orbit if they'd been docking at a planet. Given the mass they were orbiting, Kepler's third law gave a solution for an orbital period. Geosynchronous orbit happened where the orbital period matched the length of the day. It was no different for the Spider Star in the sense that the alien space station had a revolutionary period relative to the background stars.

It did not have a day the way planets did. Its star, the black widow pulsar, had cooled rapidly, relatively speaking, after going supernova. Now tiny, the size of a city, it radiated as a faint ember in the far infrared. The visible light for the Spider Star emanated from its core, which seemed to glow continuously, meaning that there were no day/night periods directly related to the revolution. And for anyone standing on a solid platform someplace on the station, the sun was *down* in the sky, not up.

They were still above the atmosphere proper, and drag forces were not large. Simple orbital mechanics guided their approach.

Griffin and her team monitored the maneuver from a staging area adjacent to their primary storage area that would become a hangar if they nanofactured shuttles or other scout vehicles. They were prepped with battle armor and three kinds of weapons each, and she hoped they were a completely unnecessary precaution.

Slyde announced, "Final burn in five . . . four . . . three . . . two . . . one."

They had killed the *Dark Heart*'s rotation, leaving them all in free fall. This last final thrust made everyone not holding on to an anchor drift toward one of the walls.

And that was it. The designated entry port steadily grew larger as they closed at the requested speed of 2.2 meters per second.

Many things could go wrong at this point. They could have misunderstood the conversion (such things, involving not only the same species but the same nation of spacefarers, had occurred previously in human history). Their docking port could differ too greatly from the Argonaut type. The docking system could have deteriorated over the span of cosmic time. Their mass and momentum could be too far from designed specifications.

Klingston hadn't seemed overly concerned, and was actually managing to come across to her as at least part cocky bastard. She was coming to believe he'd flown his scout up the exhaust plume of an alien ship once upon a time just as he'd claimed.

As the distance diminished, a spot on the Spider Star grew iridescent, the gray metallic surface shimmering with multiple rainbows, and then it moved, bulging toward them. The ballooning region split into eight pseudopodia, like a giant amoebae reaching toward them, arrayed in a circular pattern with a hollow interior. The pseudopodia stretched, thinned, and transformed into squirming tendrils, growing through space like plants recorded with time-lapse turning toward the lights that surrounded the port of the *Dark Heart*.

The eight tendrils twisted around their circle, becoming an eight-fold coil, or spring. The *Dark Heart* and the tendrils gently collided.

There was another lurch, slightly less than the last rocket burn, and in the opposite direction. Then . . . nothing. No force, no gravity. They were in free fall again.

"It's got us," Stubbs said. "As soft as a kitten's fur."

And it did. The exterior cameras showed a steady image, with the tendrils, and the hull of the Spider Star some twenty meters or so beyond, neither growing nor shrinking in apparent size.

"How'd they do that?" Griffin wondered aloud.

Robb, who in addition to the California-style martial arts expertise that had made him her pick, was an innovative materials chemist, said, "If it were me, I'd do it with a combination of micromachines and nano, using van der Waals forces, like geckopads. But they've probably got something better than that."

They continued to watch the cameras. Light filtered up from the Spider Star, through the branchy tendrils, and cast weird shadows. The strange lighting made it difficult to see the next step until it was well underway.

"Look there," Griffin said, pointing.

The light diminished as they watched, not like a door shutting, but more of a steady dimming. A thin, gauzy *something* grew between the tendrils, wispiness thickening into solid wall. Griffin felt the scene to be unclean, watching this growing thing, this tunnel, that brought images of funnel webs to mind.

"Switching camera three to night vision and camera four to thermal," Mistelle announced over the feed.

Pulsing, warm veins networked between the tendrils, colder darker shapes filling the spaces between—solid, but less active. As they watched, the heat pattern changed, inverted, as the colder, less active regions flared into warmth, and the previously active veins rapidly cooled.

A few more seconds, and the pattern began to fade as temperatures equalized, or perhaps a layer of insulation grew. It wasn't immediately clear to Griffin just from watching.

Orange lights—visible light—blinked on at the other end of the tunnel. There also came a sound, a hissing, over the *Dark Heart*'s speakers.

"That's for real," Mistelle said. "We're picking up sounds. The Spider Star is pressurizing the tunnel. There's some kind of atmosphere in there now."

Klingston's voice whispered into Griffin's ear on a private channel. "Suit up your group as if you were prepping for tactical maneuvers in a space environment—that is, no breathable atmosphere, no matter what our instruments indicate. I hope we don't need you, but be ready and let me know when you are."

Griffin acknowledged him and began implementing his orders. No one complained or questioned the breathing and pressure gear. They'd expected that, although after the announcement about the tunnel being pressurized it seemed possibly redundant.

Another five minutes passed, and, as Griffin's team was nearing full readiness, Mistelle came on again. "Tunnel conditions have reached equilibrium. Pressure is eighty-two percent Argotian sea-level standard. Temperature is two-ten Kelvin. Composition is mostly molecular nitrogen, sixty-three percent, a major minority of molecular oxygen, thirty-one percent, with trace amounts of carbon dioxide, water, and other nontoxic gases. Relative humidity is fifteen percent."

Like living in the mountains, Griffin thought. Not all that bad considering this place was light-years away from any mountains.

Klingston followed right on top of Mistelle's analysis: "We've just gotten our welcome. The atmosphere provided is consistent with that of Argo, and not too dissimilar from Earth. We can breathe in that tunnel, and likely beyond as well. Let's go meet our welcoming committee."

Klingston sounded genuinely optimistic and cheerful, without a hint of confusion or melancholy—about the only time she could recall feeling those emotions from him in the time she'd known him.

"We're still on call," she told her team. "Klingston goes in there and has problems, he's going to need us."

She garnered positive responses.

After a time, Klingston announced that he and a small group would enter the tunnel and approach the Spider Star.

Here it comes, Griffin thought. *The big moment is approaching.*

She received another private communication from Klingston instructing her to remain in a support position, where they were, so they could either rapidly follow Klingston's people, or exit the *Dark Heart* into space for exterior mobility.

She assented and they watched the historic moment on the heads-up displays of their armored helmets.

A few moments later, the cameras showed the back of Klingston's head, then the rest of his body, as he floated forward, unencumbered with breathing gear, arms outstretched, fingers spread wide, feeling his way into the unknown. Three others floated behind him—Hamilton, Madison, and Dorissey— carrying pieces of recording equipment, including lights and microphones. Safety lines trailed behind them, flying about in wild patterns in the absence of a significant gravitational pull.

"I bet their hearts are racing," Robb said.

Griffin knew hers was. Their medical personnel were monitoring their vital signs for the earliest hint of dangerous conditions, but she didn't know how they'd be able to tell what could be expected to be normal under these circumstances.

"I don't know if you can see it," Klingston's voice came, sounding uncertain and slightly choked, "but these walls are reflecting tiny rainbows. I'd say it was pretty, but it reminds me of looking at oil sludge."

She couldn't quite make out the effect on the monitor she was watching.

"Thin films," Stubbs offered aloud to the group. "He's probably seeing interference patterns. Makes sense. Growing a tunnel like that so fast could only be nanotech working at atomic levels, building layer by layer."

Klingston and the others had reached the far end of the tunnel, had touched it in fact, killing their momentum to stop before it.

Klingston said, "We're at the end now. I was somewhat concerned that the surface here might be too cold, or too hot, to the touch, but it felt soft and slightly warm. No shock, nothing like that. I don't know what the material is. It isn't metal, although it appears so at a casual glance."

He was nervous, she realized, and was providing a running

commentary about what he was experiencing as a cover. That was a smart, professional thing to do.

"The orange lights are diffuse, emanating from a broad ring about three meters in diameter. They're part of the surface, too. That is, the material just emits light in this pattern."

"What would you like to do now?" Rusk asked on the open channel. It was the obvious question. The invitation to dock had not included any instructions about boarding, just docking.

"Selene, give everyone a video feed," Klingston said.

Griffin picked up the new video and now she could see the surface as well as Klingston could. Better perhaps; she had digital zoom. The zoom didn't help much. The surface seemed perfectly smooth, but not shiny, the color of slate except for the orange light.

"I'm going to touch it again," Klingston said. He reached to his side with his left hand, holding on to one of the veiny structures of the tunnel wall, and with his right hand he reached to the surface of the Spider Star.

Klingston's fingers brushed across the surface, leaving no marks. "It still feels warm and pliant," he reported. "I'm going to push a little harder."

Griffin zoomed in on the feed from Madison's camera until she could see the individual blond hairs on the back of Klingston's hand standing straight up. His fingers bunched together, as if he were pressing a big button. His fingers slipped *into* the Spider Star.

"Whoa!" he said, and yanked his hand free.

Griffin's zoomed image remained on the again-smooth surface, which revealed no evidence that it had just sucked in a man's fingers.

"That was interesting," said Klingston. "I'm going to do that again."

That was not the response Griffin would have had, she was positive. Typically male.

Slowly Klingston moved his hand forward, pressed against the surface, and into the surface. His fingers sank in. "It feels strange. Not unpleasant in any way. No significant pressure, or heat, or cold. There is a slight tingling in the tips of my fingers, perhaps a tiny suction."

His hand slipped farther inside, to the wrist, and a little beyond. "I don't think this thing is solid. I mean, I don't know what the surface material is, although it appears solid. I think . . . whoa!"

Klingston had continued to push his arm forward, and when he was in up to his elbow he suddenly let go of his grip on the tunnel wall and fell forward. The surface swallowed him up, nearly instantly. He was *gone*, except for his tether, which emerged from the station's smooth hull.

The tether then snapped, and wiggled back, waving, toward the *Dark Heart*.

Frank Klingston was gone, just gone. His chip was sending them no vitals of any sort.

"Let's move it, people!" she shouted at her team, wondering what they'd gotten themselves into.

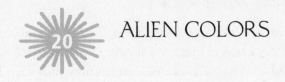

ON THE SPIDER STAR

"Easy, Sloan," Rusk whispered to Griffin on a closed channel even as he himself tensed. He felt bad immediately countermanding her order, but she was obviously keyed up and not being as cautious as she should be. "Give it a few seconds."

He started to count to ten, anticipating letting her go if he reached ten, although he thought himself more likely to start a second ten count.

At "eight" a hand pushed out of the hull and flashed an "okay" sign.

Rusk let out his breath.

While part of him wanted to let Klingston fail, so he could take over himself, he didn't want humans to experience failure here in these critical first steps. He also had to admit that he found himself respecting Klingston more as he got to know him, and really didn't want anything to befall him. And even more altruistically, which surprised him for the strength of the feeling, he knew that here, so many light-years from the nearest human, facing the prospect of encountering an entire alien civilization, he would root for any human being, no matter even if he loathed them. Call him a speciesist.

A moment later Frank popped out whole and unharmed. "We need to get one of these!"

Rusk broke in, voice stern. "What's going on, Frank?"

Frank sighed. "Come and see."

"You've lost your tether," Madison said.

Frank looked around, then down at the sheared line floating from his belt. "So I have. Hmm. We'll have to watch that."

Frank turned as if to go back inside, seemingly distracted by thoughts he wasn't expressing.

"Frank," Rusk said on a direct channel. Klingston's chip and I/O devices were on radio frequencies and the direct person-to-person query would work just fine without the tether. "What's going on?"

He responded on an open channel. "Come on in with us, Manuel, and bring Towson Field, too, if you would, and why not make it a party? Bring Jason along."

Then the bastard kicked off against the wall and vanished into the Spider Star again. His recording team followed him.

Despite his earlier altruistic thoughts, Rusk labeled them all bastards and bitches. Everyone here was dying to know what was on the other side of that hull and Klingston hadn't told them!

At least he would see soon. He rendezvoused with Field and Klingston's X-bot and made for the airlock and the alien tunnel. On the way he put Griffin officially in charge and told her to use her best judgment, and that he'd send back a timely report with more detail than their director had.

"What do you think's going on?" Field asked him.

"I don't know," Rusk said honestly, and it made him feel sick.

They came to the hull, killing their forward momentum deftly, as Klingston's group had done a few minutes earlier. Rusk had a moment of trepidation—he was contemplating walking through a wall, after all—but if Klingston could do it so could he. "Come on, you two."

Rusk did as Klingston had, using the textured wall for something to push against and leaned into the Spider Star. At first he thought something was wrong, that they were cut off from Klingston, and then he felt a tugging sensation from his entire body—every part. It was uncanny, but before he had time to contemplate it, he was moving. He felt a force, and was worried that it felt like falling, and here he was going more or less face first. The light changed from orange to a dim red, and then brightened to a cheerful gold.

And he was someplace else.

Just like that, without the sensation of actually touching anything, or the sensation of not being able to breathe, or see even. Field and the X-bot popped up next to him.

Rusk had tried to avoid having expectations after Klingston's non-explanation, but in all the years voyaging to the Spider Star he had never quite expected the reception he saw before him.

Nothing.

He was in an empty, circular room—not spherical—with glowing walls. Klingston and his three companions were the only apparent objects at first glance.

Rusk took a mental step back. There was cool air in the room, too, that seemed to match what he'd breathed in the docking tunnel. They'd seen lights, power grids, evidence of occupation and activity. He knew the place wasn't abandoned. It couldn't be.

"Two million years is a long time," Klingston said, echoing his own fears, but not his beliefs.

That's why Klingston hadn't said anything when he'd come back out. He'd been preoccupied with the notion that their trip had been a waste. That the place was automated, and empty of alien life. That wasn't what Rusk thought, not yet, anyway.

Rusk's first thought was *quarantine.* That's what he would do with unexpected alien visitors. Put them in a box and figure out how dangerous—or interesting—they were before interacting with them directly. But still, nevertheless, for better or worse, they had their entry into the parlor of the Spider Star. It just happened to be empty.

"This is fantastic," said Field, seemingly enthusiastic despite the circumstances. "I wonder what else they have in here."

Rusk exchanged a look with Klingston. Were they missing something?

Klingston asked, "What do you mean, Towson?"

The man was brilliant when it came to materials science and using unique materials, which was why he'd been selected, but he seemed to be missing the point here, didn't he? They were alone after all, wasn't that obvious?

Field kicked off across the room in the general direction of Klingston, but drifted past him. He was looking around, arms and legs spread and waving, as he drifted across. He said something, but it was hard to hear him in the low pressure, especially with him facing away.

"What?" asked Rusk.

Field turned and yelled. "The technology here is fully functional without needing form."

It could be, Rusk thought, but still leaned toward his quarantine idea. He didn't feel like floating that proposal since, if it were true, there wouldn't be much to do about it anyway.

"We're still stuck in an empty room," Klingston said.

"Maybe it's a puzzle," Madison suggested. "You know, a literal entrance exam."

"Or worse," Klingston said. "It's the equivalent of a door latch to superintelligent aliens, and we're too stupid to even recognize it as such."

"Maybe not stupid," said Field. "Maybe we simply lack the right senses. The outside entry was color-coded. I wonder if the interior might be as well."

That was an interesting take on things, Rusk admitted. Maybe he and Klingston had both made too many assumptions already. Funny how that was possible in an instant. More than possible. Field's idea got Rusk to thinking. From what they knew of the ancient Argonauts, they had a visual range that slightly exceeded that of humans. Humans could see wavelengths from about four hundred nanometers—violet light—to about seven hundred nanometers—red light. Pollux, before it had exhausted its hydrogen and swelled to become a red giant, had been hotter than the sun, with more blue light than yellow light. After the transition to giant status, it was cooler than Earth's sun, with more red light than yellow light. The Argonauts had evolved with keen blue sensitivity, but from what they'd been able to discern in the recordings, they'd altered their genome later on to give themselves sensitivity to see deeper into the near-infrared part of the spectrum.

Whether or not the room was color-coded for Argonauts specifically, or just a species with a different visual range than humans, wasn't important. The question was whether or not Field might be right.

"Jason, Selene, do you see anything in the ultraviolet or infrared?" asked Rusk. Selene had one of their multichannel cameras and the X-bot was equipped similarly.

Jason extended its tentacles to the "floor" and "ceiling" to anchor itself, and then spun its detectors around before Madison had time to orient herself in the zero gravity. An excited bald, bearded man manifested in Jason's display. "Yes! In the I-band and longer wavelengths, as well!"

"I've got it," said Madison, panning the camera about. "There are other, I don't know, portals like the one we came through, but in infrared colors rather than the orange. I'll patch forward a video feed."

"Not necessary," said Field, floating by and tapping his temple purposefully. "If you tint your contacts red, and cut down on the glare, you can make them out. I guess we just don't naturally see all that well."

Rusk tried it, let his eyes adjust for a few seconds, and then looked around. Now he could see what Madison had described as portals. They were circular rings, very similar in size to the portal leading back to the tunnel.

An entrance exam, quarantine, or simply the challenges of negotiating an artificial environment designed for another species;
no matter, they would succeed. Rusk didn't believe in failure.

Remembering his promise, he said to Madison, "Selene, can
you go back out and update the others on what's going on. I'm
afraid half of them thinks we've encountered something horrible, and the other half thinks it's something wonderful. Either
way, they shouldn't be kept in the dark any longer."

"Sure thing," she said.

"And come back and bring at least three X-bots with you,"
said Klingston. "I'm not sure which ones would be most useful—
use your judgment—but their sensors and tentacles alone will be
invaluable."

That was a good idea. As Madison left, Rusk took the opportunity to watch her go back through the hull. Very unsettling—
an unnatural movement he had no instincts for.

"Okay," Klingston said, clapping his hands and looking more
animated again. "We've got some exploring to do."

They assembled exploratory teams with a balanced mix of areas
of expertise and mapped the warren of empty rooms at the space
dock. Some were larger, some were smaller. Some were "above"
the entry room, some were "below." There was a range of colors
on the doors, mostly infrared, but a few were visible in the optical without having to adjust their contact lenses or rely on the
X-bots.

But all the rooms were empty, and their emptiness unsettled
Rusk.

Klingston seemed satisfied with their non-progression, frus-
tratingly. Selene Madison worked at the problem with special
tenacity, dropping observations and new ideas on anyone who
would listen—one example: she discovered that when mapped

in three dimensions, the rooms and tunnels between them defined a central shaft running along the Spider Star spoke. No one knew what it might signify. Gabriella Powers had the X-bots combing every surface of every room with every analysis technique she could think of. Towson Field began to actively probe the Spider Star substance, but with little success.

Two weeks passed.

At some point Rusk realized he'd become too deferential to Klingston, and didn't like it. He had to do something.

Rusk caught up to Klingston in the showers. Docked the way they were, they couldn't spin the *Dark Heart* for artificial gravity, and showers meant shower sacks: Frank was just a head sticking out of an opaque, bulging sack leaking a flowery scent.

"What are we doing?" Rusk asked.

Frank's sack continued to bulge in different directions as he washed. "We're cleaning up," said Klingston.

"You know what I mean. We had the invitation to dock. We docked. And now we're stalled, not accomplishing anything. We're dead in space."

Klingston's motions paused briefly as he stopped to look at Rusk, then resumed as he spoke. "We're following the rules, Manuel. I thought you approved of following the rules."

Of course he did! Rules were there to make things happen more efficiently, to keep people safe, to do all sorts of good things . . . as long as the rules were good rules. But Rusk didn't think they had good rules or clear rules in this situation. "Look, Frank, we didn't get an invitation to dock until we asked for one, and we asked in an alien language at that. No one has come to greet us, and at best we've got the run of a space dock where our arms are too short to reach the interesting buttons."

"I don't know that I'd say that. Selene found a way to get some sort of panel to pop up earlier today."

"What's it do?"

"I don't have the slightest idea," said Klingston, smiling at him and then looking away.

The man seemed satisfied though, scrubbing away in his shower bag, happy and clueless.

"Frank, do you really think this kind of complacency is the appropriate attitude?"

"I don't have a clue," the older man said, then turned to fix Rusk in a stare. "And you don't, either. Why not make the best of a bad situation? It could be much worse."

Rusk felt a flush rise to his cheeks. "That may be, that may be, but I have plenty of ideas and I think it's time to start discussing alternative courses of action."

"We had this discussion right at the start, didn't we? No one here to meet us could mean we're under quarantine or being tested first, and who's to say what kind of time period would be reasonable for aliens?"

"The Argonaut fairy tale doesn't say anything about them being quarantined or being tested when they arrived at the Spider Star. It just goes into the business about being greeted and then, eventually, the 'Golden Ones.'"

"That was a long, long time ago," said Klingston.

No shit, Rusk thought. But frustration wouldn't get him anywhere. He took a deep breath, and said, "I agree. It was a long time ago. The aliens, even the Golden Ones, could have died out, and this whole place just keeps going on automated systems."

"I'd find automated systems lasting millions of years unlikely if it became uninhabited."

"You and me both. I think they're out there, or down there, rather, somewhere. But there's the one arm of the Spider Star that seems damaged. This place is old. Really old now. Anything could be true."

"Your point?"

"We're limiting ourselves if we're just playing one or two possibilities. We should hedge our bets, pursue several possibilities in the absence of hard information. There's a chance we're shadowboxing here. Can you set a time limit on our current course of action?"

Klingston was silent a long time, and his arms stopped moving. Rusk looked at him and listened to the water hitting the inside of his shower bag. Finally Klingston answered, "Do you have a specific proposal in mind?"

"I do," Rusk said. "I propose we split our forces. You keep the Argonaut Specialists, and a few others as needed, doing exactly what you're doing now: exploring the space dock. I take a diverse group of the most adventurous Specialists down into the atmosphere, probably in a dirigible, and begin independent exploration. We fly down this arm and check out some of these lights and other structures we're seeing up close. Griffin maintains the *Dark Heart* with a reserve unit at the space dock in support of both our groups."

Klingston shut down the shower bag, which deflated around him as the vacuum pump worked to suck out the excess water. "Do you really think splitting up is wise?"

"We haven't been threatening, and we haven't been attacked. We've been here for many days without direct response. We could have been greeted by an automated system. The inhabitants of this place may simply not care about a civilization as primitive as ours. I'd rather pursue some options, and in the worst case manage to get us some notice."

Slurping sounds emanated from the shower bag as it finished its work and Klingston opened it up. "The worst case is we all get killed and the next Lashing destroys New Colchis."

"But doesn't that seem like a big step from where we are now, puttering around a set of empty rooms, ignored?"

Klingston said, "Sometimes being ignored isn't so bad."

That puzzled Rusk, but he didn't want to let Klingston distract him now. "You can continue with the current exploration, and I'll take a different tack. If I make a mistake and get killed, you can learn from it."

Klingston gave him a funny look, and Rusk wondered about the wisdom of his last argument, but boldly let the statement float out there without additional justification.

"Get me a specific personnel and supply request and let's discuss it."

"I'll have it for you in an hour."

"You have it made up already, don't you?" Klingston asked, with a smile.

Rusk smiled back. "Of course. I know exactly what I want to do."

"I thought so," Klingston said, getting dressed. "Let me look it over and I'll get back to you as soon as possible."

"Today?"

"Today. No bullshit."

Rusk had to admit that he liked the way Klingston handled things, even though the man didn't do many things the way he himself would. Maybe that was okay. Maybe there were many pathways to success.

"What do you think you're doing?" Griffin shouted at him.

Rusk, irritated, detached himself from the station where he and Stubbs were supervising the nanofacture of the specially designed dirigible he would fly down into the atmosphere of the Spider Star. Spinning around he confronted her. "I'm preparing an exploration craft."

"I know," she said. "Klingston told me. What I don't understand is why *you* didn't tell me."

"I wasn't sure you'd think it wise."

"Now you can be sure."

"Klingston is with me on this."

"He shouldn't be."

"Why not?"

"You didn't request I go with you."

There it was. He'd suspected she might get this way. Her core drives focused on security, safety, and caution. Despite her position on this mission, she was not, at heart, a risk taker. True, this entire affair constituted an enormous risk, perhaps the equivalent of a small band of bugs entering a person's house, not knowing when a stomping foot might be headed their way, and Griffin would be the bug recommending a thorough mapping of the first tile square of the foyer.

"Excuse us," he said to Stubbs, who nodded. Rusk kicked off to the far side of the chamber. Sound didn't carry very well in the low pressure of the *Dark Heart*. While secrets didn't keep in circumstances like theirs, the semblance of privacy still mattered.

They picked up their conversation by the armory lockers.

"Face it, Rusk," Griffin said, "you're better with me. I compensate for your weaknesses. You tend to be headstrong when you don't have clear restrictions. Remember the knock?"

She didn't need to bring that up. "I'm bringing a team with me to compensate for everyone's weaknesses using everyone's strengths. That's how the Specialist Corps works."

"But we're a team," she persisted. "A good team."

"Sure we are." They were both holding their position by their fingertips on the wire web surface of the lockers. Rusk finger-walked his way closer to her. She held his gaze with an imploring look, confirming his fears.

Griffin was taking this personally. She cared for him, probably too much, and wanted to protect him as an outgrowth of protecting herself.

Closer now, Rusk whispered to Griffin. "Sloan, if we get into trouble down there, I don't want you there with us. I want you up here, ready to rescue us."

She lowered her voice, too. "But if I'm with you, Manuel, you might not get into trouble in the first place."

What could he say that wouldn't sound ungrateful, or worse, patronizing? He said the only truthful thing that came to mind that might satisfy her, at least a little: "I'll be careful."

"Promise?"

"Promise."

"I'm going to hold you to that," she said, very seriously. "And if you're not careful, I'll rescue you. Then I'll kill you."

Well, she was getting that joking-in-serious-situations thing down. It was annoying.

FIRST CONTACT

ONBOARD THE SPIDER STAR

Klingston was huddled with Sloan Griffin and Adrian Slyde monitoring the powered dirigible's progress. Rusk and his team had departed earlier that day in a rather complicated maneuver. Dropping straight down along a radial from orbit was not something energetically sensible under most circumstances, but the Spider Star spokes carried a magnetic field and by cleverly charging the dirigible they'd been able to quickly spiral down.

"Frank," said Jason, his X-bot. "Selene Madison wants to see you in the Spider Star."

He didn't like leaving, but he didn't like making Selene wait, either—she might have made an important breakthrough. Splitting his attention this way had not cut his concerns, but had multiplied them. Frank had bought Rusk's essential argument, and had even believed that letting him take his own team away would reduce Frank's responsibilities, but he couldn't let himself focus on the space dock. Every step seemed critical and he wanted to listen to every report. For instance, Rusk had already reached the upper atmosphere and switched the dirigible to neutral buoyancy. They had dropped a deep atmosphere probe and were now approaching the core, which had already led them to a number of significant discoveries. He wanted to be on hand for that.

If he took the baby monitoring seriously, Griffin took it as sacred. She'd been glued to the monitors watching every aspect of their descent. She half-glanced at Frank and said, "Go on. I've got things here."

"Thanks," said Frank, and moved to follow Jason.

He was waylaid in the Spider Star before he reached Selene. Typical. Why have one thing to do instead of three?

"Over here!" Melinda Sergevich called to him as he came through the wall of the lobby—as they were calling the large circular room immediately beyond the hull of the Spider Star— and into one of the side rooms.

Frank grabbed on to the appropriate makeshift guy wires and hauled himself hand over hand to Melinda. This particular room was large and spherical in shape surrounded by a ring of spherical cubby holes, each about three meters in diameter. Melinda floated in the circular entrance to one of the cubby holes.

"What have you found, Melinda?"

"Come inside," she said. She had a big grin, and her blond hair was tousled, in disarray, as if she'd neglected to comb it. She was normally well coifed.

Frank pushed himself away from the wire and into the bubble toward Melinda. She reached out an arm to gently catch him and they floated together for a moment. Frank noticed some faint colored circles on the surface before him. "We didn't notice these before."

"No," she said. "They only appear if you come inside and stay for a minute or so."

"Hmm, that's interesting. I wonder why that is."

"My theory is that it works by body heat, and we don't quite radiate as much as whatever it's designed for. We have to be in here for a while before it turns on."

"But why bother? Why not have the controls active all the time?" Frank asked.

"Well," she said, smiling mischievously, "maybe it's because of the nature of the controls."

She reached out and tapped the blue button.

Hot jets of liquid and a thick mist erupted from all around

them. Frank howled, startled, and flailed at Melinda as the liquid soaked him. "Gah!" he said smartly.

"Easy, Frank!" she said, holding him and laughing. "It's okay!"

And it was okay, he realized. It had just been the abrupt, unexpected, shock of the hot liquid. Still, large amounts of water without gravity could be dangerous. He sputtered a question. "What is it?"

"I think it's just your basic, alien zero-gee shower, as far as I can tell. Nontoxic, but invigorating."

Frank looked around, blinking into the mist. It did seem to come from all directions, even from the bubble opening, but it was difficult to say for certain. He risked sticking out his tongue, and tasted what seemed to be warm water, although perhaps with a touch of chemical he couldn't immediately place. There was a scent of ozone, and mint, in the air. After a few more seconds the jets died, the mist cleared, and they floated there together again.

"Watch me," she said.

He did. Their faces were only a few inches apart. She had fine droplets of the liquid clinging to her cheeks and lips, but as he watched the droplets shrank and vanished, apparently evaporating rapidly.

"Isn't that cool?" she asked.

Frank managed to smile, although he didn't really feel like it. He should be like Melinda, taking joy in discovery, in the sheer novelty of having the run of an alien space station. He couldn't relax. He was too uncomfortable with the mantle of leadership, such as it was among this informal bunch, the responsibility of success, for him to set aside the constant stress. He couldn't even enjoy the intimacy of such a close look into her clear blue eyes, and he'd been effectively divorced for decades now. "Yes, that's very cool," he said.

"I'm going to get an X-bot in here and get a detailed analysis. This sure beats a shower bag."

That it did. Rusk was too impatient, although Frank had to take responsibility for agreeing to let him go. They weren't stalled here, rather, they were proceeding at a blistering pace in many respects. How long would it take for a clever ancient human, say an Odysseus, to figure out how to use all the technology present in a modern ground-based home, let alone any sort of space station? More than a few days, surely, given that he wouldn't speak a modern tongue, which would make the voice recognition technology difficult at best. Here the problem was compounded by the fact that the technology wasn't even designed for the same species, and, he had to admit to himself, the species this place was designed for might be smarter than humans.

That was tolerable, perhaps likely. It would just take them a little longer. A month longer, even a year longer, was not long compared to their travel time. Everyone had to trust that the swarm of doom inside Pollux would behave itself long enough for their mission to matter, or that Argo would find their own solution to the threat without them.

"That's great, but I need to see Selene now."

"No problem. She's by the cord."

That was the cylindrical, central feature that didn't seem to have interior rooms and had been hypothesized to be structural support. "Thanks."

Frank proceeded through the warren, managing to dodge additional engagements even though it seemed that Melinda hadn't been the only one making discoveries. Still, nothing he saw prepared him for what Selene had done.

Frank popped into a final large crescent-shaped chamber and actually gasped. The last time he'd been here, there had been emptiness and lights. This time, there was *stuff* everywhere. He didn't know what else to call it. It was possible to characterize it as equipment, monitors and interfaces, he guessed, but he really didn't know. What he did know was that Selene was in the middle of it all, literally.

Selene, prudently wearing green body armor, nestled with an X-bot amid lighted cables and strange shapes protruding from the walls. Multihued lights flashed across her face as her head tilted slightly, rapidly, in different directions and she blinked her eyes. She and an X-bot—Marlo, he recognized—both had appendages thrust deep into gray boxes mounted on the cables.

Selene spoke, her voice as far away and exotic as her gaze. "About time you got here, Frank. It's amazing."

Amazing. Yes, he supposed it was. Amazement held her, and was seeping into his own brain, too. But was amazing the same thing as enlightening?

"What's going on?" he asked. "What is all this stuff?"

Selene blinked, twitched, and bathed her face in the colored lights. "It's an interface, a control center, a hot zone for the space dock. I'm feeling the Spider Star around me, a part of it, anyway . . . it's *vast*. But I suppose we knew that. But, oh, it is so very, very vast."

"How did you do this?"

Selene was quiet a long moment, seeing—*feeling*—things amazing and alien. While part of him was pleased that they had made a quantum leap in understanding, part of him feared the sight of this technology holding his crewmate so enthralled. She almost seemed an alien thing.

She finally answered. "It wasn't hard. It wasn't meant to be, for an Argonaut."

That made some sense. Perhaps the Spider Star was trying to accommodate them and thought them Argonauts since that was the language they had employed.

"I don't understand everything. I'm probably missing ninety percent of what I'm supposed to be getting. Oh!"

Selene's distant look flashed surprise, her eyebrows rising and her mouth forming an open circle.

"Oh?" He thought he knew her as well as anyone on the mission, except for perhaps Manuel Rusk whose ambition he understood, but at this moment he didn't know Selene Madison at all. He didn't really *know* anyone here, not really, not like he knew his family, and he felt guilty about that. Much of the Specialist Corps' methodology was intended to engender intimacy and family. Her cry could reflect a cry of delight or of horror, and as the strange lights flashed across her face he had no clue. Only she knew, and so he waited.

"Someone's coming," she gasped, eyes darting about. "Someone's coming and they're almost here."

"Who?" he asked, more alarmed than excited.

"I don't know." Her brows knitted, her eyes squinted. "I should be able to see that, but I don't know how to do that yet."

"Keep trying." What did they need to know now? What should they do? This was like his own encounter now, those moments of greatest uncertainty before his first meeting with an alien, but worse. Now his decisions would affect everyone here, and while he could rationalize the choice he made on that occasion as the right one, that was not the sort of decision he could make for a dozen other people.

Please, he thought, *please don't let it come to something like that again.*

He took a deep breath. He needed more information, immediately, and he needed everyone's help. He wasn't alone this time. He could solicit input from others. It wasn't solely his decision.

That helped. A little. But he wished Rusk were still here. His thoughts clarified. "Selene, how is this 'someone' approaching?"

She answered at once. "I know that. Up an elevator, up the core, the shaft. There's a portal from this chamber. We found it, but it wouldn't open. The elevator car wasn't on this level, and we didn't know how to call it."

An elevator, opening here. "How soon?"

"Eight minutes, maybe nine. Close to minutes, anyway."

That wasn't much time, not at all. He needed to have everyone in the space dock drop what they were doing and assemble here. Someone needed to tell Griffin what was going on, too.

"Jason, we need everyone here, ready for everything. Get this message to Griffin that someone's coming."

"I think Gina has Phyllis next door," Selene said, indicating a direction to her right.

Jason beeped an acknowledgment.

A chain of X-bots shuttling back and forth would be quicker than individual messengers, and he'd take the opportunity to start assembling the Specialists himself.

Frank said, "Keep monitoring their approach. We'll be back in a minute."

Selene nodded, but barely, distracted by her expanded senses.

Frank went next door, as Selene had indicated, and found Gina and an X-bot working on a glowing square on the wall.

"Frank, you've got to see this!" she said.

"Not now. Right now you've got to drop everything. Someone's coming. Something, anyway."

That did it, having the same effect on Gina it had on him. "Who? Where? When?"

"I don't know, Selene's room, about eight minutes."

"What do you want me to do?"

Gina had trained for Specialist duty her entire life, with primary expertise in field medicine, but also in, what was it . . . spectroscopic analsyis, but first and foremost in basic Specialist procedures, and now Frank appreciated that training. She was ready to help in the way that military soldiers of centuries past would jump to follow orders, trusting their superiors to have the information necessary to direct them to their most useful state. Frank hoped he could live up to that ideal, and, knowing that action was required, settled for hope.

"Gina, I want you to return to the *Dark Heart*. Tell Sloan what's going on over here, then come back."

"What should I tell her to do?"

That was a good question. He didn't know. He didn't know enough about what was happening. She was good though, he knew. He shouldn't saddle her with orders that might not make sense. He said, "Tell her to use her best judgment."

"Okay," Gina said, and kicked off toward a portal.

"Phyllis," Frank said to the X-bot. "Make a circuit of the space dock and tell everyone to come to Selene's room as fast as they can manage. Highest priority."

The visage of a silver-haired woman manifested in the X-bot's display. "Roger that. I'll kick their butts in there faster than you can say 'sardines.'"

Frank didn't know that particular persona—it could have been a particularly effective Earth leader for all he knew—but he was satisfied with her fortitude. "Hurry."

The X-bot snaked away and Frank returned to Selene with Jason. He'd decided to keep his personal bot with him at this critical time. "Anything new?" he asked.

She seemed even farther away than she had just a couple of minutes earlier, and she took her time answering. "Here in six minutes. More than one . . . entity. There's more, but I don't understand it."

"Take your time," he said, even though he wanted to rush her. Something of monumental importance would happen mere minutes from now, and he had no idea if it would be something wonderful or something terrible.

Other Specialists began to appear: Melinda from the shower

room, Timothy Salerno, Gabriella Powers, Walter Stubbs, and Towson Field.

No one had any weapons. He decided that was fine. They'd likely appear distrustful and stupid. No one had any recording equipment either, beyond the few X-bots they had, and that was criminal. He yelled at a few people and they scurried to cover. Whatever happened, this was a moment worthy of documentation.

The seconds ticked on. Funny how they felt like years now. They'd journeyed years to reach this time, in hibernation so that the years passed like seconds. Okay, days.

People were whispering, giggling even. Most of the people in the room had worked all their lives in anticipation of this moment. Frank couldn't blame them for being excited. He himself felt the excitement, despite his previous unsavory alien experience. He didn't think this one could be any worse, at least not at the personal, physical level.

Seconds stretched into minutes, finally, and proper recording equipment appeared and initialized.

"They're here!" Selene called out.

Here was the welcome that the ancient Argonauts had received. It was their turn.

Frank had to force himself to relax. Floating in free fall, he had realized that he was balling up as every muscle tensed. Everyone was floating every which way, equipment was floating every which way. They looked a mess. "Be ready for anything!" he admonished.

To Jason he said, "Stay out of this and let us react to whatever comes through."

Jason beeped acknowledgment.

Unlike their transport through the other portals, nothing popped out of the wall. Instead, the gateway to the elevator faded into transparency, shimmering in a tenuous existence for a time-less moment, essentially vanishing. In that moment, Frank saw through to the elevator car beyond.

Red light emanated from the dark car. Blacks, maybe browns, writhed within, with just a few flashes of color and brief, bright reflections glinting from among the shadows. He suffered difficulty, a cognitive dissonance, in determining what it was he was looking at. Recognition would not come. He was looking at something alien.

The wall thinned to nothing, and vanished. The black, brown, glinting mass erupted forth, spewing out from the wall, separating, flying, mingling with the Specialists.

The screaming began.

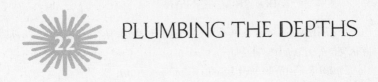

PLUMBING THE DEPTHS

Rusk leaned forward and let his weight settle heavily upon the observation rail of their dirigible. It was good to have weight again, even 35 percent of an Earth gravity—it was similar to what they had at Argo's space dock, at the end of its tether. The part that engendered more ambiguous feelings was the view.

This wasn't anything like Earth, or Argo, or any planet he'd ever heard of. That idea simultaneously thrilled him and terrified him. He was truly doing something new and noteworthy, but also something fraught with danger.

They still spiraled down around the Spider Star spoke, but all around them was cloudscape and vista. Thousands of kilometers of vista. At this altitude the atmosphere outside was cold and barely breathable, but it was also perfectly transparent and impeded one's view barely at all. Standing on this deck and looking out inspired awe, both of the place, and of one's self for having achieved this position.

This wasn't a planet, it was an infinite sky. One could fall forever into a blue abyss, the wind streaming, and screaming, overwhelming. The loss of control in the face of this infinity terrified Rusk on a level he usually refused to acknowledge.

He forced the feeling away and asked Slyde for a status report.

"Everything's perfect," the pilot said. "All systems optimal. Descent continuing at a kilometer per minute."

Perfect? How could things be perfect? There were no rules now, just a planet-size unknown waiting to challenge them. Was there any way the situation could be perfect? He could clearly hear Griffin in his head answering: *Perfectly unknown. Perfectly dangerous. Perfectly reckless.*

Thanks, Griffin. Not missing you yet at all.

"The atmosphere outside is now breathable, if you want to go outside," Mistelle said from beside him.

Go outside? Okay, it was a crazy notion, but perhaps the act would restore a sensation of control. He was supposed to be in charge, the one with all the answers, and part of maintaining that was by preserving the illusion. "Fine. Let's go outside," he said.

There was an observation deck surrounding the gondola, a cat-walk, really. They cycled through the airlock and Rusk breathed his first breath of the air of the Spider Star. Cold and searing, that breath, and he could see it trailing up and away as they dropped deeper. No particular smell to it that he could discern, nothing extreme anyway. He thought he would get a coat if he came out again, but the raw experience of seeing an infinite sky and feeling the wind slicing the flesh of his cheeks, that was worth a certain price. He was doing something real and important, something worth remembering. "Fantastic," he said quietly. "Fantastic."

Mistelle was there with him. She said, "I was holding my breath until you spoke. Funny, isn't it? I guess I don't trust my machines so much."

He smiled, a little. That was funny. The woman who told them it was safe to breathe didn't breathe. "I trusted your measurements. Perhaps it is that we simply don't trust ourselves enough."

"I suppose not." Her voice was distant, quiet in the wind and the low pressure.

This place was strange. On one level it was quite similar to flying through any planetary atmosphere, but the distances were larger, and the light coming from below, rather than above, did create a disconcerting effect. "Okay," Rusk said finally. "We've breathed the air. Let everyone have a step outside, soak up the experience, and then let's get serious."

Rusk returned to the dirigible's control deck. Air they could breathe—what were the chances? He had no idea. This was a constructed place, the station anyway, and likely the atmosphere surrounding it that sat in the potential of the dark matter.

The spectral analysis of absorption lines had indicated all kinds of gases in the atmosphere. Different Doppler shifts had indicated odd stratifications with altitude that didn't make any natural sense. Some light gases, light hydrogen, and helium sat at great depths, with neon and nitrogen at higher altitudes, and significant quantities of oxygen and water vapor at all heights. The pressure gradient was exponential, as expected, but given what they knew about the mass distribution of the dark matter, the temperature gradient was odd, nearly isothermal. It should rise rapidly with depth, like the pressure, but didn't. It rose somewhat, rising from the chilly temperatures here to toasty levels deeper down, but not the ovenlike temperatures that reasonable physical models suggested. Adrian Slyde, in addition to being a superlative pilot, was a meteorologist and atmospheric scientist, and would help him figure out these oddities.

There had to be reasons behind these properties, but what were they, and were they significant to their understanding of the Spider Star? Physical characterization they could do, and that had to be the first step toward understanding. "Mistelle, prepare a probe."

"I've already got one prepped. We can launch in minutes."

"Fantastic. Let's do it."

They dropped the probe. This category of probe didn't fly—it was more of a cannonball, designed to plummet through the thickening atmosphere. The equipment package included a sophisticated weather station to monitor temperature, pressure, and humidity; a mass spectrometer to analyze molecular composition; an assortment of telescopic cameras; and even Geiger counters and neutron detectors. The thicker atmosphere at greater depths, and various cloud decks, made the deep parts of the Spider Star fuse into a golden haze when viewed from a distance.

Mistelle supervised the probe operation, while Kat Coyner and Anatole Hamilton pressed in close to watch. Slyde kept them on their circular dive. The probe dropped much faster than they did and gave them a picture of what lay below.

"This is quite strange," Slyde reported over the open channel. "The atmospheric parameters are matching our previous measurements."

"Strange? For matching what we thought already?" Rusk asked.

"Our expectations were based on models constructed to fit the line-of-sight absorption features and their Doppler shifts given what we know about the rotation of the Spider Star and its prevailing winds." Slyde seemed to be just warming up to a favorite subject. Rusk hoped he could get to the point before the probe smacked into something. Slyde went on. "But the model fitting was wacky. Just wacky. Didn't make any sense. Temperatures all wrong, composition all wrong. Just couldn't happen."

"Seems to be happening anyway," Mistelle countered. "I don't care what the models say when the evidence is staring us in the face."

Slyde sighed. "Empiricist." He said it like a dirty word. "Data is meaningless without interpretation, without understanding."

"And theory is meaningless without comparison to data."

Rusk thought about referring to them as "children" in a joking manner, but that would be inappropriate coming from him. He settled for forging ahead. "So let's collect the data and have a look at it."

They spent several hours doing just that while they enjoyed the view.

Normally in a planetary atmosphere different gases segregated.

A common temperature meant that the gas particles shared a similar distribution of kinetic energies, but that didn't mean that they shared a similar distribution of velocities. Lighter particles, like molecular hydrogen and helium, had to have higher velocities to match the energies of slower moving but more massive particles like diatomic oxygen, nitrogen, water, carbon dioxide. The higher velocities of lighter particles let them streak to greater heights, and if the surface gravity wasn't too high, even escape the atmosphere to space altogether. Hence the correlations between planetary mass, temperature, and atmosphere.

The data coming in not only showed that some particular gases became less abundant as the probe dropped, some other gases dropped, then increased again. No natural processes could account for such a thing.

"It's just not following the laws of physics," Slyde said.

"Of course it is!" said Anatole Hamilton, whose wide eyes and loud manners tended to make him come across as a little insane. Brilliant, but insane. "You always act like your assumptions are as perfect as a spherical cow! You've simply missed something—likely a bit of engineering!"

Rusk started to roll his eyes, and then stopped himself lest someone notice. Theorist versus experimentalist was bad enough, but physicist versus engineer was worse. He was just happy they didn't have a mathematician along; then they could spend the whole trip writing their own jokes. "Fine then," Rusk said. "Let's look for an engineering solution."

"Something's got to be pumping certain things in, or selectively pumping them out," said Coyner.

"Then we're looking for some kind of structure, the Spider Star spoke, or some of these other things, tubes, pipes, whatever, connecting them," said Rusk. "Or maybe something free floating. An atmosphere maintenance center."

"Right," said Mistelle.

Rusk said, "If Adrian is correct, and this gas distribution is unnatural, then what is its purpose?"

Anatole rolled his eyes, and even his neck, to draw attention. "I said it's engineering!"

Rusk managed to avoid smiling, but not everyone did. Slyde usually didn't really care about the credit, but Anatole did. "If *Anatole* is correct, then the atmosphere has been engineered to some purpose."

Anatole beamed at Rusk, but said in a low voice he could barely make out, "I'm a theorist sympathizer, you know."

They waited for more data, people coming and going as they needed to eat, sleep, or attend to their personal hygiene. Mistelle kept fiddling with things and at one point clapped her hands to call everyone's attention. "I've got something! Two things!"

Rusk had been nursing a cooling cup of coffee and perked up immediately. "What is it?"

"A directional concentration gradient, a neutron flux, and a picture."

"A neutron flux?" Rusk asked, alarmed.

"Not too dangerously high, but someone's doing some cooking."

She meant fusion. Elemental transformation. "Where?"

"Here."

An image flashed on the big display. Rusk saw an optical feed from the probe, a little shaky and shimmering despite the electronic image stabilization. At the center of the image, situated along a fuzzy line, nestled a dark mass. The perspective changed slightly in real time as the probe fell.

"What's that?" Rusk asked.

"How should I know?" Mistelle replied. "What you see is what you get."

The image sharpened as the probe closed. The dark mass

resolved into distinct features that resembled trees and leaves—a vegetative mass of some sort. The fuzzy line was one of the tubes, or pipes, that connected the spokes at points of similar altitude. Rusk had no idea if they were structural support or if they served some other purpose.

"That dark region is where the neutrons are coming from. There's some kind of reactor there, changing one set of elements to another set of elements. To maintain these atmospheric disparities however . . . they'd have to be all over the place."

"They've got energy to burn," Anatole said. "All those microwaves from the power satellites. These air gardens don't have to be energy producers."

Air gardens. That was awfully poetic to come from a theorist sympathizer. The gardens not only grew plants, but whatever gaseous species were desired at their altitude. The perspective continued to tilt and the air garden vanished into a blur again as the probe continued its plummet.

"They are energy producers," Mistelle said, scanning some numbers on her personal monitor. "There's a thermal coming out of that place, too. Has to be important."

Perhaps they'd take a look at it themselves when the dirigible reached that altitude.

A while later, Mistelle said, "I'm plotting the gas fractions as a function of depth." She tapped a few keys into one of the dirigible's terminals and a graph popped up.

A bunch of colored lines appeared, each one representing a particular gaseous species, scrolling down as the probe submitted more data to the stream. Several of the lines did wiggle in and out, while others steadily increased or decreased. Still, nothing jumped out at Rusk.

"Can you plot that as partial pressures, in Earth atmospheres?" Slyde asked.

He was following things very closely. Rusk wondered if he

should ask him if the piloting was being as closely watched. Still, his request made good sense. For many applications, partial pressure was the key quantity, not fraction of the total.

"Just one second," Mistelle said. The scales changed and the colored lines shifted.

"Would you look at that," Coyner said.

Rusk did. Many things jumped out at him now. Nitrogen started out dominant at high altitudes, then fell with depth. At deeper levels, argon rose and then dropped. Next, helium rose, and decayed, but not completely. Finally, hydrogen, in all its perverseness, became the dominant gas at the deepest levels. Oxygen, water, and carbon dioxide maintained low but nearly constant partial pressures over the entire range.

"Slyde is right," Anatole said. "This makes no sense. I surrender."

Slyde's distant chuckle came to them quite clearly.

Rusk had to agree. The behavior was bizarre.

"Aha!" Mistelle said, sounding a bit like Anatole. "I get it. It's trivial."

Rusk hated that. His hatred of that sort of announcement of triviality went back to his days studying for honors classes. Everyone always seemed to make light of the hard problems, calling them trivial, or simple, when they found the solution first, making everyone else feel like a moron even though they were all super-sharp students.

"I get it, too," Kat Coyner said. She sported a big, white-toothed smile. "But I don't think it's trivial, Mistelle. You're a diver, aren't you?"

"Guilty," she said.

A diver? What relevance could that possibly have? "Spell it out for me. I'm a dunce sometimes, okay?"

He didn't really mean that, but he thought it sounded humble and tried to use the phrase once in a while.

Mistelle and Coyner both started to speak, then both stopped, then both started to talk again at the same time. Then they laughed. Rusk hated that sort of thing, too. He wished Griffin were here.

Mistelle said, "We're looking at diving mixtures! Human physiology wants to have a couple of tenths of an atmosphere of oxygen at all times. At pressures higher than that, for instance, a full atmosphere, inert gases like nitrogen account for the difference."

Coyner continued, looking quite pleased with herself. "At higher gas pressures, nitrogen causes problems. Neon can work. Helium can work. At fifty atmospheres, hydrogen, helium, oxygen blends are used."

"What about other inert gases, like the other noble gases? How about argon, krypton, or xenon?" Anatole asked.

"They cause a variety of problems, like dizziness, and can put you to sleep or drug you out at high pressures," Mistelle explained.

"This doesn't make any sense to me," Rusk said. "Why should this place have an engineered atmosphere at all, let alone one designed for humans to breathe?"

The silence was deafening. There was no obvious reason. This was not a "trivial" problem. The moment dragged out to minutes, an astonishing amount of time for a gondola full of such talented people.

Anatole spoke up. "I'm going to float an idea. I don't think it's completely plausible, so don't destroy me with your rebuttals. At least not until I defend myself too much."

Anatole Hamilton always carried himself in a way that seemed completely attackable, but was open and often right. For him to talk about being overly defensive seemed somewhat laughable. Rusk asked, "What's your idea, Hamilton?"

"I've got two ideas, really, although they're related. First, to answer why the Spider Star has an atmosphere at all, I propose

this answer: someone lives here, outside the confines of the station itself. The atmosphere is here for their benefit. It's engineered to taste, so it isn't just the various gases that have settled
in the gravitational potential of the dark matter." He paused and
looked around.

"What's your second idea?" Coyner asked.

"Well, that's sort of two ideas, too."

"Can't you keep it simple, stupid?" Mistelle asked. She blew
him a little kiss to emphasize her point.

Anatole smiled, recognizing the ancient admonition. "Apparently not. Definitely can't kiss. Okay, here's the second idea in
all its glory. The atmosphere hasn't been engineered for humans
to breathe. It's been engineered for Argonauts, who we know
have very similar physiologies to our own. Or," and he held up
a finger to forestall the protests that were blooming on the faces
of his listeners, "all intelligent life in this part of the galaxy has a
similar biochemistry to humans and Argonauts, either through
some sort of panspermia or parallel evolution."

That was a mouthful of a hypothesis, and individual conversations exploded between everyone at the same time. Rusk let
them go on. After all, maybe someone would get somewhere
with the seed of Hamilton's ideas, as outlandish as they seemed.
Actually, though, given what he knew now, as he considered the
ideas, he didn't see any immediate problems with them. Sure,
they could turn out to be completely wrong, but as working hy-
potheses, he had certainly operated with worse.

Coyner was saying, "The Argonauts themselves disprove
panspermia! Similar physiology, yes, but identical amino acids,
no!"

Slyde was broadcasting, "Parallel evolution is a crock! There
are myriad solutions to biological problems, and just because the
solutions appear similar on the surface doesn't mean everything
should want to breathe the same atmosphere!"

Rusk resisted smiling again. These people, these Specialists, fought over ideas the way cavemen must have fought saber-toothed cats to protect their women. He liked to think that evolution had finally started, somewhere in the last century or two, in selecting for smart people. Even after the industrial age, civilizations had continued to celebrate great athletes with the brains of bugs, heaping them with recognition and treasure, while nearly ignoring the geniuses of their time. Enough of that, Rusk thought, time to focus on the present expedition. "Interesting ideas, Anatole. I think they'll do for now."

Everyone looked at him with disappointment, except Anatole. They liked discussing ideas, and that was a good thing, usually even when the discussions became arguments. They were passionate, true, but no one lost their nose in a duel over who was better at math the way Tycho Brahe had back at the dawn of modern science.

"Hey," Mistelle said, "something's up. The probe just cleared a cloud deck and is now approaching something I don't like the looks of, not at all."

"How far from the center?" Rusk asked.

"About three hundred kilometers."

"Project it," said Rusk.

The view from the probe showed a bright, golden glow beneath it. They'd dropped the probe since they were unsure about the central conditions of the Spider Star. If the center was empty, the probe would shoot on through and eventually fall back through the center and up toward them again, with the air resistance slowing it down until it eventually settled in the center, with whatever other junk had been trapped there over the megayears. They had balloons built into the probe and could blow those to kill its downward velocity, if necessary, and let it provide them with detailed long-term surveillance of something of particular interest. They were only trailing a few hundred kilometers behind so the signal lag time was tiny and they could react quickly to what the probe showed them.

"So?" Rusk asked. "We know the light comes from the center."

"Look closer," Mistelle said, hitting a few keys, causing the image to zoom in.

Rusk looked closer, as requested, but couldn't understand what he was seeing. He'd looked at Pollux a few times through a telescope with an H-alpha filter, so he knew what the surface of a star looked like. This wasn't like that. Neither was it a solid surface radiating heat. Nor was it a bank of lightbulbs or fluorescent tubes or LED panels.

"What is that?" Coyner asked.

Anatole snickered. "You don't know already? I'm shocked."

"You know what that is?" Rusk asked Anatole.

"No! But I don't claim to know everything."

Levity in the face of the unknown—that had been Rusk's style from time to time, but he seemed to have lost that trait during hibernation. Such things sometimes happened. He preferred to keep his wits focused on the challenge at hand. But how could this be comprehended at a glance?

The probe was falling into a giant, golden wall. No, *wall* wasn't the right word. It had wall-like properties, but *wall* implied a discrete surface. What Rusk thought of when looking at the screen before him was the crab nebula, a dense supernova remnant with bright filamentary structure, glowing from both line emission as in arc lamps, and also synchrotron processes from the combination of high-speed electrons and intense magnetic fields. The crab was a combination of reds and blues, while this was a luminous, light lustrous gold, with filamentary texture. There was no solid surface, but it didn't look like a fluid or gas, not exactly.

"What do you want to do?" Mistelle asked.

"How far away is the probe from the . . . this thing?"

"I don't have a clue," she answered. "Radar's not hitting. Stereo cameras are giving contradictory results."

"How about angular size as a function of time?" Anatole asked. "That would give us an impact time at least."

"Watch closer," she admonished. "This surface, if you can call it that, is variable. I'm guessing we have five or ten minutes, but that's just a guess."

Normally Rusk would keep his own counsel here or, if Griffin had been present, consult with her. But he'd been admiring the smarts of this group, and how Klingston had been able to extract their talent by letting them work on problems as equals. He said, "I'm torn. We could stall the probe, let it study the thing, but at its depth it wouldn't pick up much velocity if we let it drop again. We could also just let it drop in and let it report back. Opinions?"

Slyde said, "I think—"

A flash of light from the display stopped him in midsentence. The display went black.

"What happened?" Rusk asked.

Mistelle tapped some keys and conferred with their X-bot, Drone, for a few moments. "We've lost the probe," she said.

"Damn," Anatole said.

"How?"

"I don't know," she replied. "I can probably get some information from the last few milliseconds of telemetry we received. But we have a bigger problem."

"We do? What's that?"

She tapped a few keys and a new image jumped onto the display. Rusk tried to make sense of it and finally figured out he was looking down onto the tops of some distant clouds.

"I'm zooming in," Mistelle said.

The cloud tops ballooned toward him and then he saw it: a silvery sphere was flying up out of the clouds.

"It's a lot bigger than us, moving faster, and it's headed directly toward us."

"I think it's a ship," said Anatole.

Brilliant, and obvious, sometimes. "Well, let's get ready," said Rusk. "Any ideas?"

Now he got silence.

He knew he wasn't fond of jokes at moments like this, but he didn't need aliens to rub his nose in it.

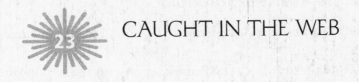

CAUGHT IN THE WEB

ONBOARD THE SPIDER STAR

"What do you mean, 'someone's coming'?" Griffin asked, looking up from her thermos of coffee.

"That's all I know," Gina Dorissey said.

"Who, where, when, how?" she asked, sure that he had to know more than the two words he'd been charged to carry.

The dark-haired woman's eyes bulged and her voice cracked when she answered. "No one knows who, and I'm not sure about the how, either, but they're coming soon and they're coming to one of the rooms inside."

That helped, not much, but a little. "Did Klingston say what I should do?"

"Yes!" Gina grinned and shook her fist with excitement, making her entire body vibrate in a distracting manner. "He said you should use your best judgment."

Terrific. She'd planned to do that anyway. So then, what was her best judgment? What did the backup do in preparation for first contact? She could do what she'd done before: assemble an armed backup. Rusk had taken most of the weapons-qualified personnel, and whether or not they would be of any use was quite unclear. If Klingston was right, if they needed weapons they were in trouble already.

Still, she thought that securing the *Dark Heart* would be wise. She could do that while they gathered more intelligence. "Gina, I'd like you to go back into the Spider Star—"

"Thank you!" she interrupted her. "I couldn't believe it when

Frank sent me away! I mean, aliens! Do you think they've arrived yet?"

"I don't know," she said simply, giving up the fight against her infectious smile. She smiled back. "I want you to take Rosetta and Lance with you. Take Rosetta to Klingston, but tell Lance to set up a communications corridor, and pop back and forth across the hull once per minute, or as warranted." Rosetta was the X-bot loaded with their general linguistics and communications experts, while the patterns imprinted in Lance featured those with expertise in security, surveillance, and intelligence gathering.

"Right! Can I go now?"

"Yes," she said.

Gina bounced toward the stairway, missed it, and clanged against the wall with a painful thump. "I'm okay!" She made it through on her second try and she listened to her clang away.

Griffin ran down her personnel roster, and was frustrated to see everyone but her and Robb was onboard the Spider Star or with Rusk. Rusk shouldn't have gone, and she didn't know if he'd taken too many people or too few. Well, she'd have to do with the X-bots, most of which they'd retained on the *Dark Heart*. She called up Robb and Kurtz and asked them to station themselves in the *Dark Heart*'s airlock. "I will join you in a few minutes."

She took just a moment to check on the dirigible. She wouldn't be able to watch over it so closely for a while, and wanted to be sure everything was secure before she left.

That was strange . . . *something* was coming up on Rusk. Something real—she was seeing it on multiple wave bands coming in from their feed. "Rusk, what's going on there?"

Rusk's voice burst onto the speakers almost immediately. "Sloan, something's after us."

"What is it already?" She didn't mean to sound angry, but she feared it came out that way. She was impatient, tapped a few keys, and in seconds had her own telescopic visual.

"Your guess is good as mine. I'm going to call it a UFO."

At first she didn't see anything, then it locked in: a perfectly reflective region moving through the clouds. It reached a higher altitude, above the clouds and, as it reflected indigo skies, the thing became clear. It was something all right, but what, who could say? This was exciting—a bit too exciting. First contact on two fronts. "What's it doing?"

"Chasing us," Manuel said flatly, replacing the cloudscape image. "I decided to play it safe and keep some distance between us—I'm sure you would approve—but it seems to have different ideas. It's going to catch us, too."

"Does it seem threatening?"

"Well, it is *chasing* us."

She realized how dumb her question sounded, but wasn't it just like Rusk to point it out in a way that made it obvious not only to her, but to everyone listening. He always did tend to find ways to build himself up, usually at the expense of others, but not usually at her expense. She was too busy to feel very offended, and she would let him know it. "Something's coming up an elevator to the space dock right now, too."

There, let him chew on that a little. He wasn't the only one with something going on.

"That's great," he said. He sounded genuine about it. "Look, I know you can't do anything for us from where you are. I just wanted to let you know what was happening."

Of course they knew what was happening with the dirigible—the airship was sending them a continuous telemetry stream that included everything from computer RAM states to control deck eavesdropping video and sound.

Rusk, she realized, was making a personal appeal. He personally wanted her to know what was going on. She tried not to read too much into things, but she thought maybe he did want her with him there, now. She softened. "The space plane will be ready in another day or so."

They'd started nanofacturing the space plane after they'd finished the dirigible. The plane was fast, but not nearly as versatile as the dirigible in this environment. Rusk had wanted to leave before the plane was finished, and Klingston had let him. She should have insisted on waiting.

"I don't know what's going to happen in the next few minutes," Rusk said.

He was downplaying the situation. He was *scared,* she realized, in a way he'd probably never been before in his entire life, except maybe for a while back on Charybdis. Indeed, who could say what would happen when that reflective ball reached the dirigible? Not a human.

"I don't know, either." Although she had a sweet tooth, Griffin was not a believer in sugar coatings, and Manuel respected her for that. Still, there was some cause for optimism. "If they wanted to destroy you, surely they have the technology to do that instantly."

It didn't sound so optimistic after she'd said it aloud.

"I suppose that's true," he said.

"Priority interrupt!" Lance announced on another channel. Rusk vanished and one of Lance's patterns appeared, an older black man with graying hair. "Klingston's party is being attacked by unknown entities."

Attacked?! She was not happy dealing with "somethings" and now "entities." All right. Lance wouldn't interrupt her without serious cause. It was an emergency. She kept her mouth shut and watched his report. "Rusk, we've got problems. I have to go for a sec."

The image of the silvery "UFO" faded to be replaced by a series of short movie clips and sound. She watched and listened to the voice-over. She saw snippets of video as an autonomous spycam popped across a portal, back and forth, collecting and relaying in alternate steps.

It was bizarre. She couldn't understand what she was seeing. Dark brown shapes, complex shapes, legs? Arms? She couldn't tell. Flashing bright glints. Distant screams. Trails of floating blood. What was this?

My God, she thought.

The voice-over provided a time stamp and identification of particular Specialists, nothing more. The worst part was, she recognized her friends without the computer assistance.

What is this?

"Forward to Rusk," she said. She didn't know what was going to happen to him, but he had a right to know what was happening up here. It might help him to know. She didn't let herself dwell on the idea that seeing this might demoralize him. She'd never seen Manuel Rusk demoralized before Charybdis, and never wanted to see it again.

Griffin had never been demoralized as long as she'd known *anyone.* "Robb, prepare to move in. This is an armed conflict. Authorized to use lethal force. Repeat: You are authorized to use lethal force."

She looked at the images again, thinking hard. She broadcast to Rusk. "Klingston appears to have been attacked by Argonauts."

Rusk said, "I don't understand what's happening up there. What is this?"

That's two of us, she thought.

She said, "You're on your own, Manuel. You were on your own anyway since we can't reach you in time to help, but I'm afraid we can't even talk to you now. You're on your own."

"Understood," he replied. "Be safe."

"Always. You, too. Griffin out."

She wondered, briefly, if that was it. If their relationship of over ten years would finish with an abrupt businesslike exchange like this. She loved him, in a way. It was inappropriate to tell him that, even if it was the last time they'd talk. Neither of them could afford distraction. He was being chased. Her people were being attacked. *Blood . . . !*

Stick to business, stick to authorized protocol. That was the safest course. That was *always* the safest course. It was designed to maximize their effectiveness, and that was what they needed now, wasn't it?

She kicked off for the airlock and the Spider Star space dock. Something awaited her, what it was she had a clue, but not certain knowledge. That was fine. She would give it her all regardless of its origin, and if indeed it required painful, forceful decisions, as seemed likely, she would make them. Rusk deserved that from her, in her position. So did Klingston, facing a cold-blooded attack, when he had been welcoming, unarmed.

If that was indeed the situation, and she had no reason to doubt it was, she'd do everything in her power to undo it. Or, if not undo it, to rectify it. Revenge it. Avenge it. This was her moment of empowerment, she vowed, for all their sakes. If Klingston and Rusk weren't lost to her already, she'd save them, one at a time, and set things right.

They hadn't traveled close to eighteen light-years for nothing, had they?

They still had nukes left to launch them on their homeward trip, but they didn't have to be used safely. Two-million-year old technology or not, she'd make them prove their superiority if she had to.

I'm coming, Klingston. I'm coming.

FIRST, BLOODY CONTACT

Seconds after the elevator doors opened, Frank had to admit to himself that he wasn't in control of the situation. Seconds after that, Frank had to admit to himself that he was in fear for his life.

He had only been in a few honest-to-goodness, out-of-control, in-fear-for-his-life situations. Once had been approaching the alien scout ship, and then with the alien confronting him, not knowing for certain how it would end. Another time, on Earth, he'd been flying his car in a storm despite weather advisories and had clipped another vehicle despite the automatic fail-safe. It didn't happen often, but it did happen. The thing that unified those moments in his mind was how the time had stretched, in some relativistic law of crisis, for him to think a multitude of thoughts that he still recalled clearly for years afterward.

While his car had been spiraling out of control, falling toward the ground, he remembered thinking something like, *No, this can't be happening.* Then he'd thought, *I have too many things to do.* He had, too—this was just shortly before he was supposed to go into deep space. A few seconds later he landed headfirst, his nanofoam had deployed, and cushioned his impact, and he'd walked away unharmed. Physically. He'd spent a few weeks thinking through those terrible moments of spinning and falling, with their memory hitting him at odd and inopportune times, and he'd feared they'd take away his scouting mission. He'd wanted to do important things and be famous, and since he was a smart, talented guy that seemed like one of the more certain ways of reaching his goals. Life was funny.

Like now, he started to think to himself, again: *No, this can't be happening.* Apparently it was his natural reaction. He'd thought it again with his first alien encounter, but the duration of the experience had diluted the thought's impact in a way it hadn't with the car accident.

Again, Frank was falling and spinning, hit in passing by some sort of creature flying out from the elevator car.

The aliens shot out, fast, dark, furry, all limbs. Legs, arms, he didn't know. He was falling and spinning, and so was everyone else.

How could this be happening? Weren't the aliens supposed to be at least two million years more advanced? They seemed to be *attacking* Frank and his people, of all things. This didn't make sense, and the spinning didn't help.

Frank reached out, trying to grab something, anything.

Something flashed, and he pulled back his hand in pain. As he continued to spin out, he looked down at his hand to see the blood popping out in a series of small globules, floating in the microgravity. *This can't be happening.*

He hadn't really been listening yet. Somehow, in all the excitement, he'd stopped hearing anything, or at least being aware of sounds. Now, with his hand throbbing, he listened to the screaming. It didn't seem to be all human screaming. No, there were alien sounds, sounds he'd never heard before, but felt safe in characterizing as "screaming." A crazy, wild, cacophony. The alien sounds were not screams of pain, but screams of exaltation; that was his impression anyway. War cries.

It felt like war to him.

Frank continued to spin, sending out his floating trail of tiny blood bubbles behind him. After a few seconds he bounced off a wall, hard, and careened back into the center of the room.

He really didn't want to be there.

There were limbs flashing, metal glinting, blood spurting, and all the screaming. He actually thought back to the alien scout, the pain, the humiliation, and how quiet it had been during the entire experience. He'd believed, at the time, that the silence had made it worse. Now he thought that the screaming made it worse. He was afraid if he thought about it he could identify some of the screamers.

His fall, his spin, stopped abruptly, as something caught him and held him, tightly. There were sounds in his ear. Harsh, loud, guttural sounds that made no sense.

Frank realized he was making sounds himself, something awful between wheezing and screaming, and tried to make himself stop. He would be dead in seconds, or not, and making awful sounds wouldn't help him either way.

Scant seconds later, and it was over. Not over, not completely, not the significance of the thing, but the initial attack. The screaming stopped, mostly, to be replaced by quieter moans and cries.

Frank looked down at his arms, at his legs, and saw limbs gnarly and hairy, dark brown, holding them, squeezing them. This alien creature held him in a death grip, and he was at its mercy.

He was cockeyed to them, but he saw another alien creature holding on to Towson, who was screaming bloody murder, kicking and biting. As he watched them, the creature lifted something gleaming bright—it seemed to have plenty of limbs to hold Towson and do other things as well—and stabbed it into him, over and over, with great force.

More blood floated out into the room, red and dark.

Frank felt as if he'd been punched in the gut, and wondered if he himself were about to suffer the same fate as well. He breathed, raggedly, loudly, and watched, and waited, and wondered how he could continue to endure what was going on. Tears streamed across his cheeks in every direction, sliding into his eyebrows without gravity to guide them. He wanted to shake his head, shake the tears off, but worried what the thing holding him might do.

He wondered how people felt when being murdered, or worse, tortured to death, and worried that he would find out soon.

Something struck him then. These weren't alien creatures, not exactly. They were *Argonauts. Argonauts!* They looked very much like overgrown spider monkeys, long, eight-limbed, screechy. They were of the technological race from Argo, who had discovered the Spider Star millions of years ago, who had apparently destroyed themselves.

But they hadn't destroyed themselves, not completely. An example of the species now held him so tightly he thought the skin on his arms and legs might just separate and spew out even more blood than already floated in the room. It was the blood of his crewmates, at least a few of whom he counted as friends. They'd all trusted him to lead them, and he had failed, oh how he had failed!

"Aaah!" Frank had started to moan loudly, and the thing holding him, Argonaut, he supposed he should think of it, squeezed him, and he decided to shut up. His heart hurt more than his wounds. What else could he do but shut up and hope not to die? Now, having a few seconds, he also realized it didn't just hold him by his arms and legs, but it pressed something against his throat.

Did it have to be so obvious that the throat was a weak point? Even in just a few seconds aliens, of all things, had figured this out. Insanely, he thought of a slight woman he'd dated back on Earth. She'd studied several martial arts and he'd kind of made fun of her, telling her that the hundred pounds of muscle mass he had on her would make the difference in any fight. She'd just looked back him coldly and calmly said, "Everyone's weak in the throat." He hadn't had any interest in challenging her after that.

The creature holding Frank made a loud sound in his ear. He

thought it was a coherent sound, not dissimilar to the Argonaut language examples he'd heard.

He didn't have a clue what it meant.

The creature made the sound again, more forcefully, and a few other sounds as well.

Frank floated in free fall, helpless in the alien grasp, the universe spinning out of control.

Over his left shoulder, he heard a high piping voice he couldn't place. "Excuse me, but they want you to surrender."

That seemed a redundant request.

There were more sounds from the aliens, and he heard someone shriek—Selene, he thought. Frank found his view rotating. The alien holding him could reach the floor and ceiling simultaneously with its extra limbs, and it turned him until he saw Selene in the assortment of interfaces that had popped out of the surrounded material. Two of the Argonauts were near her, but not holding her the same way that he, and poor Towson, were being held.

Frank realized that a familiar voice was coming from one of Jason's patterns, and that pattern likely understood and spoke the Argonaut language that was being used. He risked talking back to the bot, mindful of what had happened to Towson when he'd struggled. "Tell them we're at their mercy."

No blades stabbed into Frank, and for that he was momentarily grateful, but Jason remained silent much longer than Frank was comfortable with. Finally the X-bot pattern said, and he realized it was Virginia speaking. No—"Ginnie." He'd decided to distance himself from her pattern if he could, even now.

She said, "I advise telling them that you surrender. The most accurate translation of 'at their mercy' would give them permission to eat you. They might do that anyway, it being a common practice among some Argonaut cultures to consume their fallen foes, but I certainly wouldn't tell them to do it."

"Tell them we surrender then!" Frank said, wondering if anyone else out of sight had been killed during this exchange.

Ginnie made some strange noises and the pressure against his throat eased, but did not vanish. Insanely he thought: *Yes, that's it, we're striking back.* Such thoughts flew through his head, he seemed out of control of his own mind as much as he was out of control of the situation.

There was silence of a sort, then. There was moaning, crying, coming from all around him, but not loudly. He had a flash to what ancient battlefields must have sounded like after the explosions and yelling had ceased, and just the suffering of the shell-shocked and wounded remained.

Then Frank was moving, or his captor was moving, and Frank was moving with him. They approached Jason and Selene. As they drew near, he could make out Virginia's face in the display of the X-bot. It was crazy, but he suddenly felt embarrassed.

"Isn't this exciting?" the pattern of his wife said to Frank. "Living Argonauts speaking a recognizable Argonaut dialect?"

Frank had just watched a good, frightened man be stabbed to death by an alien creature and the aftermath of adrenaline made him feel sick. Excitement in this instance was not fun, and as much as he resented the thoughtless words of his "wife," the X-bot, how could he find fault with a robotic, scanned pattern? It wasn't really her, and it wasn't able to respond the same way she would. Besides, he was just happy these creatures couldn't actually hurt her. She was only a pattern here.

He wished that they had Drone with them. Drone was war-equipped, and might have managed to put up a fight even if instructed to take their lead. It didn't seem that the Argonauts had any weapons other than knives or some other sort of blade. A number of Specialists had skill in free-fall combat . . . and they were with Rusk or Griffin.

Frank had all the techies and Argonaut scholars with him. Well, Walter was combat-trained, but Frank didn't see him or hear him and feared the worst.

Frank was too shocked to feel stupid.

He tried not to think of his family, even though Ginnie was here with him.

The Argonaut holding him made more loud sounds, and shook him.

Jason, or Ginnie, rather, speaking from the X-bot, said, "It's rather mad. It thinks you ought to be able to speak their language, and is plenty upset you can't. By the way, it knows you're the leader here."

"How's it know that?" Frank asked.

"I don't know. My guess is that they're really good with body language, even in humans. Argonaut society, while seeming chaotic at first glance, had a very clear hierarchy to those within it."

The pressure returned to Frank's throat. Okay, they knew he was the leader and didn't question it further. "Ask them what they want, Ginnie."

The strange loud, guttural sounds issued from the X-bot again. After hearing the reply, Ginnie said, "They want your weapons, everything of value, especially your . . . um, this is a hard one to translate properly . . . 'sustenance trophy.' "

Frank didn't know what that last term meant, and the exchange overall didn't make Frank feel any better about the situation. His group had no weapons with them. All the weapons they had were back on the *Dark Heart*.

That got Frank to thinking. Griffin and Robb were back on the ship, safe at least for the moment. Did they know what was going on? Was there a way to salvage the situation? How had Griffin reacted when Gina had conveyed his message?

Sloan Griffin was a careful, paranoid woman, and he could guess what she was doing right now. He needed to find a way to stall.

The wild card in all this was that he wasn't dealing with humans. He didn't know if they lied, bluffed, or were always scrupulously honest. He didn't know how they handled hostage situations. Human governments tended to refuse to deal with hostage takers, while smaller groups and individuals always did. Which was the correct solution usually depended on whether or not there would be repeated encounters, and that was sort of a moot question given his position. He knew he *should* know more about the Argonaut species and civilization, from living with Virginia if nothing else, but the truth was that he didn't know much except for the most basic details. Who could have expected that they'd encounter living, breathing Argonauts after so long?

No one could have.

Was that a good enough excuse for his family? Sounded like something Kenny would have said to him. *No one could have expected it.*

How many of his mates were dead now? He had no way to tell. He could ask, he supposed, but how would they, aliens, react to such a question when they had just made a demand of their own? How long did aliens regard as reasonable to think over their request?

He imagined he might be able to ask more questions, win a little time, but how would they react to that?

Frank smelled something faint, but pleasant, and at the same time noticed a slickness where he was being held. Lord knew he was sweating, but this seemed to be coming from the Argonaut holding him. Did they sweat? He should remember. What did it mean when they did?

The Argonaut screamed at him, leaving his ears ringing, and

something pricked his weak throat. He didn't need Ginnie to translate that.

"Tell them we surrender! Tell them they can have what they want from us!"

What else could he do?

The X-bot spoke their language. The grip on him did not relax and the blade remained pressed into his soft flesh. The alien spoke again, still loud and angry-sounding.

"What's wrong?"

Ginnie said, "They say you've already agreed and you are to make it happen using your authority. They haven't seen any clear response yet."

What did they expect from him, magic tricks? All he could do was talk, and he assumed that everyone else was similarly held. "Please, ask them to be more specific."

It sounded stupid when he said it, already bleeding, completely cowed. Here he was, asking for more specific instructions.

The X-bot didn't make any sounds, not immediately, then it said in English, "I've thought about it some more. I'm not sure I made the best translation. You are to tell everyone to surrender, to say"—the bot made a strange sound, a sound like a whimper—"and then hand over the sustenance trophies and any weapons."

Okay, they had to say "uncle," at least those that were still alive to say it. They were dealing with aliens. If that would satisfy them, so be it. "All right. But we don't have any weapons. Tell them that."

"We don't?" Ginnie asked.

Anger flashed in Frank, and then subsided. He was engaged with a pattern—one he knew too well—but it didn't really know the full capabilities of the team's equipment. They had some analysis tools that could be construed as weapons that would be at least as effective as *knives*, of all things, and they had an entire armory back on the *Dark Heart*. No need to give all that away. "We have no weapons in this room. Tell them."

Ginnie made the funny sounds again and got a response. She translated, slowly, "They accept that seeing as how easily conquered we were, but now they insist on the surrenders or they kill more people."

Frank felt a pain in his chest, as if some small but important organ had just imploded. Kill more people. *Just how many were dead?* He wished he could look around to see, and he was happy that he could not. "Okay, Ginnie. Make the sounds again, and tell everyone to say them. I don't know if everyone can hear me."

The X-bot broadcast the alien terms and Frank forced himself to listen. He heard voices around the room—not enough!—repeating them, and he did himself. Shocked, empty. There was no meaning in the sounds. They were just sounds they had to make to let this horror show get to the next scene so maybe it could finish. He wished he were in a comedy, even one of those disgusting ones with the Swedish clowns that had been so popular when he'd been a kid.

Suddenly, Frank was spinning as he was wrapped in some kind of rope, or twine, and then he was floating, pushed toward one of the walls. He hit it lightly, and, unlike previous times when he'd bounced off the walls in these rooms, he stuck this time. He didn't know if it was something the Argonauts had done or the nature of the twine enveloping him.

He hadn't hit face-first, and had a partial view of the room.

His first reaction was to close his eyes, sick, but he forced himself to open his eyes back up and survey the situation with all the cold logic he could muster.

He got his first chance to look at a live Argonaut from a distant perspective. The creature superficially resembled a larger version of the spider monkey on Argo: dark, hairy, eight limbs—four below a body break and four above. The head sported large black eyes without eyelids and a mouth of large, squared-off teeth. None of them wore clothing, at least not that he could recognize as such, although all of the Argonauts he could see had various colored bands around their appendages—red, blue, green, maroon. He didn't know if they were decorative, or what. The Argonauts were definitely longer than humans, and wider, but he couldn't say that they massed much more. Remembering the grip that held him, he thought they were probably stronger than humans. Seemed like everything was.

Selene had been extracted from the Spider Star equipment and had been wrapped up and stuck on the wall as he was, but not all the Specialists had been so treated. He saw Towson's body floating alone, and Timothy's as well. Where was Walter? There, he saw, floating limply. He presumed they were dead. Melinda seemed to be alive, however, and for that he was glad.

The Argonauts spoke to each other. He thought there was only seven of them, but couldn't tell for sure because he couldn't tell them apart. Even more maddening, he couldn't tell anything about what was going on from their body language. Alien. Helpless, he groped for some course of action. He worked up his courage to speak, and finally said in a low, steady voice, "Ginnie, can you translate for us?"

They ignored him. The Argonauts didn't seem to mind them talking, apparently. Melinda and Selene seemed too shocked to talk, or didn't have anything to say. He wished someone had a great idea, a miracle idea, that would end the nightmare, but no human said a thing.

"As best I can," Ginnie replied eagerly. "This is a remarkable opportunity."

While the patterns were good expert systems and even reproduced personality, they were far from perfect copies. For one thing, they had no sense of self-preservation—the autonomous X-bot systems were programmed for preservation but would violate those provisions if ordered. He was glad he could think of the pattern as Ginnie and not Virginia. It helped that he couldn't easily see her face in the bot's display.

"Something about their great deeds, and bravery, and their might. Oh, not 'their' meaning the whole group, the 'their' meaning the three holding our people. They've distinguished themselves somehow and earned a bounty, a trophy."

Frank hadn't worried much about that condition of their surrender, but now an electric shock tensed every muscle. What were they going to do to them? "Ask them! Ask them what is going to happen!"

"Very well," Ginnie said, taking a moment, then speaking again in the alien tongue.

The Argonauts ignored her.

Desperation ignited in Frank, all the worse because his imagination likely conjured worse demons than reality held. "Everyone, Selene, Melinda; yell, get their attention!"

Selene's voice, high and shrill, but alert and angry, called out. He worried more about the people he could not hear, like Melinda.

The Argonauts ignored them.

Then he worried more when Melinda started shrieking. Two Argonauts used their long limbs to walk themselves along the floor and ceiling and grasped her arms from each side. The one that had held her now slid over to one side and held her left shoulder with one arm, held her forearm with another, and proceeded to wrap her biceps tightly with a rope with third and fourth hands. After it had completed tying off the rope, it placed its large, brutal blade against her right elbow.

Without pause or ceremony, the creature began to saw into Melinda's arm.

As her shrieks became loud screams, it proceeded with its

steady sawing, but took a fourth arm and wrapped its broad, splayed-fingered hand over her face to stifle the sounds.

Frank wanted to look away, but forced himself to watch. He was the executive director, and he was responsible. He had to watch. It seemed a sharp blade, but it took some time to cut through anyway.

Frank wished for a miracle, and wishing for it, realized that such a thing was possible—they weren't alone. His shock had been so deep, so profound, his demoralization so sudden and deep, he'd forgotten about Griffin. She could do something! She could save them! She was paranoid, right? She was a security freak, right? She'd do better than him in this situation. She wouldn't get surprised.

He should have told her to be careful!

As bad as watching Melinda get her arm sawed off, what came next was worse. The badly translated term *sustenance trophy* should have tipped him off. The Argonaut finished cutting of her arm just below the elbow and pulled it away. The creature immediately put it into its mouth and began tearing jagged pieces away from it.

Frank experienced another one of the those tunnel-vision moments, with stretched time, remembering when he'd been back on his farm and had torn the nasty, biting spider monkeys off his goat. He remembered hoping one of them got enough of his blood that it killed it. There was enough blood floating around the room, but none of the Argonauts had directly in-gested it like this. The toxicity of their blood was extreme and extended to most Argotian species. He assumed that would in-clude Argonauts as well. And right now he hoped so. It would be a little miracle.

He didn't say anything. He could barely make a sound. Part of him welcomed the coming revenge, and he felt sure it would come soon, but part of him feared the retribution they could receive in return. He was more afraid the creature would suffer no ill effects.

As soon as he thought that, the Argonaut chewing on Melinda's arm made an awful sound. It didn't sound like a scream, not a human scream anyway. It was more of a grating sound, the sound of something hard being polished with great force, more of a *screeching* than a screaming. The smell hit him next. While the smell from the Argonaut who had held him had been sweet, this new smell was rotten. He had read about strange plants with flowers that smelled rank and rotting in order to attract insects attracted to that sort of thing, and, although he had never smelled one, he imagined they might smell like this. And then Melinda's arm floated free to slowly tumble, released from the creature's grip.

They began screaming and yelling at each other with what seemed to Frank as ridiculous amounts of gesticulation. When an eight-limbed creature gesticulates, it is a sight, he decided. He couldn't help but smile at how upset they were. This was a perverse situation and he didn't fault his perverse thought. "What are they saying?"

The X-bot answered with Ginnie's voice: "Oh, they're quite upset. The first trophy-taker seems to be dead and they don't know why. Oh, they decided that quickly."

"What?" Selene asked.

Frank was happy to hear someone else speak up instead of merely moaning, but then he realized that the Argonauts had gone quiet and had turned their attention to him. They came toward him and didn't stop until they were close. Very close. The lead Argonaut, the one who had held him initially, he thought, put its mouth within six inches of Frank's face and began yelling. The creature paused finally, and breathed sweet breath into Frank.

Ginnie translated. "They are quite upset about what's just happened."

Frank gathered that, but didn't dare say anything with this creature's giant dark eyes staring into his.

Ginnie went on. "They want to know what you're going to do now about their loss. They want to know—"

Shots rang out.

That phrase sounded trite to Frank even as he thought it, but it was what was happening and it was the phrase that first sprang to mind. The Argonaut in his face whipped around and Frank was afforded a glance beyond it.

Two armored Specialists and an X-bot—presumably Lance, what with Drone off with Rusk—wielding automatic weapons, were floating slowly away from the portal, weapons pointed menacingly.

Frank briefly wondered what happened to the shots. Would the walls of this place absorb them, or let them bounce? He didn't know and he hadn't noticed. One of those odd, irrelevant crisis thoughts. The initial shots had seemed merely a warning, at least insofar as no one had cried out at being shot. As the Argonauts were close to their human captives, it seemed likely the shots were warnings and not all that close to actually hitting any living targets.

Focus, man, focus!

The Argonauts began howling, loud, wild, whooping noises that deafened Frank. It was a cacophony, worse even than the spider monkeys back on Argo. He knew he was old, but he thought that this would deafen the most noise-hardened teenager.

Suddenly, without warning, he was grabbed, plucked off the wall. He was being carried. Others were, too. Everything was violent, rapid motion. No up, no down, just accelerations. After all the jostling, he found himself in the elevator with the Argonauts and at least four or five Specialists and his X-bot Jason.

He heard Griffin yelling, "Stop! Stop!"

Then the wall closed up between them and he fell toward what he had thought of previously as the ceiling. The elevator car accelerated down into the Spider Star at what felt like close to Earth's gravity.

DIGESTING THE SITUATION

The silver globule rose behind the dirigible, inexorable, relentless.

At first Rusk had been optimistic, and tried broadcasting the same Argonaut hail that had garnered them the docking. The globe had not returned the hail, nor had it changed its threatening approach in any way.

It bore on toward them at high velocity, unwavering.

He'd had Slyde pilot the hell out of the ship. They'd tried hiding in clouds, but the aliens had unsurprisingly discovered radar, or one of dozens of equivalent technologies, and had not hesitated. They'd tried spiraling around the backside of the Spider Star spoke, but had been unable to keep it between them and the globe. The silver globule was faster than their dirigible.

Rusk had nearly run out of options.

He was sorely tempted to start thinking of all the things they should have done: take a space plane instead of a dirigible, not drop a probe, and stay on Argo.

No, he refused to consider that this mission to the Spider Star was an inherent mistake. After all, two million years ago the Argonauts had come here and achieved their goals. Humans had to be able to do at least as well.

"The globule is almost upon us," Slyde said.

So it was. It was within a hundred kilometers, and on the scale of the Spider Star, that wasn't all that far. Given their relative velocities it wasn't all that far, either.

Rusk wanted to curse out loud, to throw a tantrum, but he wouldn't do such a thing unless he was alone. He was being grossly outclassed by the alien technology, and it didn't seem fair.

Fair enough—things wouldn't be fair. They were not just decades or even centuries behind the times, not even millennia, but megayears. *Megayears.* That was an insane amount of time. Who could even comprehend what that meant? They were prayer wheels beseeching an unknown god, at best, asking for a miracle they didn't deserve. At worst they were ants, ants in a magnifying glass. As a kid, he'd once gotten some friends to put on ant costumes, and then while a few hundred feet up flying in a car he'd said, "Hey look, those people down there look just like ants!" His parents had ignored him and that had been the end of his career in comedy.

If the game wasn't fair, then you had to cheat to win. The problem was, even if it hadn't been against his nature, Rusk didn't know how to cheat in this situation.

Okay, if the silver globule was coming for them, did it have to be hostile? No, it didn't, even if it didn't seem overly friendly. It might well take hostile action if they provoked it, but did dropping a probe reach the threshold of provocation? If it did, they were lost already.

He made a decision. "Full stop. Let's float in the wind and wait for our friends."

There was a hesitation from Slyde, who had until now been doing his best to keep them away from the alien thing. Finally he said, "Full stop."

The dirigible became quiet, with no more wind from their passage, and very smooth.

"I'm going outside," Rusk announced. It made as much sense as any other action, perhaps more. Surely no creature living here could have seen a human before. Maybe if they showed themselves, that would display some goodwill and pique the curiosity of those piloting the silver globule. "Anyone who wants can join me, just make sure you broadcast anything important to the exterior speakers, and be listening on the audio pickups for me."

Rusk went through the airlock to the gondola and stepped out on the catwalk. There were no rules now. These were not situations anyone had anticipated in enough detail to write rules for. Rusk decided it was time for him to start making his own rules in earnest.

Outside the air was warm, if a touch humid, and altogether pleasant. The light coming from below, however, engendered a feeling of disquiet within him, a reminder that this was a whole place where the usual rules didn't apply. He slipped his fingers through the wire mesh of the catwalk cage, holding the cool composite material loosely, and looked toward the direction where the globule would approach.

After a moment he heard the airlock doors cycle again and tentative footsteps sliding toward him. Without looking he said, "A beautiful, peaceful view, isn't it Anatole?"

The man laughed. "And how did you know it was me?"

"You're the craziest one of us."

"Second craziest, Manuel. Only second craziest, now."

They stood in silence, balanced between rising and falling, in perfect equilibrium with the wind.

Mistelle came over the loudspeaker. "It's almost here. You should be able to see it momentarily."

Rusk felt strangely ambivalent. He supposed it was because the situation was beyond his control, which was very unusual for him. Why should he be invested if he had no control?

"This is fun," Anatole said.

That almost made Rusk crack up, but he resisted. Just because he felt out of control now didn't mean he would remain out of control in the upcoming encounter.

"There it is!" Rusk said.

A region of the sky before them appeared odd, warped. That

had to be it. The region grew larger as he watched, and he was sure. "Mistelle, can you estimate the albedo?"

The albedo was the fraction of light the object reflected. Mistelle answered, "Better than ninety-nine percent. I can't be more accurate right now without active scanning."

"That's okay," Rusk said. "I was just curious."

And he was very curious, especially since part of himself recognized this as a life and death situation. For all he knew this was a smart bomb designed to track down intruders and blow them to bits.

So be it. It was a done deal.

Part of him marveled at his detachment and disdain. This was a new side of himself.

Then the sky opened.

The reflective surface of the approaching globule was so good that it was excellent camouflage, but inside, it was dark. A shadowed region just popped into existence.

"Would you look at that," Anatole said. "That's fucking amazing."

"No shit," Rusk said, getting into the moment. Four-letter words distinguished the uniqueness of the event, if not the perverseness. Rusk tried to save such words for significant events, and this had to qualify, although part of him wondered why he hadn't been cursing continuously since coming out of hibernation.

The dark region continued to grow larger, apparently getting closer. The dirigible was a half kilometer long, and more than a hundred meters along the other axis. The dark region, Rusk thought, was at least three hundred meters across, maybe a little larger. Perspective was difficult to achieve. The silvery region surrounding the darkness, that was impossibly huge and hard to estimate, but it had to be measured in kilometers.

Rusk allowed himself the freedom to enjoy the experience of seeing a cave in the sky. He'd never even imagined such a thing, and there it was, hanging there before him, growing closer, growing more real.

Mistelle said, "The alien craft isn't slowing. It's continuing to head straight for us with the same velocity as when we first spotted it."

There was some famous quote about consistency that Rusk couldn't recall that probably summed up this situation. Rusk was simultaneously exalted and disappointed that ancient sayings could wrap up such an incredible situation.

"We're in for it now," Rusk said to Anatole.

"Nothing we can do."

"Not at all."

Together they watched the approaching hole of darkness flying through the sky. Anatole said, "Manuel, I know men don't say such things to each other often, but I wanted to let you know I find you interesting. You've made this mission interesting, and I'm not just saying that."

"I appreciate you telling me that," Rusk said.

Slyde's voice came over the speaker. "It's almost on us. What do you want me to do?"

Inappropriately, Rusk thought that Slyde's words constituted the perfect straight line. He responded seriously even though he was dying to release some tension. "Don't do anything. They have the power here. Let them do what they want, and we'll respond as we can."

Even as he was giving his instructions, the cavern was swallowing them, growing to fill a large fraction of the sky.

"Did you ever see such a thing?" Anatole asked.

"Of course not."

"Imagine it?"

"No."

The dark region closed on them, swallowed them, as if they were floating into a cave instead of the other way around. As the sky vanished, they began to be able to see into the interior. Well, they couldn't see much, but they could make out the general shape: oval. Maybe. It was very dark.

The hole that had swallowed them began to close, shrinking smoothly from its edges into its center. As the light vanished, Rusk felt especially vulnerable and naked. The silence became even more pronounced, even painful. "Do you want to go back inside?"

"No!" Anatole said. He probably didn't mean to be so loud, but it came out that way. "Mistelle and the others will let us know if we can't keep breathing. Otherwise I want to see things firsthand."

"All right." Maybe Rusk himself wasn't the craziest one there—which was what he'd thought all along.

The dirigible was still floating in the air in the dark cavity, lit only by their own operating lights. Mistelle's voice broadcast out to them, "We're not seeing much of anything in here, not even on the night vision or thermal systems. It's like we're in a void. I'm going to brighten it up."

"Go ahead," Rusk answered.

A ring of floodlights lining the sides of the dirigible ignited, spilling billions of candlepower into the darkness around them.

The darkness swallowed it.

"Weird," said Anatole.

Weird indeed. The interior, which he'd thought to be oval-shaped—a giant version of their own ship—had to be at least as absorbent of light as the exterior was reflective.

"How about more active probing?" Rusk asked. "Radar, lidar, sonar?"

"Yes, I'm getting bounces, but down a factor of a thousand from what I'd normally expect."

Her word *normally* made Rusk wonder how many times Mistelle had been swallowed by alien vessels, but that was a small, trite thing to think and would be an even smaller thing to say out loud.

"Personally, I'd expect a parade," Anatole said.

"Hey, I want you two back in here," Mistelle said.

"Why?" Rusk asked.

"The chamber we're inside is shrinking."

Back inside, Rusk said, "Show me what's happening."

Mistelle showed him the time series of their active sensor measurements. The walls around them in all directions were creeping in at about a meter a second.

"I can walk faster than that!" Anatole said.

"Walk to where?" Rusk asked.

Anatole shut up then, finally. Rusk said to the group, "What do you think is going on? Is it eating us?"

Kat said, "No, I don't think so. If they wanted to do that they wouldn't just have the walls close in on us, and not slowly."

Rusk agreed with her, but wanted to get everyone thinking about the new problem quickly.

Mistelle said, "I'd like to think they'd want to look us over before digesting us. I mean, we're a new, unique species and they should be interested in us."

Rusk hoped so, but didn't necessarily agree with her optimism. Maybe they were bugs here, and if you'd seen a few bugs, how interested would you be to see more? You smacked them, cleaned them up, and went on with your affairs. The few exceptions didn't help his attitude; he had briefly gone out with a girl in New Colchis who he'd watched shoo a wasp out a window rather than kill it, and that had ended their budding relationship.

"Can we see anything yet?" Kat asked.

"Let's find out," Mistelle replied. "I'm setting up some image processing routines to enhance the scientific-grade detectors. Let's see what we have."

An image appeared on the big display of Mistelle's workstation, but Rusk couldn't make sense of it. What was he looking at? Some kind of fractal pattern?

Anatole said, "That's weird! Can you get stereo, and combine it with the distance information to get a scale?"

"All right," she answered.

The workstation display shifted from 2-D to 3-D, and helpful scales appeared, along with a steadily decreasing number indicating the distance from their dirigible. The pattern changed in real time as they watched. It was like watching grass grow, with some time lapse, or a spider build its web.

"What we're watching," Mistelle announced, "is some kind of growing mesh, a foam perhaps. It's coming at us from all directions, and will impact us momentarily."

Kat said, "We have some weapons, here in the armory. We could try to destroy it."

That didn't sound very reasonable to anyone and the idea died in the air. What were they going to do, shoot it? Rusk couldn't see any alternatives, and again considered whether this foam was a threat. Was it really coming to digest them? What other purposes could it serve?

And then, during a gap in the discussion, it was upon them.

"It's on us," Mistelle said.

And then . . . nothing.

"What's happening?" Rusk asked. "I don't feel anything."

Mistelle zapped through a dozen diagnostic screens. "It doesn't seem to be doing much of anything. It's just holding us."

Then the gravity shifted.

"We're accelerating!" Porter said, redundantly.

"I know!" Mistelle said. "I'm trying to set up a display to show us where we're going."

Anatole said, "Looks like the foam is there to hold us for the acceleration. I don't think they're going to digest us! Just going to keep us from knocking about unnecessarily."

They knew where they were, at least in relation to the Spider Star, before they'd been swallowed. By keeping track of their accelerations, they could figure out their motion.

A new display appeared, a 3-D display of the spokes of the Spider Star. The red dotted path was making a beeline for the nearest spoke, albeit losing altitude rapidly.

"We should thank them if we get the chance," Kat said. "I think they can accelerate a lot faster than this. They could turn us into jelly."

Rusk didn't strictly know if that were true, but he filed away the possibility. Were they bugs, or were they a prize? He just didn't know and he'd be at great disadvantage until he figured out the answer.

They flew onward, held snugly in their quiet, dark, cave in the sky, until only about ten minutes later there came a large deceleration that didn't require sensitive instruments to feel. Mistelle's display showed that they'd reached the spoke.

Slyde walked down from his command chair on the bridge. "I'm not exactly piloting anymore, so I thought I'd come on down and join you. I hope that's okay."

He said the last part looking at Rusk. Rusk nodded. "I don't know that we're still an airship, so if all the systems are secure, welcome to the committee of confusion."

"Hey, committee of confusion . . . I like that!" Anatole said.

Rusk didn't like it. He didn't like being funny. Things were very serious and while he believed that recent events indicated they weren't going to die any time soon, that was about as much as he did believe.

"The foam, the mesh, whatever, it's dissolving!" Mistelle announced.

And so it was. They felt a slight wobble as the foam let them go and their natural buoyancy supported them again.

"I have infrared signatures!" Mistelle said, even more forcefully than her previous announcement.

"Show us," Rusk said.

The display shimmered, and a dozen white shapes materialized.

"Zoom in on one of them," he requested.

"Here you go, optical-infrared composite image."

It took him a moment to make sense of what he was seeing. It wasn't a machine, and it wasn't human, and that made it difficult.

A large, round shape filled the top part of the image. Below the large, round shape protruded an assortment of long, thin shapes. He eventually recognized these as legs, or arms, some of them at least. There were a lot of them, whatever they were. Another round shape under the larger one could be a body, or a head.

"They're balloons!" said Kat.

As soon as she floated that idea, Rusk had to admit that it was likely. The shapes were moving smoothly toward them across an open expanse without moving their limbs. The large part of them probably was floating, presumably buoyant, and holding them up. Despite their mode of locomotion, the part that struck Rusk most forcefully was the multitude of limbs, glistening, slick limbs. Even though they weren't sporting a multitude of heads—probably not anyway—the multitude of arms made him think of the old Argonaut myth.

"All those arms, legs hanging down, not heads, but I'd be more inclined to think of them as hydras," he said.

"Great!" said Anatole. "They're hydras. Still, what matters is what they *do,* or *don't* do."

The things approached, their skin slick and glistening. As they did and the resolution improved, it became clear they were holding things, devices, tools, something.

"The question is," said Slyde, "what are they planning to do with those?"

They found out soon enough. The hydras settled down just outside the dirigible and then applied their tools. There were sparks, grating sounds. Rusk even thought he felt a slight shudder pass through the floor. Part of the mesh cage protecting the catwalk peeled away. One of the creatures grabbed hold and floated off with it.

"They're taking us apart," Mistelle said. "And they haven't even asked."

"We can't just let them do that," Rusk said. "Let's do something about it. Slyde, take Drone down to the armory and prepare a light show of resistance."

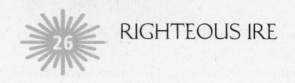

RIGHTEOUS IRE

ONBOARD THE SPIDER STAR

Griffin watched as the gray walls grew to cover the opening to the far room, to cover Frank and the other Specialists, to cover the familiar-looking alien creatures. "Lance, did you get anything from Jason?"

"Yes," the X-bot answered in its neutral, non-patterned voice. "I have a full record of the events that transpired. I infer that the room they've just entered is not just a room, but an elevator car."

Damn! They were sure moving down now, probably at high velocity. They were likely out of reach . . . at least for the time being. "Do you know how to operate the elevator? Do you know where they're going?"

The image in Lance's display shifted from neutral gray and the face of a skinny Asian man appeared. "Hell yes, I can operate a simple elevator! And I'll tell you where they're going. They're going *down*! Get it?"

Everyone was a comedian, even long-dead patterns embedded in X-bots on this ill-fated mission. It was hard to wind up with only what you wanted when you patterned someone. Bits of personality did leak through. "I get it. Get another car here as soon as possible."

Griffin didn't know if she should follow them in another elevator or not. On the Argo system, the next car would follow hours later than the previous car. She didn't know how close they needed to keep, but hours seemed like a lot.

Gina floated up to her, a little too fast, sending the pair of them flying and spinning when she glommed onto her. "Melinda needs attention. I need to get her back to the *Dark Heart*. She's had her entire arm hacked off!"

God, it was true. Melinda floated in the middle of the room, spinning wildly, holding the stump of an arm that trailed a stream of blood bubbles. It was an awful thing to see. *My God, Melinda!*

Thankfully Gina hadn't made it back here before the attack began, and had been able to follow Griffin and Robb immediately after the aliens had fled. She intercepted Melinda, grabbed hold of her, and shouted out, "Can someone find her arm? I need her arm, damn it!"

Melinda groaned obscenely.

The whole situation was surreal, and definitely not one covered in her training. There was worse than Melinda missing her arm. She floated by Towson Field, his face slack and discolored, his light blue jumpsuit stained dark with his own blood. He'd been so efficient, so productive, and now his life was cut short. She couldn't believe that a first encounter with an intelligent alien species could end this way, especially with the most experienced human in the universe leading their side.

Apparently such experience was overrated.

Griffin often adopted the position of devil's advocate when she played out hypotheticals, but she'd never imagined she'd see something like this. The smell of blood permeated the air—what was sane about that?

And now these aliens, Argonauts apparently, had hostages. Worst-case scenario indeed.

There was an additional feeling of betrayal. Humans lived on Argo, the Argonauts' home world, and knew of them from their relics and recordings. Of the tiny number of alien civilizations that humans knew about, it didn't seem fair that one of them would hurt them like this. Better it be some random, awful species. The fact that they knew of so few aliens and to have a violent encounter like this on a first encounter . . . it implied that the universe was a very, very dangerous place.

The best minds had said, for centuries, that advanced alien species would be enlightened and would pose no threat to humanity. They had said they'd be so advanced they would need nothing from us, and would be pleased to provide help and guidance.

What shitty advice. Empirical evidence trumped the best theory. Always.

Have no expectations, expect the worst, and be thrilled with the best. That was what Griffin believed before this, and that belief was only reinforced now. *My God,* she thought, *they'd cut off Melinda's arm!*

"We've got one of them," Robb said from behind her. "Not totally one-sided."

Griffin spun around as best she could and saw Jack Robb's serious face behind the diamond mask of his helmet. Then she saw what the Specialist was holding: the body of an Argonaut.

The alien was longer than a human, but not necessarily much more bulky. Long, thick bristles covered its dark body. Griffin looked at its head; greenish foam bubbled up from its mouth.

"We got it," he said simply. She'd seen enough examples of dead predators from Argo that had tried to eat Specialists out on training missions. He said, "There is some justice in this unholy place."

Buoyed forth by the notion that these aliens had already paid at least a small price for their transgressions, Griffin took action. "We're going after them. We're getting our people back."

There were no cheers, no smiles. The situation was too awful, too grim, but Griffin did think that there was a sense of determination in the eyes of the people there with her.

She hoped so, anyway.

———

There were only faint radio frequency signatures that rapidly faded to undetectablility. Whatever was in the elevator shaft of the Spider Star shielded those signals from the chips implanted in Klingston and the others.

"They're going down," Robb said. "Where else can they go?"

Griffin sat, strapped in a chair, in the *Dark Heart*'s command center with Melinda, Robb, and the X-bots Lance, Einstein, Marlo, and Kurtz.

"You need to follow them and punish them," Melinda said.

She was right, of course, at one level. If these aliens were going to interact with humans and perform unspeakable acts like cutting off their arms, they had to be prepared to face the consequences. Marlo had communicated to Lance how Selene had operated the Spider Star interface, and the fact they'd apparently used it to figure out that the Argonauts were coming up.

"Okay," Griffin said. "We'll follow them, using the alien interface, and maybe we can figure out how to operate the elevator. And we'll follow them physically, outside the spokes of the Spider Star. Inside if we can. We'll wait for them to stick up their heads, and when they do, we'll cut them off."

It was such a powerful statement for her, especially the way she said it, that Griffin repeated it. "When they stick up their heads, we'll cut them off."

Griffin prepared, working primarily from the *Dark Heart* command center, directing and delegating as she could. She had her tiny crew prepped and the space plane was ready to go. She had Melinda supervising Lance, working on figuring out the interface and the elevator. She had Gina performing an autopsy on the dead Argonaut. She had her own determination solidified. She would do whatever was necessary to protect her people. She wished there were some way to nuke the Argonauts from orbit without hurting the hostages, because she would do it. She seriously would. They were monsters, taking hostages the way they did, making people worry. Making *her* worry. She would take them out from orbit if she could.

She wondered at herself, at the elemental forces kindled inside her. She'd never hated anyone before, not like this, but her feelings seemed heartfelt. Sure, she'd had a few petty jealousies as a teenager, but for the most part she got along with people. On a small colony world like Argo, you had to get along. If you screwed up and upset people, where could you go that people wouldn't know you were an ass? And if you were an ass, they sure weren't going to send you out on a Specialist mission.

Seventeen hours after the elevator opening had shut, Kurtz announced, "We're receiving signals from Klingston and the other missing Specialists. They're down at an altitude of twenty-five hundred kilometers, on the Spider Star spoke, but moving away from it slowly."

She didn't stop to worry about how they might be moving away from the spoke. There were other structures down there, tubes connecting the spokes, platforms, stuff. She had a space plane. She would catch them.

"Jack?" she said.

His sleepy voice came over the broadcast system. "Yeah?"

"I want the space plane ready to go in ten minutes. My task force will meet you there. Can you handle that?"

"Absolutely!" Robb said, sounding instantly energized.

She licked her lips and said, more quietly, "They've poked up their heads. We know what comes next."

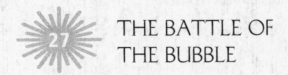

THE BATTLE OF
THE BUBBLE

27

INSIDE A SILVERY GLOBULE

Rusk remained on the flight deck with Mistelle, Anatole, and Kat. Together they watched the various monitors and hoped that the hydras wouldn't dismantle them before the situation could be resolved.

He spoke to Slyde, waiting by the primary airlock with Drone. "We're going to try a few things before we commit you to action."

"Roger that," said Slyde. "I'd be plenty happy not to go out there, and I think I speak for everyone here."

"I understand," said Rusk. And he did. From Slyde's point of view, this had to be like when Rusk had been told he was taking on Klingston as executive mission director. You did what you were told for the good of everyone, even if you didn't like it yourself. You trusted those around you, or acted as if you did, anyway, which was almost the same thing. If you maximized everyone's good, you yourself were likely to come out ahead. That didn't mean you couldn't look out for yourself, but there were situations, and there were situations.

This was a situation. And just because he was potentially placing Slyde into it didn't mean that he himself wouldn't be in it, too, and soon. They were all already in it.

He was procrastinating. He had no rules to follow. No manuals. No guidelines. He was already in deeper than his scouting plan permitted. So much for mission plans. His next actions would be judged on their own merits.

Rusk's only consolation was that he probably wouldn't have

to suffer a bad judgment if they survived this excursion. He'd get to write the history.

"Okay," he said. "Mistelle, hit them with the sirens."

He hoped this wouldn't be pathetic.

Their internal audio system maxed out and limited the screeching sounds piped in from the external mikes. Even so, the sounds were loud and they were annoying. But what if the aliens found such sounds pleasant and sweet, or perhaps erotic, resembling mating calls of their own species? He had no answers to these what-if scenarios, other than experiment. So what was the outcome of this particular experiment?

The creatures he'd christened "hydras" worked on, unperturbed.

"What's wrong with them?" Anatole yelled, plugging his ears with his fingers and grimacing.

"Maybe they're deaf?" Kat suggested, making a squinty, unattractive face.

After another twenty seconds, Rusk had to agree. They were deaf, or they were so alien they didn't care. He, on the other hand, was not deaf and did care. "Cut it, Mistelle!"

"Shit," said Kat.

They'd already hit them with floodlights, and now sound. They had no means of projecting smells. Their ability to project an exterior electric field was limited. They didn't have a lot of other things they could do to dissuade this salvage operation without sending out Slyde and the others. Crap, he just wanted to talk with them! The dirigible was a ship of exploration, not designed for military operations. They'd carried an armory to cover their bases, but hadn't expected to engage in any sort of combat.

"We could outgas the reactor," Anatole said.

Hmm, that *was* an option. They had multiple ways of cooling their reactor and could shift from full hydro to the air system, and they had a modicum of control over how the superheated gases were expelled—it was a handy feature for an airship to possess. It seemed a little extreme, but he didn't have any other ideas. "Let's direct it outwards, not right at any of them, but close enough for them to feel a burn, okay?"

"All right," Mistelle said. "Here goes."

The dirigible shuddered, and Rusk could hear a distant pinging from some air duct someplace.

He watched the camera feeds carefully.

The hydras outside shifted a few meters away from the hot zone. That was all.

What were they, robots?

He clenched his jaw, holding it in. Anger was not what was required here. At least he didn't think so, and he certainly hoped not. "Adrian," he said to Slyde. "You're going to have to go out there."

"Right," came the immediate response.

Rusk went over it one more time because it was so important. "Go outside, just outside the airlock, and let them get a look at you. Don't threaten them. Let's see if your appearance alone will do the job. Communicate with them anyway you can. Defend yourselves if necessary, but don't instigate anything."

"That's why you didn't send me," Anatole said. "I'm too scary looking."

That was true, and Rusk cracked a smile. He liked Anatole very much, but Rusk would *not* have sent the odd man even if he had possessed military training. The man lived to instigate.

"Go for it, Adrian, and good luck," Rusk said.

Adrian Slyde didn't say anything, but Rusk could see him give Drone an arm signal to cycle the airlock. Rusk watched them move inside, armed, armored, and briefly thought back to the opening line of Virgil's *Aeneid*. Would they be remembered for setting out armed, the way that hero had? Would they be remembered as heroes, or remembered at all? Most would-be epics probably ended stillborn, or strangled in their cribs. Most would-be heroes didn't survive that often to be sung about. Maybe this was the beginning of some great epic, but the time to think about that would be later. The situation was pressurizing to a moment.

Rusk focused.

The outer airlock doors cycled, and Slyde and the X-bot stepped out, weapons available but not aimed.

The hydras continued to dismantle the dirigible as if nothing had happened.

Unacceptable! He couldn't help his anger. He restrained it, but did not try to extinguish it. Were they so completely ignorable? Did their presence matter not in the slightest?

Rusk steeled himself. He knew what had to come next. He really didn't have any other choice, did he? He could not abide sitting idle while alien creatures tore apart his dirigible, the only way they had to return to the *Dark Heart*.

"Slyde," he said. "How about you yell and wave at them?"

"Okay."

They watched while Slyde jumped about, yelling. He seemed pretty convincing as a madman. Still, the aliens continued steady to dismantle the dirigible. Minutes slid by and their airship diminished with each passing second.

"Slyde," he said finally. "Wing one."

"Wing one?"

"Wing one."

"You sure that's wise?" Kat asked.

"Not at all."

Slyde was silent for a moment, then said, "Which one? And where?"

"The nearest one, so you don't miss. Shoot at one of its low-hanging arms."

"How about if I just shot beyond them, and made it clear I was missing on purpose?"

The dirigible shook as if a large piece had just been yanked off. The sounds, the light, the heat, going outside, nothing had made any difference. Additional delay would show weakness. That they were weak didn't matter.

Rusk said, "No. Wing one."

"Okay."

Rusk watched on one of the displays as Slyde slowly and deliberately spread his legs, settled into a stance, and lifted his automatic rifle. Their weapons were .458 caliber pulsed Strike Eagles, and a direct hit from one would drop a Kodiak bear (and the edits to the manual had said that was slightly more massive than an Argotian granduluk). He wished they had something less powerful since the shock wave on impact could cause a lot of internal damage even in an extremity.

That is, in the extremity of an animal from Earth or Argo. Who knew about an alien? Maybe a pinprick would make the thing pop?

Adrian Slyde took careful aim, even deliberately, toggling on a green targeting laser and letting it reflect off the glistening skin. No reaction from the alien. Locked on, his targeting computer wouldn't miss. Would he even get the shot?

Slyde squeezed the trigger.

A single shot.

The targeted hydra tentacle exploded. Messily. Gobbets of flesh flew away from the impact and the bottom meter of arm dropped straight away trailing a yellowish, faintly luminescent fluid.

All the hydras, including the one that was hit, continued with their dismantling operation. Their huge, dark, bulbous eyes didn't roll toward Slyde's smoking weapon, not the tiniest amount.

"They're like robots," Rusk said quietly.

Then, as if to spite Rusk: in unison, all the arms of all the hydras fell limp. The creatures' buoyant backsides expanded, lifted them up and away from the dirigible. They spun as one, and with a faint hissing sound floated off into the darkness.

"Whew," Slyde said.

That was it, what all of them were thinking. Well, maybe some other four-letter words than *whew*. Slyde, as the shooter, had likely feared some instant all-powerful alien retribution, striking him down even as he fired. That's what Rusk had feared for him and had not permitted himself to dwell upon.

Stay focused! "Mistelle, make sure you mark their egress points."

"Absolutely," she said. Without hardly a pause she spoke again. "I've got new bogeys. I was confused for a second. They emerged from the same place in the hull that these hydras are headed for."

"Do you hear that, Adrian?" Rusk asked. "Keep your eyes open."

"Acknowledged."

Rusk knew they would. Their HUDs gave them three decades of wavelength coverage over 120 degrees.

"Got them," said Slyde.

"What can we see?" Rusk asked Mistelle.

Their displays blossomed with visuals and tactical overlays. The general shapes resembled those of the departing hydras: bulbous, floating backend, assortment of arms holding some sort of tool. The approaching multitude of creatures with their battalion of arms raised their collection of tools.

"Something's up, Slyde," said Rusk.

"Yeah, I think—"

Dusk-red light burst out from the distant shapes. Two of their external cameras went dead. "Slyde!"

"We just had a burst in the microwave," said Mistelle.

"Slyde?"

Nothing on his channel.

Nobody answered.

The airlock was cycling open.

"Who's that coming in?" Rusk demanded.

No answer, although he could see the deadlock wheels turning on the intermediate airlock cameras. Rusk jumped into the stairwell and ran down the hallway. He rounded the corner and slid into the antechamber as the airlock door swung open.

"Damaged, damaged, damaged!" screamed Drone in three different voices as it clattered inside.

The X-bot seemed to be missing a few arms, and half of its canister-shaped body appeared molten, and reflected a faint red. Its diamond project screen was perfect and unblemished, even though it sat in a misshapen foundation. A succession of steely, hard faces flashed irregularly across the display, each one proclaiming, "Damaged!"

The screen abruptly flickered, went dead, and Drone rebooted. Whining capacitors, which should have been well-insulated, audibly charged, cycling up. The X-bot's default gender-neutral voice said, "Running self-diagnostics."

Rusk's first impulse was to step through the airlock and go get his man, but as he stepped closer to the door, he saw the X-bot more closely.

The faint red sheen, which he had at first taken to be some kind of chemical reaction in its metallic composite, or perhaps the blackbody radiation relic of the heating the bot had experienced, was neither of those things.

It was spattered blood.

Something alien had spat instant death across the chamber, and as much as he wanted to help, he suddenly realized that poking his head out would be a very, very stupid thing to do indeed.

Mistelle's voice, sounding tinny and faint, albeit steady, floated down to him from the room's speakers. "We've lost Slyde. His radio tags are dead. Moreover, there appears to be a small army closing in on us. They're not asking any questions."

And they obviously weren't taking any prisoners, either, noted Rusk.

"What do you want us to do?" Mistelle asked.

ALONG FOR THE RIDE

IN AN ALIEN ELEVATOR

The descent took hours, and, especially after the lightning-quick events in the space dock, Klingston thought it would drive him mad.

There were four Specialists in the elevator with him: Selene Madison, Walter Stubbs, Timothy Salerno, and Gabriella Powers. Like him, they were all wrapped in some sort of strong twine. They hadn't been tied, but wrapped, and that struck him as alien as anything else going on now. The only one not wrapped was the X-bot Jason. An X-bot's basic programming contained instructions for fighting—with humans. Frank wouldn't have trusted even a fighting-expert system like Drone to simultaneously fight six Argonauts and win, let alone to do it without taking human casualties.

They didn't have Drone. They had Jason, chock-full of Argonaut experts' patterns. And his long-lost wife, which didn't help one bit.

Then again, that probably wasn't such a bad thing, and, in fact, now that he had a moment to think about it, having Jason along was probably the best they could have managed. Jason contained the best Argonaut linguists, historians, and archeologists. And here they were with Argonauts.

Okay, what of the physical surroundings?

The elevator car itself was generally spherical and appeared to be made of the same material as space dock hull. A diffuse, uniform golden light seeped out of these walls to light the car.

Frank lay in a soft indentation in the floor, as did his fellow

Specialists. He realized that he was probably actually lying in the ceiling of the car, assuming they were heading down the spoke arm, but personal down was whichever way things felt *inside*. They had significant gravity, and unless the builders of the Spider Star had artificial gravity, that meant they were accelerating. If Frank was right, the gravity would diminish as they left the geosynchronous point and dropped closer to the core, if their acceleration remained constant. It probably wouldn't, though. They'd have to flip at some point if they went down far enough.

The six Argonauts who had captured them watched them from above, straddling a set of perches much in the same way he'd seen Argotian spider monkeys sit in trees: bottom four appendages wrapped tight and the upper four free for other purposes.

After the doors had closed, the Argonauts dumped the Specialists, clambered up, and began to talk. If Frank could make any sense at all of their body language, they weren't just talking, but arguing.

He had decided to chance talking. They could tell him to shut up if they liked, or gag him. "Is everyone okay?"

Everyone said they were, although Gabriella added, "They tied my feet pretty tightly. I'm not sure I have good circulation."

Timothy said, "I'm bruised. But I bet we all are."

"Ginnie," Frank began. "Can you ask them to release us?"

"Are you crazy?" Selene asked.

"Maybe . . . but why not ask?"

Ginnie said, "Okay," then sat quietly for a moment. Then it made some sounds similar to those the creatures were making. The X-bot was loud enough for them to take notice.

They all began howling—mad, hooting howls of all pitches, before settling back down to their previous style of vocalizations.

Ginnie said, after a moment, "They think you're crazy, too."

The Argonauts went on talking, or arguing, whatever it was they were doing. He didn't know why they didn't stop them from talking—he would have, in the reverse situation. He did seem to recall that most Argotian species that vocalized, including the Argonauts, didn't have separate noses and mouths, but just a single orifice. They might consider gags to be death sentences, and probably tolerated talking, especially under circumstances like these where communication was so limited.

He considered having Jason untie, or unwrap them, rather— Gabriella at least—but decided not to push things. Not yet. They were still alive and they didn't have to be. They also had all their limbs intact, unlike poor Melinda.

Frank squeezed his eyes shut, and opened them again, willing himself not to remember the sight. "Jason, please record their conversation above and translate. Try for the best translation possible, rather than a fast but inaccurate translation."

Jason spoke with Ginnie's voice, "I think we've got it down."

"Already?"

"Yes. It's identical, so far, to the Argonaut language number seven, the one used by the secondary culture of the last technological age, from the northern regions."

"That doesn't make sense to me," Frank said. "After millions of years shouldn't their language have drifted, and drifted a lot?"

"Not necessarily." Timothy's nasal voice. At least he wasn't dead. "A *human* language over that time would splinter into a thousand new tongues, completely losing the original. Look at Latin for a modern example in just the last few thousand years."

"But we're not talking a human language," Gabriella said.

"Exactly," said Timothy, sounding strangely triumphant for a man wrapped in twine and lying below a half-dozen warrior aliens that had taken him captive.

"Okay," said Frank. "Jason, can you tell us what they're talking about?"

Jason spoke, but it wasn't Ginnie's voice or the gender-neutral default voice, either. Frank recognized it as that of a senior scientist, Grace something or other. "Once the doors closed, one of them said to go down at top speed, and then they started criticizing the one who issued the command."

"For telling the car to head down at top speed?" Selene asked.

"No," Grace explained. "We intuit that one to be the leader, and that one, she, was and is being criticized for the effort they've gone to, their lost comrade, and their lack of treasure."

" 'She'?" Frank asked. "You've got genders on them?"

"Yes, they're all female."

Frank knew it shouldn't matter, but he liked to know what he was dealing with. Most Argotian species, like most Earth species, had two sexes. Most Argotian species, like most Earth species, had varieties of sexual dimorphisms. In Argonauts, the females were larger than the males and had been physically dominant in their societies, although the males had lived longer and had dominated in politics and the social arenas. Gross generalities, he remembered, but he wasn't an expert.

Walter said, "So can you tell us the kinds of things they're saying?"

Good, everyone was engaged. Small victories.

Jason spoke with a new male voice, and Frank couldn't place it or easily see the pattern's face. His neck was already feeling old and twisted from wiggling around so much trying to see his surroundings. He finally lay back, looked up at his Argonaut overlords, which seemed an apt term given their location, and listened.

"One went on with a long list of accusations about the danger of their mission, and how they now return with nothing but these weird, weak creatures. Another one is upset because of the death of the one who tried to eat Melinda's arm—by the way, note that two of the Argonauts have amputations to an extremity. Another one has been complaining that they have no food now, since they ate it all on the ride up, and we're apparently poisonous."

Frank asked, "How is their leader defending herself?"

"Well, she's suggesting that maybe we're not all poisonous, but when the others challenged her she declined to be the food tester."

That was something at least.

The X-bot went on, "She's saying that we had called in the language of the enemy, and how was she supposed to know it wasn't really them."

"'Language of the enemy'?" Frank asked. "What language did we use to get the docking solicitation?"

Timothy answered. "Argonaut number one, that of the primary technological civilization, the ones that lived on the island where we established New Colchis, and one of the reasons we settled there."

The other primary reason was that the island was on the equator, making it an ideal location for the first colonists to drop their beanstalk.

"That's interesting," said Selene. "Maybe they think they're still fighting."

"After so very, very long?" asked Frank.

"Why not? They're *alien*," Timothy said. "They haven't suffered any language drift at all. Maybe they don't change easily, generation to generation, and rigidly enforce their belief systems."

Frank stared up at the dark creatures perched above them and agreed with Timothy's assertion. They certainly were alien. "What are they talking about now?"

Ginnie's voice returned to summarize. "They're fretting about escaping back to friendly territory. We can't tell if they're afraid of us, as several have complained about being shot at, or someone else."

Gabriella asked, "Have they said what they plan to do with us?"

"Not exactly. They're hopeful that you'll be worth something to somebody—sorry, they weren't very specific and used some words not in our vocabulary. They're not going to kill you, at least not immediately, but they are very sorry you're not more edible."

Frank decided that being toxic to aliens wasn't the worst problem to have. He hoped that toxicity would extend to any creature not from Earth, but he didn't know enough about the details of the process. He suddenly thought of Kenny feeding the spider monkeys cheese, and laughing. Given the present situation, he feared that thinking of them would make him cry, and he couldn't afford to give in to those feelings.

"I want everyone thinking here, observing. Start learning the things we need to learn to survive. I don't even know what that means yet. Learn to tell them apart. Learn where their metal weapons come from. Learn their language, if we're here long enough. Learn how to be valuable to them. Learn how to escape." Frank kept his voice quiet and low, but he was infusing strength into the words, or the words were infusing strength into his voice. "Learn why they eat the arms of their enemies. Learn how they find food. Learn where they get their water. Learn why they're still here, alive, after millions of years."

A dark question interrupted Frank's train of thought and crept inside. Why *were* they alive, with the run of the place? Had the Spider Star been abandoned when they had found it? Was that why the atmosphere, interior here, and exterior down below, seemed breathable? Frank knew that the Argonauts hadn't built this place, and that some mysterious golden ones had been in charge once upon a time, but perhaps now the Argonauts were the masters here?

Luckily, Selene picked up when Frank trailed off. "Yes, Frank, yes," she said. "Everyone here is brilliant. We're all master students. We pick up entire subjects as easily as we breathe. For instance, I've figured out how to tell them apart. Notice they all have straps, holsters, utility belts—I don't know what to call them—but they're in different colors. See, the bigger one that leads them, hers is yellow."

She was right. The others had straps around their narrow midsections where they hung their blades, and perhaps other items. The other colors were brown, red, blue, green, and a dirty orange. Hmm. No black, no white. He didn't know if that was significant or not.

Timothy said, "We can call them by their colors, and try to sort out their pecking order, possibly even exploit rivalries and disagreements. Jason, which one is disagreeing with Yellow the most?"

"The one with the orange belt," Jason said.

"Okay," Frank said, "as long as they're letting us talk like this, and ignoring us, make an effort to put the time to use. Plot, scheme, plan, find their weaknesses, and tell the rest of us. We have an advantage." Frank said this directly, without any trace of irony, despite the fact that they were wrapped in twine and at the mercy of these aliens. "We know their language, we know something of their history, and they know nothing about us except that we're too trusting in initial encounters."

Frank considered that last statement, remembering back to his evolutionary studies and their connections to self-organization and emergent computer systems. There existed an ancient problem, the so-called Prisoner's Dilemma. Frank couldn't remember all the details of the problem, but it was basically a question of how did you interact with others. Did you screw them over, or did you stick by them? You got a big reward for screwing them over if they trusted you, a moderate reward if you both trusted each other, and screwed big time if no one trusted each other. The optimal mutual solution was for both sides to trust each other, but the straightforward individual analysis indicated it was in your best interest to screw the other side. In computer simulations, that strategy was indeed best, but not in situations where you would have repeated encounters. In those situations, the algorithms that worked best always trusted the other party, and then just did whatever the other party did on the previous encounter. You rewarded trust, and punished aggressiveness. Frank wondered what it meant that the Argonauts had attacked them on first sight.

Maybe they had thought the Specialists to be someone else, or simply didn't have repeated encounters with aliens. There was that part about them hailing in the enemy language, and the Spider Star saga had featured a lot of other alien species. Either hypothesis was interesting with implications worth pursuing.

They kept talking, and kept observing, and the hours passed.

There are unpleasant realities to face when being held captive for extended periods. Gabriella had to go to the bathroom, and when she confessed she did, several others also expressed their need. Frank had Jason ask permission. He had no idea where they might go, and thought that the Argonauts might be interested in the process, if for no other reason than to learn about their captives, but they denied the request.

Frank thought they learned something by what came next. One of the Argonauts, Red, climbed down from her perch, squatted over the nearest Specialist, which happened to be Walter, and urinated on him, with a powerful stream of liquid.

"Well, this sucks," Walter said.

Under different circumstances, Frank might have laughed. He bet Rusk would have.

Frank didn't know if *urinate* was the proper term, although he assumed that's what she was doing. He intended to ask Jason or one of the others about it, but didn't feel up to the task. There would be time for that later, he hoped. He didn't want to humiliate Walter and learn that the discharge had been something even more unsavory. Thankfully, Walter didn't ask.

When Frank had to go, he just went. He recalled that some of the pioneering astronauts had had to urinate inside their own suits when there had been launch delays, and that connection made it a bit easier to take.

Eventually, after what had been hours, the gravity shifted in a very perceptible fashion. It had been changed as he'd predicted: steadily lessening, consistent with a descent into the body of the dark matter planet that generated the gravitational potential of the Spider Star.

The shift was interesting, and Frank's trepidation regarding the end of their journey did not diminish his intellectual interest.

Their indented areas crawled toward the sides of the car. As the location of the indentations shifted, the Argonaut's perches extended to connect with what had been the floor. There were a few stomach-turning moments as the acceleration shifted rapidly, and, for the briefest moment, weightlessness, then gravity reasserted itself in the opposite direction. The indentations continued to shift around to what had been the ceiling, and the Argonauts rotated on their perches.

The weight Frank felt seemed like less than that of Earth or Argo. He knew the maximum local surface gravity of the Spider Star was slightly more than a third of that, nearly Mars levels. He reckoned that they might be in the upper atmosphere of the Spider Star, some two thousand or three thousand kilometers from its center, near that maximum gravity.

The Argonauts clambered down from what had previously been the floor and shifted to the ceiling, and then scooped up their hostages. Frank preferred to think of themselves as hostages, because the alternatives were worse: prisoners, booty, food—if they could neutralize the toxins.

He hoped they wouldn't consider boiling them to test the last idea.

The doors of the elevator car opened, revealing a room nearly identical to the one in the space dock where the nightmare had begun.

They moved through a series of rooms. The portals were lit as in the space dock, and they moved through the surfaces in the same way. Then they came to a room that was different.

A cylindrical object occupied much of the room. Its front end abutted a solid wall, but Frank knew not to give solid walls much credence in this place.

One of the lead Argonauts—Blue—touched some lighted panels on the cylinder and said something he didn't catch. A hole appeared in the cylinder's side and everyone climbed inside. Before they entered, the cylinder appeared hollow, but Orange said something that Frank heard, but did not understand, and cushioned seats grew from the floor. He and the others were unceremoniously dumped into them.

Once everyone was inside, the surfaces of the cylinder cleared, growing transparent, and they launched.

Launched was a strong term.

They moved, slowly, through the forward wall of the room. Slowly, ever so slowly, they gained speed. Within a few minutes, they cleared the outer wall of the spoke.

Frank rolled himself across his seat, flopped his head over its edge, and had himself a look.

Infinity dropped away below him. It was an infinite sky, with some sort of distant, golden sun shining up through the clouds. They were flying! The cylinder was flying through the sky of the Spider Star! "It's amazing," he said aloud in all honesty, happy to have something else to look at than a bunch of multi-legged aliens perched over him.

Selene, who had been tossed in next to him, and whose wrapped legs nestled against his chest, said, "We're in one of the tubes."

"Yes!" said Walter.

Frank kept looking, and didn't bother to think much. The vista held him in its majesty. It was almost enough to keep him from worrying about their predicament.

As the view slid by faster, Selene continued, "The tubes connecting the nodes of the spokes. They're just empty tubes! Just tubes!"

" 'Just tubes'?" He didn't understand.

Thankfully, Walter elaborated. "If you drilled a hole through Earth, or Argo, doesn't matter, you could fall to any other point in the surface in about forty, forty-five minutes, just under gravity. Any path from one altitude to the same altitude, if the density is similar, takes the same amount of time."

"But you can't do it on Earth," Frank said.

Gabriella, silent a long time, chimed in. "Because it's a real planet with a molten interior. Here, if there is a molten interior, it's dark matter. It doesn't react to us. We can fall anywhere in forty-five minutes or less, *if* the tube has nearly frictionless surfaces and is evacuated so that there's no air resistance."

He didn't feel any sensation of speed. That would be consistent with free fall—or the near-equivalent if they were following a cord rather than falling straight down—straight down would leave them weightless, and they certainly had some weight.

"Wait a second," Frank said. "We're in one of the tubes we saw. If we're falling through it, toward another spoke maybe, how are Griffin and the others going to find us? We could wind up on the other side of the station."

As soon as he said it, he felt stupid, remembering the embedded ID tags broadcasting their signals. He wasn't thinking like a Specialist.

Thankfully no one made him feel dumb by calling him on it overtly. Selene said simply, "They'll find us. They probably have a dozen ways to do it."

"Ha!" Walter said after a few more minutes. "I think they already have!"

Frank looked around. He didn't see anything below other

than the spectacular view. He rolled around, against Selene's legs, and reoriented himself to look up. Then he saw it.

An Earth-tech space plane paced them, maybe a few kilometers distant. He was sure Walter was right. But what could they do? They could have nanofactured an armed model, and they could attack the tube. He had no idea what it was made of, diamond he would guess, but maybe something stronger and less brittle. How could they do anything?

"It's falling behind," Gabriella said.

And it was. Were they really going so fast? Frank thought for a moment, and admitted they would be speeding as they approached maximum velocity, maybe as much as several kilometers per second. The space plane couldn't match that for a sustained period at low altitude.

And, indeed, it dropped away.

"It's gone," Selene said eventually.

"Griffin will find us," he told everyone. He truly believed it—seeing the space plane appear so quickly had inspired confidence in her talents. He even almost believed they'd still be alive when she did.

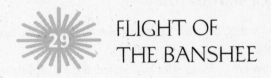

FLIGHT OF
THE BANSHEE

DEEP INSIDE THE SPIDER STAR

"What do you want us to do?" Mistelle asked again.

Rusk stood uncertainly next to the rebooting X-bot. Blood-covered Drone listed on its side chanting, "Checking, check, checking, check, checking . . ."

What did he want them to do? What could they do? Things had seemed bad enough with the first group of uncommunicative hydras that had simply started tearing their ship apart. Should he have waited for them to finish the job and start in on them? To have the problem of noncommunication back seemed infinitely more desirable than what faced them now: instant death.

This wasn't a good time for him to realize that he was more enamored by the *idea* of being in charge as opposed to actually *being* in charge. No, he liked being in charge just fine, but options were difficult to see at the moment. Here he was, cut off from help. He didn't like leadership if it meant failure, but he liked failure in no endeavor. He had to think of something.

He wished that Griffin were here with him. He always seemed to think better with her around.

He had one thought. One dull, direct thought. They'd had to hit Slyde and his team with a laser, or maser, rather, to deliver that kind of energy on target. Or at least he hoped so. "Mistelle, what kind of spectrum was the microwave burst?"

She came back immediately. "It was a maser, very tight frequency profile."

Good. That was something. His dull idea wasn't torpedoed yet. "Do we have any conducting materials with the right separation to block that frequency, or most of it at least? Or could we build a shielding mesh?"

There were several ways to block a maser. The simplest way was to put a lot of reflective material between you and it and hope it took some time for it to ablate away. If you didn't have a lot of stuff—that was, at least meters of armor when facing military masers—the next smartest thing was to distribute the material on scales similar to the wavelength of the incoming maser—millimeters. That meant reflective/conductive chaff, or mesh screens—many layers of them. The masers still had energy they would deposit, and short of perfect reflectivity, mesh seemed a better idea than mirrors or chaff, especially if the mesh was well designed and ablated away into a screen of glittery chaff. Rusk wanted to maintain, or regain, rather, some mobility. They had a small nanoforge onboard and could perhaps rapidly produce something if they had to.

"Maybe. Working on it," Kat said.

Rusk hoped so. But how simple was his idea? These military hydras had attacked and killed Slyde instantly with a weapon, and he was trying to come up with a shield against that weapon. That kind of thinking wouldn't let them come out on top in this situation. He had to find some other way of thinking, something more than reactive, or they were lost.

"Mistelle," he said. "What do you have on the entry/exit points of the hydras? If we get to them, can we use them?"

There, that was a bold idea. If staying on the disintegrating dirigible was too risky, they would have to move. Where could they move to? Into the Spider Star, or at least other parts of this globule, just like the hydras. He felt his solution was unoriginal, but natural. What else could they do?

"I know where the doors are, if *doors* is the right term. I don't have a clue how to work them though."

"Good enough. One step at a time."

Anatole said, "Kat's got something programmed in the nanoforge. She says it'll work in a pinch. How is Adrian?"

"Checking, check, checking, fail, checking, fail, fail, fail . . . ," Drone was saying.

Rusk stalled. "Later. As you can afford the time, get to the armory and suit up. Everyone needs to be in armor and to have a weapon."

"I didn't take that specialty," Kat said.

Would she be more dangerous armed or unarmed? He didn't know, but the extra weapon and armor could come in handy. "Equip yourself anyway. Make sure someone shows you."

"Okay."

Rusk took a deep breath. How close were the hydras? They didn't seem to move that fast, but how fast did you need to move when you could spit death? The aliens would be careful, sure, and Rusk and his people would be dead.

Rusk watched as Anatole and Mistelle jogged by to the armory. He hoped Kat would be along soon.

Fuck. He hadn't suited up himself. He dogged the airlock shut, and left Drone to its pathetic checks.

Rusk joined the others, who stood, apparently dumbfounded, in the face of all the weaponry of mankind. "Don't mess with the small stuff. Take the armored flak jackets—they're not so heavy in this gravity—and the Strike Eagles. Take extra clips."

Then they all moved, with Rusk pointing them at the right equipment.

Anatole said, "All my life I have dreamed of practicing the ancient art of war."

"Anatole," Mistelle said, "you're a freak."

"Yes, oh, yes!" he said, grabbing a weapon and holding it tightly. "I am *so* freaked right now."

The small man's smile didn't seem amused, but afraid. Deathly afraid. Insanely afraid, like more insane than normal for him.

What was Rusk asking of them now? Was it even possible? Even a perfect plan wouldn't work if the available personnel couldn't carry it out.

It had to work, because he had no other idea how to survive more than a few minutes.

Between the three of them Rusk judged himself the most knowledgeable when it came to personal propulsion units, or PPUs, as he thought of them. They had enough for everyone, including Drone, if it ever successfully rebooted.

Rusk quickly donned his armor, grabbed his weapon and ammo, and headed for the PPUs, which were stored in an adjacent room.

He yelled over his shoulder, "Everyone gets a PPU after the armory!" He trusted the dirigible computer to relay any directions that were too quiet to reach everyone.

Kat came hurtling down the hallway. "The nanoforge is cooking."

"Excellent. Hit the forge last."

This was all too fast, too chaotic. What chance in hell did they have? He'd screwed this up, but good. He should have treated this as a military encounter from the get-go. If he had, maybe no one would have died. And it was his fault.

Rusk stopped in the middle of the PPU strap-in. They were dead, and it was his fault. What right did he have to make any decisions at all, given his awful track record so far? Claude Martin was right to put Klingston into the position of executive director. Frank Klingston had a track record. He'd encountered aliens, and hadn't gotten himself killed. That trumped any of his own credentials to date. What did his test scores matter? What did his long list of specialties matter?

Kat tapped him on the arm. "Are you okay?"

He wasn't. He was pathetic. But how could he tell her that? "Put on your PPU."

That was what he had to do. Just make decisions, moment by moment, and help everyone else do what they needed to do when they needed to do it. If he could manage that, they would get through this. At least they would if they had any chance at all.

His PPU equipped, he said, "Mistelle, how are you doing?"

"Working on refining the doorway imagery. It seems to be spherical. I can't make out any controls, though."

Fuck. She needed to be armed, and now. "Let the ship's computer work on it. You need to be ready now."

"I just need—"

"Now!" he yelled.

She didn't respond and he assumed she was following his orders. Klingston had established an informal atmosphere among the Specialists. Rusk didn't like it, but admitted it aided smoother communications in a number of situations, but not now. Now he needed immediate obedience, or more were going to die.

He realized that he liked that sentiment. It meant that he didn't yet believe they were all going to die, not right away in any event. His subconscious must know something he didn't. *Tell me already!*

Before too long they were all back in front of the airlock, armored, armed, wearing PPUs, and worried. Those who had been well trained with this equipment were all outside and presumably dead. The one exception was Drone, who was saying, "Checking, check, checking, fail . . ."

Drone would have been helpful, but for now . . . who could say? The bot was a liability. It had expertise, in theory, but that was only useful if they could get to it.

"Mistelle," he said. "Where are they?"

She gave the dirigible's computer some specific commands, accessing specialized subroutines that she had programmed. The neutral voice, under priority, said quickly, "Closing to a hundred and ten meters."

The aliens were approaching slowly, and that was good. It suddenly dawned on Rusk that they hadn't procured the mesh shields. "Kat, what about the nanofactured shields?"

"Yes!" she said, heading back into the ship.

Rusk followed, knowing she would need help.

The nanoforge normally operated within a sealed vacuum chamber, but for something simple like the requested meshes, that was unnecessary. There was a bubbling pool, exposed to the atmosphere, and a shimmering slime floating on its surface. Rusk smelled a rusty, metallic smell that he knew he couldn't stand indefinitely.

"Help me," Kat said.

She reached in and grabbed at the slime, and, like some ancient fisherman, began hauling out a net. Kat continued to pull it out. What Rusk saw was a pile of metallic mesh piling up at her feet, spilling over her boots, as Kat kept pulling it up.

Rusk sprang over and grabbed hold of the damp, textured mesh, and helped haul it up. It was forming from the liquid as fast as he pulled it out. He tried to breathe out of his mouth, but thought he could still taste the smell. "Hurry."

Between the two of them, they picked up the mesh pile, and headed back to the airlock. "Where are they?"

"Fifty meters, and holding," the dirigible computer answered.

Well, this was it. They were boxed in, and it was time to act. They would get to the doors, get into the Spider Star, or die like Slyde. There was no other choice, now, was there?

"Systems check complete, functional capability ensuing," Drone said.

"Kat, Anatole," Rusk said to them. "We may need Drone, if it's still operational at any decent level. Kat, you make sure Drone comes with us, and Anatole, you help her out with it."

They nodded in agreement. With Drone missing limbs, the

X-bot was less bulky. At their current altitude within the Spider Star, the gravity was only about 25 percent an Earth gee.

Rusk smiled a little at that thought. The PPUs would be unusually effective.

"What about food and water?" Mistelle asked.

He had to give her some credit for her optimism. She was planning to survive more than the next few minutes. "We're Specialists. Our nanomed lets us eat and drink anything we can find. The armor has a water reservoir, and we're not carrying any food."

He switched on his tactical displays and glowing words and numbers filled his helmet's HUD. When he looked at each of them in turn, Mistelle, Anatole, and Kat, otherwise anonymous under their armored suits and faceless helmets, he had their names and vitals floating next to them. Everyone's heart rate was up, but otherwise seemed ready.

"I'll lead. Mistelle, you trail below. Kat and Anatole will follow with Drone."

They entered the airlock, arrayed themselves, and deployed the mesh. They opened the external door, hanging back from the opening. Outside, beyond the bright white of the light reflecting off the airlock frame, was pitch black.

Rusk's heart pulsed in his ears, and he tried not to think ahead more than ten seconds.

"Synchronize PPUs, slave them to mine," Rusk said. Four green lights blipped on his HUD. "Launch!"

Their PPUs ignited, transferring thrust to them through their harnesses. Under their mesh, under tremendous acceleration, the Specialists exploded into the darkness.

The PPU rumbled on his back and wind whistled through the mesh, screaming almost, its end whipping wildly behind them with accentuating cracks. Under other circumstances, it might have been fun.

Heat erupted before them. The masers were hitting the mesh. Red glowing filaments of the top layers of mesh popped, and peeled off, leaving streaks of light behind them. Seconds passed as they barreled through the dark like screaming banshees, and the mesh cooled.

They'd survived the initial maser assault. They would live another ten seconds at least.

Rusk piloted by inertial systems and their map of the chamber, adjusting their PPUs to direct them toward the doorway out of the silver ship and presumably into the Spider Star proper. Maybe he was only delaying things, but how could it be any worse than waiting to get fried?

"Coming up on the door," Mistelle said.

"Be ready for impact!" Rusk advised them. He wasn't about to slow down and let the maser-toting hydras shoot them again. The nature of the size of the mesh-spacing preventing the passage of the maser, and the insulating properties kept the underlayers from heating up, but he didn't know how long the mesh would hold up. At least seconds, but probably not minutes.

The wall approached, or so his HUD told him. He couldn't see much through the mesh even if the walls hadn't been so light-absorbing. He might as well be flying with his eyes closed, knowing he was about to crash.

He tensed. A few more seconds passed. He relaxed and tensed again, checking the figures. He—

His armor gel-packs popped with an acrid, burning smell, cushioning his body and his head as they hit. Bone-jarring, that was the word that rattled with him inside his helmet. Stunned, he knew they needed to be doing something. The PPUs were still firing, holding them against the wall, or rather, against the mesh, which was against the wall.

Their backsides were exposed.

Rusk ordered the PPUs into hover mode, released them to individual control, and rolled around. "Get covered!"

He looked back and forth, spotting his comrades on his HUD. He noted that Anatole had a cracked rib, and that Kat had a fractured collarbone, but otherwise there were no serious injuries. He spun around, holding the mesh, and the others moved in unison with him.

Everyone except Kat, who clung to Drone like a life preserver and didn't move.

"Kat! Get under!"

The masers hit then and Rusk watched her armor char and explode. Drone, released, fell into the darkness below. Kat's PPU was damaged, but partly operational, and now, finally, she spun. She spun away in spirals, bobbing, away from them.

"Kat!" Anatole called after her.

No time for any feelings, not now. Later, if there was a later. "Mistelle, we have you covered. Find their door, and get us through it."

The surface level of the mesh glowed red, then white, and began popping off. Embers drifted like slow rain under the invisible beams striking them.

"Get us through it *now*!" Rusk ordered.

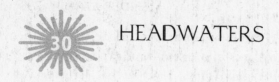

HEADWATERS

THE ARCHIPELAGO OF THE SPIDER STAR

The cylinder flew through the tube slicing through the Spider Star atmosphere at high velocity, and Frank couldn't do anything but lie there and watch. It was all clouds and sky drifting by, and it was difficult to believe their velocity was as high as Walter had claimed it would be.

Frank had to admit that the "islands"—that was what he thought of them as—zipped by too fast to see. He had to ask Jason about what they'd dropped past. They were some sort of platforms, or spherical modules attached to the tube they moved through. They passed in lightning-quick fashion. Blink, blink, and they were gone.

Jason reported shapeless, circular surfaces, surrounding forests of unrecognizable trees, and arrays of machinery, pipes, and assorted metal. No one had any idea of what they might be or do.

But Walter was right, in the end. Some forty minutes later, as he'd predicted, their pace slowed and they approached a gray structure, slower, and slower—no quick blink, blink—until Frank worried they'd never actually reach it. But they coasted in, passing through a hull as they had before, and were inside a nondescript gray room the same as the one they'd left before, as far as Frank could ascertain.

Ginnie's voice came from Jason. "They're reaching some kind of decision."

The Argonauts had been more and more vocal as the tube trip had progressed, reaching a crescendo as the new spoke approached, and a great vertical band grew wider every minute.

"Spill it," Selene demanded.

"They've decided to take us to—and we apologize for this inadequate translation—the 'big one.'"

That sounded ominous, and kind of funny.

Selene actually giggled, and Frank silently thanked her for releasing some tension. Her giggle made him smile, too, even though he knew he had nothing to be smiling about. They were all going to see the big one. Well, there it was. How could they not laugh? Frank hadn't pissed himself in hours, so why not celebrate?

"Is that a *someone,* or a *something*?" Walter wanted to know, and they laughed some more, while they could.

The cylinder gradually coasted to a stop. The Argonauts were upon them again, moving rapidly almost to the point of rushing, it seemed, and hauled them out, tossing them like packages onto the tube dock floor.

There was an argument. Frank didn't need Jason to tell him. The Argonauts' voices rose, higher in pitch, and higher in volume, until he wished he could put his fingers in his ears. He wanted to ask what they were arguing about, but was sure he wouldn't be able to hear the answer.

Eventually their screeches died down, and again they were scooped up. While Frank thought he probably smelled bad himself—reeked, his wife would have said—the Argonauts' sour stench made him gag and very nearly vomit. Somehow he endured it as the Argonauts carried them into a tunnel that sloped slightly down. They carried them, jostling, bumping, bouncing them, until Frank was sure every inch of his body was bruised, out onto a platform.

Platform didn't do the scene justice. There was a platform—a floor—but there were no walls on one side, and the ceiling barely counted. The platform opened out onto the cool, open atmosphere of the Spider Star itself.

Vertigo gripped Frank. He'd never been too afraid of heights.

As he liked to put it, he had a healthy fear of falling. But this, this was another thing altogether. The height of the drop—thousands of kilometers—was staggering. Then he saw something. The platform wasn't empty. There were piles of fluttering . . . somethings. Nothing alive, he didn't think. It looked like piles of multicolored plastic, or leather, maybe even canvas or silk of some sort. Maybe the Argonauts had some kind of craft hidden below the flapping material.

"Oh my goodness," Gabriella said, in a way that implied exactly the opposite definition. Gabriella, he recalled, really didn't care for heights. She'd been recruited as an archeologist with Argonaut expertise for in-system missions rather than being set on deep space the way most of them were. She'd managed to skip or sidestep a number of normal Specialist training programs involving heights.

Then Frank made the same connection that she must have. The flapping material didn't cover some kind of air vehicle. The flapping material *was* some kind of air vehicle.

Please, he thought, *let it be a big, smooth, slow balloon.*

It wasn't, or rather, *they* weren't.

Two of the Argonauts, Blue and Brown, went to the material. Their long, dark arms pulled wildly, lifting the gossamer material up, out, and stretched it over some kind of rigid rods, and tied the structures with the same sort of twine that bound the humans. Over the course of the next quarter hour, six different sets of wings began to form. Frank didn't recognize the shapes of the craft, not exactly, but he assumed they were some sort of glider.

The Argonauts began dragging Specialists over to the gliders and stuffing them in the bottom of a pouch that was slung underneath the web of struts supporting the wings. The constructs looked as if a good sneeze would blow them apart.

Gabriella pitched a fit, screaming and yelling, twisting back and forth, flopping around, trying to do anything but go into the pouch.

"Calm down, Gabriella!" he yelled. Up until now, the Argonauts had been inured to their chatter, but they had to have limits. They could all get gagged, or worse. He thought of Melinda, and refused to pursue that line of thought.

Thankfully, Green didn't care. Green picked Gabriella up, and stuffed her in.

There was another argument between Yellow and Orange. Their voices climbed, the sounds grating on Frank like metal raking on teeth, sinking into the bone. "What are they fighting over now?" he asked Jason.

"Me, I'm afraid," the X-bot responded with its own neutral voice. "I weigh much more than you humans do. No one wants to carry me. Yellow is telling Orange to do it, and Orange is refusing."

Panic flared within Frank. If they lost Jason, they'd have no reliable way of communicating with their captors. Losing Jason was unacceptable. Losing Ginnie was totally unacceptable. As the argument continued, Frank pondered possible solutions. He had one idea, finally. "Jason, there's an extra glider, because of the one that died, I guess. Can you fly it?"

Jason didn't reply immediately. Frank, lying on his side, watched the X-bot's facial display. All of the X-bot's patterns flashed across the display, some appearing to be in mid-sentence with pursed lips, until finally settling back on the neutral gray. "We don't know, but we think it would be fun to try."

Patterns were always up for trying things, even things they couldn't do, or that would likely destroy their host. Part of the patterning process reduced or eliminated the sense of self-preservation. X-bots had a high priority to preserve themselves, to be sure, but in situations where the risk assessment was poor, they tended to accept gambles.

Frank supposed he would have to as well, if they were to have any chance of keeping Jason. Even if Orange did take the bot on its glider, Frank had no doubt that any problems would likely result in Jason getting dumped for a long, long fall. At least it would if these Argonauts were anything at all like humans. "Jason, as carefully as you can, suggest you can fly yourself. Tell them to show you how."

Jason started speaking in Argonaut language number seven, calmly repeating the same phrase over and over. Frank thought that was a good approach. He worried about giving away too much of the X-bot's capabilities to the Argonauts. For whatever reasons, they hadn't tied it or hampered its movements. Frank hoped that meant they underestimated Jason, but still worried that the upcoming display would make them change their ideas about the bot.

Eventually, after more squawking and flailing of limbs, Yellow and Orange ceased their bickering and started to listen to Jason. There were exchanges back and forth, none of which Frank could follow. The tone settled down to a mildly unpleasant buzz, and Jason turned back to Frank.

"It is agreed," the X-bot announced. "We will pilot a glider. If we fail to follow the Argonauts, then they will kill some of you. We look forward to our first time flying an aircraft."

That hit Frank like—he couldn't think—like something really heavy. And hard.

His eloquence had evacuated his consciousness. "Okay," he said finally. "Don't mess it up."

Yes indeed, that was leadership.

Frank was last in, stuffed into a glider's pouch by Yellow. Strangely, being crammed into the bottom of a long sleeve where he couldn't see anything made him less apprehensive. The situation was out of his control; it hadn't ever been quite in his control, but now the part of his mind that worried about everything had less input. He relaxed as much as was possible in the situation, giving himself up to it.

Yellow climbed in the open end of the sack with its smelly bottom four feet, smashing them unceremoniously into Frank's face and body. That would impair his relaxation.

He stopped thinking such dark, cynical thoughts almost immediately. His side rubbed against the smooth floor as the Argonaut pulled itself and the glider forward with its upper four arms. Distantly Frank heard shouts, both human and alien, and then it was his turn.

The bottom dropped out of the world, and he was falling. Involuntarily, a scream bubbled up out of his mouth. They were falling, but gravity eased back, and he supposed they were gliding. After a few moments, he forced his muscles to relax.

He remembered the punch line to an ancient and awful joke: If it's inevitable, sit back, relax, and enjoy it.

He tried. He really did. But his mind raced. What if his family could see him now? Stuffed into a bag with an alien's stinky feet in his face. He'd traveled over seventeen light-years to have this experience. How was this preventing future Lashings? How was this saving his wife, his boys? Their home world?

Frank eventually settled down, breathed through his mouth as much as he could, and hoped Jason would manage all right. It was all he could do.

Stressed and exhausted beyond all reason, Frank somehow fell asleep.

Frank was rudely awakened. Something smacked into him with a moderate velocity, and he knew he'd be bruised. As memories of his current reality crashed back onto him, he wished he could return to wonderful, oblivious sleep, but he had no choice now.

He was still alive, and resting on some kind of surface that didn't give like the glider's silky sack, so he supposed they had landed, and Yellow had let him take the brunt of that landing.

The Argonaut's stinky feet pushed into his face and groin, and then were gone. A long, dark arm slinked into the sack, grabbed him by his lengthy hair, and dragged him out.

He was lying prone on a dark platform—an unusually dark platform. He didn't even know if it was a platform. If he didn't know better, he would have thought that he was lying on the ground back at his farm, close to twilight.

There was real *dirt* here! And it smelled more like soil than plain dirt, even.

He didn't feel very rested. He didn't know how long he'd been riding the glider, but he thought not more than a few hours. *Oh, bleh.* His mouth was like hell sprayed on. Every part of him was sweaty or worse. His pants were still damp, without a doubt his hair was a greasy disaster, and he thought he could use a good bowel movement. Oh yeah, he was hungry and thirsty, too.

He craned his sore neck around, seeking the other Specialists or Jason in the dim light. He spotted Jason right away. The X-bot's display glowed with a faint, white light. Frank called it over.

Jason waddled over on its tentacles. "We flew the glider," it said, oozing self-satisfaction in a way that bots rarely displayed.

"I'm pleased," Frank said, and he was, in a distant, abstract way. Jason's failure likely would have meant deaths or dismemberments for Specialists. Maybe. Who knew anything in this crazy world? "Where are we?"

"We're on a large, circular agricultural demesne. The altitude is a few hundred kilometers lower than we started, as you can no doubt tell by the temperature increase of two-point-six degrees Celsius, despite the nighttime conditions."

Frank decided to ignore the assumption about his ability to sense temperature. "Nighttime? How can the Spider Star have nighttime?"

Jason switched from his neutral personality to one of its patterns, a middle-aged woman with graying hair whose name escaped Frank. Matilda, maybe. "We're on an agricultural platform. You should remember the remote imaging. The platforms have mirror arrays around them. They open and close to reflect light from the core in a predictable day/night fashion down upon the platform. Dawn is still some hours away."

Frank felt wasted, stupid, so many things, none of them good. "Jason, ask if we can be untied, unwrapped, whatever. We're not going to escape. We need water, food if possible, and some place to rest if we're going to be here a little while."

"Affirmative," Jason said, and waddled off.

Frank lay there. It was all he could do. He ached, he hurt. He was thirsty. He was hungry. He stank. He wanted to piss again, and take a shit. How far he could fall in a few hours . . . It amazed him, to the extent he could be amazed.

He kept thinking of the same base needs, over and over. He couldn't plan rebellion, or escape, or even what to do next. He couldn't even picture his family, not unless he concentrated really hard, and then the images were fleeting.

Frank lay on the alien non-soil, and needed.

Jason said, "The Argonauts are accommodating you. There are other Argonauts here, you should know. Farmers, not warriors. They do what Yellow says, but they are different from Yellow, you should know. In any event, you will have what you need."

That was the most marvelous thing Frank had heard, except for perhaps the newborn cries of his sons, and the first broadcast he had heard from Argo after his alien encounter.

Yellow grabbed Frank's wrappings, lifted him, and started to drag him off. Pain he didn't know he had flared in his muscles, his bones. He was hurt deep, and they'd barely touched him.

Suddenly he was tumbling, falling, twisting, and coming undone. Yellow had flipped him, holding on to one end of the twine that held him, and let him unroll in a drawn-out fashion. Every bump, every impact, left a new bruise. He hoped all the doodads the Corps had injected into his bloodstream would do a better job than his natural equipment, because otherwise he thought he'd be useless for weeks.

His contacts let his eyes adjust quickly, lending a degree of green-hued image intensification. It was darker where he'd been unrolled—the sky was gone. He was inside some kind of enclosure.

Something grunted at him. Several somethings. Somethings neither human nor Argonaut.

He wasn't alone.

He saw them then, squat, six-legged creatures, less than a meter high, slightly smaller than an adult human. It was dark, so he couldn't discern colors, and their texture was unclear. He thought they might be hairy, but wasn't sure, and didn't want to find out. Their most striking feature was a triangular snout that ended at the corners with long, flexible whiskers. They surrounded him, but avoided direct contact with his strangeness.

Frank was free, sort of. Twine no longer bound him. The surface in this enclosed pen was damp, muddy even, and he pushed his hands into the grime and tried to push himself up. His biceps screamed, and it took him three tries to stand.

When he did, he hit his head. "Ouch."

"Frank?" said a voice. Selene.

"Yeah," he said, without enthusiasm or optimism.

"I'm here, too," said Walter.

"And me." Timothy's voice.

"Gabriella?" Frank asked.

Nothing. He thought perhaps something had happened to her, punishment for her reluctance to fly in the glider. But then he heard a loud gasp. "Uh-huh! Here. There's water and food, of a sort."

They conferred among themselves and sorted out their available resources. *Available resources, hah!* That was fucking hilarious. They were in an animal pen of some sort and might as well accept the reality of their situation.

They had a shallow pond, good for bathing and drinking. They were Specialists—they could handle that. They had food, of a sort. There was a trough filled with some kind of feed. Nothing like corn or oats, but some sort of small, leathery bean-type things that had a hint of a coffee smell. Frank trusted his modifications and ate all he could stand. He didn't know when he'd be able to eat again.

There was no bathroom. Everyone made do as they could in the corners, usually as far from the wallow as they could manage. They gave each other as much privacy as possible, and most went back to the water to bathe. Some, including Frank, took off their jumpsuits and washed them as best they could. Frank wrung out his suit and used it as a towel to dry himself afterward. No one talked about how sanitary things were. They were Specialists. It didn't matter. They would endure and prosper.

After all that, people settled down. Frank found himself a spot by the earthen wall, where it was dry, giving himself over to his exhaustion now that his other needs were satisfied at some level.

He heard a voice in the darkness, and made out a silhouette. "Can I join you?"

Selene. "Of course you can." Frank would not have refused any of them.

She nestled in against him and he put his arm around her. It was only after a few seconds that he realized she was as naked as he was. He startled.

"It's okay, honey," she said. "None of this is real. Nothing here matters."

He worried about that, what it said for her state of mind, but not for long. He was too tired. He started to fade out, his body still aching.

Later, he didn't know how long, he awoke abruptly. He was hard, and inside Selene, who was lugubriously sliding onto him, moaning softly.

He squeezed her shoulder.

"Hush, honey," Selene said. "It's okay. It doesn't matter, but I need it."

Frank, too tired and shell-shocked and erect, didn't do anything. Not anything more than he was already doing, anyway. She rode him, slowly, mournfully, for long minutes. Every time he thought he was finished, she slowed, teasing him. He didn't know if she was doing it on purpose or not, and he didn't have the energy to ask. He was in her thrall. He was in thrall to the universe, completely out of control.

Eventually, she quickened. Her movements, her gasps, made him quicken, too, and he moved in response, pumping, finishing. It did mean something, but what, exactly, he could not say. He was satisfied in the act, in its completion, and there was something about it, in the face of their captivity, that struck a note of resistance.

Selene collapsed into his body and he held her, falling asleep again.

With dawn, Frank and the others were rousted from the animal pen. In the incoming light, he saw that the six-legged creatures were a sickly pink and covered with crusty sores. He identified with them, briefly, then he was dragged into morning on the Spider Star.

Yellow pointed at the sack on one of the gliders.

Frank understood, and crawled inside, obedient.

Solidity dropped away, again, as the Argonaut launched the glider, and together they floated into the infinite sky.

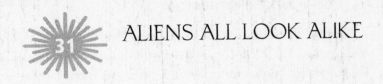

ALIENS ALL LOOK ALIKE

FLYING AROUND THE SPIDER STAR

The space plane didn't have a lot of room to move around, but to the extent she could, Griffin paced. The low gravity made it hard not to bump into things and people, as anxious as she was. She tried to make sure she didn't bump any instrument panels, but didn't worry about the bulkheads.

"You ought to relax while you can," Jack Robb told her. "You may not get the opportunity later."

Sound advice, and advice she should be distributing instead of taking. "Yeah," she said.

But she couldn't. She had been so sure they were about to rescue Frank and the others, but the tube vehicle had just continued to accelerate. She didn't dare match it. The plane was fusion powered, standard for their nanofactured exploration vehicles, and could stay aloft indefinitely, but to hit their orbital velocities they required real fuel, and they needed to save what they had to be able to return to the *Dark Heart*. She was desperate, but not crazy.

So here they were, piddling along, chasing the ID signals that faded out all too often for her taste.

"Our quarry seems to have stalled," an iron-bearded, chiseled pattern announced from Lance's display.

"Yes," said Robb. "There's some sort of solid object there. It isn't a spoke. I don't know how it's supported, but if it's floating free it's maintaining a very stable position."

"Does our tube connect to the solid mass?" Griffin asked.

"No," said Robb.

"How'd the monsters get there then?" Melinda said.

That was the first thing she'd said since they'd launched. She'd insisted on coming with Griffin. Certainly, there was room for her, but Griffin worried about her arm and her state of mind. There was damage in both places.

Despite her injury, there now existed a fire-hardened core in the once jovial woman and Griffin knew she could trust the Specialist to do anything necessary to achieve their goals. She herself had wilted before Melinda's insistence.

No one had an answer to her question, however, and she sank back into silence.

Griffin kept vacillating on their course of action. She hadn't shown any overt uncertainty, and while she did believe that four properly armed and forewarned Specialists and an X-bot could easily handle the six Argonauts who had taken their people hostage, she feared that they would be headed for reinforcements of one type or another. Just because the one group they'd encountered had appeared technologically simple didn't mean that would be the case everywhere, although she did hope it. Maybe, after all, ten-million-year time spans didn't mean ten-million-year advanced technology. Civilizations not only rose, but they fell.

The time passed quickly enough and their targets remained on this solid object, which, as they approached, appeared to be some sort of platform about five hundred meters across, lit by overhead lights, tethered to at least two different inter-spoke tubes.

"Let's get our people," Griffin said as they approached. She and Robb suited up, checked their weapons, and prepared themselves. She trusted their Specialists modifications enough that they didn't need to try to negotiate. Klingston and the others could survive a few seconds under any circumstances she could foresee. "Lance, put us down right in the middle of that platform. Stay powered, stay nimble."

"Absolutely," said Donovan.

Melinda just glared. Griffin didn't dare give her anything to do, but at the same time trusted her to jump in and perform any necessary task.

"Lance," Griffin instructed, "keep us all coordinated and informed."

As they approached, Robb said, "Interesting. The lights are changing, mirrors I think. They're illuminating the platform surface. I'd guess it's some kind of artificial day/night setup. Looks like its surface is covered with vegetation of some sort, perhaps a few simple structures. Nothing high tech."

"Lucky break for us," said Griffin. "Maybe. I bet our night vision and thermal beat the shit out of anything they have. They used *knives* of all things at the space dock, after all. Come in near the structures, and we'll just blitz them."

She was really feeling it. She was hyped. She was . . . a thousand things. This was action. This was important. And she was controlling it.

Still, she wished Rusk was with her. She knew he made her better, that she made fewer mistakes with him.

Griffin and Robb were armored, wired, armed, and primed, waiting over a quick-drop aperture out of the bottom of the plane. They approached. Griffin tightened.

"Our targets are moving," Lance reported.

Daytime on the platform. Made sense. Too late, though. The rescue was underway.

They came in under VTOL, blowing up an unholy wind, amid the low, natural buildings. Out the windows, Griffin saw Argonauts, and other strange animals, scurry about as the long maroon stalks of whatever crop they were growing vibrated in their exhaust.

She actually screamed as she and Robb dropped the ten meters from the hovering plane. Griffin *was* a warrior! Scream, shoot, scream, shoot.

She had to shoot. Argonauts were rushing toward her, attacking her. They'd cut off Melinda's arm, after all. They were brutal. She and Robb had to deal with them. Dozens of them. Hundreds of them.

The creatures rushed at them, screaming themselves.

The Specialists' Eagles screamed back, in large caliber. Griffin thought the disparity eminently fair.

Time stretched. Griffin imagined she saw her shots fly through the air. She saw the dark-hued Argonauts coming after her, blades flashing, rushing toward her, falling. She saw her shots amputate a limb off one. What did it matter? They had eight. The bastards.

She tried to settle herself. Getting emotional and losing her logical base would not be in their best interests. Focus. Evaluate targets. Eliminate them.

Griffin was right. Two well-armed Specialists were more than a match for a large number of Argonauts without advanced technology. The fight was over in about thirty seconds.

Robb said, "I don't see anything moving. Do you?"

Griffin struggled to get her breathing under control. "No," she said. "Everything is still."

"Spreading out," said Robb.

"Ditto," said Griffin.

They moved away from the noisy, hovering plane, checking bodies as they came to them, finding them harmless (lifeless or too injured to be dangerous), and moving on.

Griffin kicked open a slanted door opening onto a sunken enclosure. Beneath the door were three—no, four, Argonauts. They were smaller than the ones she'd cut down, and did not seem to be aggressive. They huddled before her and shivered.

What should she do? What was the right thing? There was no way to be sure. If she left them, one of them might rise up and attack the second she turned her back. If she shot them all, well, that wouldn't happen, would it? Did that make that the right course of action? Did it?

She aimed her automatic. The Eagle would belch death the instant she thought it. The power didn't make her feel good. It made her feel nauseous. She didn't know if that was a fair sensation. Surely she was projecting her own self onto these shivering creatures. They were aliens. Did her projections mean a damn thing?

Griffin looked at the pathetic, thin-limbed things quaking before her, and felt pity. How, and why, should they expect vengeance from the skies like this? Might they be innocent of any act against a human? If so, how would she feel in their place?

Griffin eased back and prepared to move forward. Even as she did so, she heard Robb release an extended round. Undoubtedly he was killing something. She told herself that he was trained, that he wouldn't do that unless he was sure the something needed killing.

Griffin made herself move on, paying attention to the hole. If anything moved there, she would kill it.

She found herself hoping that nothing would move. *Please,* she thought. *Don't move. Don't be stupid. I don't want to kill you.*

After a few minutes, she and Robb had the area secured. Anything that had moved had been cut into hundreds of pieces. Everything else was stationary and intact. The only structure left to explore was a large, circular mud hut filled with some kind of animal. Griffin and Robb moved in.

Something beeped at her. Lance said, "They're not here."

"Tell me more," she said, stepping carefully forward, not letting her gaze wander.

The X-bot elaborated. "The RF signals are off the platform, descending rapidly."

"Fuck," opined Robb.

Indeed. "Be that as it may, we're not leaving yet. We're making this foray count. We're not wasting—" she started, and stopped. She had begun to say that they were wasting native lives for no reason, but didn't know that she could say that with certainty. They'd made shots descending, Robb afterward. Lives had been lost. Alien lives, to be sure, but did they count out less than human lives? Part of her said yes, part of her said no. She didn't know how to weigh the two parts.

"Move into the structure," she said to Robb. "You first, me backing you up."

Griffin felt bad about the order, but it was procedure. She had to hang on to something.

Robb stepped into the darkness, stepped down, and vanished. Griffin followed him. It was her responsibility.

The enclosed area *reeked*. Another version of herself, in a parallel universe, was vomiting. This place was a sty. Literally. Filled with unclean animals, with more legs than was natural, that grunted and scurried. A part of her was tempted to shoot them all. That would make it easier to evaluate things.

"All clear," Robb reported.

So there it was. The last place, all clear, no Klingston, no Specialists. "Where are they?" she asked.

One of Lance's patterns came across the local channel. "We said they were moving. They're not actually here anymore. They've moved off the platform."

Great. How many . . . things, please, don't think of them as people . . . had we killed? Zero, twenty, fifty? She'd shot initially, but Robb had shot more.

That wasn't fair. They shared all responsibility, and she was commander. She had at least as large a share of responsibility as he did, and probably larger.

Screw that. No time to be weak. Events transpired, she had to accept that and go on, until she made the events occur that she desired. They didn't have Klingston or anyone else rescued yet.

Until her fellow Specialists were rescued or dead, there was no responsibility for anything. No worries yet. No success yet. No failure yet.

"Lance," she asked. "Where are our people?"

"They're off the platform. We've missed them."

The answer reassured her, given their lack of success. "Okay," she said. "We're coming back. We're going to rescue them. If not here, then somewhere. If not now, then soon. We're going to rescue them."

Griffin wished that she felt as confident as her words.

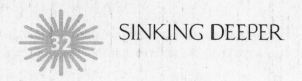

SINKING DEEPER

INSIDE THE SKELETON OF THE SPIDER STAR

"Get the door open, Mistelle!" Rusk yelled.

Their mesh shield was frayed, tattered. They'd already lost another Specialist, and every few seconds he felt one extremity or other warm up from the spillover of the hydra microwaves. Their tattered shield was fast becoming a joke. He was starting to think it likely he would die in the next few minutes and have very little, if any, warning.

Surprisingly, it was easy to work in such an environment. Rusk didn't have to think more than a few seconds in advance, trying to stay behind their shield, and trying to find opportunities to return a shot to their adversaries.

There was an undercurrent of thought, an undercurrent that terrified him, that wanted to shirk their mesh shield, blast off toward the hydras, and shoot every one of them. Intellectually he realized that they would nail him long before he would be able to nail every one of them, but the undercurrent grew in strength. He could solve all their immediate problems in just a few seconds if he could release his debilitating fear. Could he?

A cool, blue light hit them.

"We're in!" Mistelle screamed.

Rusk glanced over his shoulder to see a circular aperture opening onto a tunnel about five meters across. "Inside!" he yelled. "You first, Anatole. Then I'll back in, keeping us shielded. Mistelle, can you close the door?"

"I think so," she answered as Anatole's PPU pushed him into the tunnel.

The maser fire had stopped when the tunnel had opened, but new sparks burst from their mesh curtain and Rusk eased backward. "Hold it!" Rusk said, even as the shield began to melt away in their hands. He could feel the searing heat through his gloves. "Hold it even if your hands burn down to stumps!"

Then, almost instantly, a slate-gray wall materialized in front of them.

"I got it closed," Mistelle said, a hint of self-satisfaction in her voice, which choked off on the last syllable of *closed*. She asked, "Where's Kat?"

"Didn't make it," Rusk said. "And we've lost Drone, too. Now, come on."

"Where?" she asked.

"Where else? Down the tunnel. Do you see another choice?" Rusk said the words quickly, with an edge, and felt bad about it but did not apologize. "Let's catch up to Anatole."

Indeed, Anatole hadn't wasted any time. He was moving slowly, but deliberately, through the tunnel as it curved steadily and sloped upward. He even had his weapon armed and ready. Rusk approved. Anatole was pleasantly odd, but operative in a crisis.

From behind them came a slight popping sound, a slight change in pressure, and a slight humming noise. "We're with you, Anatole. Pick up the pace. I don't know what's ahead, but I do know what's behind."

The tunnel diameter gradually increased from five meters until it was nearly ten. They also began to hear sounds ahead of them. It was hard to judge how far ahead, or exactly the nature of the sounds—they were quiet, mechanical, rhythmic, or semi-rhythmic sounds. They were utterly incapable of preparing him for what he saw a few moments later.

The tunnel opened into a funnel. The funnel opened onto a single room.

Room was a woefully inadequate term. Rusk had never seen a single room this large. The arcology parks back in Colchis weren't so large, and the nearest equivalent he could imagine from his studies would be an indoor football stadium, but even that wasn't close. If he had to, he would have guessed the room was ten kilometers across, and shaped like a big empty ball. The light inside was golden and came isotropically from a source in the middle of the room. Its entire surface was pockmarked with faint blue holes like the one they were floating in, although the holes varied tremendously in size.

They could only be in one of the nodes that they had imaged from orbit, places where the Spider Star's legs flared out and from which other tubes and structures grew.

As Rusk took in the big picture, which required significant head swiveling in all directions, he finally began to be capable of assimilating smaller details. Hydras floated everywhere. They floated alone, in pairs, in small groups, and in three-dimensional formations that made Rusk think of the word *battalion*. Inanely, he wondered what English word would be chosen to describe groups of these aliens? *Murder* was already taken for crows. Maybe an *assault* or perhaps a *maser* or maybe even a *hug*. Words describing groups didn't always make sense.

"Don't we need to keep moving?" Anatole asked.

"Yes, we should," said Rusk. "There's a hug of hydras on our tail."

"And people say *I* make no sense!"

Rusk worried about himself, about his decisions. There were no rules to follow here! There was no word for a group of these hydras! He knew he was struggling, and every time there was a chance to stop to think about their situation, that struggle bubbled up. Anatole was right, they needed to keep moving. But to where? This place was full of hydras.

But what if they were like the first bunch that had come to

dismantle the dirigible? Might they not ignore the Specialists completely? In any event, they couldn't just go blasting straight up, hoping to follow the leg back to the space dock. They'd never reach the tunnels near the ceiling before their pursuers emerged and spotted them.

They'd have to go down a different, closer rabbit hole and hope for the best. Rusk looked around, focused again. Where now? There was no point trying to sort through the logic of the place, so he picked one at random. Not the closest, but one not so far away. "There!" He pointed.

The Specialists took off. The closest hydras was a hug of four (his own naming rule, but a rule nonetheless, and he'd stick to it), about three hundred yards away, at a slightly higher altitude. They continued in their course without pause, paying no attention to the jetting humans. None of the hydras seemed to be paying them any attention. Small favor, or a bit of luck. Didn't matter, they would take it gratefully.

Anatole led the way down the new hole, at a slightly lower altitude, off to the left about fifteen degrees. Mistelle powered down after him, their PPUs revving up for the hard turn. Rusk was about to follow when he paused to look back.

Just that instant, the pursuing, armed hydras popped out of the tunnel entrance that the Specialists had just vacated.

Damn! They barely had a lead at all, and he was still in the open.

Rusk made a snap decision. He jetted over the tunnel his comrades had just entered, radioing them a quick message: "Keep going and don't look back!" And Rusk shut down his active receiver. He didn't think they needed more than one hero right now.

He hadn't followed his own advice, and would now pay his penalty. That was just. That was his own prerogative.

Rusk quickly aimed at another hug that was on the projection of the line connecting the military hydras to himself. He hoped that they would hesitate before masering in that direction. He located the nearest funnel opening along his new trajectory and dived into it as soon as he could. He didn't feel any heat, and thought that was to be expected; he wouldn't feel anything in this range with a direct shot—his head would simply explode.

In a way, that made it easy. He simply acted. Death would strike instantly, if it would at all. It wasn't that he'd forgo caution, but it did mean he didn't have to concern himself with survival after he'd reached a decision.

Rusk dropped into his new tunnel. It was slightly larger than the one they'd exited, but similarly constricted quickly. He spied a side tunnel branching away, but decided, again in an instant, to skip it. His pursuers would investigate the first side tunnel. They'd be slower to investigate a second. This, now, was a game of margins.

Rusk whizzed through the tunnel at full thrust. The speed dizzied him. He let his autopilot navigate the turns since it was faster than him. He decided he'd turn off the main passage at the second or third turnoff. The blue tunnel, turning steadily, mesmerized him. This was a crazy way to live a life. To think, in another existence, he could be sitting with friends on a beach, sipping some wine, and petting a cat in his lap, and instead he'd wound up doing this . . . ambition made men crazy!

There, another branch! Rusk took it, spiraling off to his left, a passage with a much tighter turning radius, almost a corkscrew. He had no idea where this headed, what its purpose might be, but it was his only possibility at survival, so he dove into it with glee and abandon. Part of him abstractly mused that he was the survivor of a nearly infinite generation of survivors, so he ought to have a chance here.

Twisting blue tunnel, PPU at maximum thrust under autopilot, masering monsters behind him, the unknown before him.

Wasn't this *exactly* what the Specialist Corps had promised him? The wind whipped in his face, strange odors hit him occasionally, and nothing he saw was anything like anything he'd seen back on Argo training. This was *discovery,* no matter how it ended.

There! Another branch! Rusk headed for it, not pausing to look to see if his pursuers were visible. Part of him hoped they were, because that meant they'd followed him rather than the others. The selfish part of him hoped that no one was behind him, that he'd escaped cleanly. That was the selfish but honest part. Why shouldn't he live, after all? Wasn't life expectancy arbitrary in some sense? Why not let him die in bed surrounded by family and friends? Lots of people managed to do that, so why *not* him?

Because he'd had the ambition to head an interstellar mission, gambling the risk against the additional fame? Wasn't that a reasonable bet to make?

The new tunnel went down, very down. The angle of descent was over forty degrees, and had a sharp turn. Eventually it straightened out and increased its descent angle to over sixty degrees.

Rusk worried he was in a garbage chute. It was narrow, and dropped rapidly. Unfortunately, it didn't seem too narrow for an armed hydra. He continued to follow it, hoping it would lead someplace with possibilities for escape. What else could he do?

Suddenly the tunnel broke up into a maze and Rusk screamed his thanks to no one in particular. This was as close to perfect as he could expect. He had no expectations of complete escape and rescue, not yet, but this situation promised at least the prospect of a good hiding spot. That was as much as he could expect. If he survived the next few minutes, only then could he contemplate an escape.

Here he was, Manuel Rusk, the best and brightest of the best offspring of the Argo colonists, hiding in a maze in an alien space station, hoping for survival as the best possible outcome.

This was so wrong. But you took what the universe threw at you—how could you do anything else—and that *was* what was possible. If the best and brightest of the Earth's best and brightest who had become Argo colonists, if that was the best humanity had to offer, well, that was Rusk, here, hiding in a maze from maser-wielding aliens. That was it. That was the result of billions of years of evolution. So be it.

Still, it annoyed Rusk, and didn't seem fair. The Argonauts had a lead on humans, no matter what the ages of their stars. He assumed that the hydras did, too. Was it fair that the fairest possibility was that you'd evolved in the middle of the pack, millions of years after the early adopters? After a moment of thought, Rusk decided that, yes, it was fair. Humans might just be screwed coming from the outer part of the Milky Way, from around a lower mass, older star. It was fair. They were simply not competitive.

Still, he hid. Competitive or not, he would compete. Life didn't give up. It played until the end, and so would he.

He had minutes, entire minutes, to think. This situation was *enormous.* This was one of the first serious encounters between humans and alien intelligences. No matter the outcome, it would be significant. Even if it weren't fair, the outcome would shade future interactions. In principle, if anyone ever learned from this encounter.

A metaphorical switch shifted then inside Rusk's head. He was playing a game for the future of humanity, not just himself, and, if he could, he would find a way to pass on his knowledge.

He found a locker.

It was a space with a closing door, anyway. Enough to call it a locker. That seemed like such a trivial thing, initially, but he was able to maneuver inside it, and close that door. That was huge.

He might have just become invisible to the hydras after him, and he hoped it was true, and that it was all of them. He hoped that the other Specialists had escaped free and clear, even if he himself had not. It was possible.

Rusk powered down his PPU, and settled down on top of some coils of rope, wire, something, he didn't know for sure. He shut down most of his systems, and his lights. He relaxed his breathing, and waited in the dark box that he had found. He had no idea what sort of sensors the hydras had. His alternative was to keep running, and he didn't believe the alternative to necessarily have better chances than his current action.

Rusk tried to remain silent. He adjusted his outgassing protocols to prevent detection. He could hold it awhile, after all. A short time, under normal circumstances.

It was maddening.

Again, there were no rules about how long you needed to hide to escape detection. How long would an enemy keep looking? A few hours? A day? Forever? When might they give up?

Who knew? What was important was that they went by, at least for now.

And they did!

Rusk wanted to celebrate as he heard a parade of hydras, a powerful hum accompanying each one, proceed past him. They could be fooled! They didn't know everything that transpired on this station, even though they lived here. Rusk and his Specialists had a chance!

A few minutes after the armed hydras passed by him, Rusk powered his systems up and left his locker and backtracked to another passage in the maze. He would keep going, as long as he had food and water to keep alive, no matter the pursuit. He was one of the best Specialists ever, and now reality had a chance to confirm (or demolish) his test scores.

Why couldn't he keep ahead of his pursuers, and eventually escape?

He would try. Certainly, he would try.

He would just have to make his own rules.

TWO TRIBES

HOME OF THE BIG ONE

Yellow took Frank and the other Argonauts to another grav-tube station, which wasn't all that far away from the farming platform. Every time Frank twitched, Yellow kicked him, so the short flight was a blessing. The new tube station differed from the previous one in that the angle of descent was much steeper. Otherwise everything appeared at least superficially identical.

Frank and the other Specialists were wrapped in twine, which Walter had suggested was a natural plant derivative, and dumped into the car.

This drop made his stomach rise. The descent was *much* steeper. After the initial drop, he became accustomed to the mild gravity and confidently believed the trip would be just less than forty-five minutes.

Selene was placed next to him. He didn't know if that meant the Argonauts realized that there was something between them (was there?) or if they were just piled in at random. He wanted to ascribe motives to these aliens, but they were still alien.

He and Selene were close enough that they could converse in whispers, but Frank wasn't sure what to say to this woman. The circumstances were, at a minimum, exceptional. All he knew was that she shouldn't expect any flowers.

"Frank," she whispered. "Frank, I wanted to let you know that you'll do okay. You'll manage the situation as well as anyone is able, and if we all die, it isn't your fault."

That was supposed to make him feel better? He really, really didn't have any idea how to respond to her statement, or to their coupling of the previous night, except to feel guilty about it. He opted for the ultimate panacea, and said, "Umm, thanks."

She didn't say anything, not right away. Then she said, "Seriously, Frank. You're a greater man than you realize. When the time comes, and you have the opportunity to make an important decision, you'll do okay."

Why did this strange, fascinating woman keep saying that? Didn't she realize that his leadership had killed or maimed several Specialists, and made several more captives to violent aliens?

Did their physical act matter? It made him feel guilty, and perhaps it provided Selene with misplaced confidence in him. That suggested it mattered, in a negative way, but he didn't see any way to make up for it.

They were, after all, bound captives.

The car fell onward, downward, upward, who could say? The car moved ballistically, only constrained by the frictionless tunnel wall and the laws of gravity, as one of his old instructors would have said. Physics was so much easier than affairs of the heart. You could use calculus, after all, and find an exact solution.

Eventually the fall ended, the car slotted into a docking station, and the Argonauts hauled the Specialists out again. There were no glider rides this time. Instead, each Specialist was carried to an open platform similar to the ones they'd seen before, and tossed off.

Frank couldn't believe it! To carry them all this way, and then, with no hesitation, to toss their captives to their deaths . . . it made no sense!

Frank yelled out when it was his turn. He couldn't help himself.

But a few seconds after being thrown and believing the worst, reaching the top of his arc and falling, he slid onto some sort of angled surface. The surface resembled, at least superficially, the silky material of the sacks and wings of the gliders. It seemed quite strong, but gave slightly as they landed, and was smooth enough to slide down.

They slid. They slid for kilometers.

Every so often the slope would change, or the direction would shift, and they'd slow. Somewhat. Frank still felt, viscerally, shining-white-intestine visceral, that they were flying out of control to their ultimate doom. But at this altitude the acceleration was probably less than 20 percent of Earth gravity, and things never quite got out of control as he feared.

That is, any more than they already were.

Frank heard some yells, then Argonaut shouting as cacophonous as any spider monkey fit he'd ever heard back on Argo. He wished he had the ability to move, to look around, but he was still wrapped. All he could do was slide.

Unbidden, a thought came to him: his son Allyn would love this. Allyn loved rides.

Almost immediately, his rapid descent leveled off and he saw some sort of flat region and a wall. The wall seemed to be textured and brown, and rapidly grew larger as he looked. He smacked into it at high velocity and sank into the giving surface.

The brown was apparently a welcome mat.

Frank waited to be pulled out, smelling the unusually good smell from the dried, spongy weed. The musty, cinnamon smell was infinitely better than the animal pen of the previous night. He smelled, and he waited for his captors.

There were more wild calls, and Frank was pulled out. Two Argonauts he hadn't seen before (they didn't have colored belts) pulled him out of the cushioning pile of dried vegetation. They dragged him across the ground.

Frank saw blue sky overhead, some sort of crops, and rows of dark-bodied Argonauts lining his path. His head lolled back and forth as he was pulled along.

After several moments of irritating his bruises, the alien hands let go and he fell, heavily, onto the dusty ground.

Something loud, and something grating, made sounds that resembled the Argonaut tongue.

More yelling, more dragging, this time inside a woven hut that smelled subtly similar to rotting garlic. The smell was strange.

Frank, wrapped, laid in the dirt, then lifted his head.

He didn't like what he saw, and dropped his head.

There was a big creature, maybe an Argonaut, maybe not, making the sounds. They were louder now, more insistent. Frank had no idea what it was saying, and ignored it. The sounds repeated, several times, and he was kicked, but he said nothing. What could he say that they would understand?

Where was Jason?

Frank had been tossed on the slide before the X-bot. Had they decided to leave Jason behind for some reason?

Something grabbed Frank by his long hair and hauled him up to a standing position. Yellow, it was Yellow, and the Argonaut held Frank's head to force him to look directly at the creature seated before him.

Seated wasn't quite the correct term. *Nestled* was better, as it grasped a large assemblage of twisted, lime-colored branches with its eight appendages, and Frank couldn't help but think of a spider in its web, waiting for prey to stumble across it.

Superficially, it resembled the other Argonauts. Same basic body plan and shape, but several things distinguished the creature. It was larger, to start with, maybe 20 percent larger, and that wasn't just the fact that its limbs were longer, *everything* was larger. Its big, implacable black eyes, its fanged mouth, its bristly ears, everything. And Frank recognized it was male, and didn't need any of Jason's patterns to tell him that. The coloration was different from the others, too. Its skin was a shiny, waxy black like the others, but the thin hairs, or bristles, were not black.

They were gray. And when it spoke, it was louder than the other Argonauts, with a gravely, phlegm-filled quality.

This was the big one, then, without a doubt. But weren't the males supposed to be smaller?

And the big one spoke again, demanding something, what exactly, Frank still didn't know.

Yellow answered back and there was an exchange. It didn't scan to Frank as a conversation, but rather as a series of questions and answers.

"So what have we here?" came the voice of one of Jason's patterns, one of the female Argonaut cultural anthropologists. "Oh my!"

He heard a clang, as something hard hit the X-bot.

He wanted to turn to look, but Yellow's strong hands held his head fixed ahead.

Yellow said something, and someone answered. The big one—the Chief, Frank decided to call him, which was a little less ridiculous—said something.

Another Argonaut stepped forward, Orange, Yellow's rival as far as Frank had been able to ascertain. He didn't know if personal rivalries were something that Argonauts had, but he imagined so. He thought of Kenny and Allyn coming before him when they'd been fighting, and having to make a decision. He wondered if someone were about to get a spanking.

The three called back and forth to each other, growing increasingly loud. Frank didn't want to read things that weren't there, but he thought all three were also getting angrier. This continued for several minutes and Frank hoped that Jason was getting it all.

The Chief finally roared with enough volume that the force of it resonated through Frank's chest cavity and everyone fell silent. Except for its mouth, the Chief had remained preternaturally still throughout the entire encounter up until this point.

Now, with careful deliberateness, it released its branching nest with its top two arms and extended them toward Frank.

Frank wondered if he was the one about to get the spanking.

He didn't have a lot options. About the only positive action he could take would be to yell at Jason to tell them something, but not understanding the situation, he might just make things worse. He resigned himself to whatever fate had in store for him.

Yellow released her grip on Frank and he expected to be pushed forward into the Chief. That didn't happen. Instead, Orange sidled over to hold Frank and Yellow stepped forward to the Chief.

Yellow extended her left upper arm. The Chief took hold of it in a way that almost seemed tender. But they were aliens. Frank didn't really know if the gesture was tender or not.

The Chief leaned forward and although Yellow's body partially hid what was occurring, the crunching, slurping sounds made it all too clear how his first interpretation was so very, very wrong. The Chief was eating her arm.

Yellow stood there, taking it, and the seconds grew into minutes. The only clue that she was experiencing what Frank had to assume was incredible pain was that her bottom four legs, the ones resting in the dirt, slowly twisted, leaving behind short, curved trails.

Finally it was over, and Yellow stepped back.

The Chief leaned back and howled dominantly, the sound resonating in Frank's chest. Argonauts scurried, yelling among themselves. Two came forward and helped Yellow move off. Orange yelled some things. Jason came tumbling into the space between the Chief and Frank.

Orange, continuing to hold Frank tightly, grabbed her blade and lifted it to his throat. Maybe now it really was his turn.

The cool blade touched his skin, and started to slice. Frank let go his breath when he realized it was slicing the twine that wrapped around him up to his neck. Orange shifted her grips as she cut him free, and finally a few moments later, released him altogether.

Frank stood unbound before the Chief.

The Chief barked a few things, and Jason answered with Ginnie's voice.

The Chief roared again.

Orange started to say something, and the Chief cut her off with a quick, loud chirp. Orange, and all the other Argonauts left the hut, leaving Frank and Jason alone with the Chief.

Jason said, "I am to translate."

"Good," said Frank. "Can you tell me what's going on?" He didn't know how long Jason would have, so he added, "Quick summary."

A slightly heavy woman with short blond hair appeared in Jason's display. Judith, Frank recalled, another Argonaut language expert. She began speaking about three times as fast as a normal person did—useful now, but undoubtedly not the reason that made her chosen for patterning. "Orange and Yellow had a catfight. They were supposed to return with trophies from the enemies who had called, and should have at least returned with some of our weapons rather than run away with nothing to show for the effort but these useless foodstuffs—humans, I assume. They've been fighting about what they should do ever since, and Yellow was punished for not succeeding. Orange is in charge of the hunting party now. The big one, he wants to ask you some questions in private, and you're to answer truthfully and not misbehave, or he'll kill you with his bare . . . hands and ask the others. Keep in mind translations may be imperfect."

It took Frank a few seconds for his brain to assimilate what she'd said so quickly. She'd answered some of his questions, but he still had many more. He was about to ask for elaboration when the Chief spoke again, staring directly at Frank with his huge, black eyes.

The interview began.

The Chief gave a long drawn-out grunt with a varying inflection.

" 'What are you?' " Jason asked, neutral again, synthesizing the translating talents of all its patterns. Good. That would be less distracting.

But . . . what was he? How was Frank supposed to answer that? He was a human, a carbon-based life form, a husband and father, a mission director of sorts, and more and less than all those things. He was a citizen of the galaxy. Not as much of a gentleman as he desired. Talented and too proud, once. A man who liked a good beer. In quiet moments, a poet, he liked to believe. Definitely, at least at the moment, a man who thought way too much.

Seconds dragged out, and Frank started to worry that this interview wasn't going well, that the Chief would finish with him and move on to Selene next.

"Excuse me!" Jason said. "Better translation. The question is, 'What are you *to me*?' He wants to know what you are with respect to him. Are you a threat? Are you an opportunity? Basically, what can you do for him?"

He had been advised that the translations would not be perfect. But really, on the first question? Frank wondered what mistranslation would get him killed.

Still, this was a difficult question for Frank to answer. Less ambiguous, perhaps, but difficult to be sure.

Did Argonauts negotiate? How did they negotiate? He had an assemblage of the top experts here, extant in Jason, but little time to use them.

Frank had to say something. He turned to Jason and said, "Tell him that—"

The Chief barked something, loud enough to make Frank jump.

"He says," said Jason, "look at him when you answer."

That was consistent with the way that Yellow and the others had been treating Jason, ignoring the X-bot. They seemed to dismiss it because it was a machine. That had to mean something here.

Frank spoke again, this time looking directly into the big, black eyes that regarded him steadily. "I am an opportunity."

Jason translated his statement. Frank needed to keep things simple, learn as they went along, and see if there was room to negotiate. He just hoped that Jason's embedded patterns would realize the stakes and do their part. Despite the obvious danger, the opportunity to act unknotted a tightness that permeated his body and let a tiny flicker of hope ignite.

The Chief was gargling now, a new question. When he finished, Jason said, " 'What type of opportunity? I cannot eat you, as I am told you are poisonous. I cannot make you a worker, as you are a crippled four-arm, and weak. I cannot make you an entertainer, as you are too pale and ugly. Again, what are you to me?' "

Frank tried to think of something, but part of him stalled on the "ugly" part, quite pleased to hear the judgment. To the matter at hand, Frank thought he could offer the Chief a great deal although he wasn't sure it would be wise. Modern weapons, transport, and surveillance—the Argonauts seemed to have little of these, living as they did on these farming platforms. Why was that, exactly? They seemed to know how to operate the grav-tubes, the elevators up and down the spokes, and tap into incoming communications. And why, after two million years, were they still here at all?

He decided to play for time. They had seen the space plane out the tube, after all. Negotiate . . . He didn't know what sort of enemies they had here, but Frank bet that this bunch would have enemies if anyone would. They'd been mentioned in the arguments several times. "We have weapons to offer."

Jason translated. The Chief waved one of his upper arms and spoke briefly. " 'The scouts say you use ballistic weapons. These must require specialized materials for ammunition, special processing. Once the ammunition runs out, your weapons are useless. Try again.' "

Frank almost spoke immediately, almost offered up a nanoforge. They had several, and could make more, but that would be too much. The nanoforge would provide them with infinite ammunition, and more, much more. And if the Argonauts had been living like this for so long, he wasn't about to give them a magic bag that would upset whatever balances that existed. Not without a better understanding of life on the Spider Star.

What else could he offer? Passage back to Argo, perhaps? Yes! It wasn't like this handful of Argonauts would take over their colony. They'd be a scientific godsend. "I can provide passage back to your home world. The place your kind came from before here."

The Chief began shivering as Jason translated. Frank had no idea what shivering indicated, not specifically, but he thought it likely indicative of some strong emotion. Again he found himself hoping there hadn't been a mistake in translation that would get him killed.

The Chief's reply was long, punctuated by gestures from every limb and one clacking his teeth. Jason waited a few moments before translating, then said, " 'Home world? This airy place is our home. The'—some untranslatable curse, we think—'they have their doomed world. They are doomed for their hubris, their arrogance, their evil, blackmailing an entire'— people, we think in this context—'into perpetual slavery for second-place land holdings and suffering.' Sorry, we can translate better than this with more time, we'll work on it, continuing, 'We stay on here, making this place our home, to keep them from ever saving themselves by coming here. They had their chance, not now, we have made sure. We win, now and forever.'"

This was stunning, unbelievable, impossible. Frank knew he had to respond, and quickly, and tried to buy some more time. Another rant, and that was what it seemed to boil down to, would let him think of a way to exploit this extreme position. "Jason, only translate what I say between the word *quote*, please. I want you to figure out all the ramifications of this, if you can. What's been going on here. Now I suppose I have to say something. Pad it out if it seems too short. Quote: The—untranslatable curse— they're long dead and gone. You could repopulate your world with our help. Don't, um, turn your back or similarly appropriate metaphor, from the chance to rebuild your civilization. We've come here to . . . heal Pollux, the home-world star, to make Argo a good place to live again. To lift the curse."

Jason translated after a moment, presumably stalling for time of its own so its patterns could internally converse and work on the problem Frank had assigned them.

When Jason had finished, the Chief immediately began to laugh, at least that was how Frank read it. From its rounded black belly, bellowing croaks squeezed out painfully. The Chief spoke, finally, slowly now, with some undefined shift in emotion that might be humor, but didn't seem to be so simply interpreted. " 'My fathers and mothers came to this place, with their brothers and sisters. They spent a long time—hundreds of years—to reach this place, bringing spider monkeys to eat, dedicated to freedom and justice. You see, we came to learn to control the alien technology that held us enthralled as slaves.'

" 'One of our number fell. After his departure, the golden ones, who made the world, they heard our prayers. To be fair, they helped us learn how to control the planet movers. We called back to our people to let them fight back. If you are here now, with Pollux cursing the world, well, the'—and we're just saying 'cursed ones' from now on—'well, the cursed ones truly are cursed and the world is not a home to anyone any longer. That is their enduring legacy, and the curse they have forced us to cast upon them for all eternity. Pollux will curse Argo and make it burn with revenge.'"

Frank didn't fully understand this, but parts made sense. More important, was his side the ones who had set up the destructive engine in Pollux responsible for the Lashings? Did that mean he knew how to stop it? "Quote: You can stop the engine of destruction in the star, make Argo a place for your people to live freely again."

The Chief responded in the same manner that he'd assumed after Frank's statement about healing. "'You don't understand, and you've surely made such great sacrifices. There are no people now, not on my side. More perhaps on the other arms. Here only I remain, and old I am. Our food, we bred larger and smarter, for forces to use against my former brothers, and for recreation. There are just two small tribes, and our monkeys, tending our own spokes, sometimes fighting, sometimes trading. And my side, just me . . . I suppose the monkeys will carry on when I am gone. I can't go home, and don't want to. Now, again, what can you offer me?'"

Frank almost dropped to his knees. The revelations assaulted him physically, making his body weak. Frank had no purpose unless he could prevent the Lashings, and here was a creature that was at least partially responsible, or his ancestors, and had no interest in stopping them. He could offer this creature nothing, because there was nothing this creature could offer him that he wanted. Not if the Lashings were off the table.

Frank tensed, fury growing inside him. A mad leap, yes, he could reach the Chief. He didn't think he could kill this crazed, ancient thing, but he thought maybe he could blind it. A blind Chief . . . that seemed like justice for beings that had taken away the sun and made it an enemy. Yes.

"We advise against your action," Jason said. The X-bot could pick up his medical telemetry and draw conclusions about his mental and physical state. "We believe you'd be killed in an instant. Do not be misled by this creature's apparent lethargy."

The Chief gargled some more, foul liquids bubbling up from within its gut to modulate its utterances. Jason translated, " 'I am curious. We added a long delay into the cycle to permit threats, negotiation, and victory if possible, but we did indeed program death to our enemies. Lingering death over a generation that they would know our terrible vengeance and slowly crushed hope. How could we do otherwise? Satisfy my curiosity. Did your kind build their homes on the surface, everywhere green and lush?' "

Frank swallowed, fearful of the calm, measured words coming from the X-bot, not answering.

Jason continued, finishing the translation of the Chief's words. " 'Because if you did, and these would be wonderful places—my people admired our world, we did—they are all targets. Every place worth anything is a target. Your kind is as doomed as our enemies. If you took as long to reach this place as my people did, all your people are long extinct. The sun will burn *everything*.' "

WASP

DEEP IN THE BOWELS OF THE SPIDER STAR

His team would be trying to go up, the hydras would likely expect him to go up, and so Rusk went down at every opportunity.

Rusk no longer cared for his own survival, at least not in the long-term sense. He would do his best to stay alive, without a doubt, and even permitted himself to dream of Griffin's rescue, maybe, someday, but he vowed to learn what he could and provide periodic distractions.

Rusk learned that most of the hydras had specialized duties. That is, a hydra that maintained a power station did just that, to the exclusion of all else, and it didn't care if he walked right up to it and fiddled with its anatomy. He could study the creatures and better understand their physical weaknesses.

Their mistake, Rusk decided, had been shooting the salvage hydra. It had its instructions to do its job—their dirigible taken to be some kind of floating debris to be dismantled and reprocessed—and if they hadn't interfered with force they would have never seen the military hydras.

And Slyde and Coyner would still be alive.

He had these thoughts as he grasped a hydra tentacle in his bare hands, feeling its slick but not slimy surface, squeezing its tough, rubbery substance as it yielded beneath his probing fingers, and offering no resistance.

Rusk had been brash, and had made a mistake that had cost lives. Klingston wouldn't have been so brash. Rusk had been too bold, too aggressive. Too young and cocksure. It was his fault. It was tempting to throw his life away in some gesture, finding his pursuers, and challenging them directly. He had no illusions about what would happen. His head would explode with a high dose of microwave energy, and he wouldn't have any more guilt. The books would be balanced.

But he didn't quite believe that. He could still learn useful information, still provide a distraction that might permit Mistelle and Anatole to find a way to escape.

So he studied the nonviolent hydras, studied the equipment they tended, the tasks they performed, and he learned.

He followed one industrious hydra for three or four hours until it led him to a feeding pen. Rusk had to power up his PPU to reach the dispensers, which were holes partway up a hundred-meter wall—a wall covered in feeding creatures that reminded him of a lesson unit he'd watched once with bees and hummingbirds bobbing along a plant-covered trellis, sipping nectar from flowers.

The foodstuff had been a bland, pale paste that he'd had to scoop with his fingers and eat. It hadn't tasted bad, but it hadn't tasted good, either. He put faith in the ability of his body's modified biochemistry to digest it, and ate as much as he could stand.

He urinated and defecated when he needed to. His armor could, in time, absorb and pass on his wastes. Not indefinitely, but he didn't anticipate needing perfection forever.

He was a wasp. He flew about, stinging, laying eggs of pain. He would avoid the swats when they came, if he could.

His sabotages had ludicrous simplicity. These hydras operated mindlessly like robots, and like any robotic plant, if any stage failed to operate to specs it could cause chain reactions of damage.

For instance, down one tunnel with an especially warm and moist updraft, he found what he took to be a nursery. There were tanks, filled with a yellowish, clear liquid, aerated with bubbling gas stacked against the walls from top to bottom, filling the room with white noise. Inside the tanks floated gelatinous balls, almost transparent except for a triple set of beady, black eyes. Their appearance made Rusk think of raw shrimp. Thin, white strings, umbilicals, or guide lines connected each blob to the floor of the tanks.

They grew larger from one end to the other as they floated in their incubators, growing. Rusk followed the end of the tanks to sets of clear tubing, which the largest of the growing hydras flowed through into another room. Rusk watched what happened here, lingering for nearly an hour—much longer than he normally allowed himself—trying to understand what was going on. The embryos, infants, or whatever the appropriate word was—huggies?—ended up on brightly lit platforms. Metal arms emerged from the lights and poked and prodded them, after which they were whisked away by clawed arms on moving belts.

Closely watching the poking and prodding, Rusk realized two things. First, the pokers and prodders didn't just poke and prod. They penetrated and punctured, cutting through certain structures in what he thought might be their brains. Second, there was also one particular arm that left something inside the infant hydra brains: a small, black box extruding tiny silver whiskers.

Rusk had no idea what all this was doing, what it was for, but he didn't like it. He was busy being a wasp, a small annoying creature disrupting larger creatures and events it didn't understand. He took a unitool from his kit and broke the insertion needles on half a dozen of the stations. Then, before he could be ambushed if his activity was detected, he bugged out.

Rusk harbored ambiguous feelings about what he'd done. He didn't know if it was an awful thing, or a clever thing.

He continued to roam deeper, causing problems where he could, at random, and quickly moving on.

When he was exhausted, he located another storage closet, set up alarms, and tried to sleep. Sleep wouldn't come. Too much had happened, too many mistakes, too many incomprehensible sights. Still, the rest was good, the little he got, and he was able to save his stimulants.

Hours grew and became days. He thought.

Three times he had close calls with military hydras. They were recognizable because they deviated from the patterns of other maintenance hydras, or workers, as he thought of them, and because they carried the shiny masers extended from a pair of tentacles.

The third time, Rusk thought he was dead. He had jetted up with his PPU to a worker making adjustments to some hydroponic cages holding some sort of pale leafy vegetable that reminded Rusk of endive. He'd been planning to take a closer look, record some images, and see if there was a simple way to louse up the system. Just as he was reaching the worker, six military hydras flew out of a tunnel and spread out across the chamber.

Rusk, sure he was dead, did the only thing that came to mind. He powered on into the worker, killed his PPU, and grabbed hold of its tentacles with his arms spread wide and hands squeezing as tightly as he dared.

It was so slippery that he needed to wrap his legs around them too, and he hung there, from the slowly sinking alien, maybe fifty meters over a hard floor below. He had an unpleasant flash to an image from a movie he'd once seen, in which someone had to cut open a cow and reach inside to extract a microbomb that had been implanted inside.

He didn't know how the worker could fail to alert the soldiers to his presence, but there seemed to be little communication between different groups. Rusk felt heat on his face and arms as a meaty section of the worker warmed rapidly. Its distended air sack expanded with the heat, increasing its girth, and as the density decreased its buoyancy increased, and, together, they floated back up to the hydroponics bank.

With the extra heat came the smell of methane and other odors he associated with flatulence, all of which went poorly with his thoughts of cow innards. Still, under the circumstances, Rusk would have hidden in the most disgusting toilet in the universe if it meant surviving. The smell did fade, slowly.

Rusk held on, trying to keep the creature's body between him and the military hydras, and hoping its own heat would mask his infrared signature.

The soldiers cleared out after a few minutes, but Rusk took advantage of his forced proximity to study the hydra more closely. In particular, he watched the synchronized movements of its muscular tentacles as they groomed the plants. They moved with a machinelike precision that, in humans, he had only seen in expert musicians and video game players. Most of his weight hung on two arms in particular, and the hydra simply let these two skip the sequence. How could it just ignore him?

But he did worry then, suddenly. The soldiers had first appeared after Slyde had shot off a tentacle. If Rusk's weight injured this one, they might get called back and that would be that for him. He let loose and hit his PPU, stopping to grab some of the ochre vegetables to eat, and exited by taking a different tunnel than the soldiers had.

He proceeded downward, wondering what additional mischief he could cause.

THE HEART
OF DARKNESS

A LONELY PLACE IN THE SPIDER STAR ARCHIPELAGO

The interview with the Chief complete, Orange came to collect Frank.

The Chief and Orange exchanged words. Then Orange grabbed Frank by his hair and pulled him out of the hut.

Jason followed along, recounting the conversation, although Frank barely heard it. "The Chief told Orange that he didn't care what happened to you, that you and the others were Orange's trophies to do with as she pleased."

What did any of it matter? The doomsday machine was going to keep going, peppering Argo with Lashings for years until everything had been hit. The Argonauts remaining here had no interest in helping, if it were even possible to help at this late stage. None at all. Their mission had been doomed before they even started. The colony was lost.

Frank had failed and his family was most likely dead.

Orange led him someplace. He didn't see where. He looked, he supposed, or he would have tripped, but nothing sank in.

They had *failed*. In fact, they had never had a *chance*.

He realized at some point that he was in another hut, dark inside, with the only light filtering in through the doorway and the edges of the thatching where they intersected an overhanging roof. The other Specialists were there, still wrapped up. Jason was relating his interview with the Chief. He didn't know if they'd tried to talk to him, and didn't know that they would understand his silence. They'd have to deal with the final revelation themselves, as he was trying to do now.

Frank realized that he needed to urinate. So he did. What did it matter? He'd been forced to do it several times already in recent days. He was just an old, lonely man in an empty universe. What did any of it matter?

"Frank!" Selene said, seeing, or smelling, what he had done.

Frank didn't respond. What was the point?

He lay down and tried to sleep, turning his thoughts and all the talking around him into static. It didn't matter. Nothing mattered anymore, so he didn't need to think about it then, did he?

His head spun, here in the shadowed hut, dark with stray streams of reflected light slipping inside. Eyes closed, eyes open, it didn't matter.

"Frank!" Selene yelled into his ear. She must have rolled over to him. Good effort for her, he supposed. Good for someone. Something good. A tiny good.

He didn't say anything. She hadn't asked him anything.

"Is it true, Frank?" she asked.

Damn. There it was, a question he'd actually heard. He supposed he could answer, but it wasn't like any of them had ever known an X-bot to lie. "That's what the Chief said."

They all prattled on, and at some point someone had the balls to have Jason untie them. Frank thought it had something to do with the fact that he was unbound, and that it was worth the risk. Frank assumed that they were thinking that he could be blamed, if necessary, and that was fine by him. It didn't matter anymore.

And then, unexpectedly, a wracking sob came up from his chest. And then another, and another. It *did* matter! His sons, Kenny and Allyn, were likely dead! Or banished in some emergency orbital ark if they'd put them together in time, looking down on their lost world. And Virginia, she'd had to be there with them, facing it with them, with no way to comfort them. He sobbed on, loudly, and didn't care what he looked like.

Someone's arms were around him, cradling him. Selene. "Let it out, let it out," she crooned.

Frank did. It was a thing inside him that he couldn't stop. They were dead, they were dead, and he was alone again, absolutely alone in a way that didn't exist when he was leading this mission for them, to ensure their survival.

Tears streamed down his face and snot pooled in his sinuses, and he sobbed.

"Frank, Frank," Selene said, holding him, rocking him. "Let it out, baby."

Sometime later, he didn't know how long, he was spent. Oh, despair still enveloped him like a dark cloak, but he just didn't have the energy to cry anymore. He imagined he would again, later, maybe after he'd slept.

"Frank," Selene whispered. "How did the Chief know how far we'd traveled, how fast we traveled?"

He didn't want to think, but her question worked into his head. "I don't know," he whined.

"He probably assumed that the trip was the same distance, and at the same speed, that they had used. Those assumptions aren't true, are they?"

No. They weren't. The Chief had said centuries, so their ship had been slower. And he knew from the Galactic orbital parameters that their travel distance had been slightly less. Just lucky there. "No," he said, sniffling. "We got here much faster than they did, if Jason did his conversions right."

"He did," she said. "We all helped check it."

But did that matter? Could they even get back in time to prevent disaster? How much time did they have, if ultimate destruction was inevitably headed for Colchis?

"And another thing, Frank," she said, quietly, continuing to rock him, "how do you know they wouldn't learn to predict the Lashings, and they'd certainly evacuate New Colchis if necessary, wouldn't they? Or even find a way to shield themselves. There are a lot of smart, talented people back on Argo. It isn't all up to us. Maybe not, anyway."

What she said was true. It made sense at least. He coughed a little, and slipped his arm up between hers to wipe his face with the back of his hand. "I'm sorry," he said. "I'm sorry!"

Cripes, what did they think of him? A few words from an alien—based on an imperfect translation in an uncertain universe—that could be a lie, and here he was, their executive director, reduced to a sobbing pile. "They could all be okay. Maybe thriving, even now."

"Yes," she said. "Yes."

Hope flared in his heart. He rationalized; the days of captivity, the stress, he wasn't in his right mind. Maybe his family could be okay—that was, *alive*.

Alive was the most beautiful word there was.

But he'd been so positive, moments ago, that his family was dead, or refugees in the cold dark spaces of the universe. What was the truth?

He was totally exhausted and stressed beyond measure.

"And perhaps," suggested Selene, "the Lashing mechanism can't accurately target after running for two million years."

It was all true, everything she said, at least the possibilities, they had a good chance to be true. He'd been a weak, self-indulgent ass. What would Kenny think of him? Allyn? Virginia? "You're right."

She continued to hold him and rock him. "Now then, we've still got a job to do. Right?"

"Right."

"This isn't Argonaut technology. The Chief you spoke with, he referred to 'golden ones' that lived in the core. That's who we need to talk to. Not these jokers."

She was so right. Why had he been made executive director in

the first place? He hadn't exactly negotiated with the aliens as well
as the first time he'd been forced to do so. Rusk or Griffin would
be doing infinitely better than him right now. For instance, neither of them were the captives of aliens, now, were they?

Enough self-indulgence then. Frank snorted, tried to clear
his breathing. "You're right, Selene."

They talked then, trying to figure out what their captors
might do with them, what they might do to influence them, or
escape. Walter brought up the best point. "We're not alone here.
We have people at the space dock, in the atmosphere, and we're
all wired. I don't know that they could read us in the Spider Star
legs themselves, but out here, hell, they just boost the power and
they should pick us up from hundreds of kilometers, or farther."

Frank had forgotten that for the moment; having the chip in
his arm, that was not second nature to him. There was a chance.
There was hope. Abracadabra.

He could live with that. They were excellent, great people.
The best people.

He ignored the tears that welled up, threatening his stability
again. What was wrong with him? This wasn't what they required from him now. "They were growing a plane when we
were captured and that's what we likely saw, or they could send
Rusk and his dirigible this way. Our weapons would make short
work of this lot."

Gabriella said, "There's too much killing, too many threats. I
don't like it. We should be talking with these people."

Frank thought back to the giant, soulless eyes of the Chief, his
cavalier attitude, his scorn for what they could offer him. "We
should be, but we can't."

There was something there, in that thought. There was something that now seemed impossible regarding negotiations. He
didn't know if it was their ancient, unwavering stance, or the
way that they associated humans with their enemy Argonauts,

but there was a block there. They had to find a way to do an end around. Selene was right, they needed to talk with the golden ones, or some other species on the Spider Star.

As long as they remained here, they were dead, and their planet was dead.

"We could escape," Timothy suggested.

They could try, Frank supposed. The hut walls didn't seem all that solid, not if they let so much light through. Their X-bot had at least a dozen tools that could get through it in seconds. The hut door was guarded by a group of Argonauts, yes, but there would be ways to get past them if necessary.

He gave the idea some more thought, beyond escaping their immediate confines. "To where? To what end? We know almost nothing about this place, almost nothing about how to operate its interfaces. It would be too easy to die. No, I think we're best off waiting for Griffin to rescue us, and learning what we can. We're all together, we're safe for the moment, and we have friends in very high places."

The golden ones living in the core, the ones who controlled the technology, that was who they needed to reach. Frank had Jason go over the translation of what the Chief had said about them. Jason's patterns deferred to Ginnie. Frank decided he could live with that. It was nice to hear Virginia's voice again in this far-off place, even if it wasn't really her.

"That's one of the trickiest bits of the whole passage."

"Why?" Frank asked.

"Because the literal translation didn't make any sense. But then I realized that they had deified the aliens living in the core, and it all snapped into place."

"Explain it to me."

"Well the translation I gave you was: 'One of our number fell. After his departure, the golden ones, who made the world, they heard our prayers. To be fair, they helped us learn how to control the the planet movers.' The literal translation was more like, 'Akkai fell forever, and in falling, was consumed by the sun below. The ones bathed in endless sunlight, the life-givers and star-makers, they listened to us then. To abide their own rules of balance, they instructed us about how to control the devices of the sun.' "

Stunned, Frank wondered how literal the other translations were that he'd heard. Something bugged him, though, about this one. "As a species, humans are pretty religious, I suppose, although most spacefarers and colonists willing to leave Earth have been predominantly secular. I know the Argonauts had many religions, but I don't recall anything religious about the Spider Star fairy tale."

Ginnie's image grinned, foolishly happy. "Oh, it's been a great controversy and there are several schools of thought. You see, I personally believe that it was recast for children and so the pilgrimages of their religious elements were trimmed. Historically, the speakers of the language the Chief used had a strong belief system."

Ginnie's image abruptly faded and the face of an older, short-haired woman appeared. "Listen to Ginnie, or listen to me. I don't think we can afford to *not* take anything literally here. Do you?"

No, he didn't. Frank had much to ponder.

The thatched door squeaked open a few hours later, admitting what seemed like blindingly bright light. Green scurried in on her four lower legs and commenced squawking and gesticulating. Green threw up four of her arms, squawked especially loudly one last time, and left.

Jason translated, "She's very upset you're all unwrapped. She says that someone needs to be punished for this."

Terrific, Frank thought, *let's get punished some more.* He felt like he'd already experienced the ultimate punishment, those moments of total loss of family, and loss of hope. They could do nothing worse to him than make those things a reality. Anything else was tolerable. He told them, "If they're going to punish anyone, they can punish me."

They were led outside to blink in the bright light reflecting off the mirrors above. It was blinding, and made them stumble as they were prodded onto a trail that wended its way through a long-stalked crop of some sort. They emerged into a clearing on the edge of the platform. The clearing was devoid of plants.

Dozens of Argonauts milled around the periphery. Frank supposed that he should stop thinking of them as Argonauts, remembering what the Chief had said. The Chief was an original Argonaut, he had to assume, the last son of a species all but extinct, but these other creatures, they were the result of two million years of selective breeding of Argotian spider monkeys. Listening to their screams and hooting now, he believed it. Nasty creatures.

"Hey," said Walter. "There's not just Argonauts here."

Frank looked around and quickly spotted what the other man was talking about. Huddled in a group of five or six individuals, was what appeared to be a small shrubbery. He'd glanced over them at first, but he now recognized that they weren't what he'd first believed. They weren't shrubbery and they weren't vegetables. They were . . . difficult . . . to look at. Not because they were ugly, or grotesque, but because the mind continuously failed to recognize and process them. There was a body in there, someplace, but long blue-green needles ending in rounded bulbs covered them and reminded Frank of some sort of sea anemone.

He didn't get to look long before Orange demanded his attention. The new leader of the elite military force (as per Jason's revised translation) stood completely upright on its back two legs, double Frank's height, and pulled him to his tiptoes by his hair.

Orange began to speak, and Jason translated. "A new species has arrived. Their importance is unknown, but new things do not come into our world often. Their leader, this one here, must be punished, and that punishment will demonstrate their submission. After the punishment, the others will be auctioned off. Use them for entertainment, work, or simply enjoy the novelty of ownership. They do not seem to be good for eating, however."

At least the last part didn't sound awful. At best, they'd be scattered, difficult to rescue. At worst, many could be killed for fun, or in error, in the hands of new captors.

What could he do? One idea lurked in his mind, but it was awful to contemplate. Even more awful than his fast-approaching punishment.

Suddenly Orange bent double, grabbing him with all her free arms. Almost all. One held a blade against his left forearm. Honestly, Frank had kind of expected this. Their captors seemed quite dogmatic. The only consolation was that his arm wouldn't be eaten.

He had the Specialist biochemistry, all sorts of micromachines in his blood, his nanomed. He wouldn't bleed to death. There would be pain—how much, he wasn't sure—and the loss of an arm. The arm, if "he" were rescued, could be regenerated eventually.

Frank gritted his teeth and prepared himself.

The blade began sawing into his arm. It wasn't possible to prepare.

"Stop! Wait! One more minute!" Frank shrieked. He thought watching it being done to Melinda had been awful, and it had been, but now that memory and its horror mingled with the reality of the moment, enhancing it in terrible ways.

He noticed his wedding band tattooed on his ring finger.

Gold, for Virginia, the only physical thing directly from his marriage aside from mementoes that he'd brought with him onto the *Dark Heart*. The ring was on the arm Orange was hacking off!

Frank moaned, screamed, and cried. They were cutting off his arm, and his wedding ring.

He saw his embedded chip move, wriggling under his skin. It could elude some threats, but no way it was going to crawl up his arm far enough to escape.

The ordeal finished faster than he imagined. One claim the Argonauts had made was true: they were physically stronger than humans. Despite all his efforts, he had no chance.

Orange dropped him and Frank fell to his knees, propped on one hand. He lifted his bleeding stump to his face, smelling the coppery tang of blood. He watched fascinated as the blood flow eased to an ooze, then stopped completely as the nanomed assisted the clotting processes in the face of this catastrophic injury.

Above him, Orange started shouting something, and Frank could see the creature raise up on her back two legs again. He saw the shadow of her arms, waving his arm in one hand, its bloody blade in the other.

Jason started speaking, but Frank wasn't listening.

An idea had formed, barely coaxed, while his muscles and tendons had separated, while his bone had parted, while the pain passed his endurance, while his wedding ring was removed in the most brutal fashion possible. *Akkai fell forever, and in falling, was consumed by the sun below. The ones bathed in endless sunlight, the life-givers and star-makers, they listened to us then.* It could be taken literally, without any gods, afterlife, or death metaphor. It could save this thing, and worse, from happening to Selene and the others. Some of them would die, surely, if separated in this auction.

Frank roared out his rage and pushed to his feet, stumbling forward. The stumble grew into a run, directly for the shrub people. They scattered before him.

Frank kept running, accelerating, not knowing if he'd have another chance.

There was nothing at the edge of the platform but for a low, earthen wall. Frank hit it running, pushing off, and leapt into the infinite sky.

AN EVEN MORE ALIEN ENCOUNTER

IN A MAZE LIGHT-YEARS FROM HOME

Rusk was sleeping in a modular storage compartment among coils of transparent tubing when his alarm triggered. The faint, rhythmic thumping from the button receiver on his temple wasn't strong, but he'd been trained to respond to it instantly as if it were the loud whistle of a wake-up call.

He opened his eyes, but did not otherwise move.

His hiding place was far from the best one he'd used. The compartment was an elevated open-mesh basket resembling a giant cage, one among many, lining the upper level of a large storage room that could have held the dirigible. He rested at an angle, nestled inside one of the coils. But what his spot lacked in stealth, it made up for in access. Sooner or later a military search party would find him—he'd seen several searching places like this one. He had been becoming more and more paranoid about being cornered with no place to run. The Spider Star was so large, there was always room to run if you could get a head start. And this was a place he could run from, with many exits.

As such, he hadn't worried about covering them all with alarms. Hydras were bound to be in and out and he'd never get any sleep. So he'd carefully placed his triggers in proximity to this level, trading a little safety for a longer sleep. Sleep deprivation would kill him as surely as any military hydra if he didn't respect the danger.

Light levels were low, and he looked out over the collar and breastplate of his armor through the open cage. He looked hard, and listened, too, straining every sense to locate whatever had tripped the alarm.

All the hairs on the back of his neck simultaneously stood on end, and the accompanying tingling sensation ran from his head down through his toes.

It took all his will not to move, or make a sound, but after stifling an outburst, it was all too easy to remain perfectly still.

Something was slowly, quietly, crawling along the outside of the compartment. Something at least as large as a large dog, with tendrils feeling out the way before it.

Rusk tried to keep control of himself, and limited his reaction to flared nostrils and the on-end hair.

The thing crawled closer.

Abstractly, despite the petrifying fear that made him feel like prey, he knew his body was behaving instinctually in a way that would have protected his ancient ancestors from a predator, since all too often they had likely been prey.

But he was the commander of a Specialist mission to explore an alien world and wrest free its secrets. He knew that when he was a kid, he would have never believed a man such as he was today would feel such fear. The truth was, he supposed, that growing up and assuming responsibility meant adding to the child everyone was, but not abandoning that child.

The crawling thing, with tendrils twitching, paused before him.

Another involuntary adrenaline surge hit Rusk, and although he thought he was being quiet, his heart thundered in his own ears.

The crawling thing turned, infinitely flexible, and crawled into his compartment over the coils of tubing.

How did it know he was there? Or did it? Maybe it was just sensing heat, or maybe carbon dioxide. Or maybe it could feel vibrations with all those fine waving tendrils that were probably full of toxins.

As the thing drew closer, adrenaline came a third time, but this time Rusk brought it on and welcomed it. *He* was the one full of toxins. *He* was the predator here as much as any single entity. *He* was a wasp. Wasps preyed on spiders and crawling things of all types.

Tired of being afraid like a child, he chose to act like his model of a specialist commander. He was armored and armed, a predator in his own right. Rusk let out a low growl and exploded forward to grab the crawling thing with his gauntlets before it could touch him first.

The thing froze, and then he was on it: grabbing, growling, grappling.

It shrieked, backpedaling like it was an overgrown millipede too drunk to know which direction it was going, and it pushed away from him.

Rusk might have shrieked himself, too.

It withdrew with agility, moving backward as easily as it had moved forward, and made it out of the compartment leaving Rusk with nothing in his hands.

No, that wasn't quite true, he saw, looking down as smelling a strange, bitter odor. Bits of mashed up tendril stained his gauntlets.

It wasn't as tough as it looked.

He thought for half a second before deciding—and he didn't know how conscious the decision really was—to follow the thing. Rusk was growing accustomed to making decisions automatically, without growing paralyzed before his options. These were survival decisions. Instincts trumped rules.

As he climbed out of the tubing and out of the compartment, he rationalized his actions after the fact. Who knew what might be coming to investigate the shrieking?

More backward rationalization on the fly led Rusk to decide that perhaps this crawly thing wasn't related to the hydras but might be some sort of parasite like himself, skulking about seldomly visited warehouses.

Rusk chased the thing, catching glimpses of it climbing along the mesh front of the containers. Millipede, centipede, sea scorpion . . . these were the things that the shape suggested to him. Pincers, tendrils, segmented body with all those legs. It was faster than him, and no longer close to him, but he persisted, feeling better for being on the offensive. Keeping that fear at bay through action was worth some effort. It made him mad that it scared him.

The thing shot up to the ceiling along the metallic grill separating storage sections.

Rusk followed.

It flipped over the top into a narrow crawlspace he could barely fit inside. As he forced himself in, he just made out the thing vanishing into a hard-to-see hole in the ceiling some seven or eight meters ahead.

Rusk didn't pause until just before he got to the hole. Rather than just barreling inside, or looking in with his own vulnerable eyes, lest it be a shallow den with a cornered beast, he let his adrenaline ebb and started thinking again. A balance of boldness and caution was better than an excess of either. His wrist display sported a flat, reflective panel, and he flashed a red pointing laser off it into the hole above him.

A hole going up, vanishing far above into indistinct darkness. Okay then, not a trap with the thing waiting to grab him.

He considered his options. He would *not* go back to his spot and sleep. The thought of the thing's tendrils moving over his face, and worse, horrified him still on some deep, nonintellectual level. He preferred to keep this creature in front of him, and with barely a conscious decision he moved into the hole and stood up. He would pursue this a little farther.

What else did he have to do? This thing might be able to

teach him something about how to hide and thrive living off the hydras.

The shaft was a chimney crawl up into some unidentifiable composite material. The sides appeared to be rough, not machined, as if something had spent long hours chipping it out. Maybe even chewing it out, but Rusk refused to dwell on that possibility.

He climbed easily, but with caution and deliberation. The shaft wasn't quite vertical, which let him rest even though he didn't need much rest with the low gravity. Airflow was good, and while he sometimes thought he caught a burnt smell, the air smelled clean. The only sound he heard was his own clunks and scrapes against the sides of the shaft.

He was thinking, perhaps too much. This place was way too small for the military hydras. If there were escape shafts to other locations, this could serve his purposes well, at least for a while. He could kill this creepy monster and take over its den. It was obviously managing to survive on the edges of the hydra infrastructure. What it could do, he could do.

There was a turnoff where the shaft split into two. One passage went off to one side, close to horizontal, while the other continued up.

Rusk remembered the Argonaut base back on Charybdis. The obvious door had been no door at all, and the Spider Star seemed, so far, to thrive on the sneakier, more ruthless principles than on the obvious. Rusk skipped this first side passage, and continued upward.

He soon came to another side passage, this one spilling a little light. He didn't know what that meant, whether it was good or bad for him. Maybe the creature had its den near a furnace, or this shaft led to a hydra access corridor with lights. Time to do something—he was feeling nervous about having passed up the previous side passage and now had to worry about the possibility of something being behind him. There wasn't enough room to easily turn around, and his ass was vulnerable.

So he should move forward quickly and aggressively.

He scrambled forward on all fours, into the side passage, placing his finger on the safety of his weapon. He wondered if he'd been quiet. He'd tried to strike the right compromise between speed and stealth, but suspected the right compromise was one or the other, not both. He had no idea about the quality of this creature's hearing, but he was alert and armed, so he figured he could handle a single skulking monster. He had to be the badass wherever he went here, if possible, or he knew he'd be caught and killed in short order. Might as well play it as an optimist. He had little to lose.

He wriggled forward in small, precise motions, as fast as he could, letting himself imagine he was swimming in the ocean and a sea spider was rising below him. Go, go, go, go . . .

And the passage opened before him into a well-lit chamber.

Rusk kept moving forward, partially staggering and partially bouncing to his feet and readying himself for anything as he took in the scene before him.

The creature was indeed here, but it wasn't alone.

Rusk immediately counted off four others of various sizes and brought himself to aim on them and plan a pattern of fire. And, a split second later, he stopped himself.

He wasn't sure why for a few more moments.

The creatures didn't move, giving him time for his mind to catch up with his instincts.

Simultaneously he thought of Normal Rockwell and Cintia Nascimento. Both artists had cast scenes of pastoral community life in peaceful places, and that was his first impression. He cataloged the things before him. Two of the monstrosities were nestled in a corner with a small table with a variety of small solid objects sitting on top; it felt like two people sitting playing a game

of chess or checkers. Another was curled up in something that resembled a gel acceleration couch, fiddling with some kind of heap
of fiber and some long sticks. Knitting a blanket was what came
to mind. The last one reclined in some sort of assortment of blan-
kets and fibers that made Rusk think "nest." It made a couple of
unpleasant but unthreatening sounds as he paused.

The light in the place came from a container with an open
flame, which had a chimney contraption that sucked up most of
the smoke.

The term *cognitive dissonance* leapt to the forefront of his mind
as he watched the monsters enjoying a quiet moment at home.

From behind him, from the tunnel he'd just crawled through,
came a sound. A high-pitched wail, varying in tone, and continuous.

Rusk stepped aside, keeping the four covered and also enabling himself to cover the entrance.

Another one of the things crawled out of the tunnel behind
him. Rusk suppressed a shudder as he watched it. He thought it
was probably the one he had originally followed.

The thing moved slowly in his direction, holding up its multiple tendrils.

Rusk flipped the safety, and prepared to spit death.

The things exchanged high-pitched sounds back and forth,
but didn't move, except for the one that had come out of the
tunnel after him.

"Stop right there, asshole!" Rusk screamed.

It did. He didn't believe it understood English, but he
thought it understood something. All these things did. These
weren't things at all. They were some kind of thinking beings
that cared about each other. Damn . . . he felt a little sick.

Despite the visceral horror they incited within him, everything
he'd been seeking in the robotic hydras and not finding was here
in these monsters. Evidence for feelings, values, sentience he could

recognize as similar to his own. The small ones were playing a board game of all things, he was sure.

What was he becoming in this place, living this existence?

This world, a microcosm of the universe, was full of diverse life. Everyone, everything, everywhere, was just trying to get by, competing for a slice of the limited available resources. And in between the constant stream of dog-eat-dog moments and instances of paralyzing, instinctual fear, it reached out to itself for support and comfort.

Except for him. Alone. Living to destroy and spread havoc. He had to get away from his mind-set, and find a way to escape from this existence.

He feared for himself and what he was becoming. He yelled again, "Stop right there, everyone! Give me space."

Rusk took small side steps, rocking his body with each movement back toward the exit. He watched everything and kept his weapon ready. The creepy creatures all turned in small steps to continue to face him in response.

"Stay away from me," Rusk said. "I'm trouble."

He backed into the passage and eased himself away, with a vague plan to move on and out of this area. His presence could only be trouble for this monster family.

And even as he thought it, he wondered who exactly was the monster here.

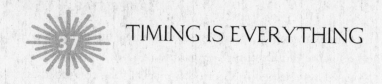

TIMING IS EVERYTHING

PART OF A RESCUE ON THE SPIDER STAR

Griffin smiled for the first time in days. The RF signatures were stable, out in the open, and within minutes of their position.

She was going to get Klingston and the other captives back. They all seemed to be alive still, and while their vitals had strayed from their norms, they didn't seem to be in bad shape, all things considered.

"Let's be sure about what we're getting into this time," Griffin said. "Robb, slow our approach and launch a swarm."

"Good idea," he said. "Launching swarm."

The Specialist surveillance arsenal had a variety of probes, spysats, and drones. The sneakiest were swarms, sets of eighty-one tiny robots designed to resemble small insects. Earth and Argo both had creatures that filled similar niches: flies on Earth, dangbits on Argo. The thinking was that most living worlds would have a similar niche in their ecosystems and that they'd be camouflaged. And in any event, they were small, quiet, and distributed.

Initially, all the displays showed the same thing: a round platform covered with various colors and textures. Upon closer inspection, more details were apparent. The largest detail was a raised set of mirrors ringing the platform, catching light from the core and reflecting nearly uniformly across the surface. There were geometric figures etched onto the surfaces, a sort of patchy grid, with some squares having different colors. She didn't know if the platform was agricultural, or perhaps a waste processing station—the two things that first sprang to mind.

The swarm closed, and it became apparent that this was an agricultural platform, with irrigation channels and reservoirs. The images were blurry. Diffraction limits on such small optics were physically insurmountable, at least when they were taken individually. "Robb, can you lock in an interferometric solution?"

"Almost done," said Robb.

Lance announced, "Executive Director Klingston's vitals are becoming unstable."

Damn. They'd lost too many people already. "Hurry," she said.

"There," said Robb.

A central synthesis image appeared in the primary display, infinitely rich. "Okay. Hold this in memory and let me know when we lose our fringes." They'd have to, eventually, as the swarm grew near and the individual bugs went their separate ways to collect their individual images.

In the meantime they had a sharp picture to study.

Melinda had her own display and was poring over zoomed images. "Oh, those fucking bastards!"

"What? Where?" Griffin asked. "Link the primary."

The image ballooned outward, zooming in on a region near the far edge. There was a clearing there full of Argonauts. In the middle of the group were the missing Specialists, their blue jumpsuits clear enough, and one X-bot.

"That's them," Robb said.

It was them, all of them. Dirty, bedraggled, dragging, but alive and whole. But what was going on? She recognized Klingston ahead of the others, right next to one of the Argonauts, towering over him. The creature bent over to grab Frank.

Scant seconds later, Melinda began to scream.

"Shut up!" Griffin screamed back, realization about what was happening sinking in. "We can't do anything about it."

Thankfully, she did tone it down. Griffin asked, "Lance, what's our ETA?"

"Three minutes if we push it. The swarm will beat us there by about thirty seconds."

There was an unspoken question in his second statement. The swarm units had limited offensive capability that could be employed. Griffin, however, just didn't see the point. "We'll come in as planned. If these Argonauts only have low-tech weaponry, we'll be able to take them quickly. Bring us in and hover, per plan."

"All right," Robb said.

"Lance, arm your weapon systems, and plan to target Argonauts, nonlethal when possible."

"Acknowledged."

"No!" Melinda screamed.

Griffin saw Klingston's arm, sans Klingston, raised by the Argonaut, and tried to think of something to say to Melinda to comfort her, but then she realized that the woman might be screaming about something else.

Klingston was running away. What was he doing? He was sprinting as fast as he could, she judged, and it just didn't make sense. Where did the fool think he was going?

"Oh my God," Melinda said.

Griffin watched, dumbfounded, as the aliens around him parted and Klingston went right over the edge. "No. What's he doing? What in the hell does he think he's doing?"

Melinda wailed. "It was too horrible for him! It was just too horrible!"

Could she be right? She would know, if anyone would know, what could go on in a mind after such an event. But why, oh why, had they just lost Klingston? They were *so* close!

She'd lost Frank.

"I'm coming in as planned, as fast as I can," Robb said stiffly.

He had the right attitude. This changed nothing. They still

had the others to save, and they had to do it, and do it now. "Right. Everyone, prepare yourselves and check your weapons and armor. We're hitting hot. We're taking back our people, and no one or no thing had better get in our way."

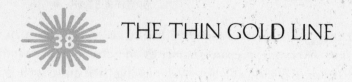

THE THIN GOLD LINE

DEEP, DEEP, IN THE SPIDER STAR

Rusk lived a nightmare.

There was no other way to describe it. His life had that never-ending quality that some dreams had, a pseudoreality that was impossible to escape, but while within it, the dreamer bought into it in its entirety.

The lighting was all wrong. The shape of things was all wrong. The smells and tastes were all wrong. The gravity was all wrong. Moreover, the air itself was all wrong.

Rusk had gone deep enough that the gas mix had changed substantially. He could still breathe it even though the pressure had to be over ten atmospheres, but he avoided talking now. There was so much helium that the sound of his voice had changed, the pitch ratcheting up into frequencies he could barely hear. Everything seemed louder, too, and closer. He used his PPU sparingly, sure that its exhaust could be heard and traced for kilometers. The gravity was only a small fraction of Earth's, however, and he could bound around, leaping like a superman, nearly flying. With the high pressure and low gravity, he thought he probably could fly if he had even rudimentary wings. These effects all just added to the surreality of his situation, his waking nightmare.

His mood swung from extreme to extreme. He would get an ordinate amount of glee from spinning the dials on some sort of manual override, laughing when he heard the alarms echo through the tunnels. He would cry—just a couple of times— when he would snake his arm into a hole to scoop out the sour gruel that he and the hydras fed upon.

His laughter and his cries sounded the same to his ears: high-pitched squeaks, like a mad tatinka bird.

What did these hydras *do* anyway? What was their purpose in life? What was their future?

He knew he needed to sleep more, knew he needed to eat more. Hell, he even had to worry about how he pissed and crapped. He tried to hide it, lest he become too easy to follow. He urinated into the food stations once, and giggled about it.

What was wrong with him?

Manuel Rusk was a highly trained product of the most advanced civilization humans had ever created. Moreover he was a top Specialist, and under other circumstances would have become a full mission director.

Here he was, flitting about an alien artifact, living like an animal, committing sophomoric pranks, alternately laughing and crying about them.

In a more lucid moment, he wondered about the gas mix. He knew that many gases had narcotic effects at high pressure. Maybe their initial analysis had been superficial. Maybe humans couldn't breathe the atmosphere safely at all altitudes.

Maybe he *had* gone mad.

If so, did it matter what he did? Whether he lived or he died? Could he, as a madman, even answer those questions with competence?

Rusk decided he had to operate as if he were sane, and could answer them positively. And, reaching that conclusion, wondered if it proved him to be sane. Or not. How could he tell?

He tried to sleep more, when he was happy with his hiding places. He tried to eat regularly, when he could locate food stations. He tried to create serious mischief that rose above the level of pranks, although he hesitated with starting fires. While he knew the relative oxygen partial pressure had to be a few tenths of an atmosphere, he also knew that at some depth the hydrogen partial pressure rocketed. Hydrogen and oxygen would combine, explosively, to make water.

The lights in this warren did change with a predictable pattern, perhaps a day/night cycle, although the change was more of a wavelength shift than an intensity shift. The only way that made sense to Rusk was if the hydras originally came from a binary system with stars of two different masses. The high mass star would be brighter and bluer than the low mass star. If he were right, then the hydras were a transplanted species here.

Maybe humans were now, too.

Rusk went on this way, floating through the netherworld, a twilight zone of impossibility, losing track of time, losing track of himself. Until something triggered him.

He was in the middle of a descending tunnel, on his PPU at the moment. Suddenly he felt he was in danger. He didn't know if he'd heard something, felt something, or what, but he had learned to trust the adaptation of his senses to this strange, old world.

He'd become a creature of instinct in the preceding days. If he hadn't transformed in this way, he wouldn't be alive now.

Rusk rolled his eyes around, seeing no place to hide.

Fine then. If he were going to die sometime soon, then why not now? All times were equal as far as he could tell—he'd either succeeded in leading the military hydras away from his team by this stage, or he hadn't.

Rusk shimmied into a half twist, so that he was facing backward while the PPU propelled him downward. He raised his Strike Eagle, and flipped off the safety. He accelerated down, scanning for the enemy.

They were there and he fired off six shots at the first glimpse.

The shots did not make the air explode, and he didn't know enough chemistry to know if he was lucky or not. He thought their masers might do the same thing, so screw it. If they were after him, he was firing.

The tunnel curved, like most of them here, and by keeping his speed high he could prevent them from getting a clear line of fire back at him. But to what end? How could this end for him? Presumably they knew where this tunnel led. He did not.

His one saving grace was that their coordination seemed poor. It wasn't like hydra drones below would suddenly drop what they were doing to pick up weapons and peg him as he flew by. He supposed he wouldn't expect human workers to do so either, but, hell, there was something unnatural about these aliens!

He would shoot them at will, if they poked their heads up. He didn't ask for this sort of hostility, after all.

He had never personally shot at another sentient being, except in simulations, and he steeled himself for the task. He thought these hydras were just some sort of organic machine, but he knew he didn't know the whole story.

Rusk fired as he needed to, and neither his weapon nor his head exploded unexpectedly. That was good, he thought, watching for bulbous white floating things.

He bumped off the tunnel a few times, rather hard. His armor compensated for the impact. How fast was he going? The PPUs were nominally configured for near atmospheric pressures, and he didn't know quite how their performance specs changes in high pressure, or if they'd even been specified for such extremes. This was not a natural atmosphere, after all.

Like some monotonous video game, Rusk shot down the ever steepening tunnel, faster and faster, waiting for his enemies to present a target. The nightmare had intensified to an intolerable situation, and Rusk feared that it could end in no good way.

The quality of the light changed, brightening and growing golden. Rusk ignored it, keeping alert for the hydras trailing him. The light continued to intensify, starkly illuminating every feature of the curved tunnel zipping by Rusk. Its surfaces weren't all that reflective, a composite slate gray like most on the Spider Star, so the light welling up had to be overwhelming. Was it a furnace? Was he in an incinerator shaft?

No, there wasn't much heat associated with the light.

Then Rusk finally got it.

He turned just as he pierced the heart of the Spider Star, exploding the same way their first probe had exploded.

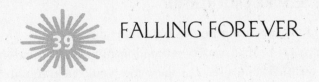

FALLING FOREVER

FALLING THROUGH THE SPIDER STAR

Frank fell.

Frank fell, and Frank screamed.

He couldn't help himself. He'd made his decision with cold logic, but his animal instincts were more powerful in the moment.

He tumbled in the cold, loud wind, out of control, falling and screaming.

After a minute, he gained a little stability, managing a slow spin, facing down. He remembered something of skydivers and how they held themselves. The spin slowed a little more.

The wind ripped by, but seemed quieter than it had been just moments before. He realized he'd stopped screaming, and with that realization, resumed.

The remainder of his arm hurt, and he twisted it up against his body and lost control of his fall again, chaotically tumbling.

Frank stopped screaming, and regained a measure of control.

Maybe two minutes had passed.

He guessed he'd fallen a couple of kilometers.

Another twenty-five hundred to go.

He continued to fall. What else was there to do?

After about five minutes, coherent thoughts began to breach the wall of terror in his mind separating rational thought from conscious thought. After all, below him was a general golden glow, gentle and diffused by kilometers of atmosphere and clouds. He appreciated the way his contacts permitted him to keep his eyes open in the gale-force winds buffeting him, and he used his vision to try to put his situation in context. There

368 * MIKE BROTHERTON

weren't too many structures visible at this distance, aside from the elevator spoke that steadily receded from him (his rotational velocity was different, although the wind would help minimize that effect). His speed became difficult to judge in this limbo land. He figured it had to be some kind of terminal velocity, perhaps a few hundred kilometers per hour, and likely somewhat variable as he fell into higher pressure regions.

Still, that velocity was slow. In the evacuated grav-tubes the top velocities were measured in kilometers per second rather than kilometers per hour.

Another five minutes, and he was still falling.

"Shit, shit, shit," he whispered, trying to remember to breathe.

Breathing was important. Crap, he didn't know if it was or not. He didn't know if he was going to *live* or not. But the pressure of the Spider Star's atmosphere increased exponentially toward the center. At the altitude the Argonauts held sway, the pressure was only about half a bar, but it increased to nearly fifty bars at the altitude of the golden core. Since the oxygen partial pressure was maintained at a few tenths of a bar at all altitudes, he'd be okay breathing. The danger was holding his breath—he needed to keep the pressure outside and in his lungs equalized.

Wasn't this crazy? Hadn't he just jumped to his death?

Under what circumstances was this a sane action?

He was going to die, and soon.

Soon was hours. At two hundred kilometers per hour, he'd reach the core in about eleven hours.

Frank had had a car accident once. He'd been an advanced student, back on Earth before becoming a deep-space Scout, and his collision sensors had failed in a thunderstorm. That was the kind of thing you couldn't do anything about, even if you were a great driver. Well, you could avoid driving in poor weather, but at that age he'd thought himself immortal. It had happened fast. He only had a handful of seconds between the problem and the anesthetic foam filling the car. He had only had a handful of seconds to come to the realization that he was in deep shit and likely to be seriously injured, if not die outright.

Frank had looked toward his instruments, with the foam streaming out, with no time to articulate anything sensible. No control at all, no time to establish control. Out of control. The thoughts came back easily to him now. He'd thought to himself, *No, this can't be happening.* But it had been, and it did. He'd also had time to think, *I'm going to be hurt.*

He hadn't been, and neither had the other driver. The safety devices operated as designed, protecting him even as the car around him shattered.

This was nothing like that.

Frank had thought *No this can't be happening,* and *I'm going to be hurt,* maybe a hundred times in the first few minutes.

Could he handle falling for eleven hours? Well, what choice did he have? Besides, maybe he was wrong about that time. Maybe it would only be ten. Or maybe it would be thirteen. Or maybe he would hit some structure before then. If he didn't, he supposed he had time to figure it out, if he wanted to, even making some numerical approximations in his head. He'd been good at that sort of thing, once.

The grav-tubes took about forty-five minutes for a trip. He recalled that for an evacuated tube, with minimal friction, the physics were essentially the same as for a simple harmonic oscillator, a pendulum, for instance. The fact that the timescale was about forty-five minutes indicated that the dark matter indeed had a density similar to terrestrial worlds. It didn't matter if you had a planet like Earth or Argo, or smaller planet like Mars, for a terrestrial density of close to five grams per cubic centimeter you ended up with a transit time of about forty-five minutes. The tube could go straight through the center of the planet, or just connect two surface points a few hundred kilometers away.

From anywhere to anywhere, as long as you started and ended at the same altitude, was forty-five minutes.

The wind blew, like a gale, in Frank's face, relentlessly refuting his thoughts. It would be a lot longer than forty-five minutes for him. Air resistance would slow his fall tremendously.

He didn't know if that was a good thing or a bad thing.

Did it matter?

He was falling at hundreds of kilometers per hour into the heart of an alien satellite seated in an invisible, intangible planet. This was not planned, and could not be expected to end well.

Frank saw a shape loom before him. He thought it was close, but it took nearly half a minute to come into focus. A line stretched before him, below and in front of his trajectory. He didn't know what it was, but assumed it was another grav tube.

He realized it was not just a grav tube. One of the gardens swelled along the tube's length below him.

He felt a warm wind, a thermal upswell. In a way it was pleasant. The omnipresent wind had been so cold, so cutting, for so long. The warm air also carried moistness, and interesting, organic smells. Absurdly, he considered trying to enjoy the moment as he fell at two hundred kilometers an hour into a planet of dark matter.

Then Frank realized what it meant to be caught in a thermal. The source of the heat, the garden, was directly below him. He would fall into it, hit it, at high velocity.

He would die in seconds.

He refused to believe this was his fate. He hadn't jumped to smack into something like this. He had to be able to do *something*. Let him be blasted at the core, or fall into the unknown, but to hit an obvious obstacle like this . . . that was unacceptable.

Frank moved his stiff and sore limbs. He shifted out of the flat, stable, face-down position, and pushed down with his arms and brought his legs together. His left arm throbbed in protest.

He dove, asymmetrically, in a spin. It was still a fall, but a faster fall, with a different trajectory. Different enough to miss the garden anyway, he hoped.

He lifted his chin away from his chest, looking down, catching sight of the green and maroon mass of the garden looming larger on each spin. The urge to scream grew in the tightening muscles of his jaw.

Frank let it out, a little. He groaned, a low sound lost in the whipping wind. He only knew he was making it from the vibrations he felt in his throat.

Sky—spin—garden—spin—sky—spin—garden—spin—sky—spin—garden—spin—garden—garden!

Suddenly he was in it, among branches, plunging through great veined leaves that felt like razor blades at his speed. His thigh brushed a more substantial limb, a bright flare of new pain, and his spin reversed direction, and he was tumbling and flailing again, his fall barely slowed.

And then he was in the clear again, cold wind burning into new cuts on his face and body, and below him only sky.

He fought through the new pain in his leg, the old pain in his arm, and the new lesser pains, and tried to once again stabilize his fall. The adrenaline rush and the spinning had left him feeling sick.

Something above him squawked loudly.

Frank swallowed, twisting, and craning his head around to see what he could.

Five or six creatures dived after him. They were splotchy, and light colored, and he imagined they'd be difficult to see gliding through the sky, but they were easy to see against the dark mass of the garden. They were becoming even easier to see because they were closing in on him.

Frank didn't have a lot of options. He could try to dive himself, and perhaps outdistance them, but they looked streamlined enough to catch him if they were determined. He decided to stand his ground, so to speak.

Another few heartbeats, and the first of the creatures shot past him. It popped out its wings, slightly, and, from Frank's perspective, appeared to bounce back up to him. Two others passed him, and bounced. Three of the creatures matched his velocity, ringing him.

He looked from one to the other. *Pteranodons,* was his first thought. Their heads had long beaks and long crests, and from tip to beak was at least two meters. Their wings enveloped much of their bodies, and extended at least another five or six meters above them. Their splotchy camouflage broke up a smooth, porpoiselike skin, marred only by a rippling musculature.

One of the creatures drifted closer, a single platelike eye on the near side of its head regarding him coolly. No, they weren't perfect matches for the extinct Earth dinosaurs, despite their similarities. At this closer distance, the sense of the alien was clearer—colors he'd never seen in nature on Earth or Argo, a star-shaped iris similarly foreign.

The creature's altitude changed, and the eye rose out of sight as its beak ascended to the level of Frank's head. There was a nostril there, about two-thirds down the beak. The skin around the nostril rose, the way bubbles rose on pizzas he used to make with his kids, and the entire region of the beak elongated until the nostril had become a flared tube—an intake nozzle. The end of the quivering tube, several centimeters across, slid toward Frank's face.

He considered his options again. Should he try to hit the creature, or maybe grab this extendable nostril? If it didn't rip off, could he somehow ride this thing back to a solid surface? The sharp-looking teeth in the beak, each as large as his finger, didn't seem encouraging for this plan, or his immediate survival.

As the nostril closed to within scant centimeters of his cheek, Frank heard a rhythmic sucking sound even over the rush of the wind. It was sniffing him.

The nostril suddenly snapped back into the beak, which cracked open as the creature emitted a deafening squawk.

Frank heard several loud bangs and the creatures opened their wings into parachutes, immediately arresting their dives, and found himself again alone in his plummet.

His blood! The new cuts he'd gained falling through the leaves . . . they didn't like the smell of his blood. Smart move on their part. It killed Argonauts. It might kill them, too.

Frank continued to fall for a few hours. He didn't have anything better to do. He talked to himself in bursts. He knew that the gas mixture and pressure would change as he fell. He would sound louder as the pressure went up, but against the rippling white noise of the wind he wasn't sure he could tell any difference. He was pretty sure that when he hit the helium- and hydrogen-rich layers he'd be able to tell from the squeakiness of his voice. So he talked to himself.

"Some crazy people would pay an arm and a leg to do this," he said, grinning in the wind. "I got half price."

The view was magnificent, and he sometimes marveled at it, watching thunderheads build hundreds of kilometers away with spectacular lightning shows—one he got to watch for nearly forty minutes, it was so huge. There were rainbows, strange rainbows, with a truncated spectrum weak on the bluest colors, but he noticed that there were more blues at lower altitudes than at the higher altitudes. Atmospheric dust helped redden the core to its golden color—it would be more of a bright white the deeper he fell.

He thought of poetry for the sights he saw, but with the pain, his cold, numb lips, his verbal updates to himself would come out something like, "Shit, piss, fuck twenty-seven." That was especially true when alien bugs exploded on his cheek or forehead with sharp smacks, or when he fell into clouds.

Most of the clouds were water clouds, and it was like falling through a thick fog. While he was thankful for the moisture, he knew the evaporation would be dangerously chilling falling out the other side. He'd been cold for hours, and went through shivering episodes. There was a slight warming trend as he fell, but he believed he was on the edge of hypothermia. The worst part about being in the cloud was a loss of vision that was somehow much worse than the agoraphobic vistas, and sometimes a cloud passage lasted many minutes. He imagined unseen things in the fog flying toward him, wondering if he were about to die, as he anticipated an unanticipatable collision.

"I'm sorry, Selene," he said. She'd had so much faith in him, in his ability to find a solution. And they'd dragged her off, just like that. He'd had no power to do anything at all about it. He briefly wondered if his leap had been a well-disguised suicide, a way of atoning for his guilt. No, he reaffirmed, he really truly believed there was a chance this would work out. The only chance he saw. If he were wrong, well, Rusk, Griffin, and the others might still have a chance on their own and it wouldn't matter if he were alive or dead. But if this were the only way . . . well then, who else would be willing to jump? He surely wouldn't ask anyone else to do it. Selene, Selene, Selene . . . he couldn't help but feel guilty. Intellectually he knew that her mores were not his own, that she had wanted the physical intimacy they had shared, that she had enjoyed it. Still, he could not help but feel that he had exploited her youth, her naïveté, that he'd taken advantage in a way that should be forbidden. Not only was he much older, he was the one in charge—he felt that way even when they both held the same status as prisoners. That look on her face, that last look, had appeared to hold betrayal. Why shouldn't he feel guilty? He *was* guilty!

Frank continued to fall, and realized he needed to urinate. "Damn."

This would make Kenny laugh. Kenny was raised in the country, outside. Frank had felt funny about it, but he had encouraged the boy to "take a whiz" (which always made Kenny giggle when he said it) whenever he had needed to. Walk a few paces to the nearest tree or shrub, and take care of it. Simple.

"Not so simple here."

Frank recalled something crude he'd once heard Virginia tell Kenny: "Don't piss into the wind."

Despite the crudeness, it seemed sound advice. Into the wind was down, away from the wind was up. Frank tried to flip onto his back, but just managed to start a runaway series of somersaults. Escaping the tumble back to stability left his arm and leg aching. Even if he managed to get stable on his back, there were other problems to consider: opening his tattered jumpsuit and fishing out his equipment. Worse, he realized that from his back, his own body was likely to block the wind, letting his urine fall faster with less air resistance. He was likely to make a mess. He also didn't think there was any way he could manage a sideways position and remain stable as he opened his pants.

Frank remembered something that gave him some measure of resolution. As part of his Scout training, he'd had intensive lessons on the history of space exploration. One of the first astronauts—or maybe it had been a cosmonaut, he always got the sides confused—had experienced an extended launch delay. After laying in his launch vehicle for most of the day, he'd informed the controllers that he had to urinate. He didn't have a catheter or other collection device as no one had planned on such a long delay. The engineers called meetings, and discussed it, and discussed it, while their man endured his agony. Finally, they told him to just go. He went. It was okay.

Frank went.

It was cold and uncomfortable, but it was okay.

He giggled, and the wind caught in his mouth making his cheeks flap. "I'm so not okay it's funny." Bathrooms were apparently one feature that the Spider Star seriously lacked when compared to Earth technology.

He giggled again, just because he found he could.

His emotions were all over the place. He was laughing now, but the truth was that everything hurt so much. His giggles turned into sobs. "Kenny, Virginia, Allyn," he said. "What have I done?"

Every choice he had made had seemed like the one he had to make. He'd had to act to protect his family when Pollux had Lashed out, hadn't he? He'd followed the very reasonable recommendations from Rusk and the crew for exploring the Spider Star—what else could he have done? He'd have been dangerously paranoid to have greeted the elevator with an armed party, right? He'd have been suicidal to have tried to overpower the Argonauts, yes?

Had he been foolish to have read things into the big one's statements that perhaps weren't true?

His conclusions *had* to be true. Too many lives depended on his analysis being accurate, starting with his own. But what were the odds? Could he calculate them? Should he have tried to do so before leaping? He might not have had another good chance. But maybe he'd ruined his chances, the chances for the whole mission. Griffin or Rusk could have rescued him, maybe, or there might have been a chance to escape. Something. Something other than leaping into an abyss several thousand kilometers deep.

"What have I done?" Frank asked.

His voice sounded strange.

"Piss crap fifty-nine."

He had the voice of a cartoon character. The atmosphere around him was no longer nitrogen or neon dominated. He'd moved into the helium, and perhaps the hydrogen levels. The total pressure was probably tens of atmospheres.

He'd grown accustomed to it. As long as he got a few tenths of an atmosphere of partial pressure from oxygen, and the other gasses weren't too physiologically hazardous, the increased pressure wasn't a huge health risk. He knew that the overall pressure climbed exponentially toward the core, and that the increase would be rapid. He'd been falling for hours already. He had no idea how long, exactly. Perhaps he was nearing the end of the line.

The exquisite view stretched before him, under his numb body, below the rushing wind. Cloudscapes, alien structures, and towers of light.

Towers of light? The only way to get clear light beams was if the light was not multiply scattered. That meant Frank was close. There wasn't much atmosphere or many clouds between him and the light source at the core of the Spider Star.

Frank fell through another cloud, and this time realized that the sensation was cool and refreshing rather than chilling. The temperature was definitely up. Before long, water began to collect on his skin and hair.

He emerged from the cloud in a rain shower.

Bright, scintillating light, refracted into a million rainbows by the water droplets, grew before him.

"Lux fiat," Frank squeaked as his contacts darkened. "Lux fiat!"

The light blazed away: a wall of photons, a wave of heat, a curtain of rainbows. He was in a zero-gee sauna with a thousand sun lamps before him. The air pressure, he knew, was high—close to fifty atmospheres. The increasing pressure hadn't bothered him too much so far, but now he found it nearly impossible to breathe. It was like trying to breathe from inside a geyser.

This was the end. He was heading into the light at over a hundred kilometers per hour. He didn't know if it had a sharp surface, or even what it was really. The golden core of the Spider Star represented advanced and alien technology.

Frank suddenly felt like one of the poor bugs that had flown into his face, a small creature in a universe of another species' making, subject to powers and forces beyond his ability to comprehend. He'd known, intellectually, since they set out, that was the situation for them all. But now he felt it, physically, permeating his body as the luminosity overwhelmed him.

If there was an afterlife, he would soon discover it.

He continued to fall through steaming rainbows. He had no sense of the distance, no sense of impending impact. The light was swallowing him, laying bare the shadows lurking in every corner of his heart.

"Selene," he squeaked loudly, frustrated that his voice betrayed his intent here in his last moments. He went on with his list of names, paying homage to those who fed his guilt. "Virginia," he squeaked-croaked. "Allyn, Kenny."

All his actions leading him to this place and time, this fate, had been motivated by other people, people he cared for. And now he was alone. He'd even lost his wedding ring. He was completely, utterly alone in a way that perhaps no man had ever been alone before.

In his isolation his fear grew—not the instinctual, physical fear of falling, which he'd compartmentalized and held at bay—but a deeply held and powerful fear of failing. He was afraid he'd failed everyone who had trusted in him. He was afraid that everything he'd striven for had been a sham, a waste. Afraid he'd made a mad, desperate choice. Afraid he was seconds from death. Afraid he'd failed his loved ones, his family.

Frank repeated the names, over and over, as the light and the rain washed over him, rinsing away the blood encrusting his face, soothing—somehow—the injuries to his arm and leg.

The names left him, and instinctually he screamed, "Abracadabra!"

Frank fell into the light, and the light ripped his body apart.

HEAVEN AND HELL

THE HEART OF THE SPIDER STAR

Rusk floated snugly in a warm place. No thoughts. No cares. No pains.

A sense of an enveloping, golden light filled him.

He felt like a child. No—younger than that, an infant, floating in a womb. Secure. Fetal. A young species.

Now, why had he thought that?

He recalled—no—he *was* stumbling after a puppy, and the creature had the temerity to yelp and bite him. Pain! The bite hurt. The universe was not all warm and fuzzy, even the parts that appeared to be so.

Rusk bawled.

Someone, Mommy, cradled him in her arms, warm, supportive, letting him float in security.

Cake, spankings, present ripping-open . . . more! Orbit ball, played in a rotating cylindrical satellite. Some boring speech, trying to drag his parents away, tugging on their sweaty-slippery hands in the middle of a crowd listening to someone talk about nothing he understood.

Bicycles, oh yes, he liked bicycles, even when his foot got caught in the spokes and his father had to wash out the blood. The red-tinted water swirled down the sink, oblivious to his pain. Getting back on the bicycle that same day, determined.

Discovering the TV teacher, exploring everything from bees, to rivers, to government, physic, and astrophysics. More and more, coming faster and faster.

Enrolling in the academy, aspiring to the stars. Knowing he

had to know more than everyone else, knowing he had to be the best. More images, more, coming faster, faster.

Being a Specialist, waiting on the Corps to send him out. More training, more work. More, more, faster, faster.

Rifling through his head. Memory activation accessed like computer links—

The trip from Argo, exploring the Spider Star. More, more, faster, faster.

Rusk slipping, firing, screaming as the glow shredded his body.

Rusk screamed out and opened his eyes.

He panted, mouth dry, eyes wide, disoriented. He was floating, and he was comfortably warm, also, surrounded by golden, uniform light. It took long seconds for his mind to process and assemble what his senses were telling him beyond those obvious things. First, he was naked—he didn't even have hair, not even eyebrows. Second, he felt good. Surprisingly good. His injuries were gone, healed as if they'd never even existed.

His life had passed before his eyes, and now he floated peacefully in a place of golden light. While he personally was not religious, this smacked very much of some people's version of heaven.

"I have two hands," someone said from behind him.

He wasn't alone! Rusk made a garbled sound, but didn't manage anything articulate. He paddled like mad, trying to spin himself around. As he did so, another figure came into view.

It was a man, a human man, naked and hairless like himself, taller and lighter complexioned, maybe twenty-five years old. A little on the fat side. He floated, like Rusk, but at a skewed angle.

Rusk's spin carried the other person out of view. He furiously back paddled, trying to bring himself back around. He'd trained often enough in zero gee that this really shouldn't be too difficult, although he admitted he'd rarely permitted himself to get stranded in an open space like this.

The man reappeared, and Rusk managed to kill his spin so that he wouldn't quickly vanish again. The man looked familiar. Then it hit him. "Klingston?"

"Yes, Rusk," he said, patting his hands against his chest. "I think."

"You're not old," Rusk said. It was true. Sometimes bald men looked rather ageless, but Rusk remembered Klingston's appearance quite clearly. He had skin that had seen too much sun, or at least too much radiation, and had a lot of wrinkles, particularly around his squinty eyes.

"And you're fat," said Klingston.

Rusk looked at himself again, rubbed his hands down his sides. He did indeed sport love handles. "So I am." This was most strange. More alert now, he was also more sure that this wasn't heaven. "I thought I'd died. Maybe I did. Now, trapped with you, I'm starting to wonder if I'm in hell."

Klingston laughed. "That's exactly what I was thinking."

Rusk chuckled, too. He'd resented Klingston usurping his position as mission director, resented taking orders from the man. But now, Rusk knew he was in above his head, in a situation beyond his understanding, and was truly thrilled to have someone else here with him. He didn't believe that made him less capable, or less of a leader, just a little more human. There was an old Spanish saying he knew: It's good to have friends, even in hell.

"At least my voice isn't squeaky," Rusk said.

Klingston nodded.

It was a bizarre, outrageous situation. He'd thought he'd died, and here he was, floating fat, happy, and naked in a big golden tub (for all practical purposes), with one of his less favorite people in the universe.

Rusk blinked, and blinked again. He tapped his eye, and flinched. "I don't have my contacts. You?"

Frank closed his eyes and rubbed at his eyelids vigorously for a moment. "No." He opened his eyes and said, "I'm coming over."

Klingston tilted his head down, pursed his lips, and blew. At the same time he waved his arms and kicked like a swimmer. Klingston drifted toward Rusk.

They reached each other and grasped hold without rebounding away from each other. They clapped each other on the shoulders and grinned like fools.

"It's good you see you, Klingston."

"It's good to see you, too."

Rusk related what had happened to him since they'd separated. Klingston did the same. When they had both finished, and had finished questioning each other, a long silence descended on them. Too many of their fellows had died.

"I don't think we're dead," said Klingston. "But I don't have any good way to explain what's happened. I'm young, fat, and I have my hand back."

"I have a possible explanation," Rusk said. "I don't know if it is a good one, but it's an idea."

Klingston said, "Go on."

Rusk wondered a bit at himself. He was accustomed to just telling Klingston how it had to be, especially when he didn't see any other options. He no longer felt the need to assert, or try to assert, dominance. Rusk said, "The only place we know for sure in the Spider Star with no gravity is the core. The symmetry of the problem makes the gravitational force cancel out. The last thing I remember is falling into the core."

"Me, too," said Klingston. He wore a strange smile. "I fell in, too."

"I suppose you did," Rusk said, remembering the frightening details of Klingston's story. Rusk believed that he, himself, could have done the same thing under the same circumstances, but was far from sure. What kind of desperation, or faith, did it take to jump into an abyss a thousand kilometers deep? He liked to think that he was superior to Klingston in most ways, but he was far from sure he had the balls to do that, desperate or not.

They smiled at each other some more, like silly goofs. Klingston said, "So what else do you have to your explanation?"

That caused Rusk's goofy smile to waver. "We're in the core all right, with no gravity. The dark matter planet that makes up the Spider Star is pulling at us equally in all directions, leaving us floating free. But the other things, our fatness, your youth . . . we've been reborn."

"Reborn?" Klingston lost his smile. "Resurrected?"

"What else? Our bodies aren't the same."

"Couldn't we just be fattened up, and shaved, after being drugged and fed intravenously while healing for an extended period?"

Rusk looked at him, looked into his light blue eyes. If their situations had been reversed, Rusk would have been thrilled to have shed decades, but this seemed to be bothering Klingston quite a lot. "You told me you'd felt like your body was ripped apart. Felt like you'd replayed your whole life."

"Yes," Klingston admitted. He and Rusk held each other by their forearms and their heads were only a third of a meter apart.

"So bear with me. The light field tore us apart, read our memories, and put us back together from scratch. That's why we have no hair and no injuries."

They were silent a moment, contemplating this extreme interpretation of events. The phrase "put us back together from scratch" had just come out, without a lot of premeditation. If true, what did that mean for them?

They were dealing with multiten-million-year-old alien technology. As far as they could comprehend, there might as well not be any rules, any limits.

Before they could pursue that line of discussion further, the light altered. It kept its bright, golden quality, but altered nonetheless. Rusk looked over Klingston's shoulder. "Do you see that?"

"Yes. Well, I'm seeing *something.*"

Rusk was seeing something too. The opaqueness of the surrounding light had diminished. There were shapes around them. He wasn't able to see them very clearly, but that situation improved as he watched, with the contrast improving with every second.

The shapes resolved into one of two basic types. One type he classified as "boxy." This included an array of dark, metallic boxes, for want of a better word. Some weren't boxes, but more complex shapes, but they still shared boxy qualities—assemblages of smaller boxes, or rectangular shapes. Size was difficult to judge, but he estimated that the boxy shapes ranged from a few meters across to tens of meters. They were presumably some sort of machinery. The other type of shape he saw he classified as "spider." Sure, he'd been thinking of this place as the Spider Star for years, but it struck him as the most appropriate name anyway.

Yes, *spiders.* The things were all legs, long legs, and yes, eight of them. If he'd estimated the machine sizes properly, the spiders had leg spans of at least fifty meters. They attended the machinery. Sometimes two or three flitted about a single machine. Some machines had only one, or no, attendants. Rusk craned his neck around. In every direction there were machines and spiders.

As he watched them, Rusk realized that these giant spiders were quite different from Earth spiders of any species. For instance, the eight legs were arrayed symmetrically, and had a mix of discrete joints and flexible sections. They seemed well suited to a zero-gee environment.

"Look up," said Frank.

Rusk looked. Above them, to the extent there was an above, one of the spiders grew larger, approaching them. It coasted toward them, legs splayed out, leading, slightly, the smaller body.

It was going to fly right into them, like a predator on prey.

Rusk flinched as it neared, but it drew up sharply, stopping abruptly some ten meters from them. Four of its arms seemed to rest, equidistant, on an invisible surface between them. The other four were drawn in closer to its spherical black body, pointing toward the two men. On the ends of those limbs were clusters of digits, appendages, fingers the size of arms, that reminded Rusk of sea anemones. On the ends of several of the digits on each arm were dark globules as large as a human head. Rusk immediately recognized them as eyes.

The spider was looking straight at them with at least a dozen eyes.

"Our apologies," came a smooth, mellifluous voice, seemingly straight into their minds with the intensity a laser might shine into their eyes. "Your form of communication, the aural language known as English, is flexible but not very sensible. We had to apply some very old systems to understand it.

"Welcome. Now then, I imagine that you have some questions. What do you want to know first?"

GOLDEN OPPORTUNITIES

IN THE CORE OF THE SPIDER STAR

Frank didn't know what to say, what to ask for. This was the first time since their arrival at the Spider Star that someone had apologized, that they'd been asked anything, and here was an opening the size of a planet. What *did* he want to know first?

While Frank was still trying to formulate his first priority, Rusk spoke. "Where is my missing team? Are they still alive?"

Rusk's heart was in the right place, immediately thinking of the other Specialists, but Frank thought they needed to worry about their overall mission first, and suspected that they needed more background information to be able to ask the right questions. Still, he eagerly awaited the answer.

The spider—Frank just couldn't think of it as a "golden one," as it was the light that was golden and not the being before them—did not respond immediately. It just floated there, quiet, for a long moment. Frank didn't think he'd ever have a chance to read what it was thinking, and decided not to try. He'd take things at face value.

Finally the spider responded, again with that rich, sonorous voice that came from nowhere and everywhere. "They are alive. Where they are would not mean anything to you."

"Are they captives? Are they free, and in danger?" Rusk demanded.

"They are barricaded in an arboretum in a spoke. More information would not mean anything to you."

"Tell the damn hydras to stop shooting at them, will you?"

"It is done, although the command will require approximately fourteen seconds to be relayed to the besieging units. Is that acceptable?"

"Yes, thank you," Rusk said.

"You're welcome."

They were polite. He had to give them that.

"You came up with that pretty quickly," Rusk said, a strange tone in his voice. "How was I able to escape detection as long as I did?"

The spider responded immediately. "The hydras aren't as thorough or as fast as we are, and your crew isn't as careful or disruptive as you are."

"Oh. I see."

Time to move on to the key business. Without fear or hesitation, Frank said, "If you've learned our language from our very minds, then you know why we are here."

"Yes," said the spider. "You desire that the devices in the core of the star you call Pollux be placed under your control or destroyed. We cannot do that."

The beautiful voice belied the ugly answer.

"Cannot, or will not?" Rusk asked.

"Both, and neither," answered the spider. "What's the difference? First, the devices may only be controlled from close proximity, and we do not leave this place. Therefore we cannot. Second, we made an exchange with the Argonaut species for control of the devices, and it would not be fair for us to give control to another."

Frank looked at Rusk, who stared back at him, eyes similarly wide. What did this creature mean? Frank looked back into the spider's gold-reflecting eye, the one on the end of the arm closest to them. "Fair? Was it fair for the Argonauts to invite us to dock, and to then attack us? To kidnap us? To torture us? Was it fair for the Argonauts to sabotage an entire star system for millions of years of future habitation? Is it fair, now, for you to facilitate this state?"

Rusk picked it up. "Was it fair for the hydras to capture and dismantle my airship? Was it fair for them to kill members of my team?"

With its smooth voice, sounding neither angry, nor upset, the spider responded. "Was it fair for your would-be rescuers, Frank Klingston, to kill twenty-seven Argonauts? Was it fair for you, Manuel Rusk, to kill 3,713 hydras in your sabotage efforts?"

Frank looked at Rusk again.

The man looked away from both Frank and the spider and didn't say anything immediately. Then taking a deep breath, Rusk said, "I didn't know it was so many. I told you, they were like machines. They weren't truly living."

Frank, thinking about the twenty-seven, said, "There was a rescue attempt?"

"Yes, two, actually. The second one was successful, just moments after you jumped. We monitor everything, although we seldom act."

He'd been right to advise waiting. Then why had he jumped?

Deep down, he knew. Part of him still believed they were too late, that a new Lashing had destroyed the colony and killed his family. Another part realized that while his fellow Specialists being sold as slaves and novelties was bad, he couldn't tolerate the idea of Selene being poked and prodded for some alien's entertainment. Or worse. He didn't think the Argonauts would do worse, but there had been that other alien race at the auction. Humans might not be poisonous to them.

Frank asked, "How many sentient alien races are there on the Spider Star?"

"At last count, seventeen, although there is one reclusive species we haven't seen in many years."

"How many intelligent races are you aware of in the Milky Way?" Rusk followed up, also apparently willing to drop the issue of who killed who, and how many.

"We are aware of one hundred thirty-two intelligent species in the galaxy, but of those, we estimate that only fifty-seven are still extant."

Frank's world whirled. This was amazing. He could ask anything, wild things, and get real answers. He wasn't a scientist or mathematician. He figured if he knew what the right questions were, he could make history. Hell, he *was* making history. Then he thought of Kenny, and remembered what had to remain his top priority.

"What are you doing here?" Rusk asked.

That was a good question. What was the purpose of this place? Why had they built it?

"Talking to you."

"No, in general, in orbit around this pulsar."

"You wouldn't understand," the spider replied.

"Try us," said Frank.

"Very well. As simply as I can put it, we were created to study the time evolution and phase changes of a form of dark matter, as you would inadequately call it, that you have not yet discovered. The timescales post-assembly have implications for the nature of this universe."

Frank appreciated the simplification. He could understand that much, and worried that any additional levels of detail would indeed be incomprehensible.

"What sort of implications?"

"Well, there's an equation of state parameter that cannot be theoretically determined and can only be measured, and we will eventually determine it to our specification. There's also a hypothesis we're to test regarding detection of the phase change."

"And there are other universes?"

"By your common understanding, yes."

"You were created?" Rusk asked, jumping topics.

Frank wanted to hear more about the cosmological issue, but

had to admit that Rusk's question interested him as well. There were too many questions to ask.

"Of course," said the spider. "Obviously we're optimized to live in an oxygen-rich, microgravity environment. Such things don't exist naturally."

"So who made you?" Frank asked.

"Our creators, an ancient race interested in such issues."

"Are they here? Can we talk to them?" Frank asked.

"No, they're not here. We haven't seen them in almost one hundred million years."

That was crazy. This whole thing was crazy. They were all using English words, but how could they actually be communicating, really communicating, using a human language with beings that had been designed and created when the dinosaurs stalked the Earth?

"Given what you know about us as a species," Rusk said, "and Frank and myself as individuals, what do you think we'd most like to know?"

Another good question from Rusk, but jumping around again.

"That's easy," the spider answered. "You want to know how to be happy and satisfied with your existence, and how to preserve it indefinitely."

Frank smirked, guessing that he could have guessed as much himself without vastly superior intelligence. But what he couldn't do, perhaps this alien could. "So what's the answer?"

"There isn't one. No one designed you to have one. Any happiness you achieve is only transitory. Your desires are too diverse and contradictory to long be satiated. Very typical for a species such as yours."

Frank frowned. He probably should have been able to guess that one, too. Still, there had to be thousands of fundamentally important questions with clear, quantitative answers that they could ask. That thought triggered a memory.

There had been a document that had been part of his Scout training. He had looked at it exactly once since leaving Earth, just before his first alien encounter, and laughed. The document was a manual for encountering intelligent aliens, containing a long discussion of philosophies and protocols. It was supposed to provide guidelines to follow, and its first assumptions were dead wrong for the present circumstances. They involved long chapters about how to determine how the alien communicated, building up to math and symbolic logic, and developing a common vocabulary. It had been written, presumably, by some high-paid government experts who, of course, had never met an alien in their entire lives. Perhaps they'd put some effort into it, but in his more cynical moments (which were too common) he believed they'd enjoyed the luxury vacations that the work had enabled.

There was an old quote Frank half-remembered. Something about how with solvable problems experts showed extreme virtuosity, but with the truly hard problems, they demonstrated nothing all that detailed or useful. So after these detailed, long passages about how to establish and build communication— ironic when you considered that Scouts had been chosen as people who could manage for long periods of time alone— there was precious little concerning what to talk about or how. He supposed they had probably written some drafts and deemed them overly stupid. The primary directive was to bring the alien back to Earth if at all possible. That was kind of dumb, Frank had thought at the time, and still believed.

But that document . . . it had still had an entire section on key questions to ask of older, more technologically advanced species. And he couldn't remember a single one.

Frank took a deep breath, half-heartedly wondering how the alien spider regarded moments of silence. Did it feel awkward? Did it think so quickly that what he would consider a normal conversational pause was like an empty eternity? If this creature before him, with its body so clearly defined for free fall, also possessed a mind designed for efficient, logical thought, how could it think him and Rusk quick-witted?

Well, he always told Kenny and Allyn to forget about appearances and ask questions they didn't know the answers to. These beings had scanned their minds, and, in principle, knew everything about them. They were completely naked. As naked as they were already, floating together. Time to stop overthinking. They couldn't float there forever.

Frank blurted out, "Is there free will?"

Rusk made a short noise that sounded like support for the question.

The spider did not answer at once. After maybe ten seconds, it said, "We don't know for certain. To the extent that faster-than-light signals appear impossible, it seems possible. Fully deterministic mechanics appears unlikely on enough levels to support that position."

Rusk grinned at Frank, and he understood. The golden one, this spider, had just illustrated a clearly skeptical, scientific worldview consistent with a perspective that he could understand. As advanced as it and this place were, they were also potentially understandable. Rusk added on, "So it's impossible, in theory, to determine exactly what will happen and what people will do?"

"For a sufficiently sophisticated intelligence, yes, that's correct for any technology we are aware of. Although you're not that difficult to predict. We've noticed that you yourselves have figured out how to predict responses from your experts with a high probability, at least for a subset of environmental stimuli. That's easier than predicting the long-term behavior of many nonlinear systems."

That wasn't the clearest answer, but it seemed clear enough to move on. Frank decided to hit a big one. "Does God exist?"

There wasn't nearly so much hesitation before the spider

replied. "As understood by the majority of your cultures and religions as you and your fellow see them, in recent history, no. We've found no evidence for miracles, for instance, and we have watched very carefully for violations of established physical laws. More than you could appreciate.

"It is possible, and our creators thought likely, that the nature of existence itself implies something more, powers and knowledge underlying everything that some in your species have labeled 'God.'

"However, and perhaps this is more telling, the concept of God as an individual entity for a species is significantly correlated with a number of characteristics, such as mode of sexual reproduction, social unit hierarchies, civilization age, and twenty-two other parameters. The primary correlation seems to be with the expected biological lifespan, which does lengthen dramatically with technological advances."

That made sense to Frank, especially given his recent fall. God was a concept most sought after in the face of death.

And he had a disturbing thought then, that should have occurred to him sooner, but things had been moving too quickly. *He had died,* his body torn apart, when he hit the golden glow. He wasn't himself anymore. He was a copy. He was a new being, not the original Frank Klingston, but some sort of facsimile. He had the memories, they'd recorded somehow—a much more advanced version of the X-bot technology humans possessed.

Did it matter?

He *felt* like himself. Sort of. He was young, fat, healthy and whole. With the memories of a much older man, his memories . . . that he remembered. Was he really Frank Klingston? Should he ask?

If he had been expertly taken apart, and reassembled, perfectly, then he was the same. Protons, neutrons, and electrons were all interchangeable after all. But they hadn't done that. They'd reassembled him with a number of real differences. Could he even count on any of his memories being real?

Frank thought he would ask about this, but reluctance seized his jaw. How could the answer really help him, even if he could fully accept it? He didn't quite believe it, but maybe there were questions better left unanswered. There was no chance he wouldn't have asked when he was younger. He'd been too impulsive then, and he could say that even now as someone who had just jumped off a ledge many hundreds of kilometers high.

Rusk asked, "Did Frank and I die when we hit the golden wall?"

So much for wisdom.

"Yes, but not very much."

Frank wanted to both laugh and cry at that answer, and supposed he cared so much because he was a social mammal that gave birth to live young and his species hadn't been around long enough to extend lifespan much past a century and a half.

So be it. He was what he was, and small changes were hard enough to make even in a lifetime.

They continued to talk, the spider seeming to have both near infinite patience and near infinite obtuseness. Frank didn't know if that combination was the best possible, or the worst possible. The silky delivery made the conversation pleasant even for its strangeness, but the same silky delivery made Frank distrustful, even more so than the circumstances would warrant.

"Can we go back to our ship?" Rusk asked.

"Absolutely. Any time you want. Do you want to go now?"

That seemed like a trick question to Frank—who knew how and when they would get this chance again without falling a few thousand kilometers—and thankfully Rusk didn't bite on it. "No. Why didn't you answer us when we approached the Spider Star?"

"You didn't ask any intelligible questions, and at the time we did not know your communication protocols or your languages. When you asked in the Argonaut language, we assumed you wanted to speak with the Argonauts here. They answered. Why should we say anything? We have our own tasks."

Hours of this . . . illuminating, but maddening. It was everything they wanted here, except what they really needed, and every time they worked back around to that . . .

Frank asked, "How did your creators charge you to treat visitors here?"

"We are instructed to be fair and friendly, as long as that does not detract from our duties here."

"Look," said Rusk, "you basically read our minds, right? You're more advanced than us, right, so why can't you tell us what we want to know that you're allowed to."

"We're allowed to tell you anything we want. There are no rules about such things. How could there be? It must be very confusing to be your species. And as for mind reading, as you call it, if you were presented a . . ." the voice paused, ". . . Rosetta stone, enabling you to translate one language to another, that would not permit you to determine every wish and desire of the speakers of those languages. Some fundamentals, but only some, are easy to determine and we've shared some of them as you've requested."

This was crazy, floating naked in a bubble with another man, asking a giant spider for ultimate knowledge, and having it talk circles around you. Somehow they had to find the intersection of their own needs and "fair and friendly" as defined by an alien.

What was fair? Did that mean they had to treat all other species equally? Or did it mean they could only provide assistance for some sort of return in kind? What was friendly? Did that mean simply not killing visitors? Or did it mean giving them anything they asked for within reason? Frank would be happy with less than friendly—his first contact had been too friendly for his preference.

The spider seemed to have as much time as they wanted to take, so they started playing what seemed like a crazy version of twenty thousand questions. *Fair* did indeed seem to imply an equitable transaction, however they defined *equitable,* and *friendly* was sort of mind-boggling to Frank.

"So the second batch of Argonauts traded you their ship, including three grams of the stable isotope of element one twenty-six, and you provided them with the technique of controlling the planet movers, right?"

"Right."

"And to be friendly, as you call it, you gave the Spider Star an atmosphere that they could breathe?"

"Right."

They'd given this place an entire atmosphere, and all the engineering that went with it, because some visiting aliens had no choice but to stay there after trading away their ship.

Rusk asked, "Could we learn how to control the planet movers for the price of our own ship?"

Frank's pulse pounded in his ears. That was a good question!

The spider responded immediately. "Do you have any significant quantities of the stable isotopes of elements one twenty-six, one eighty-four, or four eighty-four?"

"No," Rusk answered. Humans hadn't even discovered them yet, and Frank knew that it must really annoy Rusk that the Argonauts had had, and used, element 126. It annoyed Frank, too, but just learning that there existed stable isotopes of elements 126, 184, and 484 was valuable. Physicists would be thrilled.

"Are there other items or knowledge that would earn us the control of the plant movers in Pollux?" Frank asked.

"Yes, of course. We're very fair about such things. If you offer us something more valuable than what the Argonauts provided, that would be fair, and then we could help you."

This was ludicrous. The Argonauts had destroyed their own civilization by warring, and now their leftover doomsday machine threatened a human colony. What was friendly or fair about letting it be destroyed, too? Frank took a deep breath, and tried to think of the next question they needed to ask.

He didn't know if it was the result of his rejuvenation, or the fat they'd added to his frame, but he felt like he had the energy and persistence to keep at this as long as necessary. After the events of the previous few days, it was a great feeling.

Time to backtrack. "When was the last time your creators were in contact with you?"

"Approximately twenty-five million years ago."

That was a long time by anyone's measure. "Have you fulfilled your duties yet?"

"Oh no. We're still making measurements. There's plenty to learn here."

It seemed like the spider's English was improving, becoming more colloquial anyway. The voice was still as smooth as melted butter. He tried to keep it from distracting him.

Frank thought there was something here, however, in this line of questioning. "How often were you accustomed to being in contact with them, say, thirty million years ago?"

"About every twenty-seven years."

"So what happened to your creators?"

"We don't know."

There! That was interesting. "Don't you want to know?"

"We would like to know, but we continue to perform our duties as designed."

Rusk asked, "Why don't you go look for them?"

"We listen," said the spider, "and we watch. But we are, as we said, designed for this environment. We cannot endure significant gravity as would surely be required. Moreover, none of us can leave here."

"You *can't* leave?"

"I suppose that your kind would say 'won't,' but is there really a difference if you have been designed to have that preference? We are here to perform our task, and that is all, for as long as it takes."

"Part of that task is to provide your data to your creators, is it not?" Frank challenged.

"Most certainly."

"I have a proposal for you then. We have a technology, perhaps primitive by your standards, but capable enough: X-bots. An X-bot is a mobile expert system that can store extensive knowledge bases and behavioral patterns. You could imprint an X-bot, and we would provide transportation to take it on a search for your creators."

"And in return?" countered the spider.

Frank had thought his desire clear, but had to admit that any direct request had been declined smoothly.

Rusk spoke up. "You say it wouldn't be fair to provide the control codes for the planet movers. What if instead you just provided us a way to disrupt them, without actually providing us control?"

Frank grinned at Rusk. If that wasn't the right idea already, it was on the right track.

"We will consider your proposal," the spider said, and kicked away, propelling itself with a jet of air suddenly spouting from the middle of its head.

"One more question," Frank said, suddenly aware that a golden opportunity was slipping away. "What's the ultimate fate of the universe?"

The spider was dwindling in size, its impossibly long legs pointing back at the men. The voice came in as clear, and close, and compelling as ever before. "That," said the spider, "is still being determined."

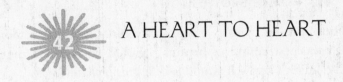

A HEART TO HEART

BETWEEN THE SOULS OF TWO MEN

Rusk watched the spider depart, shrinking to a small, unresolved dot, dark against the golden light. He noticed seven other spiders leave their machines and float off in the same general direction. Did their proposal merit such a powwow?

Rusk's hand was growing sweaty hanging on to Klingston's shoulder, but he didn't let go. He turned away from the spiders beyond the bubble's edge and looked into the other man's blue-gray eyes. "What do you think? Will they go for it?"

"They *have* to," Frank said. "What other chance do they have back on Argo? The apparently random nature of the Lashings, well, that's going to keep them from evacuating, won't it? But the old Argonaut, the Chief, he said they'd get it, complete destruction, and I have no reason to doubt him."

"Wish we knew when it's supposed to happen."

Klingston just nodded his head, in small quick motions, dropping his eyes.

This was the man that he'd resented so much for usurping his directorship? This man, motivated by the love of his family and adopted home? Rusk looked into the mirror of this man's eyes, and wasn't sure he liked what he saw.

"Frank," he began, "I wish I could say that I'd fully supported you since day one, but I—this is difficult to say—I wanted to be the only director of this mission. I wanted the recognition. Claude Martin had a space hero in you, and how could I compete against a space hero? *I* wanted to be the hero. I'm afraid I haven't always supported you the way I should have. My scouting mission, with twenty-twenty hindsight, that certainly wasn't the best course of action. I should have stayed, moved slowly. I didn't know it would be like this. *I didn't know.*"

"How could you have known? How could anyone have known? And as for the scouting jaunt, I approved it. It's my fault, too."

Rusk had just confessed something selfish and awful, and Frank Klingston was taking blame. Was that fair?

"You're a hero, Frank. You were the first man to encounter an intelligent alien species. You brought back the dark drive."

"I'm not the hero you think I am."

What was wrong with the man? He was as humble as a saint. It made Rusk want to confess the whole deal. "I'm an even worse faker. We're here because of me."

"I know. You found the base and the files about the Spider Star and the Lashings."

"I did more than that. I caused the Lashings." Rusk paused, letting it hang there, perversely hoping for a little hate from Klingston. He got it.

Klingston's face scrunched up. "What? You set them off? How? What were you thinking?"

"I was thinking I'd let the archeologists go at it, but I had to knock on the door."

"You knocked on a door?"

"Yes. There was a booby trap. It was a fake door, and only that faction's enemies would make the mistake. Or some ignorant alien like me."

Klingston's face relaxed. "Manuel, that wasn't your fault."

"Of course it was. I set them off. I started the Lashings. They might have killed your whole family by now." There. Let him deal with that.

Frank looked down, closed his eyes, then opened them and locked in on Rusk's own. "Look, maybe you could have been super slow and super cautious, and even if you had been, the trap would have been sprung. If not when you did it, a week later, a year later, or ten years later. It was a ticking time bomb."

How dare he be so reasonable?

"Hey!" Frank said suddenly.

Rusk realized he'd been digging his fingers into Klingston's shoulders, and eased off. "Sorry," he said. Here he was apologizing to the saint now. *Damn him!*

"Aren't you mad at me?"

"A little, I suppose. But the Argonauts . . . they were, are, completely evil bastards. That's not your fault. They're the ones I'm mad at. Here we are, after millions of years, still fighting their battles. Millions! That's just fucked up."

Like most fathers of young children, Klingston didn't curse lightly. This did seem like a decent time for it. Rusk said, "You're too good to be true. Why don't you ever screw up like me? You're good, but never seemed razor sharp. Not as sharp as me, anyway."

"Thanks. Your ego wasn't lost coming here."

"You've got an ego, too. Everyone does."

"I've got an ego, but diminished in old age." The man was young now, and it sounded strange. "Getting married stripped me of most of what I had that way."

"Come on, Frank. You met aliens before. You brought back the dark drive, priceless technology. What did you do that was so special?"

"I did what had to be done," Klingston said.

Emotions played on the man's face, and his gaze kept sliding around, avoiding Rusk's own. Finally Klingston said, "Don't you find it curious that such an important event is so poorly chronicled, at least in the Argo system?"

Yes, he certainly did, and on one or two occasions had blamed Klingston aloud for keeping secrets for his own purposes. He had assumed that he'd been under instruction not to make it public, that there were details some official like Claude Martin had deemed dangerous for the general public. Or perhaps there were secret instructions from Earth that Scouts had to keep. Klingston hadn't helped the impression by refusing to answer questions in public about it, and then avoiding the public eye. Rusk proceeded cautiously. "Yes, I do. Can you tell me why?"

"There was a lot of debate among the Specialist command back on Earth about how to crew Scouts. You could do it entirely robotically, which made plenty of sense. You could have a crew of one, which was eventually chosen. Or you could have crews of two, perhaps three, and still meet the scout specs for speed and longevity. Everyone preferred to send humans if the expense and life support specs weren't too extreme, but there was a big split between advocates for one or two shipboard."

"I recall reading the abstracts of the analysis papers. It's the kind of thing that concerns Specialists."

"I recall watching a few live debates. Basically it came down to one versus married, sterilized couples. Divorce statistics and a few historical experiments in bad taste settled the issue, finally, along with the resource savings for a single crewman. It was fine with me—I was one of the loner Scout candidates."

"You seem well adjusted and social," Rusk offered, not sure where he was going with this.

"I am, now. I was okay, then, too. I'm fine, but I have strong introvert tendencies—a 'rich interior life' was how they put it. And you spend a high fraction of time asleep shipboard, so it didn't seem like a big issue, and the potential payoffs were huge."

Rusk nodded, understanding, and happy to see Frank engaging him so directly now after the tentative start. It was more than a little weird having the conversation floating naked with him, appearing decades younger and bald. "Yes, you were alone."

"I had books, videos, music, games, and long, long stretches of sleep. I even conducted a few research experiments, some astronomy. Still, one goes a little crazy from time to time."

"I imagine."

"I was a little crazy, I suppose, when I entered the system with the alien ship." Frank paused then, a faraway look in his unblinking eyes, looking right through Rusk and seeing something amazing and long gone. "If I hadn't have been, I wouldn't have caught it."

Rusk knew this part well enough. At least the official version. The Scout ship had had no dark drive at the time, just using interstellar hydrogen to propel itself in ramjet fashion. The alien ship had used both normal matter and dark matter to move forward, but its wake was rich enough in expelled hydrogen for Frank to catch up. "You rode the alien's exhaust plume, right?"

"Right." Frank paused again.

Rusk thought about it. Frank had exceeded design specs, plowing through a high-velocity, high-density plume, that was fuel rich but oh so dangerous. "Why did you do it?"

"I was lonely."

The way he said it, with a small squeeze of Rusk's shoulders, and the look on his bald, naked, fat face . . . well, Rusk felt for him. He had a flash of insight to what he would feel like now, floating alone, waiting for the spiders to return.

"There's a reason why, historically, solitary confinement has been one of mankind's greatest nonlethal punishments, no matter how rich your interior life. Humans are a social species."

Rusk said nothing, but let the silence be his acceptance.

"It wasn't suicidal what I did. It had some logic behind it, but it was certainly risky."

"Yes," said Rusk. "I know about this part, and the technical details. We study it as Specialists. Damn nice piece of flying."

"Thanks," Frank said. "It was. But it was the only solution to catch something going that fast when it didn't initially answer my radio signals. I flew up the plume, and caught up, exploiting the rich fuel supply. Did some damage to my engines, but nothing too awful."

"I remember those technical points." All too well. Overly anal as usual, he'd memorized them on the off chance they'd come up in some exam or other.

"What do you know about after I caught up?"

"The technical details of the docking, and that you shared your nontechnical library in exchange for the alien's spare dark drive. A few things about the alien, anatomy and such."

"Good. If that's all you know, no one who knows more has been talking." Frank closed his eyes and bent his head down into his chest.

Rusk could feel the deep breaths the man was taking. What was the big secret here?

Frank looked up and made solid eye contact. "Our species isn't the only one that gets lonely. And we're not the largest or strongest sentient species in the universe, or even this section of the Milky Way galaxy."

Rusk didn't understand, not immediately. Then it hit him. The descriptions of the alien had been like something out of an old monster movie: all scales, muscles, and teeth. Like Frank, it had been out in the deep alone for many years. And lonely. "He took what he wanted from you?"

"Yes, you could put it that way. Called himself something that sounds like 'Crotx.' Creepy, huh? What struck me then, and sticks with me now, is that the more experienced, more technologically developed species holds all the cards in such interactions. It wasn't much different than when the Europeans first encountered the Native Americans, and raped them for their land. What's the famous story? Manhattan Island for a handful of colored beads?"

"What? He raped you for your land?" he said, smiling.

Frank didn't say anything, nor did he smile back. His pulse thundered through his body, and Rusk could feel it under his warm skin.

Was it really possible? "The official account said you'd traded entertainment for the star drive! I always thought that meant the alien wanted movies, books, artwork, so they could study humanity."

Frank's pulse eased, somewhat. "It wasn't rape, not entirely." Frank took a deep breath. "He needed my willing assistance, and traded me for it."

"Did you . . . ?" Rusk started to ask, then stopped. How could he ask this? "Was it . . . ?"

"What do you think?" Frank responded abruptly, then continued after a reflective moment, looking away. "It was weird and I didn't like it. I suppose I'm standing in the way of science, not recreating every lurid detail in a three-dimensionally rendered model for the xenobiologists to drool over." Frank spoke rapidly, as if he'd thought about this many times in the years since the event. "As it was going on, all I kept saying to myself was that it was *for* our advancement, that this was a small price to pay for such a technology. Of course, by that stage, I was a little less naïve and a little more worried about a double cross."

"But you brought back the star drive," he said.

Frank sighed. "Yes, and that bothers me, too. Crotx was physically more able than me, and technologically more advanced. He could have double-crossed me, I'm sure, killed me or destroyed my ship. But he didn't."

"Why not?"

"I've lain awake many nights wondering. It could be a sense of honor, abiding by the bargain. Or maybe it's that we're so far behind them that a secondhand engine wasn't a big deal. Or maybe he was mad about being out there alone, and giving away technology was a way of spiting his bosses. Maybe it was a joke, and it simply amused him. I spent three weeks docked with him, and I didn't get a clue about what motivated him beyond the sense of loneliness that we shared."

They were silent for a long time.

"Damn, Frank. Really? You went along with it."

"He made it worth my while. And humanity's. The part I'm ashamed of is that it wasn't as awful as I think it should have been."

They went quiet again, and Rusk couldn't help but feel awkward. Given their state of undress, and the story, he didn't feel comfortable giving Frank the hug he probably deserved. Rusk didn't know what to do, or to think.

If he'd heard that story about Klingston secondhand in a bar, he'd have called "bullshit" on it and laughed, but hearing from this old man turned young, literally in the middle of a giant alien space station embedded in a planet made of dark matter, well, it was hard to doubt the smallest part of it. After a long, silent moment, Rusk said, "Shit, Frank. I had no idea."

"And that's the way I like it."

How do you respond to something like that? Those details should have been in his personnel file. You think you know someone, understand them, and sometimes you just didn't understand anything.

"Frank, listen, if they accept the proposal, you don't have to go looking for this ancient race," Rusk said.

"Still bucking for sole directorship?" Klingston asked, smiling.

"No," Rusk answered, too quickly. "I mean, I thought you just wanted to save your family and world, and be with them."

"That's the idea. But I'll do it. If the colony can still be saved, and if they can help us save it, I'll leave again."

"But your family?"

"They'll understand. It wouldn't be the first time I've run out on them, would it?"

"Frank, that's being unfair to yourself."

"But true, isn't it? I mean, Virginia will likely be dead by the time we get back, or old and remarried at least, or evacuated to Earth or parts unknown. Or something more crazy. In any event, how would she feel about being with a man so much younger? And my boys, Kenny, Allyn, will likely have families of their own, assuming they haven't become Specialists themselves and left Argo. With that angry sun, I'd be more likely to leave. Guess I did."

How was Rusk supposed to respond? Was he supposed to tell Klingston that reuniting with his family would be easy, when it was likely impossible? The man had made a sacrifice, and had accepted the price.

Rusk decided to say nothing more on the subject. To break the spell, he said, "I have to take a piss."

"There's that high-powered Specialist education speaking again," Klingston said without derision or mirth. Then, "Me, too."

"What do you think? Should we just go?"

The slick, angelic voice entered their heads without warning, nearly making Rusk lose control of his bladder. He didn't suppose it should startle him—why did a spider have to be in eyeshot to communicate with them?—but it did. "Please feel free to eliminate your wastes without risk or repercussions."

Klingston said, "I always had trouble with other people watching."

"I'll close my eyes."

"Or listening," he said.

"Tough," said Rusk, and let loose. They were floating, heads together, holding hands, safely not pointing at each other. A few moments later, Klingston managed to join in.

It was strange, and felt stranger, even though it had to be one of the least strange things they had experienced since coming to the Spider Star. And strangely intimate.

The walls of their bubble absorbed the liquid and that was that. No big deal.

Rusk realized that they should be talking about the staggering revelations they'd heard from the spider. Alien races, all over the galaxy, all over the Spider Star. Races so ancient that their spans had to be measured in megayears, or perhaps it was gigayears. He wished they'd asked. He also wished he knew more science questions to ask, fundamental questions.

He supposed he shouldn't beat himself up too much for asking questions about saving his people and his planet, but, when he considered the big picture, he wondered what opportunities he'd so far missed.

Klingston said, "Hey, over there," and gestured with his head.

Rusk craned his neck around to see.

Something was moving toward them with purpose, and it wasn't a spider. "What is it?"

"I don't know," said Klingston. "It does look familiar though, *hey*! Something's not right here."

Now Rusk managed to get a better look himself and understood Klingston's consternation. "It's an X-bot. Sort of."

There was something wrong with it as it drifted toward them on its anemic free-fall thrusters. The bot was not symmetrical; it looked melted or something on one side.

"Drone!" Rusk called out.

Drone, lost in that initial flight from the dirigible, had also apparently made its way to the core of the Spider Star. And now to them.

"Drone," said Klingston thoughtfully.

The X-bot fired a retro-jet and coasted neatly to a stop in front of their confining bubble. Its display window showed a single dark orb that both emitted and reflected the golden light around them, looking just like one of the eyes the spiders had at the end of their legs.

"Your proposal is acceptable," said Drone, or whatever Drone had now become. The voice was no longer perfect and rich, but rather the gender-neutral X-bot default. Still, it was impossible not to realize the intelligence guiding the machine.

Both the men were silent for three heartbeats, then Frank erupted, "Excellent!" He was smiling like a fool. "Say, just how many patterns do you have in there?" he asked.

That didn't seem like the first question to ask this spider wearing an X-bot suit, but the answer proved illuminating to Rusk.

"Just one," it said, "and some capacity and information had to be sacrificed. Enough functionality remains to accept the proposal."

Rusk decided not to consider the immediate implications. Drone, previously, had been able to store over a dozen human expert patterns and ancillary data-processing capability. If the spiders wanted to show off, well, he supposed they just had.

Worse, he imagined they probably weren't showing off.

"Now then," said the X-bot formerly known as Drone, "we should work out the details of our arrangement."

OUTLIERS

DOCKED TO THE SPIDER STAR

Griffin was in the shower bag on the *Dark Heart* when the broadcast came. The space dock shower was superior, but Griffin wouldn't trust it, or trust being over there, unarmed, let alone naked for an instant. So she was shipboard.

Selene patched the message through to her. Stunned, Griffin didn't immediately feel anything, just continued to wash herself. The words' meanings couldn't reach her entrenched heart, not without additional assaults.

The voice was Rusk's. It repeated: "Again, we're coming up to the *Dark Heart,* me and Klingston, up the elevator. We'll be there in about eight hours. Be ready for us."

She'd seen Klingston jump to his death. She'd had no word from Rusk since his entire ship had vanished, presumably lost with all hands.

"They're alive, Sloan," said Selene, speaking after the broadcast. "They're alive!"

Griffin kept scrubbing. Finally she said, "Run a voice match, and a retina scan if they sent video."

"It's *them.* They're alive!"

Griffin didn't say anything, not right away, but then repeated her order, more quietly, "Run the scans."

Then she blinked rapidly, trying to clear her vision. Her hands were inside the bag and she couldn't use them. Without gravity, the tears wouldn't fall.

———

Griffin and the remaining Specialists, all well armed and armored, were there, waiting, when the elevator opened at the space dock. She had two levels of backup, armed X-bots, serving as relays. She had gas, grenades, and computer-controlled lasers ready to deploy at the slightest hint of trouble.

The doors opened and Manuel floated out toward her. "Sloan!"

What she wanted to do was launch herself into him and intersect him in an embrace. Instead she shouted, "Catch the guy wire, mister, and hold position!"

Thankfully, he did exactly as he was told. He knew her too well not to.

When she got a good look at everyone inside the car, she knew she'd been wise in her caution. First, Rusk only had part of his team with him, and they were in sorry shape, while Rusk himself was bald and seemed kind of pudgy, like he'd spent the entire time he'd gone missing eating ice cream. Worse, Drone was seriously messed up and ran a strange, dark display with glinting highlights that she'd never seen before, but that wasn't so suspicious; the X-bot was clearly damaged, after all. No, the problem was with Klingston, or the man who appeared to be trying to pass himself off as Klingston. He was way too young, and, most damningly, had *both* his arms.

Griffin had seen his arm cut off. She'd seen the tattoo on his ring finger, before, which was now missing.

What kind of bad joke was this?

"Everyone hold position while I sort through this," she said. "I need some plausible explanations for what's going on here, and I needed them yesterday."

Rusk smiled at her and said, "There isn't one. What can I say? We're outliers."

She felt a flutter of adrenaline. That was exactly the sort of thing that Rusk would say to her in a situation like this. Some-how, maybe they were who they said they were.

"There is an explanation," the young, bald Klingston said, "and here it is."

Klingston and Rusk began to tell their friends their stories at gunpoint, and while hope flared in Griffin, she held her weapon steady throughout.

REVERSALS

A DIP BACK INTO THE SPIDER STAR ARCHIPELAGO

Even as the space plane's VTOL systems wound down, he had popped the hatch and jumped out. Frank stepped into the clearing where he had lost his arm, an arm he once again possessed. He had lost his wedding band, but he was still fighting for his family. And, at the moment, perhaps the honor of his species as well.

"Hold up, Frank!" Griffin called from inside.

Frank did hold up, but not because of her request. Two other things gave him pause. The first thing was that this really was a beautiful place, with perfect temperatures, clean air, magnificent views, and—most important—a solid surface. The unusual lighting gave it the feeling of a late afternoon, with hints of twilight, but still plenty of light to feel alert. It was just beautiful.

The second thing was the armed war party of Argonauts facing him, led by Orange.

Frank considered the group. Orange had six other Argonauts—pseudo-Argonauts, evolved spider monkeys, whatever the hateful things were—armed with their curved blades. Frank had a sidearm with him, two X-bots, and heavily armed Specialists in the plane behind him.

Griffin had told him that the Argonauts had scattered when she had rescued the rest of his group after he'd lost his arm, and after he'd jumped. Would they scatter again? Or would they show resolve and want to make up for last time?

He thought he might be able to tell if he could count how many arms Orange still had.

Frank held up his left hand and flipped off Orange. The brutal creature was fully limbed. With his right hand, he liberated his .500 magnum Raptor Enforcer from its holster and brandished it. "Give me an excuse," he said.

He regretted the statement as soon as he'd said it, even though none of the aliens could understand him. He wasn't a cheap cowboy or a drama queen. Still, he had to admit he liked the way the phrase rolled off his tongue. An excuse. It was all he wanted. Why not revel a bit? Here he was, on the edge of triumph . . . but he thought about the interview to come and what it might mean for the fate of his family, and the entire Argo colony, and lost his joyfulness.

There could be no triumph here. Everything he truly cared about was over seventeen light-years away.

The Argonauts eyed him, balancing on their hind toes, and looked ready to act. He still sort of hoped they would, the emotional part of him that didn't weigh the consequences. It would take more than a few trophies before things were close to balanced.

Jason crawled next to him. "What do you want me to tell them?"

"Tell them we've come to talk to their big one, and if we can do that, we won't hurt them."

Jason popped a loudspeaker out of its top and spoke in the appropriate Argonaut language.

Orange started yelling, louder and louder, waving its six upper arms up, and up, over and over again. Frank decided to upgrade the yelling evaluation to ranting and raving.

Jason translated, but had to slip into Ginnie mode to avoid internal arguments among the patterns and to keep up with something like real time. "She's going on about how last time they weren't ready, but now they are, and who is with her, to reclaim honor—or glory, maybe—and take back their . . . trophies won in battle, as opposed to trophies won by commendation. She's saying . . . oh, she's going to attack!"

Frank could tell without the translation. Orange had pulled a second blade from her belt and was hopping up and down, each hop slightly ahead of and higher than the last, each one accompanied by a guttural call. Frank eased off his safety.

He could just shoot her now, he realized. Head this off immediately. The Argonauts would respect that, and not hold it against him. In fact, they were probably surprised that he didn't simply attack. He wasn't here for vengeance though, and even if it would be sweet, he wouldn't take it for its own sake. He was here for hope. He was here for—

Orange's attack came faster than he imagined possible, and caught him off guard. Later he would say he didn't know if it was because of the hypnotic jumping, or the fact that attacking him would be suicide, or because he subconsciously wanted it to happen. And honestly, he didn't know for sure, but he thought he knew why what happened next did.

Melinda, bereft of her arm that was not yet regenerated, similarly armed only with a sidearm like Frank himself, dropped Orange with a single shot to her head.

Fast, shocking, and brutal.

There was a moment of surreal quiet, and then the Argonauts facing them turned and scattered into the fields, bounding away on eight legs.

"Thanks." Frank didn't say anything else aloud, but he had mixed feelings about what had happened. Seeing Orange laying still in the dirt really didn't please him in any way, despite how he'd first felt upon exiting the plane. It was just another waste in this wasteful place that regarded limbs as tools of barter and standing. He thought, also, that Melinda wouldn't get as much out of the act as she might have thought. He'd talk with her later, if the opportunity arose, he promised himself.

"Come on," he said. "Jason, Gold Eye, let me know if you pick up anything coming back that seems unfriendly." The X-bots had more senses and faster reaction times than any human, and likely any pseudo-Argonaut evolved from spider monkeys. That whole idea still disturbed Frank on levels he hadn't considered deeply, thinking back to Kenny playing with the critters back on Argo.

The large, old hut still stood as he remembered it. Really, not much time had passed, even though he was, in some sense, an entirely new person. Did the Chief await him within?

He had better.

Frank walked straight in, unafraid, flanked by the X-bots and backed by a trigger-happy Melinda.

The Chief sat there, darkly, in his dark nest, as if he hadn't moved since Frank had stood before him. Perhaps he hadn't. Didn't matter. This time, the Chief was before *Frank*.

"Shall I shoot off your arm?" Frank asked, and Jason translated.

"You are not missing an arm," the Chief answered through Jason.

"True, I am not," said Frank, waiting for Jason to translate, then continuing. "We want information that you have. Will you tell us what we want to know?"

" 'Maybe,' " Jason said, translating for the Chief. " 'More specifically, this particular response implies "what's in it for me," or sentiments to that effect. It's a conditional response.' "

Frank wanted to tell the Chief that he was in no position to bargain, that getting anything at all out of this exchange could be regarded as a significant victory. But, instead, he managed to ask, "What does he want?"

This wasn't about vengeance, or about who was in power now. It was about hope for Argo.

The Chief sat there, unmoving as was his predilection, for long minutes. Frank waited. Finally it spoke at length. Jason translated. " 'Part of me longs for an end to this, for death, but I do not want that and do not request that. I long for change, for excitement, but do not have the energy. Why is everything the same? Day to day, more of the same. I send my agents to contest the other arms, and vice versa, but there is no movement. I know not what I want. My default response is to destroy my enemies, but what enemies do I truly have? I don't know. Ask your questions, foul beasts. Mayhap I will respond.' "

" *'Mayhap'*?" Frank asked Jason.

"Sorry—that's what I have in my vocabulary list."

Fine then. That wasn't important. It was time to ask the question, and ferret out a precise answer. "When I was here before, you said that the Lashing would strike everywhere at Argo, destroying all. I want to know specifics. How long it takes, and how it proceeds."

Frank waited impatiently while Jason translated. *Everything* depended on this old thing's response. Frank could only hope that it knew the details. They'd passed on so much from the days of war, verbatim, that perhaps the Chief knew this, too.

Jason finished, and the old thing sat there, in its nest, its web after a fashion, and said nothing. Frank kept cool, patient, and waited for him to decide what it would say. He failed to make his mind blank, however, and started to consider extreme scenarios. Was torture justified? How would an apparently immortal Argonaut respond to torture? Would Gold Eye, the pattern inhabiting the rebuilt Drone X-bot, tolerate it? If not, what would it do?

Frank waited.

" 'How fast is your ship, four-arm?' " Jason translated for the Chief.

Frank made a mental calculation about the creature's intentions, and answered. "We can reach just under ninety percent light speed."

"Ehh," said the Chief, a noncommittal sound that Jason did not translate. Frank could almost hear the cogs turning, the gears whirling. How would he make his decision to talk? Given his previous experience, he predicted the creature would talk only if its answer wouldn't be helpful. It seemed that the Argonauts, at least this race of the species, were just that way.

It croaked out an answer, slowly, with a rhythmic response. Jason translated: " 'We could not easily manage the destructive swarm. Designed that way? Perhaps, perhaps not. We threatened the cursed ones, tried to force them from their lording ways. Why should everyone be slaves to their effort? They should be slaves to our effort. We gave them a choice. They would be given proof, and escalation, in time. They would have a deadline to hand over the power, the control. The sequence, could be shut down, but it was all or nothing. They would pay! Pay, I say! They would have to shut it down! Them, the slave mongers!' "

This was all ancient history that Frank preferred not to engage in, just or not. "How do the Lashings proceed?"

The Chief screamed something, screamed himself hoarse for over a minute.

"This is important," Ginnie said. "We're going to take a moment to get it right."

Frank waited.

Then Ginnie spoke slowly and clearly. "This is what the Chief says: 'First, sputterings. Hitting military targets on the moons and in orbit. Shows of force on Argo itself. Time to ponder, built in, to recover, and see sense. See our rule. And a generation. After a generation, the entire swarm brings the core of the sun to Argo, and it's all destroyed. For all time. Vengeance is complete. We rule, or all die. It is fit, it is just. Vengeance, vengeance, vengeance!' Then he curses for a while more, apparently without content."

A generation? What was a generation to an Argonaut? "How long?"

Ginnie said, "Approximately forty-four years and three months."

Frank did the calculation in his head. He didn't need an X-bot. They were screwed! As fast as it was, the *Dark Heart* couldn't quite get them back in time. His adopted home world was lost, and his family would likely be killed. He took a few deep breaths, and reconsidered. They were dead if they needed the Specialists to return in person, but there was another way, and his panic subsided somewhat.

They'd have no choice but to radio back an evacuation order, which probably would get back in time to save everyone, just. Maybe. Everything would have to be checked. Frank suddenly wasn't sure. The math was complex, and maybe he was making a mistake.

The Chief croaked, and Ginnie translated. " 'You can't stop it. Can you? Your ship is faster than those of Argonaut design, I grant you that. Indeed, I grant you that. But it isn't fast enough, is it? Is it?' " And the old, blackened creature began to bark and wheeze, in what Frank could only consider a laugh.

Fine, the old thing laughed at him.

It was maddening, this near miss. Einstein's light-speed limit would still permit them to save Argo if it was possible through a radio signal, but not if it required their physical presence. That might still be okay, if they could send back instructions about how to dismantle the planet movers. Frank voiced this notion to Gold Eye. There was a course to salvation that didn't require complete evacuation and abandonment of the colony.

"From what we can ascertain about your technological accomplishments, no. You don't have the ability to build the converters you need."

Converters? What sort of converters? Was Gold Eye sure they couldn't manage if they had to? "Then we're lost, and the deal is off. You can't help us after all."

"Why," said the alien-inhabited X-bot. "We can proceed to Pollux fast enough, can't we?"

"We can?" Frank challenged.

"Of course," said Gold Eye. "We only need a few years compared to what your ship can manage. We can provide the extra speed. And you will hold to your part of the bargain."

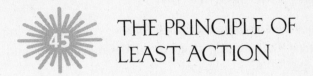

THE PRINCIPLE OF
LEAST ACTION

OVERSEEING SPIDER STAR ENGINEERING

Watching from the *Dark Heart*'s engineering deck, Griffin was in awe.

The hydras, under direction from the spiders, were building the most powerful particle accelerator she'd ever seen. The station comprising the accelerating ring exceeded the diameter of Talos. It wasn't for any scientific purpose, like nearly every other one she had seen, ranging from table-table cyclotrons for instructional purposes to pictures of the lunar supercollider, but this one was solely for them. It existed solely for the purpose of propelling the *Dark Heart* to within a heartbeat of light speed over the next eighteen something years of travel.

Their own part in the enterprise was much more modest. They had to build a superconducting ring to transfer the momentum of the particle beam to their ship. The X-bots, headed by Einstein and Marlo, made sure it happened right. The tolerances were insane, but possible. They had enough engineering expertise on their end to manage their meager responsibilities. Really, a particle beam craft wasn't so difficult to create, and such a craft held many advantages over the *Dark Heart* with its intrinsic engines. The most difficult part was to gather the power and sustain it over the years that a voyage would take.

They had to trust the spiders would maintain their particle beam for the duration of the trip to Pollux. What choice did they have other than to trust the spiders now?

They would return to Pollux at close to light speed, and relativity would shorten their subjective journey to a mere year and a half. They would shave the necessary few years off their travel time to beat the Lashing that would destroy Colchis and its space bridge.

This mission would be a success.

Still, Griffin maintained a cadre of concerns. The foremost was deceleration. They weren't really planning for it as far as she could tell, and Klingston wasn't pushing the issue. They would achieve light speed, for all practical purposes, but how did you shed that speed? Would they be doomed to spend the rest of their lives slowing back down? Would a bit of interstellar debris slightly too large to ionize with their lasers smack into them with the force of a planet and destroy them? Or, and this was how her brain tended to work, was this the direction the spiders wanted them to go, to look for their creators, and were they all being drafted into the search?

"What are you thinking about, Sloan?" said a voice behind her. Rusk.

"The usual. Threat analysis." True enough.

"I should have guessed. Now, come on. We've won. No more threats, right?"

How could he *think* like that? There was always a threat. Safety was *never* certain. And, moreover, they hadn't saved Argo yet. You didn't win until you'd won. All sorts of things could happen, both natural events like her fearsome debris theory, and betrayal, like the particle beam failing. How could they afford to spare so much energy? Was it really so cheap to them? Still, this was the reason she was such a good partner for Rusk—she could stay alert after he had ceased. "Maybe."

Rusk floated closer to her, and latched on with his arm around her waist. It felt good. He said, "Have you given any thought to what happens after?"

See, there it was. *That mindless thinking ahead that made you miss the threat right in front of you!* There was no after until they'd finished their current task. "Manuel, we've got a long time until then, and some important things to do. So, no, I haven't."

"I have," he said.

Of course he had. He'd been planning his whole life from the cradle. That was his strength, and his curse.

"Frank and I were the ones who promised to haul Gold Eye around the galaxy. He shouldn't do it. He has a family to go back to. I don't have anything to go back to."

Griffin wasn't sure how to take that. She really *hadn't* given much thought to what happened after. But some part of her, deep inside, shivered. She and Rusk were a team, and a good one. He was off making plans again, and she wasn't sure that was right. Was their relationship over when they returned? Did they even have a relationship?

"I mean," he stumbled along, apparently in an effort to explain, "I always wanted to be the one in the history lessons, to be immortal and important. I've followed every rule I could figure out to be center stage. But you know what? There are no rules. Anyone can do anything. It just takes will and luck."

Was he just figuring this out now? "That's what I've been trying to tell you for years, Manuel."

"But I *get* it now!"

He irritated her. Everything was still about him, his revelations. If there weren't any rules, why weren't they a couple, married even? They'd only avoided becoming serious because family complicated mission selection, an unwritten rule that Manuel had followed scrupulously. They could have done it. Maybe he didn't feel the same way she did.

Of course he didn't. They were very different people. How could she be so stupid?

"I've got some things to do," she said, shaking off his arm and leaving the deck. Thinking, paramount among them. She had a little over a year until they saved Argo, or didn't. Little over a year to figure out what to do with her life. She was sure that Rusk wanted her to go with him, with Gold Eye, on a mission of indeterminate length, one that they'd probably die on, eventually.

Was that what *she* wanted?

It sure didn't seem like the safest option.

POLLUX PASSAGE

ZIPPING ACROSS THE UNIVERSE

Rusk heard a woman's scream broadcast over the intercom. The ship's computer said, "Assistance required, lounge two. Medical emergency."

He was close, but he tried to be careful and take his time. The *Dark Heart* was accelerating under the particle beam at close to three gees. You didn't make any fast moves under three gees.

He wasn't far, but he had to climb a ladder. Weighing over three times normal and just walking around was bad enough. Climbing with the extra weight was much worse.

Rusk was breathing hard by the time he reached the next level. He took a blow, and wished circumstances would permit him to lie down on the padded floors (every surface in the *Dark Heart* was now padded).

Gina Dorrissey, still primary medical doctor onboard, announced she was on her way, but he was the first one on the scene. Sloan Griffin sat, crumpled on the floor before him, a bone protruding through her shin, a nasty compound fracture.

Part of his mind analyzed the situation this way. Her Specialist biochemistry would prevent the wound itself from becoming infected, but she'd need help setting the bone and medical attention. Three-gee acceleration was akin to torture, and no one avoided bruises, or worse. Given Griffin's ultra-cautious reputation, at least she would set a good example, poster child for being even more careful.

Another part of his mind did this: *Sloan!*

His consciousness wanted to reject the simplicity and neediness of the second thought process, but it was a true and honest reaction. Where had it come from? He and Griffin had always maintained a professional relationship, not letting things go too far. Why should that have changed now?

In either case, he responded as he needed to, and rushed to her side to render assistance.

When he reached her, Griffin said, "I need Gina."

Right. She was a lot more useful than he was.

"She's on her way. What did you do?" he asked. The question sounded inane even as it left his lips.

"I fell down, moron." She made a noise, a small shriek, something, indicating great pain, and he sat by her, helpless.

Rusk didn't think he should try to set her fracture, which he knew how to do but deemed unwise, or anything else. He didn't think there was anything useful he could do except be with her while they awaited more expert assistance.

Suddenly part of him melted. This was Sloan, injured, in need. He was here and would do anything to help her.

The worst thing was that, even though there were a number of things he knew how to do, with more professional medical help minutes or seconds away, there was no point. He did the only thing he could think of that might help. He whispered, "Sloan, I love you."

She turned to look at him, her face twisted with pain. "This isn't the time."

Rusk felt dumb, and could only watch stupidly as Dorissey and two X-bots showed up to take better care of Griffin than he was apparently able to.

He needed to figure this thing out.

Most of the crew spent the following months in the dens, lying on their backs, and watching movies and other entertainment on ceiling displays. The days passed slowly, and the literal weight of their burden made optimism difficult to maintain.

Although they lay side by side together often, especially during her recovery, usually watching thrillers of one sort or another, Rusk didn't know what he should do about Griffin. He thought—hoped, anyway—that they had a solution to cure Pollux of the infestation at its core.

This situation inside his own heart was less clear, and it was so dark inside Griffin that he thought he needed night-vision goggles.

"She is so stupid," Griffin said one night, while they watched a remake of *Casablanca*. "She should just appropriate one of those machine guns and mow down all the stupid people, starting with the Jihadists, and not finishing until she's alone on the entire continent."

"That's not the point," he said.

"Why not? Why can't she be more proactive? Do you think the fundamentalist regime engaging in that world war was sane?"

"No, of course not," he said, but uncertain about how to proceed. His answer seemed safe. He used to have no uncertainties talking with her, but now, lately, everything seemed to be a minefield. He decided to just watch the end of the movie in silence.

It ended too quickly.

He started a search for something else to watch, but Griffin started talking.

"Why did you kill all those hydras?" she asked.

"What?" he said, tapping through some menus to find another movie.

"What 'what'?—you did kill thousands, didn't you? How do you feel about that?"

He tried not to, mostly. But Griffin was his oldest, best friend, maybe more, and he owed her more of an honest answer than even he owed himself. "Honestly, I feel fine about it. They threatened my people, and were not trying to find a solution to our conflict that didn't end up with me dead. As far as I could tell—and I've heard nothing to disabuse me of this notion—the spiders just use the hydras as machines, lobotomizing them, or whatever, from birth. The poor critters never got a fair shake, and it was tough for them that I didn't give them one, either."

Griffin was quiet a long time while he continued to search for something else to watch. He was torn between looking for something good and something mindless, which didn't have a great overlap, but he feared starting a new movie that would just get him into more trouble.

"Okay," she said.

"Okay?"

"Okay."

They seemed good, and very close right now. The relationship felt right.

They watched another movie. It wasn't like sex was much fun when you weighed three times normal. No one wanted to be on the top or bottom.

Pollux loomed before them, although *loomed* was far from the right word. Given that their velocity was nearly light speed, relativity changed everything.

Doppler-boosting made Pollux into a point of hellishly intensive gamma rays before them, and relativity ensured that the rest of the universe was dark, invisible. And while the trip to the Spider Star had taken nearly a decade, subjectively, the trip back was only a year and a half.

Rusk had never been completely clear on what was supposed to happen when they reached Pollux. They had set up all sorts of contraptions around the ship that made no sense, in addition to the superconducting ring that let them ride the particle beam. Gold Eye always managed to weasel out of complete explanations, and Klingston kept letting it. It was like he'd committed to trust, but how could one ever completely trust the alien?

This frustrated Rusk. This deal that they had struck with the spiders, he thought they should push it for everything it was worth. Having one of them here, even in X-bot form, was a golden opportunity to learn more. Every statement the thing made potentially had the chance to advance entire new areas of science and technology.

Ignoring Klingston, Rusk took every moment he wasn't with Griffin to pump the spider pattern. While it didn't seem to dismiss his questions, it did seem to manage to avoid providing him as much information as he would have liked. A typical exchange:

"Those stable heavy elements that you mentioned," Rusk would fish. "Of what practical use are they?"

The X-bot would reply, "Many."

"For instance?"

"None that you can yet exploit."

"Give me an example."

Gold Eye said nothing for a long time, then said, "Your science and language cannot yet express the interesting properties. The simplest exploitation you would understand is in ballistic weaponry, akin to the ways your species has previously employed depleted uranium."

"A more complex example that I can still understand?"

"Simple applications include high-temperature superconductors, smart materials, quantum computation, but in no way you would yet have technical understanding."

Rusk got a lot of that sort of thing from Gold Eye, even concerning matters closer at hand. For instance, Rusk asked one day, "How will we disrupt the planet movers?"

"With direct action."

That was not clear despite its simplicity. "How, exactly?"

"With an energy transfer."

"But they're in the heart of a star!"

"Yes."

"They're already in the middle of a massive energy sink! They're in Pollux."

"Only in this universe."

"So what are we going to do, hitchhike to the next universe over?"

"Yes."

"How do we do that?"

"No way that you would understand. I could spend a year explaining it to you when we leave this place."

He repeated the conversations to Griffin, in between movies. While she didn't spend much time talking with the frightening X-bot, she seemed very curious, and very disturbed, but wouldn't articulate her concerns. That was fine by Rusk. She worried too much.

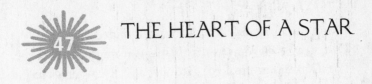

THE HEART OF A STAR

POLLUX

Frank had to admit that he had second thoughts, but he was the man who had jumped willingly into the abyss. How could he back down now?

But this was that jump again, a million times worse in some ways, a million times easier in others.

He sat in central control with Sloan, Manuel, Selene, Anatole, and Gold Eye. Before them in the central display was Pollux, or as he preferred to think of it now, the gamma level of hell. Since they were flying toward Pollux at nearly the speed of light, even this relatively cool star's photons were blue-shifted into high energies, into the hard X-rays and slightly beyond, into the gamma-ray regime.

It was going to get hot, and soon. Their lasers and magnetic fields kept them safe from particles in front of them, even as the particle stream pushed them forward, but electromagnetic waves obeyed the principles of superposition. Photons passed right through magnetic fields.

"We should have particle-stream cessation in sixty seconds," Griffin announced.

This was one of the many moments of truth that would come now, furiously, at the end of their journey home. They had trusted the spiders to provide them with thrust, and to cease the effort at exactly the right moment.

They waited.

Rusk asked, "Gold Eye, what is the probability that the beam won't go off on schedule?"

"I don't understand," the X-bot responded.

That answer was not as reassuring as it might have been.

The *Dark Heart* creaked, groaned, and the oppressive gravity they had lived with for over a year was gone. Frank could hear distant cheering drifting up from the lounges and dens.

"Mark," Sloan said. "The beam is off. Right on schedule."

Okay, Frank felt a sort of reassurance flooding back into him. The spiders were bang on, and tens of millions of years more advanced. Who was he to doubt them at this point? He'd had more faith when he leaped.

Was it the fact that they were close to home, close to success, and to his final fate, that made him doubt? He ignored the disastrous thought. Now was not the time.

Gold Eye said, "The devices activate now."

The X-bot meant the spider devices that had been added onboard, meticulously aligned, and scrupulously calibrated. They had been explained to some of the more technical Specialists, and they had told Frank that they didn't understand what they would do.

Something . . . happened.

Frank's stomach turned, and sweat broke out all over his body, but without discernable cause. "What's going on?"

He felt stupid for asking, but he was nominally in charge, if that still meant anything, and it was his duty to ask the stupid questions. In this case the question was stupid because they *knew* what had happened, but it was a completely novel experience.

Selene said, "Look at the sun!"

Frank looked, and looked again.

It wasn't there.

Rusk said, "Brilliant!"

Griffin said, "I was going to count down our relative impact time to Pollux, but that doesn't make a lot of sense now, does it?"

Frank looked at where Pollux had been, where the gamma-level of hell had been. Nothing. Gone. Vanished.

Not quite. There was something still there before them, in the display.

The swarm.

Thousands and thousands of points of faint light moved, hypnotically, zipping back and forth

Somehow, here he was, seeing it, without the assistance of gravitational telescopes.

"*We're* dark matter!" Rusk crowed.

Yes, that was it, and that was a simple way to state it. That was what Gold Eye had been telling them. The spider pattern was probably being direct, as direct as it knew how anyway, but it hadn't ever put the transformation into the simplest terms. The planet movers, they were dark matter capable of carrying a powerful electrical charge.

The spider devices had converted the *Dark Heart* and its crew into the same kind of matter that constituted the swarm of planet movers inhabiting the core of Pollux. They *weren't* in the same universe. Christ, that stuff that Rusk had been telling him was all true.

He felt a bit of déjà vu, similar to what he'd felt when he realized that his current body had been copied or grown, and he wasn't exactly himself anymore.

The swarm grew as they rapidly approached. Frank wanted to think that they were still approaching at light speed, but he didn't know if light speed was the same here or not. His mission, his entire existence, was in the hands of an X-bot hosting an alien pattern, and he didn't trust aliens.

But he had forced himself to do so now, and he was committed. The point of trust was a willingness to accept the consequences of decisions when you put your faith in others. He was a trusting fool, once again. He hoped that the costs would be less than the deal he'd made for the dark drive, because it was all beyond his powers. Any positive action he took now would likely be destructive and stupid.

Frank sat there, and watched. He was made of dark matter, and he was seeing dark matter, at least one of its forms. He was a ghost of sorts, except everyone was a ghost, the ship was a ghost, and the universe was a ghost.

"Mark," said Griffin. "Activating secondary fields."

This was the part that directly exerted the force on the swarm. They would witness, soon enough, the fruits of their efforts. As Frank understood it, the force exerted was exactly analogous to electromagnetism, still the strongest, most easily manipulated force, even in different universes.

The *Dark Heart* shuddered, skipped a beat. There were real forces in play here, powerful forces, and Frank was hitched to them.

The swarm shimmered, the motions of the individual points warping from their dance. Even as Frank tried to grasp what he was seeing, the motions changed. A new pattern emerged, the ballistic launch and fall transforming into a spray.

A gentle hand pushed him back into his crash seat, a strange, unwelcome weight after the minutes of blessed free fall. They were pushing on the planet movers, and the planet movers were pushing back. Newton, in action, again. Equal and opposite, nothing more basic in all of creation, even in other universes.

If he got the chance, and had to worship someone or something, he thought Newton would be it.

The planet movers continued in their spray, accelerating away, dispersing. They flew into the infinite darkness of this dark universe.

Gold Eye said, "Reintegrating."

Frank thought he would vomit. His world, the control center

of the *Dark Heart,* spun wildly. The feeling was similar to what had occurred before, but not identical. It was worse, causing more nausea. Frank wanted to hurl.

Another part of his mind wondered what, exactly, was going on. Were they reappearing in their original universe? If so, was it within Pollux, which would kill them all immediately? Was someone worrying about this? Even though he trusted Gold Eye, how far could the X-bot be trusted?

Frank didn't die.

He imagined that meant that they weren't manifesting back inside Pollux.

"We have stars," Griffin said.

The implications there were enormous. They were back in their own universe and no longer moving relativistically.

"How did that happen?" Anatole asked. "All of it, since we left. How did it all happen?"

"It happened," said Rusk, "because as a species we don't sit on our asses and we look after our own."

Frank thought of his family, and said, "Amen."

BROKEN HEARTS

The *Dark Heart* limped home, at such a slow velocity that Griffin couldn't help but think of some wind-dependent sailing vessel becalmed upon an uncaring sea. They used Pollux to give them a gravitational boost, blew through their nuclear fuel, and picked up a respectable speed. It still took days to reach Argo.

There was a reception—a party—for the Specialists at the space dock, of course. New Colchis, the elevator and orbital stations, were all intact, although there were a few visible scars on Argo and its moons that were clear reminders of recent and violent Lashings.

Surprisingly, Claude Martin was still in charge, in space anyway, and looked better than ever despite the forty-plus years that had passed for him. "Earth has made big progress on several medical fronts," he explained. "I might be running things forever, unless you want to make a play for my job, young Manuel."

Griffin stood with him and Rusk in one corner of the party, sipping champagne out of extremely long low-gravity flutes.

"No," said Rusk. "I won't make a play for your job. And I won't be staying, either, not longer than necessary to resupply and refit the *Dark Heart*."

"What?" Martin blurted out, almost sounding like he'd gotten some champagne up his nose. "And just where do you think you're going with the *Dark Heart*?"

"The Hercules Cluster," said Rusk. "That's the first place anyhow. And I'll need to recruit a new crew as well." He turned to look at Griffin before continuing. "As you know, we lost people, and not everyone wants to go on with the *Dark Heart*."

"I do though," she said, quickly, startling herself. She'd been putting off a final decision for months, and Rusk had respected her silence and avoided hounding her, but she'd been leaning this way for some time and the flight through Pollux had crystallized her intentions. "You see, there are dozens of intelligent alien species in this part of the galaxy with technology much more advanced than our own, and I'm by no means certain that they'll be friendly. In order to safeguard all of humankind, we must learn as much as we can, as fast as we can, and make allies."

"Yes, yes," said Martin. "We have to explore, yes. But I simply cannot allow you two to make this decision yourself. We didn't expect the *Dark Heart* back for several more years, if at all, and we've been preoccupied with the Lashings. This isn't how decisions about Specialist missions are made. *I* make them, with a committee."

"Not this time, Claude," Rusk said, steely, not deferential in the least. "You see, I've already made a promise, and I have to keep it."

"Promise? What promise?" Martin's face flushed.

"Ah, there," Griffin said. "You need to talk it over with this X-bot here."

"An X-bot?" Martin seemed befuddled at the challenge to his authority. He'd been in charge for decades, and now was being told how things were, and by an X-bot of all things!

Griffin rather enjoyed it.

Gold Eye crawled over. "The arrangements are made?"

"Nearly," said Rusk. "But this official here needs to understand that he cannot impede our mission. Will you explain it to him?"

"Of course," said Gold Eye. "This is something I can clearly explain to one of your species. It is very simple."

Griffin didn't like the overtones of that message, and she imagined Martin would like them even less.

Well, they were committed.

"Come on," Rusk said, smiling. "Let's join the rest of the party."

They strolled off to leave Martin and Gold Eye, neither having any doubt about how that conversation would end. Spiders were very smart, and very forceful. They kept their deals, as they saw them anyway, and expected others to do the same. It was strange to see the two of them, Gold Eye and Claude Martin, looking so similar, on their bunched tentacles, head to eye.

"There's Klingston," she said, spotting him talking to Selene.

"Let's leave him alone," Rusk said. "Selene already told me she wants to come with us. She knows Frank won't. I'd just as soon not intrude on them now."

She should have realized that, as well. They'd been sort of a couple, at least by Specialist standards, on the flight home. "Well, then, let's try to recruit the best and brightest from this bunch and put together our new crew, Director."

He reached over and squeezed her shoulder at the title. She knew it wasn't what he cared about now, not so much anyway, but he had for most of his life wanted it and he seemed happy to hear her say it. "We'll need a pitch."

Griffin agreed, and had been thinking about it. "I was watching a historical documentary about dangerous exploration last month and it gave me an idea. How about this: 'Men and women wanted for hazardous journey. No wages, bitter cold and sweltering heat, long hours of bright darkness. Safety doubtful. Wonder certain. More of the same in event of success.'"

"I like it," said Rusk.

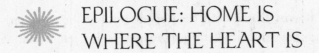

EPILOGUE: HOME IS
WHERE THE HEART IS

POLLUX SYSTEM, 2494 AD
KLINGSTON HOMESTEAD, ARGO

Frank stepped out of the car onto the green grass of Argo for the first time in decades. Getting out from under the tinted windshield made him blink and squint into the warm afternoon light. He missed his contacts, and should have gotten a replacement set already.

A breeze brought the smell of flowers and manure, in nearly equal parts. The Klingston estate still appeared to be a working experimental farm.

He smiled, loving the smell.

Overhead Pollux glowered, blazing, too bright to look at without his contacts, but again a life-giver rather than a life-taker. Externally all was right with the world.

"It isn't quite the same as you remember," his driver said.

Frank finished his deep breathing and looked at the driver he'd been assigned to take him from the shuttle port to the farm, a young woman with long dark hair, no more than eighteen years old. She reminded him of Virginia. "I didn't think it would be. But it's actually not that different."

"If you say so," she said, wearing a small smile. "We can go inside anytime you want to."

So, she was going inside, too? She looked and sounded familiar, and he'd been thinking about who she might be throughout the flight to the farm. He'd thought something might be up when she'd been coy about her name, and in a light yellow sundress and sandals she sure didn't look like an official driver.

They'd flown slowly, with the top down, and he'd soaked up Argo and they hadn't talked much. She hadn't tried to volunteer anything, although he did catch her watching him more than once, and he thought that his family might be pulling a surprise, that she might be his granddaughter. She looked like Virginia, but he didn't see much of his own features in her. Still, maybe his family had prospered.

He hoped so, very much.

The house looked much the same as he remembered it. Sure, it needed painting, and there had been an addition, but it was still essentially familiar. Frank liked that.

A troop of spider monkeys milled around near the addition. Frank tensed up and glowered at them, scanning his surroundings for something to throw. When he'd lived on Argo before, he'd never minded them, but after what he'd gone through on the Spider Star he'd just as soon smash them all with a heavy stick. He knew that once, long ago, he'd have found such a notion repugnant, but no more. He looked around for a weapon.

"They won't bother us," his driver said.

He let his breath out. "No, I don't suppose they will."

He stood still, regarding the house. "I guess it's time to go in."

"Yes," she said.

He'd been away from home for years by any measure, but here he was, younger than when he left, and subjectively gone for less time than had passed on Argo. He fancied himself a time thief, and that designation made him feel guilty about showing up at home.

Since the promise that he was expected at the farm, Frank had resisted the impulse to make automated queries to discover what had happened to his family. He was expected. That had been enough.

Frank took a few steps toward the house, surreality descending upon him. Not only was he standing, and walking, on a planetary surface again, he was at his own estate. His *family's* estate, he corrected himself. Kenny and Allyn would be gone by now, but perhaps they had made a trip back with their own families. Virginia, he hoped, was still here. He expected her to be remarried, that this welcome would be a show of sorts. That was fine. He'd left a long time ago, and he possessed no preconceptions about his homecoming. It was enough to know he'd protected his family and that they were safe.

What happened to him now didn't really matter. He'd done what he'd set out to do.

Frank spied faces in the windows. Small faces, low. Children? Not Kenny or Allyn—they'd be grown by now, and then some. Maybe they'd had kids and had come back when they'd heard he'd returned?

"Go on, Frank," the driver said.

She was a little more familiar than he was comfortable with, but she did seem sweet and attractive, and he let it slide. He had more important things to worry about.

He made his feet move some more. He found himself walking across the lawn and onto the porch. Only the screen door was closed, and he noticed a crowd of people milling about beyond. So they'd made a party of his return? Fine. That was fair enough.

There had been a party waiting for Ulysses, too, when he'd eventually returned from the Trojan War. He'd had to kill most of that party, but what could one expect after being away for decades, really?

Frank's heart raced. Funny, that. It was likely a *hundred* times faster than during most of his voyage.

The driver stood there with him, which seemed strange, but he was comforted by her. She was surely more familiar than most of the people in the house would be.

"I'm not the same as when I left," Frank said. "And besides, that was a long time ago."

She said, "The people in the house aren't the same as when you left, either. They know what you've done, and why you did it. This is your *home*. It'll be fine, mark my words. You're still much loved here, even if you were too headstrong."

Frank rubbed his sweaty palms on his pants, glanced at her briefly. She sounded too balanced and wise for her years, too knowing. But might not someone say the same thing about him, now in his youthful facade?

Together they stepped up on the porch, his boots plinking the wood, through the door with the squeaky hinge, and into the house. The inside was quite dark after the sunny afternoon, and Frank blinked, trying to get his bearings. He told himself again that he needed to get a new set of contacts.

"Everyone's waiting in the family room," the girl said.

"I know the way," Frank said, not moving. He heard people down the hall. A cacophony of voices suggested a crowd of people. He was afraid Martin had planned something, some ceremony, here in his house. This was nerve-wracking enough without having to entertain such silliness. The fact that his family, his home, still safely existed was the greatest reward he could imagine.

He moved forward, the prospect of a fight helping to settle his nerves regarding the uncertainty with his family. Tinted skylights filled the family room with a glow that struck him as especially inviting as he emerged from the hallway.

People packed the room to nearly overflowing. Frank scanned them, just counting, not really seeing at first. He counted five women, four men, and at least eight children. All of the smiling adults looked to be no older than forty, most younger than that; so where were Kenny, Allyn, and Virginia? Had Allyn become a stud, impregnating right and left on a mad spree after Frank had departed? Actually, that idea kind of made him smile, which really was the appropriate response to this warm reception, whoever these people were, however they were related to him.

"Is that him?" one of the boys asked. "Cool."

Frank looked hard at the boy, at all of them, and saw facets of himself in many of their faces. Could all these people really be related to him? "I know it must be strange, me being this young, us not knowing each other. It's strange for me, too. But can someone tell me what happened to Virginia and the kids?"

Frank hoped they were alive and happy someplace, perhaps wisely moving on to a safer colony not beset by an angry sun. He hoped they weren't dead.

"Frank," said his driver. "You were told that there had been changes while you'd been away, right?"

"Right." Of course there had been changes, and he didn't need anyone to tell him that. He'd been away for a long time, for the second time in his life. And he himself had probably changed more than anything.

She nodded, then put one hand on his shoulder and pointed with the other as she began to introduce the people in the room. "The couple on the loveseat are Janet and Ismail. Janet is Ken's oldest. Their baby is Jessica. Then over there you have Keith and Svetlana—Keith is Allyn's oldest. Their kids are Brian and Igor."

Igor was the one who had spoken before. "Yeah!" he shouted, thrusting his fist into the air and striking a pose. "Igor!"

Frank smiled at him again.

She went on, "Then you have Ken and his wife Eliza there—"

"Kenny?" Frank asked.

"Hey, Da!" The man she'd called Ken grinned and raised his hand to wave hello. He didn't look quite forty. Maybe he just looked young.

Frank held his place and resisted the urge to go hug him. Yes, it did look like Kenny. Kenny had been six when he'd left, and while he seemed happy, for all Frank knew at this point he harbored deep-seated resentment. But, oh, he did look happy!

"Now then, over there is Allyn, and his wives Faruka and Babette. Their other kids are Jonathan, Eric, Ionnis, Hera, Perseus, and Atlanta."

Frank looked at Allyn, trying not to be impressed that he could manage two wives when one always seemed like plenty, and tried to estimate his age. He just didn't seem old enough. "What gives, Allyn? You don't look much older than I do now, and you should. And you shouldn't have two such fine-looking wives, either, should you?"

Allyn shrugged, smiling. "Things change. Don't forget, we're not just a small colony here on Argo. We also have Earth sending us technology. Aging is a disease, and we've all but beaten it."

As Frank considered that, his driver turned to face him. "And really, cosmetic make-overs aren't that difficult, either."

He squinted at her, leaning close, considering her in a new light. Was it possible? "Virginia?"

"You always were a little slow, husband."

His hand slipped into his pocket, and he was ashamed he'd lost his wedding ring. Lord, was it really her? It had been a long time since he'd seen her, but cosmetic alterations or not, could he really have not recognized her? And what sort of relationship were they to have now? He was young, she was young, but what if she had someone else? What if she didn't want him anymore? Did he want *her* anymore? He'd been with Selene, after all. How could a couple just pick up after what they'd been through, the time, even if there was no one else in the equation? But she'd called him *husband*. That had to mean what he thought it meant, didn't it?

"Slow, slow, slow," she said, wrapping her arms around his waist and pulling him to her, and kissing him.

He fought it a moment, then kissed back. He still had a wife, family! He had grandchildren!

Virginia pulled back. "You're crying, kiddo."

So he was. Nothing wrong with that, was there?

Ken stood up. "Come sit down, Da. We want to hear all about it."

"Yeah," said Igor. "Tell us about the aliens."

Frank let Virginia lead him forward to sit in the middle of the sofa, the spot Ken had vacated. Ken went and pulled another chair out of the kitchen and sat down.

Frank sat, with Allyn on one side, Virginia squeezing in on the other, and several of his great-grandchildren at his feet. "I'm overwhelmed."

Allyn said, "No. *We're* overwhelmed. Our home is safe, and you're back where you belong."

It was all Frank could do for the moment not to break into tears and start bawling. In the darkest moments he had not imagined such a moment. He sat quietly, breathing deeply, inhaling the light of his family. "Where do I even start?"

Igor said, "The Spider Star is no star!"

The Argonaut fairy tale? Yes, he remembered it, how most of it went, anyway. He could indeed start there. He would share with them the true story of the Spider Star, because they deserved it, because they'd been there with him in his heart, because they were his family. He began, " 'The Spider Star is no star, and the Spider Star is no planet, but it is a place anyway, and its golden heart is the source of all good and evil. But mostly evil.' "

Frank sat quietly, tears wetting his cheeks. "That was how the ancient Argonauts saw it, but that wasn't how I saw it. Let me tell you how I saw the place, and what happened there."

448 ✳ MIKE BROTHERTON

"Why?" Kenny asked, smirking.

Frank smiled back. "You can just shut up and listen, okay?"

Everyone laughed.

Frank began to speak in a simple, compelling voice, and his family listened to him.